THE
CONTEST

THE
CONTEST

A NOVEL BY
CARNE MAXWELL

ISBN 978-0-473-39917-7

NZWG Registration No 16/045

Cover art and design and interior layout by Carne Maxwell
Island illustration by Carne Maxwell
Typeset by Carne Maxwell
Headings in Arial - Text in Bembo

Proofread edit by Lel Scott
Hawkeyeproofreading.co.nz

Printed and bound in New Zealand by PublishMe
www.publishme.co.nz

https://www.carnemaxwellauthor.co.nz/
https://www.facebook.com/carnemaxwell/

For
John, Roy and Hayley

A poor man with a conscience
is wealthier than a rich one without one

Carne Maxwell

THE CONTEST

This contest is open to ten teams, made up of two or more participants in the same family, who will reside on an island for three months and compete for the chance to win thirty million dollars. Should more than one team remain on the final day, three competitions will take place and the team to finish first will win.

Conditions of the Contest

1. Must be over the age of thirteen and hold a current passport.

2. Must not have a criminal record.

3. Must not take any items that have not been authorized by the police and our management.

4. Must be in good health. You will be given a medical examination and any necessary vaccines. We will intervene if someone falls ill and have medical staff ready to evacuate anybody who needs hospital treatment. We will not take responsibility for actions that do not comply with the terms and conditions of the contest.

5. Pets are not permitted.

6. If incidents occur requiring official involvement, the police in charge of the island will attend the initial investigation. However, should the investigation need to go further, the people involved would be investigated in New Zealand, according to New Zealand law.

7. Any entry form not marked with a tick in the 'I have read and agree to the terms and conditions' will be disqualified.

This contest will take place on a remote Pacific island of average size. A tropical paradise, with lush vegetation and palm tree-lined beautiful sandy beaches. An inner reef helps protect the northern sides of the island, so it is regarded as safe for swimming and fishing. The island is uninhabited by humans, but alive with animal life and insects. Fresh water can be found on the southern side and edible fruit and vegetables on the northern. There are no man-made shelters. There is no reception; technical devices are of no use.

Each team will have two flare guns, in case of emergencies.

A detailed summary and information pack will be handed out to the teams that make it through.

You will not know the island's location before you board your flight.

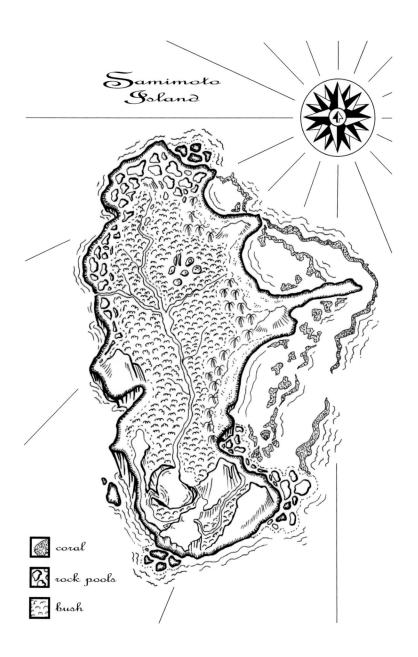

Samimoto
Island

coral

rock pools

bush

THE CONTESTANTS

BOOTH FAMILY	Drew and Trudy/Ritchie and Celia
CROMPTON FAMILY	Jack and Rosaline
DAVIDSON FAMILY	Matt, Moana, Sammy and Zach
DOWNS FAMILY	Stan, Yvonne, Harvey, Mary and Jessie
HENDERSON FAMILY	Henry, Nancy, Peter and Candice
JENNER FAMILY	Aron and Helena
LONGS FAMILY	Eric, Bridget, Sara and Warren
SMYTH FAMILY	Ian, Kate, Josh and Logan
TILLER FAMILY	Karl, Greg and Terrance
WENTWORTH FAMILY	Nigel, Linda and Mark

PROLOGUE

I didn't expect it to be like this. It was meant to be a chance to start over; the money was supposed to make everything right. How could it go so wrong?

Was it my fault? No matter how many times I ask this question, I get no further. I still can't find an answer ... this guilt is too big, and am I worse than them? If we hadn't let our feelings get the better of us, then none of this would have happened.

They tell me I'm not to blame, but I see it in their eyes, just as they see it in mine, and it hurts; it hurts like hell. I love him, but it's never going to be enough. This will hang over us like some invisible shield, but there's no protection – or maybe there is in some bizarre way. Maybe it's there to prevent us from telling the truth. Anyway, what good would it do now? It would only destroy more lives.

Of course, Greg makes it better. Dear Greg – so like him. He is the one thing that makes this bearable, and yet the one thing that makes it so hard. Sometimes, I can't bear to look at him but then that moment is gone. He has become our rock, poor thing.

I'm getting sleepy now and it won't be long. Sleep has become my very own Groundhog Day. I know when I close my eyes it will begin.

CHAPTER ONE

A beautiful, blue crystal sky merges into the sea as the midsummer's parching heat stifles New Zealand's largest city, Auckland. Ten selected families make their way to the Midway Convention Center, located at the Viaduct Harbor.

Martin Fallaway waits inside with his team. He is dying. Bowel cancer. Crept up on him without warning. He went for his medical two years ago, took the usual tests and there it was. Low white blood count. More tests, more bad news. They operated, unsuccessfully. Chemotherapy made him sick. He wasn't going to waste his final months feeling like hell. He would leave nature to itself and get on with things while he still could. Painkillers are wonderful things.

With no family left, he has already made generous donations to charities, but now that time is his enemy, the bulk of his fortune will go to his last adventure.

He purchased an island back in 1995 and planted fruit trees, in the hope that someday he would build a resort. He named it 'Samimoto Island'. Sami: meaning sea and Moto: meaning island. He hadn't gone ahead with his plans. Other projects had taken his attention. In the end, his failing health made the decision for him. Being an explorer, he wanted to do something he felt connected to, and he channeled his thoughts into having a contest. He liked reality programs and knew people would enter anything for money.

Over the last two years, with the help of a top management team and the input from the police, careful, meticulous planning has made his contest as safe and fair as possible.

He employed a further five scientists and three horticulturists to investigate the island. They tested the water and found it safe to drink. The island's vegetation was prolific, due to the fair amount of rain the island received, and charts were constructed with pictures of edible plants. Around the beaches, caves can be found.

Martin is happy with all he has done but, still, he can't quite stop that nagging feeling that deep down inside, is he being irresponsible? The words reckless, thoughtless, stupid play on his mind and he knows this is true, but he isn't forcing anybody to enter. People got hurt or worse everyday doing things they wanted. He prays regularly, but can't figure out why. He knows he is a hypocrite; he never attends church, has never read *The Bible*.

He could have handed the money to some family, but where was the fun in that, the adventure, the achievement? It had to be earned; it had to mean something.

He is thoughtful for a moment, as though in these last few seconds he might be let off the hook, but the doors open, putting an end to any second thoughts.

Martin smiles as Ella Goodwin, his live-in nurse, gently touches his arm. He has grown very fond of her over the past two years. She is a good nurse, a treasured friend. He places his hand over hers and watches the people filtering through the door. They wipe their brows, displaying their expanding sweat pits, and stand like limp flowers before ambling towards the ten tables facing the stage and Martin is thankful for modern technology. He surveys the teenagers. *I hope their parents have their eyes wide open. It was not much more than winning 'Lotto', but the chances of winning – ten to one.*

It is 11:15 a.m. and the tables fill up. At 11:29 a.m. the last contestants appear at the door. Martin looks at his list. *The Tiller brothers! They seem casually calm for people who have made it with seconds to spare.* He wonders if this is deliberate — part of their plan? His eyes scan the other tables. *Incredible. Not one family has pulled out.*

Once everyone is seated, Martin takes to the stage, introduces himself and his team and gives a brief summary of the contest. A short film will be shown about the island. Lunch will follow and then each family will receive their medical examination, followed by their police check. Before they leave, an information pack will be handed out to each family, giving them twenty-four hours to read and sign all the documents before a member of his team will call and collect it.

Jessie Downs is out of her seat the moment they are invited to eat. She grabs a plate and walks along the counters full of dishes she has never before seen. She notices the man next to her. "Oh boy, this looks good." She glances quickly at her sister, Mary, still sitting at their table.

"Sure does. What's your name?"

"Jessie ... Jessie Downs. That's my family over there. They're a bit slow, aren't they?"

"Yep. I'm Terrance. I'm with my brothers, Karl and Greg."

"Oh." Jessie peers over. "Just you three? Don't you have any girls?"

"Nope."

"How come?"

"How come?" Terrance scratches his chin. "Well I guess a girlfriend isn't family, Karl is between girls and Greg ... just doesn't have one."

"That's weird." Jessie mumbles from her ever-expanding mouth. Terrance smiles.

"Gosh, this is delish." She gets another piece of crumbed fish, devours it and glances towards her family. "Oh God, hope Dad didn't see that!" She piles more food on her plate. "See ya."

"Enjoy!"

"I will." Jessie makes her way back to their table, fully aware of Mary's expression. It is a look she sees often. She pokes her tongue out at her sister, sits and attacks her food.

Amused, Jack Crompton turns to his wife. "So, she's not keen on her sister talking to poster boy."

Rosaline smiles. "Interesting description." She takes a sip of water. "What I can't understand is why you'd enter this thing with children. I mean, the boy looks … maybe eighteen? The older sister's quite pretty … guess she could be seventeen, but the little one, well, surely she's only just thirteen. Bit stupid to bring her."

"Yeah, suppose. Could prove interesting. Notice that boy on your rights been watching. So has the one with the homely parents."

"Really!" Rosaline looks at Jack. "Well just as long as it's them and …"

Jack's face hardens. "Don't go there. We're the perfect couple – remember."

Rosaline's hand reaches across the cold table. "I didn't mean …"

Jack's chair screeches along the tiled floor. "I'm getting lunch."

"Sure," Rosaline smiles timidly and glances across to the table where the man Jessie had been talking to sits. *Jack is right; he is very attractive.*

"Looks like you got yourself another admirer?"

"Oh yeah, very funny!" says Terrance shaking his head.

"Personally, I think it's stupid bringing kids. They can be very problematic."

"Karl, kids can be pretty smart."

"Nah, Greg. I think you've forgotten there's no phones or computers. I mean, what are they going to do if they can't Google?"

Terrance laughs. "Absolutely … complete shut-down."

Karl chuckles. "Anyway, didn't mean her, meant the blond."

Terrance looks to where Karl indicates. It is the woman he noticed when they arrived. She is gorgeous with her mane of long, curly blond hair and olive skin.

"Been looking in our direction, no doubt sizing us up. Think they had words. His face looked like thunder. Name's Crompton – Jack and Rosaline. Reckon something's not right there."

"Karl, we've only been here five minutes. How can you come to that conclusion?"

"Watch and learn buddy, watch and learn. It's all about observation. You should try it sometime."

"Sarcasm is the lowest form of wit, Karl."

"Geez, Greg, don't be so sensitive. Karl's right."

"I know that. I'm not stupid. I mean … it's like what they were doing, when we got our food, isn't it?"

Karl looks at Terrance and pokes Greg with his fork. "Exactly, Greg!"

During the afternoon, the medical examinations and police checks take place. Everyone in the room passes. No one wishes to be excused. Several questions are asked; some answered, some not.

Martin and his team thank everyone as they leave. They know the day has gone well.

CHAPTER TWO

The following afternoon, John Sedden's car pulls into Martin's driveway. He gets out, proceeds up the flight of stairs to the front door, rings the doorbell and is greeted by Edward, Martin's butler. Edward shows John the way through the foyer and out to the extensive lounge, overlooking the city's harbor and Rangitoto Island. Martin and Ella greet him as two more cars arrive. Edward excuses himself and makes his way back to the foyer to let in Bill Reese and Alison Meadows. Together, they and John manage Martin's team.

"Nice to see you," says Martin. "Help yourself to a drink."

"Thank you," replies Alison, taking a glass of white wine. "I hope the others aren't too long. The suspense is killing me."

"Hey, did anyone notice the friction between the Cromptons? That Rosaline's a good-looking woman. He looks like a control freak."

"Maybe he just gets jealous, Bill."

"Don't think there's any maybe about it, Alison."

"They seemed okay to me," John says, catching Alison's coy look. "She might be one of those ladies that likes a bit of dominance."

Alison flutters her eyelashes. "Well, that could make life interesting."

Ben Smith, Duncan Knight and Grace Williamson arrive and place their envelopes on the table, followed by Phil Neils, Owen Mills, Karen Holland and Penny Goodings.

"God, this is sooo exciting, isn't it?" Penny says to no one in particular. Her head turns towards Martin. "Come on, Mr. M, don't hold us in suspense. Rip these babies apart."

Martin picks up the envelopes, but suddenly finds himself nervous and decides to hand them out. Doing this almost seems like it is their idea.

Ten yeses.

"Shit," says Owen, chucking his envelope on the table. "Let's just hope they don't regret it."

Martin stands up quickly. He doesn't want the conversation to go any further and gestures everyone into the dining room.

After dinner, Martin and Ella wave off the last of his team. It is decided that January 18, will be the day they will meet again. The contestants will get their instructions tomorrow, via courier, informing them that attendance is compulsory.

At 10:30 a.m. on January 18, all the contestants have arrived at Martin's "Essential Living" warehouse. They are ushered up the stairs, into a large reception room casually decked out with tables and chairs. A cafeteria runs along the left wall, distributing the aroma of coffee and freshly baked bread into their wanting nostrils.

John and Alison greet everyone warmly. John tells them that each family will be called up alphabetically and taken through the door on the right. There will be an approximate wait of half an hour until the next family. Tomorrow they will be picked up at 9:30 a.m. and taken to Auckland Airport.

The Booths are called first and follow Alison into a narrow room. Martin sits at a long table that stands adjacent to the glass windows, overlooking the interior of the warehouse.

"Hello Drew, Trudy, Ritchie and Celia. Please have a seat. This is our viewing room. We can see everything from up here, and what we can't see, our security screens do. On the table, you will find cards with the warehouse's layout. You have five minutes to study the cards and work out what you want to take to the island. The cards also state items which are banned." Martin holds up a large black travel bag.

"You will each be given a trolley. You have ten minutes to grab anything you think necessary and then you will put what you can fit into one of these bags. You will be given these bags once you have landed on the island. Remember, you may have to travel some distances. Each family's bags are color-coded. Yours is black.

"We are supplying a chest with tools, knives and utensils for food and building, a first-aid kit, pillowed sleeping bags and mosquito nets. For the women, we will provide all your requirements for your menstrual cycle. Ladies, please fill out the form inside your envelope."

"Terrific," whispers Trudy. "Totally forgotten about that little inconvenience."

Celia grins.

Martin continues. "When finished, you will be taken to another room where your bags will be checked. Afterwards, you will be able to leave. Are there any questions?"

"So, we get five minutes to discuss what we're going to take and ten minutes to grab what we can?"

"Yes, that's right, Drew," replies Martin. "Ten minutes is quite long. Now, are you ready?"

"Yep, let's do it," says Ritchie.

"Once the clock stops, you must not discuss anything else. Good luck." Martin and Alison leave and their time starts.

"Okay, Ritchie and I will get the heavy things," says Drew.

"Good. Trudy, we'll get food. Get your own clothes?" says Celia.

"Okay, but don't get much. Shit – torches, can we take them?"

Ritchie scans the list. "Doesn't say we can't. Batteries … I'll get them. Hey, girls, get oil. We can use that for loads of things." Ritchie's fingers drum loudly on the table.

Celia's hand moves instantly. "Ritchie, stop it, I can't think."

"Rice, canned food … we need a can opener," bursts out Trudy.

Drew rubs his forehead. "Wet suit booties?"

"God," interrupts Trudy. "Just grab whatever."

The bell rings and the door opens. Martin gestures for them to follow Alison through the door and down the stairs. The clock starts again and they take their trolleys and dash to the nearest aisles. Trudy realizes she has forgotten her map.

"Damn it, Trudy. You start down one end and I'll start at the other. Let's do the clothes first."

The girls grab what they can and hunt for food. There is so much. With no time to think, they snatch anything in cans or packets.

"Oils must be the next one. I'll go," says Celia. She gets several bottles and notices vinegar. She knows it has multiple uses.

Meanwhile, Drew and Ritchie grab rope, nails, screws; anything that will help construct a shelter.

"Gloves. Ritchie, you seen any gloves?"

"Nope."

Drew shouts, "Girls! Look for gloves. We're running out of time."

The girls look at their map and notice a section on gardening. It is six aisles down, so Celia takes off. She reaches the aisle with seconds to go, notices the gloves, panics, and in her haste knocks several to the ground. The bell rings. *Damn it!* She looks at the pile in her arms. *Christ they're small.* She makes her way back to the others and they are taken to the room on the right by two security guards.

Alison greets them as they enter. "Well done! That was quite an effort. Let's get this packed and then you can go."

The Cromptons are called up. After them, the Davidsons, then the Downs, followed by the Hendersons, the Jenners, the Longs, the Smyths, the Tillers and finally the Wentworths.

CHAPTER THREE

On January 19, the contestants board Martin's private plane. He purchased a 2000 Airbus A319 CJ and customized it to his requirements, splitting the interior into two zones. The first class compartment is used for comfortable seating, dining and general relaxation. It has a total of thirty-eight seats, a division for four beds, a luxury bathroom, a shower and toilet. Another toilet and washroom is located near the middle of the plane. Martin has chosen soft white for the walls with Rimu wooden paneling throughout. To compliment this, the furnishings are white leather, the wooden tables and wall cabinets aged Rimu. A dark ebony carpet, with a mustard diamond design is carried throughout the plane. Martin has all the latest audio, video and telephone systems in place. The front compartment has been made into an office and a bedroom, with an en-suite bathroom for his private use.

The outside of the plane is Artic white, with two gold waving stripes, which run along its length and then carry vertically up the tail. The words 'Martin Enterprises' in midnight blue lettering are centered above the wave. The plane looks clean and expensive.

The contestants are told it will take approximately five-and-a-half hours before they touch down at Papeete, in French Polynesia. Caroline, their hostess, will be supplying food and drinks and the movie *'Castaway'* will play, because it might prove useful to those interested.

The Davidsons take the front seats. Moana dreamed of the day they might take their first flight, but never thought it would be this one. To be on Martin's private plane is something else. It is pure luxury, completely foreign to them.

They live in the South Island in a small town called Hokitika. Have never moved, never gone anywhere. Moana was born in Hokitika and will probably die in Hokitika. She cleans and sells jams and chutneys, made from their garden; being half-Maori, she knows how to live off the land. Money is tight. It was worse when the boys came along. Zach first, then Sammy. Her husband, Matt, is in and out of work after a job at the local bakery ended with a careless accident involving hot oil. A badly burnt leg led to months of visits to the local hospital. His leg improved but left him with scarring, a limp and an ever-increasing waistline. He has grown lazy and looks older than his forty-nine years. The boys do what they can and help out with money from their jobs at the dwindling local timber mill.

Moana studies the menu. She decides to indulge in the lemon and chili oven-roasted chicken. The wine list is extensive and she has no idea what to choose. She remembers liking a white wine at her Uncle's wedding a few years ago, and settles on a Chardonnay. Beside her, Matt orders a steak and beer. She knows he doesn't care too much for wine. He seldom has it. He likes his beer and it shows.

The Downs are seated behind the Davidsons. Jessie is full of excitement and is ravenous. She finally settles on the chicken, as it sounds the most delicious. Mary orders the same and Harvey picks the ravioli. Being a special occasion, they ask their parents if they can have a glass of wine. Stan and Yvonne allow Harvey to have a beer, but the girls are to have juice. Mary pulls a face and Jessie giggles. Harvey tells them to shut up so he can concentrate on the movie. This sets the girls off and, instantly, Yvonne's head towers over them.

The Tillers watch and listen while drinking an expensive bottle of Cabernet Sauvignon. The wine goes perfectly with their ravioli. They start their second bottle just as their dessert arrives.

"Your friend, Jessie, looks to be having fun," says Karl nodding in the Downs's direction.

"Yeah, she's a lucky girl."

"Maybe!" Karl smirks and nudges Terrance. "Trouble coming our way."

Terrance sees Mary approach, swishing her dark wavy hair. Her sensuous ruby red lips glisten with her deliberate pout.

"Hello. This is cool, isn't it? It's Karl, Greg and ..."

Terrance watches her scrunched-up nose raise the left side of her lip. *Man, she's provocative for her age.* Karl elbows him "Terrance," he says nonchalantly. "As if you didn't know."

Mary cocks an eyebrow. "Faces I remember, names not so much."

"Toilets at the back," says Terrance smugly, as her face changes color.

"Could you hurry, dear, as I'm heading there, too."

Terrance sees Rosaline. She is like the sun, shining bright, sending a warmth into his skin that finds its way to his heart. His pulse quickens. He sees her mouth move but doesn't hear her words. He is mesmerized by her sparkling emerald eyes, her pink, full lips and her hair, which frames her face, falls onto her shoulders and ends somewhere down her back. Mary's shrill voice interrupts his thoughts. Irritated, he blinks and is back.

"Well, you'll just have to wait for me then, won't you?"

He takes in Mary's cool smile; the deliberate flick of hair. Rosaline doesn't blink and Mary continues down the aisle.

"Kids, huh!" Rosaline says teasingly.

He shifts in his seat as an awkward silence takes hold and she smiles tentatively and walks on.

"Oh, boy!"

"Shut up, Greg."

"Mary not your type then, Terrance?" Karl takes a delicate sip of wine. "Not like Mrs. Crompton?"

"Okay, you two, knock it off. I'm not going there."

"By the look of it, think you already are, mate!"

Greg bursts into boyish giggles.

"Relax, Terrance. Just winding you up." Karl winks at Greg.

Terrance watches Mary on her return. She turns and smiles before she sits. *Man, she's either extremely thick-skinned or bloody stupid!*

The flight goes quickly and they touch down a little after 5:00 p.m. Everyone disembarks, are cleared through customs and escorted across the road to a modern building named 'Martin Enterprises'. They enter its chilled foyer, a welcome respite from the hell-like air outside.

"Since it is quite late in the day, we have decided that everyone will be better off spending the night here. We will leave for the island tomorrow morning at eight-thirty.

"We have a very comfortable dining and relaxation area. If you would like dinner, the restaurant will be open from six-thirty to nine. You are welcome to help yourself to the refreshments on offer, at any time.

"Ella will show you to your rooms. Oh, just one more thing," says Martin with a warm smile. "Please do not leave this property. We wouldn't want any accidents before you get to the island."

Nancy Henderson leans into her husband, Henry. "Bloody typical. If I had known this, I would have had a drink."

"Oh well, you can make up for that now, but don't forget we have to be up early tomorrow." Henry unlocks the door to their rooms. "Not bad!"

Their son, Peter, pulls his sister, Candice, into the room and makes a beeline for the sofas. "Cool, a huge TV."

"Hon, the fridge has the usual and …" Henry looks up. "Hey, you two … got some delicious looking chocolates here."

"What?" answers Peter, eyes glued to the TV.

"For God's sake. We've been here five minutes. Turn the damn thing off!"

"Geez, chill, Dad. It's crap anyway. Nothing we haven't seen, like two years ago."

Candice snickers. "Yeah – lame. Hey, let's go take a swim." She spies the chocolates in her father's hand. "Oh, can we take those with us?"

"Good idea – go get some exercise."

"Hey, Peter, look. He's got a large toilet."

"That's enough, young lady."

"Dad, lighten up. He's fat."

"Well, that may be, but you don't say things like that."

"Why not? You do."

"I do not!"

"Yes you do! It's like when you call black people ogga boggas."

Nancy points to the bathroom. "Get changed … and behave."

Peter and Candice's shoulders move in unison as they open their bags and pull out their togs.

Henry whispers to Nancy. "Got to admit, he's pretty big."

"His wife's on the fat side too. They don't look overly fit, do they?"

"Nope. What was their name?"

"Can't remember."

"Oh, I know. It's Matt and Moana."

"An ogga bogga." Henry chuckles as Nancy tries to suppress her smile. "Seriously though, we should watch them."

Candice and Peter rush past, arms flying.

"God, I hope we're doing the right thing. When I look at Candice … she's so young and vulnerable."

"She's got a good head on her shoulders. Peter will take care of her, even though he acts otherwise."

"I know. It's just … what if something goes wrong? We'll never forgive ourselves?"

"Bit late for that now. We'll be fine."

"I've had my doubts. Gone along with this. You seemed so determined. I thought, well, maybe this would be good. Get the kids out and about."

"Things aren't that bad, Nancy!"

"Really! Well, I'm not enjoying it much. All this shouting and having to justify myself all the time. Now Peter's moody not being with his friends and I never thought in a million years we'd get through. We never win anything!"

"We haven't won this yet."

"You know what I mean."

Henry puts his hands on her shoulders. "Look, this will be good for us, whether we win it or not. I'll spend more time with the kids, especially Peter. We just have to be careful, use our heads. If something doesn't feel right, then we don't do it. Come on, let's see what havoc they've been causing." Taking her hand, he gives it a squeeze. "Or, we could stay here, lock the door and amuse ourselves?"

"No, I'm not in the mood." She pats his back. "Maybe later when they're asleep."

"Yeah, right." Henry grabs a couple of towels and takes two more. Instinct tells him the kids didn't take any. *God they're hopeless.*

So lazy. Perhaps the problem is we do everything for them … it's just easier. I must make an effort to change that.

At 8:45 a.m. the next day, the mini bus Martin hires leaves the hotel. All are aboard, full from breakfast and excited about getting underway. They are taken to Papeete's ferry terminal.

Sara Long watches her husband's jaw drop when he sees Martin's launch. She sees in his eyes that the Horizon P110 is his ultimate cruising vessel. She remembers back to when they were first married and how his love of boats eventually led to his becoming a partner in her father's fishing business. Warren squeezes her hand as they board.

A buffet is set up and although everyone frequents it, there is little mingling between the families. Harvey Downs scowls as he watches his sister. "You're such a pig!" he hisses. "Mum, look, she's doing it again."

"Please, Harvey," cuts in Martin, appearing at his side. "It's perfectly fine. It is good to see Jessie has a healthy appetite."

Harvey glares at Martin and feels a tap on his shoulder. It is the dark-haired boy with the nice-looking sister.

"Silly old fart. I'm Peter," he says extending his hand. "How old's Pippi Longstocking, then?"

"Thirteen and that's sick."

"Thanks, remember it from when Mum made us watch it … so not cool. What about your other sis?"

"Sixteen going on nineteen." Harvey suddenly finds himself wanting to talk. "Thinks she's going to be a movie star or international model – she's got no chance."

"Yeah?"

"She's a pain. Trust me, she's okay to look at, but you wouldn't want to go there."

"'Course," agrees Peter, trying not to sound patronizing. "Best get back." He leaves Harvey and scoops up a slice of watermelon and chomps away, spitting out pips like cannon balls. His eyes find the Booths. *That Drew looks like some bulked-up marine. Wife's small, kinda cute. Brother's ridiculously good-looking. Pretty wife though … like her black hair!* His eyes travel her body and go to her face, rendering him momentarily paralyzed as his skin turns to fire. Feeling exposed, he looks away and concentrates on the older boy and his parents. *He seems chilled, a little bored. Probably wishing he's elsewhere. Parents look smothering; no doubt Christians. Certainly dress like them.* He moves on to the three brothers. *That Greg's probably queer. Too immaculate. The old one with the trendy beard thinks he's mister cool. Guess he looks like he knows what's what though, like he could win this thing easily, and the other one's like some surfer dude with his long blond hair. Bet that's what's got the woman's attention. Certainly got Harvey's sister's. She can't stop leering.*

His eyes go to the man called Warren, who is running his fingers over the railings. *Christ, you'd think he was a god the way his stupid wife looks at him.* He guesses the man knows about boats and fishing. He bites his thumb and sees the older woman, with the ridiculous orange hair, smile at him. Feeling foolish, he turns away.

The launch begins to slow down at approximately 3:30 p.m. It has been a long day. Martin's voice comes over the intercom, saying they are going to reach the protective reef in a few minutes. Everyone below deck scrambles up. A few kilometers away stands Samimoto, towering above the ocean. The waters in her tropical turquoise lagoons are separated from the deep indigo ocean by white marshmallow ribbons.

As they draw near, they can see she has a long, white, sandy beach, lined with palm trees and hibiscus plants in various shades of reds, pinks, oranges and yellows. There is dense vegetation behind. The island climbs to a sheer rock face on the left side – the remnants of an extinct volcano – and drops away into the ocean, where the sea smashes against the rocky shoreline. This side of the island, being volcanic, is quite exposed. It curves back inland and this provides shelter for the beach they are approaching. Heading back right, the peak of the volcano descends down to a crescent shape and rises up again to a smaller peak that runs out like a child's arm, almost dividing the lagoon in two. A break in the reef provides the launch its entry point.

Nigel and Linda Wentworth think it is the most beautiful sight they have ever seen. They have never been to an island before and to arrive at one, on a gorgeous day, with the sparkling waters glistening in the sun and the island standing majestically in front of them, is alluring.

Linda draws a big breath and Nigel hugs her. Mark, their son, smiles, his eyes filled with excitement.

Nigel stands transfixed. "It's just like you see in the brochures, absolute heaven."

Mark is glad his parents are impressed. He knows they entered this contest because of him. They are out of their comfort zone but Nigel, his father, had considered the facts and said he thought they stood a good chance of winning. All three of them are fit and healthy. His mother, Linda, has a degree in nursing; his father is a landscape gardener. Both have extensive knowledge of plants. They are not afraid of hard work. They are practical, homely people. Mark puts his arms around his parents. He knows they are here because he told them he is going to leave home.

The launch enters the lagoon and anchors a few meters off shore. John, Bill, Grace, Ben, Martin and Ella appear on the deck. Bill goes up the few stairs to a platform.

"Hello. We hope you enjoyed your passage. Couldn't ask for a nicer day and better conditions. In a moment, we will assist you over to the island in our dinghy. This will mean several trips to get you and your luggage ashore. Any questions?"

"So, do we hang around, or do we get our stuff and go?" asks Terrance casually.

"We would like you to stay until the last family arrives. We will go over a few points again." He runs his eyes over the contestants. "Now, if you can get ready to leave, we will take the larger families first."

The waters of the lagoon are crystal clear and as the Downs are slowly taken across, Jessie points out the different fish, while Mary chatters about the coral's beauty.

Jessie eyes are full of anticipation. "Oh, Mum, Dad, this is going to be so much fun. Can we swim when we get there?"

"We'll see," laughs Yvonne, enjoying seeing her children interested in something outside. "Remember, we have to construct our sleeping quarters tonight."

"Oh, got that covered," Harvey says with pride. "Remember, I grabbed those tents."

"Good idea, that!" replies Stan, rubbing Harvey's back.

"Yeah, I know."

Yvonne feels grateful that Stan has acknowledged Harvey's sensible action, even though other items were compromised. She is happy to see her husband's face beaming with that beautiful smile she fell in love with. *He's still tall and fit … wearing the same hairstyle. Always loved his fringe swept back.* This, together with his sideburns, olive skin and come-to-bed eyes, had mesmerized her from the start. It had been a while since she remembered this.

It takes nearly two hours to get everyone and their luggage onto the beach. Martin has not been feeling well, so he and Ella stay on the launch with half of his team. Back on the beach, John, Bill, Alison and Ben address the contestants for the final time.

"Okay, guys, just a few things to remember. You have to be the whole family to win. If someone gets sick or hurt, use your flare; don't try to be heroes. We're anchored out at sea and we have a helicopter on stand-by. If anyone from your team can make it to this beach, it would be helpful."

"Just one more thing," says Alison, a serious tone to her voice. "Please do not contaminate the fresh water. Any rubbish that is not biodegradable, including your body waste, can be put in the specially designed green bins. They are chemically treated to break down materials and odors. Their positions are marked on your maps."

"Right, that's it. Take care," says John, as his eyes sweep over the group of people in front of him one last time before they leave.

CHAPTER FOUR

Everyone opens the envelopes attached to their chests. They find a basic map of the island, locating the waterfall, dangerous areas, fruit trees and shorelines with swimmable beaches. Another sheet of paper shows photographs of poisonous plants and sea life. Inside each chest are the two flares, a first-aid kit, a hammer, a moderately-sized spade, a pick and garden fork, a pocketknife, large plastic bags with the word 'rubbish' in white bold print, a compass and a colored flag. For each member there are food utensils, plates, cups and bowls, a water bottle, mosquito net and a sleeping bag.

Clever! Any items missing can be easily identified if another team takes them. Aron Jenner hopes it won't come to that. He takes a mental note to watch out for the Tillers and Jack Crompton. He can't put his finger on it, but there's something about Jack that makes him feel uneasy.

"Aron, if we take the chest, it could come in handy. I know it will slow us down, but in the long run, could be worth it. What do you think?"

"Huh?"

"I said, what about this chest?"

"You want to take it? Good. We should." Aron places the map on the sand, studies it then looks around. "The waterfall's to the left. Looks a pain with all this vegetation, and there's hills … probably be wetter. I reckon we go right, to the far end." He points. "This smaller beach area looks flat. Fruit trees are close. We can make day trips to the waterfall."

"Sounds good to me." Helena stands. "Let's see how heavy this thing is." She grimaces. "Bloody hell! We'll have to make stops."

"Fair enough. Let's go, before the others make a start."

They walk in silence, headed for the inviting shade the palms.

The Hendersons set out in the same direction. They want to reach a small cove they like the look of, in time to find a suitable place to set up camp before nightfall.

Mark Wentworth watches his father study the map. His dad's finger drums repeatedly on an area towards the middle of the island. It is slightly inland from the next cove. Mark knows his dad is thinking of protection, in case the weather turns.

"It's a good idea, Dad, but it's kinda late. Might be wise to go in the morning. Looks to me as if most are heading north. I think the Downs are camping here but, with the kids, we can easily lose them." Mark looks down the beach. "As to those brothers, don't think we have to worry about them with the amount they put away. We should make a tent up there, to the left, between those bigger palms."

Linda gets up, stretches and yawns. "Golly, it is awfully hot. Makes sense to wait, don't you agree, dear?"

"Absolutely. Let's get our bags and make our way up."

While Nigel and Mark construct the shelter with the tarpaulins they brought, Linda gets to work pulling out mosquito nets and sleeping bags. She finds the picnic rug with the plastic underside and lays it down. It will keep any dampness from seeping through into their sleeping bags.

Rosaline, aware that some families have already left with their chests, looks at their orange one and groans. Jack is taking everything out of their bags, gesturing to her to do the same with the chest. She opens the lid, spies the rope and suggests they use one of the tarpaulins; they could fold it up, put some rope through the holes and place the chest on top, so that they can drag it behind them and carry it when they need to. Jack's expression delivers another wound.

"What the hell are those two up to?" Karl says, somewhat amused.

"Who cares?" mutters Greg.

Terrance pushes himself up. "Gotta pee. I'll check out the rocks."

"We should look at this chest."

"Jesus, Greg, he needs a piss. *You* do the housekeeping."

Terrance stares at his brothers and nudges Greg with his foot before he departs.

The Longs pack up their gear and move to the shelter of the overhanging umbrella-like foliage. They also decide to stay overnight. Their plan is to cut northwest, where there looks to be another small beach, marked suitable for swimming because of a coral shelf. Eric and Warren get to work and attach a tarpaulin between two palms. Bridget and Sara connect mosquito nets overhead. The invisible humidity takes hold as darkness descends. Exhausted, they sit, munching biscuits and drinking orange juice.

"Where do we go to the toilet?"

"Knew you'd ask that, Sara, so I kept a bucket out," says Eric.

"Warren, can you come and hold the torch?"

"Sure. You need to go, Bridget?"

"Yes, think I will."

They walk a few meters into the lush, green foliage, find a suitable spot and Warren hands over the torch.

"Guess we won't mind about this in a few days, darling. You go first."

Sara's body trembles as the scuttle and bustle of nearby insects intensifies. She hastily changes places with her mother.

"Lord, it's a bit awkward, isn't it? Bridget chuckles. "Hope I can get back up again."

Oh God! Sara shudders; she has no intention of seeing her mother naked.

"All done. Sara, you take the bucket." Bridget touches her daughter's shoulder and walks over to Warren. In the dim light, Sara catches her foot and loses her balance.

"Shit!"

The torch bounces over her and Warren shakes with laughter.

"I wouldn't have bloody fallen if you hadn't taken all the goddamn light." She furiously brushes herself. "Guess I don't have to empty the wretched thing now. Oh, great. Now it's broken."

Bridget smiles. "Doesn't matter, darling. We have more."

They arrive back at their shelter and Eric stands instantly. "What happened?"

"Nothing!" replies Sara, frostily.

"I'll tell you later," whispers Bridget. "Sara, where are you going?"

"I'm going to wash my hands? That all right?"

Warren reaches for her. "Sorry, babes. Want company?"

"No, I won't be long." Sara briskly walks to the water's edge. Her eyes adjust quickly in the moonlight.

"Hi."

"Who's there?"

"Karl Tiller. Was about to take a dip, care to join me?"

"'Course not!"

"Okay, okay! I was just being friendly."

"We're not friends." *Arrogant bastard!* She washes her hands, glances at Karl's disappearing silhouette and hastily retreats.

"Who was that, babe?"

"One of those brothers. Make sure we camp away from them."

"I agree," says Bridget. "Acting too carefree for my liking. Did you see the amount of booze they put away?"

"Well, let's get some sleep. Best be up early and off before any of them." Eric places his sleeping bag next to his wife.

As the sun rises above the horizon, casting a coppery gold streak across the waiting ocean, Eric wakes his family. They quickly eat cereal, followed by bananas, take a quick drink of water and pack everything up. Eric levels the sand and they disappear into the lush greenery as though they were never there.

Their progress is hindered by the masses of ever-expanding undergrowth. The vines wrap onto anything they can and the dense leaves cleverly mask what lies beneath. Ferns grow, tucked into trunks; hibiscus plants become scarce and banana clumps send them off course. They rest in a small clearing and Bridget sees a breadfruit tree.

"What do you do with the fruit?"

"Well, Sara, we can cook them. It's really nice with coconut milk and if you wrap it in banana leaves, it has a wonderful flavor, similar to baked bread ... hence the name."

"Impressive, Mum. So glad of your island blood. That list we got is good but it doesn't say how to cook anything."

Back on the beach, Mark wakes and quickly nudges his parents. It is early and he wants to go. Linda gets out three water bottles and muesli bars so they can eat as they walk. She packs the last remaining items away, makes them rub on insect repellent with sunscreen and they set off. Mark and Nigel go first, carrying their chest.

Jessie wakes with a jolt. The vision of a giant crab eating her vanishes as she catches sight of the Wentworths disappearing into the trees.

"Dad, Mum, wake up. The others are leaving."

Yvonne yawns. "Stan, come on, get up. We need to get going."

Stan groans, rubs his eyes, unravels himself from his sleeping bag, stands and stretches until he hears a pop somewhere down his spine. He whips off his shirt, grabs Jessie's hand and runs down to the water. She squeals uncontrollably as he washes her then piggybacks her back up.

"Oh, that was so fun. You guys should do it."

Harvey groans. "I'm a bit over piggybacks, Jessie."

Stan snickers. "Come on, take a dip. It'll wake you up. Jess and I will take care of this."

"Do I have to, Dad?" asks Mary. "It's so early and it looks cold."

"Go with your mother right now, both of you."

Mary and Harvey reluctantly follow Yvonne into the water. Harvey yanks Mary's legs and she surfaces, spluttering and cursing.

"If you need to go number ones, do it now."

"Oh, gross!" Mary dives under and resurfaces quickly. "Oh, my God! Did you go?"

"Of course," laughs Yvonne automatically. "Don't be so silly, Mary, everyone does it!"

Harvey bombards Mary with a wall of water. "Boy, I can't wait till you have to do number twos."

"Just hurry up you two, so we can get the best spot."

"There's probably more than one spot here, Mum."

"Don't get smart, Harvey. Five minutes then we're off."

Yvonne strides out of the water and smiles to herself as she hears Harvey and Mary behind her. Mary heads straight for her bag, wipes herself down and ties her towel around her waist.

"Hey, Dad, my bag's really heavy!"

"Really, Mary? What a surprise." He stops packing and looks at his daughter. "We'll take breaks, or you can leave some of it behind … no, I didn't think so."

"You need to harden up," says Harvey smugly.

Stan frowns at Yvonne, motions for them to move and they veer southwest towards the waterfall.

The Smyths head for a small cove further north. It means traveling more or less in a straight line through the middle of the island. The reasoning behind their decision is that Ian and Josh believe it to be sheltered and close to the fruit trees. Kate happily lets her husband, Ian, and brother, Josh, take charge and follows behind her son, Logan, as they set off.

The lush bush becomes dense quickly. Josh says it's hardly surprising, as there hasn't been much human interference. He identifies a few plants and trees along the way and Kate takes a mental note of where they are. None of them thought to bring a pen and paper but they have a compass and, as Ian says, as long as they keep going north, they'll be fine.

Moana notices the Smyths heading right. By her calculations, there are at least three families going in that direction. Last night, she studied the map before she fell asleep and came to the same conclusion; heading north was best. She likes the look of the protruding arm-like land that juts out significantly into the lagoon. *Staying close to the sea will be vital. If it's safe, fishing could be choice.* She found fishing tackle, comprising of hooks, sinkers and some synthetic long-line rope and nylon lines, when they were in the warehouse. Matt had been thankful for her wisdom. She knew he and the boys hadn't thought about any fishing parts, since rods were not allowed.

She rolls up her sleeping bag, takes out some crackers, eats a few, walks down to the water, strips and takes a dip. She isn't too worried about people seeing her naked. It's not as though she's a great beauty these days. She knows she's let herself go over the years, but being here will change that. *I'll lose weight. Matt and the boys will be better off, too. They'll have to make do. Matt's tendency to eat all the wrong foods won't be a problem.*

Getting out of the water, she dresses and heads back. The boys stir. She tells them to eat while kicking Matt awake.

"Been for a swim, Mum?" Sammy asks, trying to roll his sleeping bag while shoving a cracker into his mouth. It unrolls with a life of its own. "Fuck!"

"Slow down, love. You eat, I'll do your bag." Moana shakes out the sand, rolls it up and, holding it between her legs, gets the cover on before Sammy finishes his mouthful. "Now," she says, "I did go for a quick dip to wash! It wouldn't be dumb if you did the same."

"Okay, Mum," says Zach. "Any ideas where you want to set up camp? Noticed you studying the map."

"Yes, I've had a thought." She kicks Matt again. "Get up, lazybones."

She watches Matt roll out of his sleeping bag. *He looks like a disheveled hobo … bloody hair's full of sand – skin looks like shit.*

"Yuck, my mouth's rough." He rises and stumbles down to the water, wades in like a duck and takes a leak. Zach and Sammy whistle, while Moana looks away. *God he's hopeless. Worse today.* She turns around to see if anyone is watching.

"Right, you two can carry the chest. No one else is leaving theirs, we won't either."

Matt's clothes cling in all the wrong places as he trudges back. He helps himself to food and juice. Zach and Sammy exchange looks with their mother.

Sammy rolls his eyes. "What's the plan, Mum?"

Moana tells them of her idea to go right and stay near the sea. The boys don't argue with her logic and she knows Matt won't care. They pick up their bags and chest and leave. Moana sees the smaller woman from the Booths family watching them. She smiles and waves.

"Nice of you to acknowledge her, Trudy," Celia says, as she packs the last of their things away. "They seem a bit basic."

"Where's Ritchie?"

"Oh, he got up early. Boy Scout stuff. Fancies himself as an explorer."

Drew smiles to himself.

"Really? I'd never of picked it."

Celia raises her right hand "Was in the Scouts, you know."

"Well, well … Quite the little trooper, isn't he? Better come back with some useful information, then."

Drew has cleared up their campsite spotlessly and is sitting on the chest, deep in concentration, studying the map. *Right looks best, but maybe we better re-think. Hope Ritchie comes back saying he's found something … Kinda like it here, sitting halfway between the waterfall and the fruit trees. Get the morning sun; be cooler in the afternoons and this beach is good. Can fish off those rocks under the cliff and the rock pools should have shellfish.* He looks up. *And it looks as if everyone else is leaving.*

Ritchie appears out of the palm trees, eyes sparkling with all the promise in the world. "There's a fucking ginormous banyan tree, 'bout ten meters in. Shit load of exterior roots that make a hollow area in the middle. We can use them to build some kind of platform."

"My God. You really do like this Robinson Crusoe stuff, don't you?" says Trudy.

"And I'd like to know what a 'fucking ginormous banyan tree' is?" asks Celia playfully.

"Ha fucking ha," says Ritchie dryly. "As you know," he says looking directly at her. "I've been investigating tree houses and this tree is a doozy."

"Never heard of them," says Drew lazily, folding up the map.

"Neither had I till I Googled it. They used them in the film 'Avatar'. They're amazing ... leaves are huge. We'll be protected from the weather and if we build something off the ground it should be dry and keep pests out. We can use our mosquito nets and tarps for extra protection. What do you think?"

"You're not just a pretty face are you?" says Trudy impressed. "Sounds as if we better get a move on before someone else grabs it."

"Let's go, then." Celia picks up her bag. "Good job it's close, 'cause I'd hate to have to carry this too far."

"I figured on that, hon," smiles Ritchie tenderly and the four of them head off. They come across the tree within minutes. It stands like a protector, dwarfing anything near it, surrounded yet left alone, as if the other trees know not to intrude. Golden rays reach its branches, giving them an ethereal beauty.

"God, Ritchie, you're right. It does look like something out of a film," squeals Trudy with delight.

"Yeah, I know, and see these? Well, maybe we can make some kind of ladder out of them to get up."

"Vines, eh?" says Celia biting her nail. "Yes, why not? It says on this map that there's some bamboo to the right. If we cut some and use them for poles, then I guess we could make some sort of ladder."

"That could work. Bamboo's pretty hardy." Drew dumps his bag down. "Let's get started, 'cause this is gonna take a while."

CHAPTER FIVE

Terrance wakes with a start. His eyelids open, but focusing is difficult in the muted light. He blinks twice, momentarily forgetting where he is. They hadn't gone far before deciding to camp and even though it is morning the cave lacks definition.

"Greg, Karl, you awake?"

Greg rubs his eyes. "Just."

Karl mutters a barely audible hello, rolls over and farts.

"Jesus, Karl!" hisses Terrance as he reaches for their torch. Greg stretches out his hand and feels the cold damp wall.

"Not sure about this, guys."

"Why?"

"Don't bats hang out in caves?"

"Bats? Geez, Greg, don't be such a girl. Terrance, shine that further in."

They see that the ceiling descends quickly, leaving a half-cylindrical black hole.

"Perhaps we should explore that, before we make up our minds."

"Of course we're going to explore it. Honestly Greg, did you really think we're going to stay here? Duh … Anyone would find us instantly."

Terrance shakes his head. "Greg, stay put. We'll go."

"Well, don't be long."

"Woohoo," moans Karl, towering over Greg.

"Knock it off." Terrance pushes Karl forward and before long they are on their hands and knees. Terrance stops when the beam from the torch splits and he reaches out to touch the smooth frigid surface.

"I'll take the torch, see if we can get through?"

"Okay, but remember I'm bigger than you. And don't take too long."

Terrance crawls forward, leaving Karl in blackness. The walls are icy yet not moist. He hears Karl yell, but is unable to make out what he's said. Smiling, he makes his way back.

"Man, that's tight. You'll be fine though. It opens into this huge space. Got two more tunnels. The roof's really high. Good thing is, there's this opening, so there's plenty of light. Greg should be happy … no bats, nothing. Don't need to do a thing."

"Sounds good to me."

They get back to find Greg has everything packed and ready to move.

"So, how are we going to get the chest in there?"

"Jesus Greg, do you even have a brain? We'll push it."

"Push?"

"Yeah. Well, not you, obviously. Me and Terrance."

"You can go first."

"First?"

"What's the problem now? Terrance's been down and it's fine. No coffins; no vampires."

"Oh ha, ha."

"Greg, you gotta man up."

"All right, all right. I just don't like dark spaces."

"It won't be dark, 'cause you'll have the torch and if you turn it on, you'll be able to see."

"Sarcasm is the lowest …"

"Knock if off. We'll come back for the chest." Terrance shoves his bag forward and vanishes into the tunnel, leaving his brothers' bickering behind.

Terrance watches Greg inch out of the tunnel and pick himself up, sending sand in all directions. "So, Greg, you like?"

"Yeah, it's good. Great, in fact."

"Yeah, pretty cool, huh. Ready-made shelter."

"So how about you set up and Karl and I'll get the chest and then go check out these other tunnels."

"Suits me."

"Hey, Greg?" says Karl, toying with the sand directly under the opening in the ceiling.

"Yep."

"We'll make a fire here. Smoke will rise and go out the hole."

"I hear you, Karl."

"Hey ..."

"Yeah?"

"Was only teasing before."

"I know. Done and dusted. Scoot."

After getting the chest, Terrance and Karl leave Greg doing what he does best and descend down the tunnel, towards the salty-seaweed breeze. The opening comes out just as the cliff turns towards a small cove. The shelly sand becomes a sea of black rocks, some glistening, some covered with slippery green velvet upholstery. Crystal clear, mirrored ponds lay trapped, in wait for a top-up. To their right, the reddish-brown precipice ascends quickly then becomes a mixture of over-hang roots and boulders, where seeds have survived and sprouted into various shades of green. At the top, pine-like warriors stand tall, protecting what lies inland.

Collecting stones, they head back and see spoons protruding from three baked bean cans. Karl takes one and empties it in seconds, then downs a can of apple juice.

"Okay ... yep ... where's a bucket? Hmm ... wonder how deep this sand is?"

"Whoa, you're not going here, bro, and put one of those plastic bags over it when you're done."

"Terrance, I wasn't about to dig here."

Terrance cocks an eyebrow.

"I'll be off then," replies Karl as he waves the bucket around like Julie Andrews on a summer day, high on a Salzburg hill.

"Fucking idiot," laughs Terrance.

Karl reappears, clutching his bum. "Did you guys bring dunny paper?"

"Shit, I didn't," says Terrance glancing at Greg.

"Fortunately for you guys, I did. Just a sec! Here you are. Three-ply, extra long. Took up a bit more room, but figured we'd …"

"For Christ's sake, give it."

Greg tosses.

"Damn it, Greg, you throw like a girl. It's full of fucking sand now." Karl retrieves it and storms down the tunnel.

"It's not as if your bum will notice."

Greg snorts. "Oh, that's good, Terrance. Crikey, hope he's not long."

Terrance smiles teasingly at Greg's screwed up nose. "You know he's probably filled it by now, right?" He folds the map and puts it in his pocket. "We should get going."

They see Karl returning and Greg exists down the tunnel before Terrance has moved. "Shit he can be devious when he wants to be."

Karl hollers. "Just follow your nose, Greg."

"You finished? 'Cause it's already ten-thirty and we've done nothing."

"Not true. Had breakfast and … I've done poooos."

"Dick."

Karl shrugs. "These gloves for me?"

"Yep. Take a hat and get some sunscreen. It's got repellent in it. If there's mossies, they'll be at the waterfall."

Greg comes back and Terrance leaves, asking for them to wait a couple of minutes before joining him.

"Oh, good, you're got the pocketknife and … rope. Yeah, guess we might need that." Greg makes a final sweep of their cave and, satisfied they haven't forgotten anything, he and Karl make their way down the tunnel.

"Hey, Terrance. Tide's on its way out, that'll make life easier."

"Still have to be careful, it's pretty slippery. You go last, Greg."

As they get closer to the cove, the rocks get bigger and drier, making their progress easier. Karl buries their excrement. Terrance waits till he's finished before he says it might be wiser to turf it in the sea in the future or at least find one of the bins on the map.

Terrance starts their ascend with Karl and Greg in tow. Being mostly volcanic, the cliff is quite solid, making it relatively easy to climb. They reach halfway and take a breather, surveying the view. There is nothing but blue in front of the reef. They wonder where the launch is anchored? Terrance motions for them to start moving and grabs hold of the vines and tree roots readily available. Sweating profusely, they reach the top and realize they have no binoculars.

"Well, that was smart!" says Greg, using his hat like a fan.

"What's to see? There's just 360 degrees of ocean out there," voices Karl. "Hey, listen. Is that the waterfall?"

"Reckon so. We'll follow the noise." Terrance moves towards the inviting shrubbery. "This could be some sort of track."

They sip water and start descending. Going down is harder than coming up and the twisting flora slows them down.

"Hold onto the vines," yells Terrance, as he carefully maneuvers himself around a large tree, where he finds the shrubbery has been replaced by rock. Inching forward they become surrounded by a fine mist. Cascading water drowns the bird and insect orchestra and Terrance finds they can go no further.

"Back up guys," he shouts. "Unless you want to dive." He sees the nervous shake of Greg's head. "We'll find another route."

They continue on until Terrance stops suddenly. A chasm halts their progress. Its cliffs tower over a stream and Karl suggests the rope. They tie a knot on one end and Karl goes up a large tree near the edge and wraps the other end around its biggest branch.

"Greg, it's okay. Watch." Terrance grabs the rope, steps backwards, runs and leaps out, pushing his body forward and makes it to the other side with ease.

"Piece of cake," he bellows, as he thrusts the rope back.

Karl grabs it. "You sure you want to go last, Greg?"

"Oh, yes, perfectly."

Terrance signals to Greg, puckers his lips, bends his legs and scratches his armpits as Karl leaps and lands beside him with a thump.

"Oh, very funny, asshole."

Terrance snickers and gives Greg the thumbs up. Karl hurls the rope back. Greg misses and it swings back.

"No matter. Try again," yells Terrance, catching Karl's raised eyes.

Greg leaps like a frog and manages to grab hold of the swinging rope. He signals tentatively to his brothers, who stand waiting with crossed arms. *I know what they think. Please, God – don't let it be like school.*

"Are you praying, Greg?"

"No," yells Greg quickly.

Terrance looks at Karl. "You ready to catch him?" Karl nods, as Greg lingers near the edge.

"No, don't look down," yells Terrance. "Turn around!"

"Okay, okay." Greg hesitantly ambles back. "I will not be sick," he mutters. "I can do this." He closes his eyes and runs. He is off. His spring is good and he flies past the outstretched hands of Karl, smacking straight into a tree. Karl and Terrance grab him as he starts to dangle back.

"You okay, Greg? That was quite a smack. You've won a few bruises there, buddy."

"I don't care, Terrance. Chest's a bit sore, though."

"Winded yourself, mate," states Karl. "Here, drink. We've done the hard part. Soon be having that swim. See down there … not far now. Doesn't she look good?"

"Amazing," says Greg rubbing his chest.

The sun shines down, forming small white diamonds, which glisten and dance over the still pond. The waterfall cascades about seven meters, sending spray upwards, forming the mist-like veil that they experienced near the top.

"You two go. I'll … just get my breath."

"Sure."

Karl and Terrance easily make their way down, leaving Greg to follow when ready and find an open patch of grass, strip off and enter the water. It is brisk but forgiving and, after seawater, it feels silky and clean. Karl swims over to the waterfall and finds a ledge. He begins to shower. Terrance joins him and looks back to see Greg slowly getting in. He watches his ungainly dog paddle and waits to help him out. They wash and then make their way towards the lighter water.

"I'm going to take a dive over by those rocks. See if there's anything worth getting. Coming Terrance?"

"Sure."

"I'll stay."

"Yeah, you rest, Greg, that chest's pretty red," says Karl as he and Terrance swim towards the rocks. They do a couple of dives and head back.

"Anything?"

"Yep, some type of prawn. Could be similar to yabbies. Terrance reckons he saw an eel."

"Really?"

"Don't get your hopes up, Greg. Eels are fast and masters of camouflage. Catching them won't be easy. Spear might work," says Karl. "Anyway, time to go. Give me that bottle Greg. I'll swim to the waterfall and fill it."

"Why don't we just fill it here?"

"'Cause it's cleaner where it's flowing." Karl snatches the bottle and re-enters the pool.

"I think it's cleaner near the middle, 'cause the crap would have sunk."

"True," says Terrance. "Doesn't matter, 'cause we're boiling it anyway."

They follow the stream back towards the beach and veer right where they hope to find the tunnel's entrance. The bush is dense and they have to step over fallen trunks and navigate the many tangled vines trapping their feet. The lush tree canopies deny the sun from entering, making it seem late in the day. All three wear gloves to protect their hands, constantly under attack from the foliage's razor sharp edges.

Twenty minutes in, the bush becomes clearer, they forget about the tunnel, make it back to the beach and discard their clothes.

"Nice cold beer would be good about now," says Karl.

"Yeah, it would," answers Terrance, as they float on their backs, limbs spread out like starfish.

CHAPTER SIX

The Wentworths notice the Jenners, Davidsons and Cromptons have decided to reside at the cove that they want. Nigel and Mark head into the bush, find a tree that will enable them to make some sort of tree house, get Linda and then spend the rest of the day collecting palm leaves and bamboo canes.

Jack Crompton watches, unnoticed. He sees the canes lying ahead, and crouches down, observing Mark as he drags more. He waits till Mark is a comfortable distance away and silently creeps forward, takes two and leaves them in the cover of the undergrowth.

Rosaline makes herself busy while waiting for Jack. She knows he is furious the others have stayed. He said the cove was theirs – they reached it first. She told him he was being ridiculous and he had stormed off.

She was so relieved when they had stumbled upon their small cavern. If she hadn't insisted on resting at the north end of the beach, they would have missed it. She had climbed onto the rocky ledge, sat beneath the cover of protruding branches and noticed a small chamber in the rock face behind her. Pulling back the needle-like leaves answered all her prays and she stood inside and called Jack over.

She now finishes hanging a mosquito net from the tree when she hears a noise and sees Jack striding towards her.

"We have a door," she says, proudly.

"Terrific!"

"Where did you get those?"

"You'll see."

"But you didn't take a knife."

"Didn't need it."

"I don't understand."

"Come."

Rosaline follows Jack till he pushes her down. He points to a pile of canes a meter ahead and then further on.

"Oh, Jack – no. You need to bring them back."

"Don't be stupid. They shouldn't leave them lying around. We need four more, then we leave."

"We just can't take them."

"Sure we can. We're not here to make friends. Sometimes you need to get your hands dirty."

"It's not right."

"Fine." Jack grabs her arm. "You go back, get the knife and cut them down. Call me when you're finished."

"What?"

"You heard."

He's so unfair. Always got some answer, making me do things I don't want to. She sighs giving the faintest of nods.

"Good girl. Now, stay here – watch and be quiet." Jack moves silently while the Wentworth's backs are to him. He grabs four canes and with Rosaline's help they carry them to their shelter. Rosaline grudgingly helps construct a wall between the closest trees. The sound of his cheerful whistling incenses her and she feels the bond with her husband slip further away.

Back at the Wentworth's shelter Mark is puzzled. He is nearly out of canes. He asks his parents but they can't shed any light on the situation. Feeling pissed, he knows they will have to get more and their knife is now useless. Nigel tells him not to worry. They have plenty of time.

The Davidsons have been busy all day, gathering palm leaves, bamboo canes and banana leaves. Zach even managed to get a bunch of bananas that Moana had seen and they have hung them up to ripen.

Matt found some pieces of volcanic rock. One is shaped like an axe and he has been trying to make it sharper. He plans to tie it with thin vines to a bamboo cane, in which he made two holes, and is now finishing a notch to wrap the vine around for extra strength.

"Looking good, Dad," yells Sammy counting more canes. "Got fifteen!"

"Good. If we use that larger palm over there as a support, we can line them to that one over there. We'll get more tomorrow if we need them. Can use the tarps for shelter again tonight."

Moana has woven palm leaves into a mat. Having learned weaving as a child, it is second nature to her, but now her hands ache. She looks at her work, then at Matt and the boys, stands and wanders down to the water, climbs up the rocks to the ledge that protrudes out to the reef and walks along its flat, dry path. She stops, takes off her clothes and dives into the clean, lukewarm bath. A few curious fish dart back and forth. She can see the bottom is sandy and decides to stand, carefully placing her feet down. The water comes up to her shoulders and envelopes her body. She relieves herself, gets back onto the warm ledge and lies down. The black rock's heat soothes away her aches and pains. She lets herself relax for a few minutes, then rises, puts on her clothes and walks back. She opens a bag to see what she can muster up for dinner, while Matt and the boys bang in the last canes.

Feeling proud, Moana tells the boys to use the mosquito nets again and puts her arms around Matt. Once they have them up, they collapse onto her mat. It is eight-thirty and they are exhausted and hungry. Moana opens tins of smoked oysters and salmon, while Matt gets four cans of beer.

"Whoa! I didn't know we'd brought beer," says Sammy, thrilled.

"Yep – gotta few more, too."

"Choice, Dad," says Zach, pulling the tab of his can. "Man, there's nothing like the first taste."

A pleased grin lights up Matt's face. "You're not wrong there, son."

Sammy hands out the stale bread. They dip it into the tins to soak up the brine and sit in silence, admiring the perfect sunset. The sea is a glorious mixture of gold, copper and aquamarine, and against the burning sky of reds, oranges and yellows it is dazzling.

"You know," whispers Matt, "I'd forgotten how much I like making things."

"Hmm, I can see that. You've got that look again. This is going to be the making of us, hon, just wait and see!"

Matt puts his arm around his wife and drinks his beer. Usually, he would have downed it by now, but tonight he feels no need. He hasn't felt this untroubled in years. He sees Zach and Sammy exchanging looks, knowing it has been a long time since they have seen their parents sit together, smiling. It feels good.

A little further west, Aron Jenner finds himself knackered. His arms ache. Helena tells him to take a plunge in the sea before they put up their tarpaulin. He strips off and walks tiredly down to the water. Even though he has worn gloves, his hands are red and sore. He hopes he isn't going to get blisters, but thinks it inevitable. He gets in and falls back in the cool water, letting it cleanse him.

The salt stings, but he knows it will do him good. He gazes up at the dazzling lights, thinking how magnificent the night is. His stomach rumbles, wanting food, and he gets out and strolls up the sand to see Helena has the torch going. He inhales the salty air; rubs his chin and decides tomorrow will be about fire.

Helena gives him a towel and kisses him. "This is brilliant," she purrs, pressing against him. He spies the picnic rug they argued over bringing, lifts her up and forgets about his stomach. They make love to the gentle song of the waves and the constant drone of insects.

The Smyths noticed the cove they chose was already harboring three families, so they went on to the next one. They found a broad, raised piece of land on the western side, sheltered by a protruding cliff, which provides protection from the southerly winds. They now have little time to erect anything decent before darkness and Kate has them gathering bundles of pine-like needles to place under their sleeping bags.

Finishing for the day, they put up tarpaulins and mosquito nets. Kate gets out tinned spaghetti and gooey chocolate biscuits. They decide to go to bed so they can get up early to make a huge effort on their shelter. Josh says the weather might turn anytime.

CHAPTER SEVEN

It was overcast when the Longs woke the next morning. They traveled inland, straight across to the larger beach on the western side, liked what they saw and put up a makeshift tent.

Now, after rising and having breakfast, Eric and Warren go to cut down canes while Bridget and Sara set to work dragging foliage for walls and a floor.

The Downs set up their camp slightly southwest of the main beach. They decided to go towards the waterfall and found a raised ledge protruding from the bottom of the volcano. It is dry and sheltered on the west side by a huge She-oak tree. Its branches are perfect for Stan to tie a tarpaulin to make an awning between their tents. The ground is solid but over the years the fallen debris has made a thick layer deep enough to hold their tents' pegs. They use the two tents to sleep in and store their gear under the canopy. Both tents have netted windows and flaps for the doors, enabling the breeze to blow through.

Yvonne thought to bring weed matting and they place it on the south side of their shelter and tie it to the awning. Pulling it taut, they use rocks to hold it, cover it with fronds for extra insulation and then place their mosquito nets on top, making their shelter comfortable, dry and sheltered from wind.

"Er, Mum, where's Dad?" asks Jessie timidly.

"Why?"

Jessie points and Yvonne stops what she is doing. The spider is large, brownish in color, with long matchstick-like legs. "Okay, let's not panic, they're not poisonous." She hurries to the doorway and sees Harvey. "Where's Dad?"

"Gone to the waterfall."

"Goddammit … Grab your net and go inside. Where's Mary?"

"I'm up here, Mum."

Yvonne raises her head.

"I'm getting flowers for you. They're so pretty."

Yvonne sees the orchids with their spectacular white, pink and yellow blooms and smiles at their welcoming contrast to the palette of earthy colors.

"Okay, be careful."

"'Course, I'm not stupid. Be down in a mo."

Yvonne heads back inside, where Harvey is trying to entice the spider into his net by poking it with a stick. It descends down its silvery thread and Jessie runs outside, shrieking. The spider is fast and Yvonne curses as it easily maneuvers out of harm's way. She instinctively raises her leg and slams her foot down. Feeling repulsed, she flings her shoe outside.

Harvey retrieves it and shoves it near Jessie's face. Horrified, Jessie screams and screams.

"For God's sake, Harvey." Exasperated, Yvonne cradles her daughter. "Shh now … it's dead!"

"I hate him (sniff) … I do. What … what if there's more? Oh, Mum (sniff) … I want to go home!"

"Oh, darling, don't be silly. It's gone. Harvey, go and check there's no more."

"Oh, what?" Harvey takes in his mother's glare and begrudgingly marches inside. He instantly reappears holding a can of insect spray. "Look, Jess, I brought this. It'll kill anything."

Yvonne holds Jessie tight. "I don't know, you guys. One moment you're at each other's throats and the next you're nice as pie."

Jessie dries her eyes and smiles. "That was smart of him, wasn't it, Mum?"

"Yes darling. Feeling better?"

Jessie nods, hears her father's cheery whistle and quickly wipes her eyes.

"Hey, what's all this?"

"Spider," mouths Yvonne as Stan sits down and lifts Jessie onto his lap.

"Spider, huh?"

Jessie nods.

"Gone?"

"Yes – mum squashed it."

"Mum did?"

"Well I got it down," corrects Harvey, throwing the insect spray down.

"Don't worry, Harvey, I haven't forgotten what you did." Yvonne's words do not fall on deaf ears. She knows her son is well aware he needs to tread lightly. She turns her attention back to Jessie and hears Stan telling their daughter about where he's been. How there's a huge pool with a waterfall they can shower under and if you dive around the rocks, you can see little prawns. She hears him promise that if the weather holds, he'll take them there tomorrow.

"Harvey, that fire okay?"

"All good, Dad. Went down before, got a bucket of twigs and that dried grass – burns good. Can we go to the rock pools – see if we can something?"

"Sure. How's your line coming along?"

"Ace." Harvey grabs his rod and passes it over. "I cut down a young bamboo cane like you said. Used the pocketknife to make a groove to tie the line around. It works perfectly, Dad."

"Off you hop young lady." He rubs his legs. "Think you're

getting a bit big for sitting on my lap." He opens his bag and takes out a hook.

Mary jumps down. "Is that all you need?" She hands Yvonne the flowers.

"It is. This kind of fishing is called angling. We'll cut up some sardines, place a bit on this hook, wave it around in the water, and whammo – we have fish."

"Can I come?"

"Me too!" shrieks Jessie bouncing excitedly, the horror of the last few minutes forgotten.

"Guess that's okay. All right with you, hon?"

"Actually, why don't we all go? And thank you, Mary, these are lovely." Yvonne takes the flowers and places them in a bucket. They pack what they need and Harvey puts a few larger twigs on the fire before they head off. Reaching the beach, they clamber around the rocks and see the Tillers.

"Hi there guys. Catch anything?"

Terrance looks up. "Oh, hi. Yep, there's cray off those rocks … got huge coconut crabs. You kids wanna see?"

"Choice!" Harvey peers into the sack Terrance opens. "Jesus, they're huge. Dad, – look at this!"

"I'm not a kid," Mary whispers to her mother.

Yvonne grins as she gets the chart from her bag. "Mentions here, those crabs could be poisonous."

Harvey ignores his mother's words. "They're awesome. They look like those red and white toadstools."

"Precisely, Harvey. They're most likely poisonous."

"You're half-right, Mrs. Downs," intervenes Karl. "However, you can usually tell if they're off, 'cause the birds won't eat them."

"I don't get it? What if there's no birds?"

Yvonne rubs her daughter's shoulder. "Oh, there are always birds, darling."

"You're Stan, aren't you?" asks Karl getting out of the pool and coming across to shake his hand.

"Yes. You mind if we fish here?"

"Can't stop you."

Yvonne sees Mary's eyes lock on Terrance. She can see why her daughter is so transfixed. *Those cool blue eyes and tanned skin ... And those dimples are to die for. Even his blond hair pulled back looks sexy.*

She watches Jessie give Mary a shove and frowns as Mary unbuttons her shirt and slips into the pool beside Terrance. She notices the grin Greg gives Karl and quickly looks to her husband, but his attention is elsewhere.

"Harvey, come, let's see if we get any bites."

"Okay, Dad!"

"Mind if I join you?"

"Guess not."

"Great." Karl studies Harvey's handiwork. "Hey, not bad. You've been careful. Tell you what? We have some shrimp – let's put one on, see if we can catch ourselves a fish or two."

"Bought our own sardines," interrupts Stan, glancing at his wife.

Karl leans into Harvey. "Of course you did."

Stan and Harvey follow Karl to the end of the rocks and while Harvey casts his line out, Karl shows Stan where he found crayfish. They catch two more and surface to see how Harvey is doing.

Terrance and Greg show the ladies the sea life in the pool. Greg spots a small octopus. Jessie stays behind her mother, saying she doesn't like the long tentacles; they remind her of the spider. Yvonne finds her a midnight blue starfish.

Stan, Karl and Harvey return; their lines empty.

"Dad thinks we have to go out further to catch anything worthwhile."

Yvonne sighs. "Never mind, love, you can try again tomorrow."

"Cool, we can blow up my boat and …"

"What boat, Harvey?" questions Stan.

"Oh, the one I stuffed into Mary's bag. I bought the inflator thing as well."

"My bag?" screeches Mary. "Oh my God! That's why it's so heavy."

"Stop moaning, I took out some of your stuff."

"What?"

"Christ, you had like a million pairs of bikinis."

Karl winks. "Girl can never have too many bikinis, can she, Mary?"

Greg and Terrance give a short chuckle and Harvey grins triumphantly. Yvonne looks to Stan, her eyes like saucers.

"Mary, Harvey, that's enough."

"But, Dad?"

"Enough."

Terrance smiles at Mary and Stan quickly leans over and rubs Jessie head. "Find anything in here, Pumpkin?"

"Oh, yes, the starfish are so pretty. One's sort of purple, and there's those shrimpy things and prickly sea-eggs too. They're not very pretty. We didn't touch them."

"Good girl. Well, we best head back. Wind's picked up." Stan sniffs the salty air. "Could rain. You guys camping round here?"

"Not on the beach," answers Karl quickly. "You?"

"Yes, we're …"

"Just around to the west," cuts in Stan, putting his hand on Mary's shoulder. "Like I said, we'd better be on our way."

"Yes we had. It was nice to see you."

Karl gives them a quick wave. "Thanks, Yvonne."

"Yvonne?" she whispers to her husband, as Harvey and Jessie nudge each other, delighted with Mary's redness.

"Well, well, Mary. Find Terrance attractive, did we?"

"Oh, shut up, Harvey. You're such a dick."

"He's probably queer," laughs Jessie, poking Harvey.

"God!"

"Stop it. It doesn't matter who's what, and you three think before you speak. We need to keep our location secret."

"Really, Dad?"

"Mary, we don't know them from a bar of soap. This is a competition. Be friendly by all means, but just not too friendly, because things will change."

"What things, Dad?"

"Well, we have to be clever, Jessie. Not give away much. People might get nasty." Stan sees Yvonne frown. "Well maybe not nasty, Jessie, more like not so friendly but that's okay, cause we'll keep to ourselves."

"Oh, but Dad, what if they see our smoke? They'll know where we are."

"I don't think so, Pumpkin – too many trees. You can't see it, can you?"

"Yeah, Jessie, if we can't see it, no one else can."

"That's what Dad said, Harvey."

"Not helping, Mary." Yvonne's kneels before Jessie. "Do you understand what Dad means?"

"S'pose so." Jessie thinks about her diary. *Yes, tomorrow I will take it from behind my pillow and make a nice place for it, which no one will find … but not before I write down about Mary being in love with Terrance Tiller!*

Greg, Karl and Terrance pack up after watching the Downs depart.

"Told you. You got a right little admirer there! How old is she again? Very pretty and quite mature, don't you think, Karl?"

"Very! Mind you, anyone would look mature in that bikini. You agree, Terrance?"

"Don't be fucking ridiculous!"

"Language, Terrance, language!" says Karl. "After all, there could be kiddies around."

Greg erupts into laughter. "Oh God, that's so …"

"Juvenile." Terrance takes off for their cave and is busy stoking the fire when Karl and Greg return.

"Hey, man, sorry," says Karl, giving him a slap on the back. "Seriously, though, noticed the way she looked at you. Be careful … girls like that … trouble."

"I'm well aware of that." Terrance puts the large pot over their makeshift fire.

"I know but *that* doesn't always work out with you, does it?" Karl smashes up the crabs and plops them into the pot. Greg cracks open a coconut and pours the fluid in. It smells good and he gets out their last lemon.

"We need to go look for those fruit trees tomorrow."

"Okay, Greg … and Karl – it's fine."

"I believe you, mate. All I'm saying is, I've seen the looks she gives and you know … you're here, she's here … it's a beautiful island."

"Nothing's going to happen."

"Good, glad to hear it."

Terrance sees the silent communication between his brothers and looks away. He partly entered this contest as an escape. He wasn't expecting Mary and he certainly wasn't expecting Rosaline, but he was okay. Mary was a kid and Rosaline was married. He wasn't going anywhere.

"Chef Greg at your service."

Terrance takes the bowl, sits back and listens to the whistle of the wind as it tries to penetrate their domain, just as the anticipated rain starts to fall.

The Hendersons' progress has been slow. In the morning, Peter twisted his ankle, carelessly tripping over a fallen tree. Feeling mortified, he vented his frustration and blamed his sister for walking too slowly, until the arguing spiraled out of control and nobody knew what they were arguing about. The rest of the day was spent in silence, while they found a suitable place in the bush to make camp.

They finally arrived at the small cove and saw the Smyths on the piece of land they wanted. Annoyed, they begrudgingly moved, finding a part of the cliff with a wide overhang, providing ample head height and protection from the wind. By adding canes to increase the wall size and using large leaves for insulation, they now rest and watch the weather set in.

The Booths listen to the rain falling, from inside their tree house. Earlier, Drew and Ritchie worked like Trojans. They had drawn a rough plan, which had impressed the girls, and had pretty much kept to it. They now have two rooms coming off a larger central room. Because the banyan tree offers so many arterial roots, the walls were easy to construct by filling the gaps with the many large leaves on offer. They covered the floor with layers of needles and put the picnic mats on top, making it soft and comfortable. The girls weaved a flap for the door and by using vines they are able to roll it up. A fire burns at ground level, protected by the tree's spreading branches. Ritchie has constructed a half-meter high oven apparatus out of rocks and bamboo canes.

Celia helps Trudy put the finishing touches to her crayfish curry and Trudy spoons it over the cooked rice already in bowls.

"We should crack open that wine."

"Good idea, bro." Drew gets up and goes to their bags.

Celia feels warm and fuzzy. She watches her husband's hair fall over his face. He lifts his head and she smiles intimately.

Trudy hands out bowls. "A perfect curry for a perfect night."

"Smells divine, love," says Drew as he opens the bottle of Pinot Gris.

"I'll say," purrs Ritchie softly to his wife as she sits beside him. Celia shivers and wishes they were alone. *He's so incredibly good-looking. Of course he knows it … Still, only makes him more attractive.* She feels light-headed, so completely happy when he touches her hair and tucks a piece behind her ear. Warm breath plays on her skin as he whispers 'later babe' in his husky, exotic voice.

"I'll open the other!" says Drew unfazed by his brother's open affection. "Who cares if it's gone?"

"I'll second that." Ritchie licks his fingers. "Trudy, that was ace. Give me your bowls. I'll wash, you guys relax, drink your wine."

"Thanks, bro."

Celia smiles at Trudy. She remembers the effect Ritchie had on Trudy when they were first introduced. How Trudy stammered away, goggle-eyed, blaming it on the incense and how she couldn't handle the smell. *She looked so damn guilty with her flaming cheeks and puppy dog eyes. God, it was funny when Ritchie got her drink and she dribbled.* Over the years, Ritchie's effect on Trudy has lessened and they are now more like brother and sister. *I can't blame Trudy; Ritchie's just plain gorgeous.* She still finds it hard to believe Drew and he are brothers. While Ritchie is tall and athletic, with dark hair and a face to die for, Drew is taller, built like a tank, with golden hair, and although somewhat good-looking, his face is friendly rather than sexy. Luckily, he possesses an awesome smile, full of honesty and safety. She laughs every time Trudy likens him to a bear. 'Big, soft and cuddly!' she says, happy as Larry. *Yes, he's no Ritchie, but he doesn't have to be.* Her thoughts turn to the other men on the island and stop at Terrance.

Ritchie comes back and she wriggles into his body as he fills her mug. She lifts her head and kisses him. He tastes like curry and wine.

"Babe, what say we retire?"

Without hesitation she says goodnight to Drew and Trudy, takes his hand and heads for their room. She slowly takes off her shorts, unbuttons her shirt and slides her finger delicately down her smooth cleavage. Her moan is barely audible when he grabs her and she sinks beneath him as his hands find her naked breasts, sending shivers of anticipation to her hardening nipples. They made love to the sound of the rain hitting the branches above them and she hopes that maybe tonight she might get pregnant. Her thoughts melt with the passion that seeps through her, turning her mind and body to jelly.

CHAPTER EIGHT

The storm rages all night and well into the afternoon. Thunder booms from the menacing black clouds like continuous cannon fire and lightening strikes tear the sky. The torrents of rain and gusts of wind break off tree branches, sending them crashing to the ground, where streams flow swiftly, creating new paths. The dirty-coal sky creates a sooty darkness, making the island gloomy and unnaturally intimidating.

The Tiller boys creep along the tunnel that leads to the sea. They come to the exit but cannot go any further. Waves batter rocks, ejecting cream spray and slimy weed bombs; rain slices the air horizontally and wind howls across the mouth of the cave.

"Jesus! We'd better check the other tunnel."

"Yeah, I agree, Greg," shouts Karl, as he battles against the storm's force.

They turn and make their way back into the cavern and come face to face with a vertical slide of runny caramel.

"Oh, bugger, that's not good. It'll put out our fire!" Karl rushes to their chest and pulls out their gloves. "Quick – put these on … have to move those stones."

As Karl kneels, a huge torrent of water falls into the cavern, drenching him and their fire. "Shit, shit, shit!"

"No good mate, it's dead!" Terrance kicks the wet porridge-like sand. "Better try making a channel." He gets down with Karl and Greg and they work frantically. The water flows sufficiently away to avoid disaster, but with no fire to dry them they crawl into their sleeping bags to wait out the storm.

Meanwhile, the storm attacks the Cromptons' tarpaulin. The relentless wind starts to rip the plastic and Jack battles to try to save what he can before the storm claims it. The mosquito net is getting hammered and Rosaline folds it to one side and hooks it back onto itself. Their dwelling is drenched. Leaves and debris fly into their belongings, leaving them soaked and soiled as the wind gusts threaten to take whatever they can with them. Rosaline rushes around, pushing everything to the back. She is soaked and cold and can no longer see Jack through the blanket of rain. She makes her way against the wind to their entrance and sees him struggling. She grabs one of the ropes flying around but as she pulls it taut, a large gust of wind catches the tarpaulin and the rope is ripped through her hand instantly. She howls, rocked with pain from the fire spreading itself through her palm and watches Jack seize the rope and secure it around the She-oak. He takes hold of Rosaline and they stumble into their shelter and nestle down at the back. He manages to get their chest open, takes out the first-aid kit and a blanket, shutting the lid quickly. He wraps the blanket around her, opens the kit and attends to her hot, red hand. Tears fall freely down her face.

"Oh, God, this is a nightmare. I've never seen a storm like this. Look at this rain … When's it going to stop?" Jack rubs in antibiotic cream and bandages her hand.

"We'll be fine, Roz! It will die soon. Guess we took things for granted, didn't we?"

"Yes!" They get into their sleeping bags and snuggle into each other.

Aron and Helena Jenner are in trouble. The wind has taken out their bamboo wall facing the sea and has pulled down their roof. Aron is trying to pull the ropes tighter so it doesn't take off and leave them without protection. Helena is still in her sleeping bag.

"Hon, you got the torch?"

"No." Helena reaches out in front of her. She feels something cold and metal, picks it up and switches it on.

"Yes!" Aron leans over and takes it from her shaking hand. "You okay?"

"A-ha. Bit cold ... Can't move much. Damn roof's on me."

"I'll just fix this." Happy he's secured the ropes, he makes his way to Helena and climbs back in their sleeping bag, hoping his body heat will warm her.

They lie for hours, listening to the deafening storm's fury. By 3:00 a.m. the winds finally begin to abate. Aron and Helena fall asleep in each other's arms and don't wake until daylight.

Rosaline watches the helicopter until it becomes a small speck in the sky. The others have gone and Jack is taking their share of Aron's and Helena's leftover belongings back to their cave. She closes her eyes, trying to shut out Aron's and Helena's departure, but it is useless. Helena's distress is too fresh and she goes over the past few hours again, feeling hopeless and uncertain about the situation she now finds herself in.

She had seen the carnage of Aron's and Helena's shelter through the binoculars in the early hours of the morning and had got up immediately. Jack had held her back. It was their fault, he had said, but she had looked at him in disgust, saying that they might be hurt; need help. What if it was them? He shrugged, let her go and reluctantly followed.

When they got to them, Aron explained that Helena was pinned down. A branch was embedded in her foot and he wasn't sure he could get it out. She had looked at Helena and saw the pain and fear in her eyes and had asked what they could do. Jack just stood there and she loathed him for it. It was when the Wentworths showed that some good fortune prevailed. Linda used to be a nurse. She watched Aron talk to Linda and remembered the look Linda had given him before they went over to Helena. Rosaline hadn't wanted to see. She had known it wasn't good. They couldn't get the branch out without causing more distress and even if they did, they didn't have anything to really stop the bleeding; stop any infection. Linda had put her hand on Aron's shoulder. Rosaline remembered how calming it was, together with Linda's soft, kind voice. Her words were full of wisdom and Rosaline knew that Linda would have been a very good nurse.

She thought about the honesty in Linda's words and how hard it must have been for Aron to hear that the best thing for Helena would be to get to a hospital. Helena's health was worth more than the money. Aron had put his hand over Linda's and nodded, saying it was quite funny, really. They had never even thought they would make it to the first part, let alone end up here. Just did it for a laugh – didn't need the money!' No one said anything. There was nothing to say. His disappointment was obvious. It was bad luck but it was what it was. Mark, Linda's son offered to let off their flare somewhere down the beach, so Helena didn't see, and that was that. Nigel, his dad, had gone with him and it was then that Jack had offered his bottle of whiskey. Said he thought it might ease Helena's pain.

How stupid of her to think Jack had felt bad about his earlier display and wanted to make amends. Not to Helena or Aron but to her. That feeling was short-lived when she thanked him for being so considerate and he had replied that everyone now would think he's one hell of a nice guy and he had grinned that sickly grin of his, she'd seen once too often.

The Hendersons had shown up then, with Nancy trying to squash the argument that her son persisted with. Peter was not letting up about the fact they had bought along their first-aid kit. He was going for it. She recalled his words. 'They've already got theirs. They don't need ours. We do. It's you that doesn't understand, Dad.' Henry's face had been thunderous and Candice seemed to be silently backing her brother, which was confirmed later when she overheard Candice say to him that their parents shouldn't be so nice and he had answered back saying they weren't going to win anything with their attitude. That was when Peter had looked at her and she had to look away. There was something about Peter that made her feel uneasy. His face was friendly enough but his eyes were cruel.

It was the same when it was decided, after Aron and Helena had been airlifted away, that they could divide up Aron and Helena's belongings that were left. Little arguments here and there! She thanked God Nigel had taken on the role of deciding how it was to be done and, surprisingly, no one disapproved and she thought it was even more surprising that he had been the one to step up and show some authority.

She glances back over to their shelter and sees Jack attending to their tarpaulin. She won't go over, as having to be near him at this moment makes her sick. His lack of compassion has hit her hard and again she wonders if she really knows the man she has married, or if she even wants to.

CHAPTER NINE

The Downs wake early the next day and head inland to find the waterfall. It is a golden morning and with their backpacks filled, they travel south and find a stream. Stan checks their map. It leads directly to the waterfall. They notice that when the stream is not more than a few inches deep, the mosquitoes are abundant and are glad Yvonne insisted they apply plenty of repellent.

When they make it to the waterfall, they see Jack and Rosaline bathing. Rosaline and Jack wave and swim over. Stan extends his hand to Jack. "Hello."

"Hi! Survived the storm then?"

"Yes."

"Shame about the Jenners," says Jack blatantly, trying to gauge a reaction.

Harvey looks puzzled. "The Jenners?"

"You don't know? Didn't you see the flare?"

"No!" Yvonne looks from Jack to Rosaline.

Jack grins. "That big old wolf got them good."

Jessie's eyes widen. "Wolf?" She looks to her parents. "Is there a wolf on this island?"

Jack's laugh echoes and the bush goes silent. Jessie's arms wrap around Yvonne's waist.

"Seriously, kid?" roars Jack before Stan and Yvonne can answer. "The wolf ... oink oink. Oh, come on ... the three little piggies?"

Rosaline takes hold of her husband's arm. "I'm so sorry. Jack's got this weird sense of humor."

"I'm shocked." Jack moves closer, but Jessie edges behind her mother and Rosaline thumps her husband's backside.

"We're leaving."

"Jesus … Look, sorry, kid. Didn't mean to scare you."

"She's fine," cuts in Stan, stepping in front of his wife.

"Jack, I said we're leaving." Rosaline stares at her husband, her face a mixture of embarrassment and disgust. He shrugs and walks ahead of her and she mouths a silent apology before following.

Yvonne and Stan get the kids into the water and Jack's words are soon forgotten. Yvonne gets out, happy to hear their uncontrollable giggling, and sets out their picnic rug. When she hears footsteps, she looks to the edge of the clearing and sees the Longs approaching. She says hello and tells them about the Jenners.

"Wow!" says Sara. "It's only been what, six days? What happened?"

Yvonne shrugs. "Didn't ask. Jack wasn't very pleasant, so his wife insisted they leave."

"Wonder if anyone else got into trouble?"

"Don't know … Warren?"

"Good memory. Guess we'll find out soon enough."

"Yes, guess so. Are you going to try and catch something?"

"Sure are!" Sara takes off her outer clothes. "Still, with all this noise, it might be a waste of time."

Yvonne smiles. "Sorry about that."

"Oh, no, Yvonne. It's lovely to see the kids having fun. We can try a bit later."

"Absolutely, Mum. Hey Warren, you want to swim to the waterfall?"

"Sure. You two coming?"

"No, thank you, Warren. We'll take a rest and chat with Yvonne."

"Suit yourself." Sara grabs Warren's hand and they amble

happily down to the pond, wave to Stan and the kids and leisurely breaststroke across to the cascading water. Yvonne, Bridget and Eric look on lazily.

"I noticed Rosaline had her hand bandaged."

"That's Jack's wife isn't it?"

"Yes, Eric."

Bridget yawns. "Probably hurt it in the storm."

"Probably. I don't like Jack. He was very inconsiderate. He really frightened Jessie."

"What did he do?"

"Tried to be clever," sighs Yvonne. "Maybe they don't have children."

"Maybe," agrees Eric. "Changes people, having children."

"Yes, it certainly does. I think I'll go and join mine for a bit." Yvonne leaves Bridget and Eric and walks elegantly into the pond. Jessie squeals, swims to her and bombards her with a wall of water.

"You know, I'm beginning to like this life," says Bridget. "It's no wonder we like islands." She lies back and closes her eyes. "Listen … you can hear is insects at work. Oh darling, is that a wood pigeon?"

"Could be."

"You know, yesterday Warren showed me some swallows and petrels. He's very knowledgeable about birds now, isn't he? Guess he has you to thank for that." She reaches across and rubs his arm. "It's nice you and him have formed this bond. All those Sundays out fishing, watching birds, have really paid off."

"What's making you so sentimental all of a sudden?"

"I don't know. It's just nice being here."

"It's nice to see you relax."

Bridget's fingers find his just as Sara and Warren join them.

"Man, I'm starving," says Sara, shaking her head furiously, sending shards of spray everywhere.

Eric looks at his wife. "So much for the relaxation."

Bridget laughs.

"What's so funny?"

"Nothing, darling. Today we've got cold fish in a lime coconut sauce."

"Mum's famous poisson cru," says Eric proudly.

"And to finish off ..." Bridget winks, "my delicious mangos."

Eric snorts, watching the Downs exit the pond. Stan's hand goes from Harvey to Jessie as they chat and laugh their way towards them.

"We are just about to eat. Why don't you join us?" says Bridget warmly.

"That would be lovely," replies Yvonne, handing her children a towel.

"I just love mango." Mary sits down next to Sara and Jessie immediately plonks herself next to her.

"Did you get these where the fruit trees are?"

"Yes, we did. You been, Yvonne?"

"Nope! Plan to go tomorrow. Good is it?"

"Very." Eric looks at his wife. "Bridget's the one to ask though. Knows all about island stuff."

"Well, I know a bit here and there. My mother was Tahitian."

"Would it be rude of me to ask for a few tips?" Yvonne takes a piece of mango.

"Depends. What do you want to know?"

"Well, what do you do with this breadfruit it mentions?"

"You can cook it or eat it raw, but they have to be very ripe. It's very creamy and sweet. Good for cereal. Really – you can use it for lots of things. Find ones that are yellow-green in appearance, soft and have a lovely sweet aroma. One thing to remember, and this is quite important, twist off the stem and turn it upside down, let the sticky latex run out." Bridget doesn't offer any more advice.

"Thanks." Yvonne raises her eyebrows and looks at her family. "We'll try to remember that."

"Mum, can we go and get some today?"

"Maybe tomorrow, darling."

Jessie's mouth opens in protest but she glimpses her father face and quickly closes it.

After a relaxing lunch, swim and catching the night's dinner, the Longs are packing up when the Tillers arrive.

"Hi there. You leaving?"

"Yes. It's Terrance isn't it?"

Terrance nods.

"Been here a while." Eric gets up. "You three hear about the Jenners?"

"Nope."

Eric gives them the news.

"Man, that's a bummer," Terrance looks at his brothers.

"Yes, I guess it is." Eric picks up the last of their gear and follows his family back into the bush. "You boys have fun."

Greg notices Mary's gaze has fallen on Terrance. He sees his brother watching her tentatively as she packs up her things. She deliberately wipes her hair back and then very slowly does up her small blouse over her even smaller bikini.

"Mary!"

Irked, Mary's eyes divert to her mother.

"Do get a move on or you'll fall behind. God, Stan, look at her fluttering those eyelashes."

Terrance turns his head to his brothers. "She's wasting her time."

"Oh, it never rains but pours with you," laughs Karl on his run to the pond. He dives in, rises and shakes his head from side to side, like a walrus making a kill, then sinks back on his back to look up at the clear blue sky, where a few gulls squawk overhead, and he watches them, admiring their gliding. He decides to head to the waterfall for his daily shower. Each morning they trek up the side of the cliff, swing across the chasm, make their way down to the waterfall and then follow the stream back to the beach. It helps them keep fit; keep clean.

An hour later, the Smyths arrive. Josh sees the Tillers lying on the grass and gestures to Logan to be quiet. Logan tiptoes into the water but can no longer restrain himself and falls face down, waking Greg.

"Sorry, mate."

"No problem." Greg gets up. Karl and Terrance glance over, wave but don't move.

"Oh, do you know about Aron and Helena Jenner?" Greg holds out his hand to Ian. He winces. "Crikey, you have one hell of a strong handshake there, Ian."

"Sorry, what were you saying about those two?"

Josh comes over and extends his hand. Greg nervously takes it. Josh's handshake is manly but not hard and he relaxes and holds Josh's gaze for a moment longer than he normally would.

Josh pulls his hand away slowly, causing his fingers to brush the length of Greg's hand.

"So, are you going to tell us about them?" asks Josh, smiling.

Greg focuses on Josh's bemused expression. "What … oh yes, that. Well, they had to leave. Got hurt or something."

"Blimey!" Kate looks at Ian. "That's terrible."

"Mother of a storm, that one." Josh strips off his t-shirt. "Can't wait to cool down."

Greg's eyes follow him. "He's your brother, right, Kate?"

"Yes, he is. Lives with us. Actually we're twins – obviously not identical," she gives a small laugh.

He likes her open friendliness. *I think you guys are very alike. Same brown hair and eyes and even your builds are similar. Solid, but not fat!*

"We're fifty-six, if that's the next question?"

"No, oh God, no." He feels foolish, trying to think of something to say. "Gee, you don't look it, neither of you."

"Really? How charming. Are you and your brothers close in age?"

"Yes. I'm the middle, thirty-three. Karl's thirty-six and Terrance, the good-looking one is the baby – thirty one."

"Oh, come now, you and Karl are good-looking." Kate looks at him openly. "You're gay?"

"Yes … I am."

"Hmm, thought you were," she says as if she has known him for years. "So, Greg, are you staying close by?"

"Well, sort of. So many went north. How about you?"

"Well, we're one of those many. We're quite near the fruit trees." Kate pauses. "If you don't mind Greg, I might just join them. It's so very humid after that rain."

"Of course, you go right ahead. Your lad looks like he's enjoying himself."

"Logan. Yes he does, doesn't he? Josh is great with him," she pauses. "I wouldn't waste your time."

He takes in the sympathetic look Kate gives him before she takes off her shirt and shorts. He notes the modest black swimsuit, which compliments her age, and as he studies her walking towards the pool he thinks Kate is probably a very wise woman.

"What were you talking about?"

"Not much, just being friendly."

"Didn't tell them about the cave?"

"No, Karl, I didn't. I'm not stupid. And you could have said hello."

"Frankly, we're better off keeping to ourselves. This is a competition and there's only one winner. Let's not forget that."

"Great, so we're just supposed to ignore everyone."

"Maybe?" Karl closes his eyes.

Greg knows the conversation is over, looks down at Terrance, snoring ever so gently and thinks about Mary. *Girls come to Terrance like bees to honey. Nothing seems hard for him.* He looks back to the pool and spots Josh, sitting on the far side. *Is he looking at me?* His instincts tell him he is, but sometimes his instincts are wrong. Sometimes he wishes he wasn't gay. Today he's not so sure. A private smile spreads across his face, his concerns vanish and he lies back and closes his eyes.

CHAPTER TEN

Trudy Booth wakes the next morning feeling hot and cold. "Oh, crap!"

"What's up babe?"

"Feel shitty. We got any lemons?"

"Come here, I know what you need." Drew grabs her waist and pulls her onto him.

"Idiot, you don't want it."

"Babe, I think after what we did last night, I'm probably well infested."

Trudy's head pounds and dulls her reasoning. His warmth takes over and she sinks her teeth into his flesh as he licks her ear. His whiskers tickle as he draws with his tongue.

"Oh baby, you're burning."

Trudy closes her eyes and gives herself to him. It doesn't take long before the passion overwhelms her.

"Snuggle into me, my little flower." Drew tucks a piece of her flaxen hair behind her ear, kisses her and cocoons her with his body.

Ritchie and Celia cover their mouths and can barely breathe.

"You think they're finished?" Celia whispers as she carefully undoes the zip on their sleeping bag.

"Yep, sounds like Drew's snoring. Let's go."

They rise and quietly make their way outside and down to the beach. It is another scorching day and they run carelessly over the pearly sand to the awaiting crystalline turquoise waters. Ritchie scans their surroundings.

"Okay, coast clear!"

They strip, hold hands, wade into the refreshing water and swim along the beach, where the coral hasn't intruded. They then get out and spread out their towels.

"Heaven."

"You're heaven." Ritchie kisses her.

"Hmm, that's nice, but someone might see us."

"No one's here."

"We can't be sure."

Ritchie looks up. "Absolutely deserted. Just you and me, babe."

He pulls her over and she sinks down onto him. He tastes of the sea and she is soon aroused. Her breathing deepens as he grabs her breasts and caresses her nipples. She moans. He is the best lover she has had and she never takes long to reach her utopia. She opens her eyes and a blinding burst of light pierces her vision. A chill descends her body and she freezes. "Someone's watching us."

"Don't be silly." Ritchie sits and looks back at the bush.

"No, up there, on the cliff – in the trees."

"Just be the sun hitting something."

"Hitting something? Like what? Come on, I want to go."

"Hon, who cares? It's too far to see anything. Hey, maybe they're masturbating right now."

Celia thumps him. "Don't be disgusting. It's not funny, it's creepy."

"Yeah, it is, if someone's there, but I seriously doubt it." He rubs her arm. "Boy, you're tense."

She shrugs.

"Seriously, Celia, you've gotta chill."

She gives him a nervous smile.

"That's better. Now, lets go and get that fruit. Something nice and juicy."

"That's gross."

Ritchie chuckles. "Yeah, but you love it."

She grins. *He's right, and I am way too tense. I have to lighten up or it's never gonna happen.* They quickly get dressed, pick up their towels and run back to their tree house. Celia's eyes dart over the cliffs, but see nothing.

Harvey gets more than he bargained for. He had been out with the binoculars, trying to see whales off the reef, when he noticed movement on the beach. He knows he should have left but when they started making out, he couldn't tear himself away.

Now as he spies, his excitement mounts. She is sitting on top, pulling her torso back, pushing her breasts forward. *Oh, shit, shit, shit.* Harvey's right hand yanks furiously while his other hand tries to hold the binoculars steady. *Fuck, she's staring right at me.* Mortified he comes instantly and drops the binoculars, before his limbs solidify. *Stop it. You're being ridiculous. She's too far away. There's no way she's seen me.* But still, the nerves take over and he scrambles around, withdrawing further, until the greenery consumes him. He picks himself up and runs. He feels dirty, a little ashamed, but also euphorically free. More alive than he has the whole time he's been here. Boredom has given way to elation. He makes it to the waterfall and is thankful it is deserted. He dives in and swims over, takes off his clothes and rubs them under the cascading water. Satisfied that he has washed away his sin, he swims back, gets out and places his clothes on the grass. *I'm definitely going back tomorrow.* The thrill of doing something he shouldn't excites him. After a while, he puts on his clothes and heads back to their shelter. He thinks about the others on the island. The other women; the Henderson girl ... A smile of satisfaction creeps across his face as he goes up the cliff to the safety of his family.

"Oh, hi, darling. See anything interesting?"

"Not really, Mum. Watched a few birds. Mind if I take the binoculars every morning?"

"It's not a problem is it, Stan?"

"Nope. Be good for you, exploring. Just be careful up those cliffs."

"Dad, I'm not stupid."

Jessie looks at Harvey baffled. "What's so interesting about a bird?"

"I'm looking for whales. Birds are just something to watch, numbskull."

"Jerk!"

Harvey grins. *If only you knew, Jessie, if only you knew!*

Stan grabs a few bags and heads for the door. "We've decided to take a trek to the fruit trees. You may as well come now you're back."

"Harvey, put some of this on. It's pretty hot out there."

"Sure, Mum." Harvey takes the lotion and starts rubbing it on his arms. It is a task he hates, but today he will do it without complaint.

Harvey walks at the back, listening to Jessie's inane babbling, and wishes he was elsewhere.

"Stan, there's bananas." Yvonne says delighted.

"How are we meant to reach those, Dad?"

"Easy – you can climb up and get them."

Jessie faces her brother and pokes her tongue out.

"Oh, that's very mature. Just what I'd expect from a monkey."

Jessie's face goes blotchy as her eyes bubble over.

"You're such a baby."

"Harvey, stop it. What's the matter with you? Do you have to pick at each other all the time?" Stan's body stiffens and the kids take a step back.

"Please, stop." Yvonne sits and rubs her forehead.

Stan sighs. "Headache?"

"Uh-huh."

"Sorry, Mum," Jessie wraps her arms around her mother. "We didn't mean to upset you. We'll be good from now on."

"You know, I read about bananas on the Internet," intervenes Mary.

"Oh, this should be good."

"I'll ignore that, Harvey. Would you like me to tell you what I found out?"

"Not particularly."

"Harvey – enough." Stan turns to Mary. "Is it in any way helpful?"

Harvey snickers. *Not a chance.*

"Well, for a start, the trunks are not …"

"Oh, for God's sake, Mary. We don't need a detailed description. I'll just cut them down."

Harvey scoffs and Stan eyes turn to fire. "Harvey, got that knife?"

"I wish we'd never spotted the bananas," says Jessie quietly.

Harvey ignores her. "Yes, Dad. I brought two."

"Good. Yvonne, are you up to catching them when we push this thing over?"

"Yes."

"Girls, you get between your mum and us and help lower this thing. Don't want it to fall and hit the ground."

"Okay." Jessie positions herself between her mother and Mary. "Like this, Dad?"

"Yes – yes Jessie." Stan slides the knife and it easily penetrates the trunk.

Harvey smirks. *What a fucking palaver. It's just a bloody banana tree. Should just kick the damn thing over and be done with it. Everything has to take so long and Mary is such a pain. Always trying to act all grown up.*

He knew whose benefit that was for – Terrance. *Boy, she's got it bad. Might be able to have a bit of fun with that. Put her in her place when the time comes.* He smiles at his dad. *Yep, better be nice for now, he's in one of his volatile moods. Can't afford to be in the line of fire if he erupts.* He looks to his sisters. *But I'm outta here if we win. Get a flat with a mate – cause there's no way on earth I'm bringing home a girl with them around.*

"Concentrate, Harvey" Stan pushes his arm back. "Okay, that's it." He gives the trunk a gentle push and it gives way. They lower it gently to the ground and Stan cuts off the semi-ripe fruit.

"Brilliant. Some of these top ones are ripe and we can hang the rest up. Yum, they smell good, don't they?" Yvonne opens her backpack and takes out a plastic bag and string.

"What are you doing, Mum?"

"Well, Jessie, pretty sure bananas ripen quickly in a plastic bag."

"Okay, everyone have a drink and then we'll head off. Can't be far now." Stan slings the bunch of bananas over his shoulder. They continue and come to the part of the trail that splits in two and follow the left path, which has been made easier by the other teams' efforts to reach the fruit, and arrive to see the Longs and the Wentworths.

Eric gets up and comes over to greet them. "Hot, isn't it? Nice place to be, other than in the water, but even that's a little warm at this time of day."

"Waterfall's good," replies Stan, shaking Eric's hand.

"Hi, Yvonne, Harvey, Mary and … Jessica?"

"Jessie!" giggles Jessie, as she shakes Eric's hand.

"Hard to remember everyone's names at my age."

"Hard to remember at any age, darling! Now, Jessie, you look a bit hot," Bridget smiles. "Would you like some mango?"

"Oh, yes, please." Jessie sits next to her. "I just, um … love your hair. It's so cool. You're like an island princess cause it's so red and curly and long … and your skin's so gold."

Harvey shakes his head and is whacked by his father.

"Jesus, Dad," he mutters. "Why do you have to be so embarrassing all the time?"

Stan's voice is low. "No one noticed, and if you grew up I wouldn't have to."

Harvey hears the warning signs and keeps his eyes down. *Treats me like I'm five. I'm fucking sick of it.*

Bridget hands Jessie a piece of mango. "Well, thank you, Jessie. I'll let you into a little secret. It's not totally natural. I dye it redder than it actually is. My hair is black but I've always loved red."

"I want to dye mine, too."

"Do you now? Well, I'd wait a few years, sweetie."

"Mum wouldn't let me do it anyway."

"Well, she's right not to let you and why would you, anyway? You have lovely hair."

"Thanks!" Jessie's eyes shine.

Harvey is standing beside his father, listening to the meaningless discussion, when Ritchie, Celia and Drew arrive.

"Hi, guys." Warren holds out his hand to Ritchie.

"Another burner of a day!"

"Yes Ritchie. Hi – Drew isn't it?"

"Yeah."

"Your wife not with you?"

"No, she's feeling a bit off, so she's resting."

Harvey retreats behind his dad as Celia comes over and extends her hand to his father and then to him. He hesitates, then with everyone watching, puts his hand in Celia's. Perspiration drips from his cherry-red face and he closes his eyes, welcoming the darkness. *Go away. Everyone's staring. Fucking hell, they think I like her.*

"Teenagers," laughs Stan, whirling his finger.

Oh, thanks, Dad. Embarrass me more, why don't you?

"Harvey, come on. We'll get some fruit, while your mother rests."

What? Why the hell would I want to go with you? He looks around. *Then again I don't fancy staying here, either.* Harvey reluctantly follows his father and is relieved when Ritchie and the other men follow.

"Poor Harvey," says Celia, watching the men depart. "You know, this is kind of nice seeing you all. Why don't we arrange a catch-up? Everyone can bring something to eat and we can make a fire on the beach. Be nice for the younger ones. Lunch would be good. Any thoughts?"

"Yes, I think it's a great idea, Celia," says Yvonne.

"Absolutely," agrees Linda.

"Jessie's got some paper. The girls can draw some posters and we can put them up."

"Brilliant," says Bridget.

The women sit down in a circle and Jessie undoes her shoulder bag and takes out a small pencil case full of pencils, pens and markers. "I want to be an artist when I'm older."

"Do you? That's nice," comments Bridget.

"Shall we have it at the beach where we landed?"

"Good idea, Sara." Bridget looks at the others.

Yvonne nods her head in agreement "What if it rains?"

"Oh, I know!" gushes Jessie. "Why can't we fly something from the top of the cliff at the waterfall on the morning of the do … like my bright orange scarf! It can be our flag. We could tie it to one of the trees so everyone can see it."

"I suppose that could work, darling."

"Clever little thing, aren't you?" Bridget rubs Jessie's arm and Jessie's face beams with pride.

"There you go, Jessie, Mary. Make them look good. We need at least three of them, four if you can manage it," says Sara.

"Well, I think we're done. I'm going to go and see how the men are doing. I'd like to see what's on offer, rather than leave it up to them."

"Hold on there, Yvonne. I'll come with you."

"I'll stay here with the girls, Mum," says Celia as Bridget, Sara, Yvonne and Linda walk off, chatting away like best friends.

"Thanks for staying with us, Celia. Mary thinks Ritchie is really handsome."

"Jessie!"

"But she likes Terrance Tiller more. Greg's queer, you know."

"Oh, it's okay, Mary. Everyone falls for Ritchie. I'm used to it and Terrance is quite dishy, isn't he? And yes, Jessie, I did wonder about Greg."

"Well, we'd better get this done or we'll be told off." Mary looks at Celia and hands Jessie the black marker.

"I can't wait. Harvey's been such a grump. He wants to go out in the mornings by himself. He's weird!"

"Oh, I don't know, Jessie. Boys of his age like to be alone sometimes."

"He takes the binoculars, says he's looking for whales."

"Yeah, he's such a dork." Mary nudges Jessie, giggling. "You okay Celia? You look weird?"

"I'm fine, Mary. Just hot."

"Okay, then. Jessie, hand me that red marker."

The adults arrive back with their bags full. Stan crouches down next to Jessie.

"Good idea huh, Dad? It was mine to put the scarf up."

"Was it, indeed?"

"Why don't you men have a rest while the girls finish?" asks Linda.

"Fine. We'll do that, love. That avocado tree's got plenty of shade." Nigel leads the men away and they rest under the tree's canopy of glossy foliage.

"Jesus Christ!" Stan stares exasperated. "Get them together and all common sense flies out the window."

"Totally," agrees Drew, shaking his head.

"Do you think they even realize it's a competition?" Ritchie frowns. "I'm really surprised Celia agreed to it."

"Yeah, talk about dumb."

"Oh, come on, Drew – what's the harm. It's early days." Nigel looks at the other men calmly. "When I think about it, it could be nice."

"Guess so."

"Suppose," utters Stan hesitantly. "Anyway, nothing we can do about it now."

"Hate to imagine what they'll come up with next," says Ritchie chuckling.

"Coffee group?" Drew says and they all burst out laughing as though they are old mates.

CHAPTER ELEVEN

The Downs rise early the day of the feast, eat a quick breakfast and Stan and Harvey go down to the beach to get a fire started. The sky is lifeless and even the melodies of the bush seem lackadaisical. Perspiration finds its way into any crease it can. Harvey yanks his hat off and slaps his lank hair back as he squints at the millions of tiny lights that flicker over the tropical paradise.

He takes their magnifying glass and angles it towards the sun. Sweat drops plummet onto his carefully placed grass and he hopes it will catch quickly. A delicate gray snake swirls and he is not disappointed. He spies Peter and Candice and waves as he watches their feet kicking the lapping water as they make their way towards him.

"Hi! Mum and Dad said we could come early," Candice says, dumping her bag down.

"Well, I've just suggested to Harvey that now might be a good time for a swim before everyone arrives. I'll go and see how Yvonne and the girls are doing. I'll let them know you're here."

"Thanks, Mr. Downs," says Candice sweetly.

Stan watches Candice sit down and take off her already wet shirt and shorts. Peter and Harvey, immersed in conversation, are already walking towards the lagoon, and it brings a smile to Stan's lips. He wonders where the Hendersons' camp is and hopes it is near, so the boys can spend time together. He yells to them to stay near the shoreline and makes sure the fire has plenty of fuel before leaving.

By the time Stan, Yvonne, Mary and Jessie get back to the

beach, Harvey, Peter and Candice are drying off. Henry and Nancy arrive, arms full of beach gear and food.

"Morning. Those planks over there are for food. Henry, I wonder if I could grab you and the boys and we'll go and get a couple more."

"Sure, Stan. Let me just put this stuff down and I'll call the lads. Yvonne, this okay for you?"

"Yes, thanks."

"Boys, can you come and give us a hand?"

The boys look at Henry, nod and carry on talking.

"Today would be good," shouts Henry, shaking his head.

"You have that problem too?" smiles Stan.

"That and many others," laughs Henry, gesturing the boys to follow. "We live in hope, but nothing ever changes."

"Yeah, Harvey's pretty uncooperative. Apparently, we know nothing."

Henry snorts. "Remember *Hogan's Heroes*? God, I loved that program. Tried to get Peter to watch it but he called it 'dry', whatever the hell that means?"

"Blame the phones. Kids today – the techno-dead," moans Stan, head cocked to the side and dragging his left leg. Henry snickers while Harvey and Peter roll their eyes.

Stan wipes his brow. "Here we go, guys."

Henry scratches his head. "Guess these must have washed up from some ship. How about Harvey and you take one and I'll take the other with Peter."

The planks are battle-scared and heavy. Stan and Henry hold the front ends while the boys, still deep in conversation, take the back.

"What are you two plotting?"

"Oh, nothing, Mr. Downs. Just thought we might start running in the mornings to keep fit. See if we can spot any whales."

"Now that's a great idea, guys."

Harvey and Peter share a private grin. They get the planks in position and see the Wentworths and the Cromptons arrive, followed closely by the Smyths, Booths and the Davidsons. The Longs come a few minutes later, with a wide variety of delicious looking food and drink and, just as they settle themselves down, the Tillers come into view, carrying a huge pot.

"Smells good," says Yvonne taking in the inviting aroma.

"Crayfish stew. Greg's work," replies Karl.

"Wonderful." Trudy inhales deeply. "Hope it tastes as good."

"Oh, no worries there. Greg's a damn good cook. It'll be just like being at his restaurant."

"Oh, are you a chef?"

"Yep, but it's not exactly my restaurant. Mind you, if we win this, it could be."

"Oh, what an advantage, Greg."

"I guess, Rosaline. Still it's not hard to cook something here, is it?"

"Depends how good your cooking is."

Rosaline glares at her husband. Furious, she walks off to see what the others are doing with the ball Mary bought down.

"Can I join in?"

"Absolutely. You go on the other side. It's volleyball, really, and the line in the sand is our net."

"Great."

"Ready," calls Drew, preparing himself to serve.

"Ready," answers Harvey from his side of the net. Drew serves. The game begins, proving a welcome amusement to those playing and watching. After Harvey and Peter end up on their backsides, Jessie laughs so much that she blows like a trumpet. Everyone convulses with laughter, making her fart again and again. Mary and Candice roll around, holding their stomachs and when Drew lets out his rumbling flatulence, the game comes to a stop. Lunch is called and they make their way up.

"What's so funny?" asks Karl, bemused.

"Jessie farted!" laughs Mary.

"It wasn't only me," jumps in Jessie, defensively. "Drew did too!"

"It was priceless, just what we needed." Bridget chuckles, giving Jessie a pat on the back.

"Well, it sounds it. Better out than in, eh Jessie," says Nigel winking. "Anyway grub's up so tuck in, everyone."

Jessie forgets her embarrassment and grabs a plate. There are fish cakes, baked fish, stews, a vegetable curry, rice, salads and fresh fruit and nuts. The colors and smells draw everybody together. Bridget has made her version of 'Tahiti Drink' and everyone finds it palatable. They sit down and eat, most going back for seconds, until there is nothing left.

"Oh, boy, that was amazing." Rosaline appreciates the time and effort taken to prepare the food. Like many, she has eaten way too much. She notices Jack licking his fingers. She decides to ask how everyone managed to make it taste so good, but before she gets a chance Linda asks Moana about her salad.

"If you get kumara, remember to let it air for about six to ten days. You don't need to always cook it."

"Really? I didn't know that," Rosaline moves closer to her. "Then and again that's hardly surprising. I'm a hopeless cook."

"It's not hard, Rosaline. Use some herbs – they make all the difference."

"You make it sound so simple, Moana."

"So, what did you bring today, then?"

"Oh, I did the fruit platter, Bridget."

"Well luv, you may not be able to cook but your presentation was great." Moana gets up to rinse her plate.

"I second that, Rosaline. Had a bit of a cold but am feeling much better. Fruit is just what I needed."

"Oh, yes, Drew mentioned you weren't well, dear. Glad to hear you're feeling better." Linda pats Trudy's leg, smiles fondly at her and then takes her plate down to the water.

"She reminds me of a mother chook," says Rosaline, smiling. "It's nice."

Jessie runs over. "Are you guys joining us for another game?"

"Why not! Go ask the men, love."

Jessie runs straight to the Tillers, pleads and gets her reward.

Greg nudges Terrance. "Best you go on the side that Mary isn't."

"Okay, Greg. Keep your voice down."

Everyone but Nigel, Linda, Rosaline and Warren decide to play. They tidy up what they can and sit down to watch.

Rosaline notes Terrance's irritation as Mary meanders her way next to him. Stan serves the first ball. It flies to the back of the opposite team, where Drew is prepared for it. He thumps it high and Mark jumps into the air and hits it forward to Celia who manages to push it over the net. It falls in front of Terrance and as he lunges forward, Mary intercepts him, causing the ball to hit the net as Terrance and Mary collide.

"Sorry, Terrance."

"I think we both know I was perfectly capable of getting that ball."

"Oh, don't be like that. I'll be more careful next time."

"There won't be a next time, Mary."

Mary's eyelashes flutter as her pearly teeth bite her rosy lip.

"Not interested, Mary." Terrance leaves the game and sits himself down next to Rosaline.

She inhales his obvious displeasure. "Teenage girls, huh?"

He sighs. "Oh, yeah."

"Poor thing's got it bad."

"I know."

"Goes with the territory, I guess."

He turns to face her with a flirtatious grin. "Guess you'd know."

She feels warm, instantly euphoric. "Well, okay, but I'm not the one with a teenager hanging around, now am I?"

"No, you're not, but if Jack wasn't here, I bet it would be different."

"Maybe."

"Hon, there's no maybe about it."

Her eyes follow Terrance as he rises and heads for the water. His words are printed in her mind and she shivers when she sees Jack staring and gives him a coy smile. He doesn't smile back.

The game continues on in good spirits, with some of the players retiring because of the heat. After a while, when there are only Stan, Andrew, Sara and Trudy left, the game wraps up and they follow the others down to the water. Late in the afternoon they decide to part ways, but arrange to have another lunch in seven days' time.

CHAPTER TWELVE

Over the next week, everyone finds the days pass slowly, each seamlessly rolling into the next. The little amount of relief the breeze offers is useless against the relentless burning yellow ball overhead.

Mary is restless. She desperately wants to see Terrance, but her mother and father say no every time she suggests a trip to the waterfall.

Two days ago, her family had met the Hendersons on the beach. It had been all right but she didn't even get a glimpse of Terrance and today, the day before they all meet again, is worse. It is sweltering, so her parents are lying down and Jessie is being a pain, asking to play some silly game of hide and seek.

It isn't fair! Harvey is allowed to go with Peter for the morning but I have to stay. "Please can I go? I'm so hot. I'll take Jessie and let her draw me. Please, Mum?"

"What do you think, Stan? If they both went, at least they'd be together and we can get some peace and quiet."

"Yeah, I suppose."

Hearing her father's voice brings a smile to Mary's face. She will get her wish.

"Okay, Mary, but on two conditions."

"Thank you. What are they?"

"You're back in two hours and you never let Jessie out of your sight – and you only go to the waterfall."

"That's three!"

"Mary, I don't care if it's forty-three. Those are the conditions and if that's too much, forget it. Do I make myself clear?"

"Yes, Dad. Jessie, grab your stuff, we're going."

"Can I really draw you?"

"We'll see, just hurry up."

"I'm not going if I can't draw you. Dad said ..."

"All right, all right, you can draw me. Geez. Can't you just sketch flowers?"

"No, I want to draw you on the rocks, like a mermaid."

"Oh God, isn't that just a little babyish, even for you?"

"Right then, I'm not going." Jessie puts back her art equipment and plonks herself down on her sleeping bag. "I'm staying right here."

"God – you're such a baby. You act more like an eight-year-old than a thirteen-year-old."

"I'm just thirteen and I do not."

Mary sighs. "Look, Jessie, I just want to go. You can draw me if you must and I'll pretend I'm some mermaid."

"Really?"

"Really! Now, can we go?"

"Just a sec while I get my things."

"Okay, Mum, Dad, we're off. Have a nice sleep." Mary shoves Jessie out the door and they make their way down the ledge and walk beside the stream.

"Slow down, Mary, you're going too fast."

"Stop whining."

"Why do we have to rush? It's not as if ... oh, I know why. You think Terrance is there."

"No, I don't," states Mary, brushing away the ferns, which grab at her legs, slowing her down. "I just want to take a swim, cool off."

"I don't believe you, because those men said they go up to the waterfall every day. Oh, Mum and Dad are going to be so angry with you."

Mary stops and Jessie slams into her. "Why, Jessie? Why are Mum and Dad going to be angry with me?" She grabs Jessie's arm and squeezes. "What are you going to say to them?"

"Nothing. I don't care what you do. He's just a stupid man."

"Jessie, if you say anything to anyone – anything at all, I'll take that diary of yours and show it to everyone."

"How do you know about my diary?" squeals Jessie, biting her thumb. "Oh, please, Mary, I won't say anything. You can't tell about my diary, you just can't."

"Keep your hair on. I won't tell if you don't – deal?" Mary extends her hand. "And don't start crying, it's pathetic."

"Deal!" mumbles Jessie desperately. "But Mary, he's way too old for you, even with your big boobies and pouty mouth."

"My God, Jessie, they're breasts, not boobies, and that's just your opinion and you know nothing."

Mary continues on with Jessie scampering behind. They make the waterfall in good time and Mary scans the area for Terrance but only sees Karl.

"Geronimo!"

Mary and Jessie look up to see Terrance plummeting towards the pond and then he is gone, hidden under the exploding water.

"Oh, my God," says Mary, transfixed, while Jessie giggles and claps with joy.

"Hello, you two," says Karl, as Terrance surfaces, swishing his hair back.

"Oh, he's a god!"

"Close your mouth, Mary. You look stupid."

Mary's look is murderous. "Shut up, Jessie."

"Maybe I'll draw you as the sea-witch."

"God, you're so pathetic." Mary turns her attention back to the pond. "Did you guys make that swing?"

"Yep, wanna turn? Mind you, you'll have to wait for Greg. He's a bit of a girl when it comes to this sort of thing."

Jessie starts laughing, clapping and jumping with excitement. "Oh, please can we have a go?"

"'Course you can," says Karl. "You want to go first, Pumpkin?"

"I don't know."

"You just went on about having a go," reminds Mary, annoyed, her hand furiously scratching her leg.

"Well, how about we go together and you can hold onto me."

"Oh, yes please, Karl. Can we go first?"

"Fine with me," says Mary. "You go ahead, Jessie. I need to find that blasted repellent." Jessie skips off with Karl and Mary's eyes fixate on Terrance as he exits the water. She quickly rubs lotion on her leg and stands in wait.

"Your parents not with you?"

Mary nods delicately and deliberately pushes out her chest, while removing her shirt.

"Might pay to put that back on. You hit the water with some force."

"Oh, I'll be fine, Terrance, but thank you for your concern. Oh, look, there they are. Did Karl just push Greg?"

"Yep," replies Terrance, snorting, as Greg's feet kick air. His arms and legs oscillate in all directions as he hits the water. Terrance and Mary roar with laughter.

"You okay, mate?" chuckles Terrance.

"'Course!" Greg swims over and gets himself out, tugging at his shorts. "Oops, nearly lost these. Hi, Mary – you having a go?"

"Absolutely! Just waiting for Karl and Jessie. You know how it is."

"Sure."

"Oh, there they are."

Karl and Jessie take a mighty leap and Jessie squeals with laughter as they splash down. She emerges, beaming, and asks Karl if they can do it again and again, while Mary makes her way up the bank.

"This should be interesting." Greg nudges Terrance as Mary pulls on the rope, takes a huge leap and swings towards the middle of the pond, lets go and falls into the water bottom first. She pushes herself up and out of the water.

"Oh, that was so much fun," she sings as she raises her arms and slides her hair back.

"Mary!" screams Jessie. "Your boobies!"

"Oh, my goodness." Mary slowly sinks back down into the pond and starts swimming over.

"Holy Mother of God!" says Karl. "Right, Jessie, your turn. Let's go."

"I'm coming, too," shrieks Greg, moving with more speed than he has all day, as Mary exists the water. Terrance turns quickly to follow.

"Terrance, would you mind?"

Terrance curses, knowing he is caught.

"Thanks. I can't seem to tie it tight enough."

He takes the ties from her, with hands that are not his own. He steps back and Mary turns to face him.

"Sorry about that. Bit embarrassing, really."

"Yep."

"Still, it's not as if you haven't seen a girl's breasts before?"

"I usually see women's breasts, not girls', Mary."

"I'm not a girl. I'm very mature for my age, Terrance."

"Yeah, well, you made that perfectly obvious, didn't you?"

"And did you like what you saw?" Her lip curls to one side. "No – no need to answer. I think you did."

"Look, Mary, I'm just not interested."

"Oh, I think you are, Terrance. A girl can always tell." Her eyes travel down to Terrance's shorts and back up to his face. "Like another look?"

He shoves past her and dives into the pond, just as Karl and Jessie hit the water. A slow victorious smile spreads across Mary's face. *I'll get him, one way or another. It's just a matter of time. I'm nearly sixteen and I know exactly what I want.* She gets out a towel and places it on the grass. Jessie jumps out and runs up to her.

"You did that on purpose didn't you?" She kneels next to her sister. "You'll get into trouble."

"Oh, don't talk about things you know nothing about Jessie. Now, I'll sit here and you can draw me if you like."

"Really! Do you want some fruit?"

"Yes," says Mary inspecting her fingernails.

"I brought oranges. Here you are, Mary." Jessie passes one over and they sit together watching the Tiller boys in the water.

"Right, I'm going to draw you now."

Mary sighs loudly. "God, you're so easily distracted, aren't you?"

Jessie starts her masterpiece. It is a terrible likeness but Mary doesn't notice. Her eyes never leave Terrance.

"Oh, cripes, Mary. Look at the time. We only have half an hour to make it back."

"Oh, it's all right."

"If we're late, we won't be able to come anymore."

You might be right Jessie. If we're late getting back, my chances of coming here again are slight. She quickly puts her gear back into her bag and stands. "Hurry up, Jessie." Mary hastily puts on her shoes.

"Bye, guys. See you tomorrow," she yells, as she shoves Jessie in front of her.

"Thank God she's gone," says Terrance, "and I don't find it amusing that you two took off like that."

"To be honest, I thought I'd better put some distance there, bro. Christ, she's stacked."

"No kidding."

"Sorry, Terrance. We should have stayed."

"Yeah, Greg, you should have," says Karl. "She is a little vixen, that one."

"Won't affect me, of course, and maybe not Josh."

"Josh?" says Terrance questionably.

"I reckon he's gay."

"Jesus, Greg, Terrance's problem is enough for now."

"I was just saying …"

"Well, don't. Let's go. I've had enough excitement for one day." Karl collects his things and heads back towards their cave. Greg and Terrance follow in silence.

CHAPTER THIRTEEN

By noon on Sunday everyone has arrived at the beach. While the younger ones set up a game of volleyball, others bathe in the lagoon and Linda, Bridget and Nigel finish off attending to the food. Bridget has made banana bread combined with breadfruit and, as she unwraps the foil, its aroma escapes, enticing those nearby.

"Lunch is ready," calls Linda proudly, causing Nigel to smile at the pleasure she takes in the game being abandoned so abruptly.

"Oh, who did this bread? It smells heavenly."

"Mum did this morning, Yvonne. Bananas and breadfruit – delicious."

"I thought it would be nice for you to try something different."

"It's a welcome addition, Bridget." Nigel takes a bite. "This is very good. Now, are you going to be nice and let us know how to make this?"

"Of course not," Bridget chuckles, "but making chips is fairly easy. I'll tell you how to do that."

"Chips huh?" says Karl digging into Moana's curry. "Greg, you listening? Man, this is good."

Matt nudges Moana. "Our secret."

Moana chuckles. They share a private look and Matt slips his arm around her. They take their food and sit together, observing their competition.

"Greg certainly seems to like the Smyths."

"Yeah, he does seem to hang around them."

"You reckon he's gay?"

"Hadn't really thought," comments Matt, tucking into a piece of bread. "But now you mention it, reckon he could be."

"Hmm, hard to tell – perhaps he's bisexual."

"Perhaps they all are?"

Moana snickers. "Hardly!" They look at Karl and Terrance and start laughing. "Oh, the thought of …"

"Don't, you'll give me the stitch."

Moana laughs harder. "Oh, shit." She wipes her eyes and a piece of bread spills out of her mouth.

"You're a disgrace, woman." Matt wipes her chin and licks his finger, causing Moana to howl. Sammy and Zach decide not to intrude and sit down with Mark and his parents as Karl walks past, winking, before joining Terrance, who is sitting watching Greg.

"What are you so deep in thought about?" Karl inhales deeply, ejects a loud belch and rubs his stomach.

"You think Greg's right about Josh?"

"Hope not," replies Karl, yawning.

Jessie wants to stay with Mary, but she is talking to Candice about men. Disinterested, she wades over to Harvey and Peter.

Peter stares at her. "Yes?"

"Wanna go for a swim?"

"No."

"Can I sit with you?"

Peter's eyes bore into hers. "Push off, Jessie, we're discussing something."

"What?"

"Jesus, don't be a pain … go."

Harvey's words hurt. She gets up and runs to her mother.

"Peter," calls out Nancy.

"Oh, for fuck's sake."

"You'd better answer them, Peter," says Harvey shielding himself from his dad's steely eyes.

"Peter," yells Henry. "Come here."

"Jesus, could they be any more embarrassing?" Peter saunters towards them.

"Peter, we know you like to be with Harvey, but don't be nasty to Jessie."

"Yeah, but we're trying to plan things."

"Just let her join in sometimes."

"Fine. Now can I go, 'cause Harvey's trying to tell me something?"

"Yes, yes, Peter, just take heed of what your mother said."

"Is that it?"

"Put some of this on first. It's really hot."

"I'm fine, Mum. I'll put some on later."

"Peter, put it on, otherwise you'll end up burnt."

"Look, I'll do it later. When Harvey's finished telling me."

"You'll do it now, or you won't be moving from this spot."

"All right, all right, keep your hair on, Dad."

Exasperated, Nancy shakes her head. "Why do you do this, Peter? We're just trying to help you."

"Nagging me, more like."

"We wouldn't have to nag you if you just did what we asked."

"Keep it down, Mum. Why do have to shout?"

"Because you don't listen. Honestly, Peter, it's not hard."

"Give me the bloody stuff, then."

"That's enough, young man. Don't swear at your mother. Do that again and you're grounded."

Fuming, Peter rubs the lotion over his face and half-heartily over the rest of his body. "There – done, can I go?"

"Will you change?"

"Yes."

"And, Peter ...?"

Peter looks over his left shoulder. "Yes, Mr. Downs?"

"Tell Harvey to be nicer to his sister or he'll have me to deal with."

"Sure." Peter looks back to his parents. "Can I go?"

Henry nods. "Change, remember – and mean it this time."

Peter runs back to Harvey, shaking his head. Harvey rolls his eyes and gives Peter an amused grin. "Usually me that gets called up."

"Yeah, well your dad wasn't happy, either." They both give each other disparaging looks and Harvey tells Peter that he will show him something that'll make him forget this. Harvey won't say what it is, but Peter has an inkling that it may be something they shouldn't be doing. He doesn't care, because being with Harvey is better than being with his family.

"You think your sister has a thing for that Mark guy?"

Peter shrugs. *Gross – I'm not thinking of my sister with a guy. Wonder what Harvey's parents really think of Mary and the way she acts around Terrance. Maybe they can't see it, being her parents. Maybe they're blind to these things.* He smiles. *Mind you, they'd have to be deaf too.* He looks at Mary and over to Terrance. *He can't be interested? He's way too old.* He looks at Mary. *She's quite mature, though, and if she's throwing it about, I'm more her age. Maybe she isn't so slutty after all, just bored like me and maybe she likes Terrance cause he talks to her, which is more than I've done.*

Peter taps his head to banish his thoughts. He doesn't want to ruin things between him and Harvey. *Better leave alone. It would be too weird.*

"So do you?"

"Do I? ... Oh, Mark – I don't know. Candice's not like Mary."

"Mary's a pain. Thinks she's all sexy and grown up with her tits "

They watch Mary flaunting herself at Terrance. "Poor guy."

"Yeah, poor guy," mutters Peter.

Greg is discussing restaurants with Josh. Greg tells him he is the head chef of one, back in New Zealand. Josh lets on that he has also had some training as a chef, but wanted to be an architect and had left the food industry to further his dream.

"So, you live with Kate and the family."

"Yes. Had a health scare in my thirties and they rallied around me. Have been with them ever since. Wonderful people."

"So, you never married, then?"

"Nope."

Hmm – not very forthcoming. "So … I'm pretty happy with life at the moment. Single, but open to any suggestions," sings Greg, as his shoulders and legs twitch as though listening to a song.

"Sounds like you're in a good place, then," says Josh nonchalantly. "Now if you excuse me, I'm going to help the others pack up. Nice talking to you."

Greg gets up and wanders back over to Karl and Terrance.

Karl grins. "So, what's the verdict?"

"Not sure. He's very protective."

"Fair enough. Best left alone, then."

"Guess so. Hey, noticed you talking to Stan, Terrance. What did he want?"

"He told me Mary has a crush."

"He did what?"

"It's all good. I told him I knew and he didn't have to worry."

"What did he say?"

"Not a lot. Just smiled and left."

"Yeah, well, keep your distance."

"Yes, Dad."

Greg hits Terrance playfully on the back. Terrance winces. "You're such a brute."

Greg flexes his muscles and Terrance wraps his arm around Greg's neck, squeezing him tenderly.

Candice, Mary and Jessie join Harvey and Peter who are trying to plan what they will do the next day. The boys decide to let them hang out with them after their earlier humiliation.

"Well, I don't think Mum and Dad will let us go far. We could go to the waterfall. Perhaps you could come with us, Candice?"

"I wouldn't be allowed to come by myself. Hey, maybe I should come with you, Peter, and then I can met you guys on the beach?"

"No way."

"Definitely not!" enforces Harvey.

"You guys are so mean. I'll have to ask Mum and Dad if they can bring me to the beach, then, so we can meet up."

"Great. So all we have to do is ask our parents then," says Mary sarcastically.

"It'll be fine. I'll ask." Jessie jumps up. "Come on."

Mary gives Candice a mocking smile. "Bound to say yes to her."

"That's a splendid idea, girls," says Nancy.

"I'm not sure Dad will agree, Jessie, but it's fine with me."

"Thanks, Mum, and Dad won't mind. It's going to be so much fun." Jessie takes Mary's and Candice's hands and they head back down to the water.

"You really okay with the girls going there themselves?"

"Well, I think it's safe enough, Yvonne. There's usually someone else up there."

"Yes, I suppose. Maybe I'll go up a bit later – check on them."

"Oh, I wouldn't do that, Yvonne. They'll feel like babies."

"I'm worried about Mary, though. She seems infatuated with Terrance. Stan isn't happy with the way she's behaving."

Moana intervenes. "Well, it's probably some teenage crush. You remember how it was at that age, don't you? And he's awfully good-looking, isn't he? I mean if I were any younger, I'd have a crush on him, too. Hell, I think I have a crush on him now."

Yvonne bursts out laughing. "Oh, you're so right. He's very good-looking and it is perfectly natural for Mary to be attracted to him, isn't it?"

"Yeah, like you haven't got just a little thing for him too?"

"Trudy!"

"Well, come on, he's gorgeous. I've even seen Celia here take a look, and she's got Ritchie."

Celia blushes.

"See."

"Yes, well, I think we probably all agree he is one attractive man." Bridget states. "But you know, Yvonne, your Stan is mighty handsome. Like a man with a touch of gray above his ears. Gives him that distinguished look."

"Must have been one hell of a catch," says Trudy suggestively.

Yvonne smiles. "Yes, my friends and I used to just hang out, hoping to get a glimpse of him and his friends. Nearly died when he asked me out a few years later. Been together ever since."

Kate smiles wickedly. "You know, Terrance isn't the only good-looking male here. Oh, if only we were younger and weren't married."

"Oh, stop it. We haven't done too badly for ourselves, have we? Your Matt, Moana, is looking better and better these days and there's Jack – very tasty."

Rosaline glances nervously at Yvonne before answering. "Yes, we couldn't really be any luckier, could we?"

Celia pulls her hat back over her face and lies down. "It's a good job we're all content then, isn't it?"

No one answers.

"Hey, wonder if they're scrutinizing us?" says Sara.

"Oh, they wouldn't dare," says Trudy with a glance across at the men. "Hey Celia," she whispers. "Can't imagine why no one mentioned Drew."

Celia lifts the brim of her hat and they share a private smile.

CHAPTER FOURTEEN

Matt, Sammy and Zach are in good spirits. They have collected various pieces of foliage and canes, along with plenty of vines and palm leaves. Logan, Ian and Josh arrive at the beach and casually amble over.

Logan looks at their pile. "Building a raft?"

"Trying to," replies Matt matter-of-factly, shaking Ian's hand.

"Be happy to help. We're at a bit of a loose end at the moment."

"Yeah – well what do you say, boys?"

"Sure – we could use a little help," admits Sammy. "Boat construction's not one of our stronger points."

"Dad's knowledgeable on boats, aren't you, Dad?" says Logan with pride.

"Yes, I am," replies Ian, crouching down.

"We're using the canes for the base. Tied them with vines."

"Right, well that's a start, Matt." Ian suddenly feels the longing to show them what he sees; how it can be done.

"Look here." He finds a stick and, going down to harder sand, starts drawing. He can't help himself; boats are his hobby. The others watch transfixed as a raft materializes in the sand.

"Hey, that's pretty cool," says Zach.

"Yeah – could we do that though?" asks Sammy, rubbing his head.

"I don't see why not. We have a spare sheet. Be perfect for a sail," says Ian. "Josh, what do you think?"

"I think Kate might have something to say about that and on that note I'll leave you guys to it. I'm meant to be getting dinner tonight so I'm off to the waterfall. See you later."

"You want one of us to come?"

"No Ian, I'm a big boy. Think I can handle it." Josh winks at Logan. "Have fun."

"See ya, Josh," says Logan. "Catch plenty, 'cause we're going to be really hungry tonight."

Josh waves, cuts into the bush and follows the path by the stream. Enjoying his solitude, he imitates a cricket, thinks of Kate and picks wild herbs growing along the stream's edge. A rustling in the trees overhead catches his attention and he spies a few wood pigeons. Smiling, he decides to test his slingshot. He is in no hurry. He knows the secret to a good kill is the wait. He sees four but knows he will only get one and concentrates on the surrounding drone of busy insects while he waits for the right moment. Focusing, he draws back his arm and fires. The pebble rockets through the air and the pigeon falls quickly, unaware of its plight. It hits the ground, dead. The whoosh overhead is instant and in a blink of an eye, the other birds vanish. Josh springs to his feet to retrieve his victim, feeling a mixture of sadness and pride. It will be good to eat something different.

As a small boy, he had gone out with his father and shot ducks. To his surprise, and his father's, he became very good and, after several trips, had even began to enjoy himself. His father told him humans ate all kinds of meat and fish that someone had to kill, so it wasn't any different. But it was to Josh. Fortunately, as time went by he began to understand what his father meant and the killing got easier.

He arrives at the waterfall in good time, places his equipment down, then swims and showers. The water is refreshingly cold.

He notices the rope tied to a tree above the rocks, grins and starts to climb.

He swings out, with a smile full of memories, and lets go, curling his legs as he falls into the water. He emerges like a euphoric adolescent and gets out to do it again.

"Someone's beat us," shouts Terrance reaching the pond. Karl and Greg arrive to see Josh catapulting above them.

Greg brings his hand to his throat. "Oh my, oh my!"

Josh surfaces and swims over. "Morning – this yours?"

"Sure is," replies Karl.

"Brilliant, mate. Hope you don't mind me using it?"

"Crikey, no. It's for everyone," gushes Greg. "Here alone?"

"Obviously," answers Josh wryly, getting out and heading for his gear.

Karl walks over to him. "What have you got there, mate?"

Josh undoes the piece of cloth he has taken out of his chilly-bin.

"A bird?"

"Yes, Greg, wood pigeon."

"Wow! God, I would kill to cook one of those." Greg peeps at his brothers. They stand motionless with their arms folded and eyebrows raised. "How'd you get it?"

"Made a slingshot."

"Thought about making one, myself," cuts in Karl.

"Karl, you get me a wood pigeon and you'll dine like a king."

"Calm down, Greg. Came here for a shower. Might make one this afternoon."

"Brill." Greg watches his brothers walk to the water. He decides to stay with Josh.

Josh listens to Greg's advice on the numerous recipes he volunteers. "Thanks, Greg, but tonight I'm cooking it the way my mother did, with herbs, wrapped in foil. In fact, I'd better go. There's sage on the top of the cliff. Found some the other day. Could you look after my gear? I'll pick it up on my return."

"Sure, no problemo."

Josh gets up, takes a bag and a knife and departs up the bank just as Terrance and Karl get out of the pond.

"Where's he off to?"

"Gathering sage. Actually Karl, I might go see where it is."

"Uh-huh."

"Hmm … see you in a tic." Greg departs, sprints up the bank and quickly disappears. He finds Josh admiring the view.

"Hey, Josh. Hope you don't mind but couldn't resist it when you mentioned sage. Thought I'd get some."

"Help yourself, it's not mine."

"Thanks. Wow, it's great up here, isn't it?"

"Certainly is – peaceful."

"You like the quietness?"

"Yes, good for the soul. You?"

"Sometimes. To be honest though, I always seem too busy."

"You do yoga?"

"No, do you?" Greg moves closer.

"Yes … sit."

"O … kay."

"Good. Now cross your legs and put your hands together in front of your chest like this."

Christ, this crossing your legs stuff hurts. "Is this going to take long?"

Josh smiles. "Close your eyes and breathe in through your nose and out through your mouth. Long, slow breaths so you can feel your chest rising, your stomach tightening."

"Gotcha, chest rising, stomach tightening." He watches Josh and sees him close his eyes. *No way!* He finds himself mesmerized by Josh's expanding chest. He jumps when Josh's low, calming voice interrupts him.

"Close those eyes Greg – breathe with me. Keep in time. Clear your mind."

Greg obliges but can only keep his eyes shut for a few seconds. *Oh boy, this is a bit weird. Is he in some sort of trance?* He looks around. *I feel ridiculous.* A bee buzzes between them and he swings his arm around like a sword. *Goddammit! Bloody thing's on his hair now.* He slowly reaches out when Josh's hand whips up and his hand catches Josh's chain, causing it to break.

"What the hell are you doing?"

"Nothing, there was a bee." Greg bends to pick up the chain.

"Don't give me that. I've seen the way you look at me."

"No, Josh, really there was this bee and …"

"Jesus! Look Greg – you're a nice guy and all that but I'm just not interested."

"Okay," says Greg inching forward.

Josh takes a step back.

"Look, there really was this …"

"Whatever."

"It was going for your ear."

Josh fumbles with his bag, spilling the contents. Greg bends to help, and Josh steps back, catching his foot on a vine. He falls towards the cliff's edge and frantically reaches out as his body goes over. Greg rushes forward, dropping the chain and clutches at vines but they slide through his hand with ease. In desperation, he manages to clasp them but finds himself laid flat, his body inching towards death. When his body stops, his face and upper torso are suspended in air and he looks down at Josh's dangling body and his terror-stricken face. Birds squawk as they leave their perch. They are all that are between Josh and the dark angel waiting below. He lowers his free arm and winces when Josh's nails dig deep.

Bits of rock crumble and Josh blinks, trying to expel the dust from his watery eyes. He frantically looks for a foothold. "Yell, Greg. Your brothers might hear you."

"Help!"

"Louder."

"I can't. I've never had a strong voice."

Josh's face cringes. *Be a fucking miracle if they hear that.*

"My arms hurt." Greg gawks at Josh's face, not sure if it is terror or disgust he sees. "I don't know what to do!"

Josh's bulging eyes stare at his mountain-white knuckles, straining to hold Greg's hand.

"Please listen to me, Josh. There really was a bee. I mean, yes, I fancy you, but I would never do anything without … thinking you wanted it."

Disgusted, Josh watches a trickle of blood run down his wrist. "Shit, you're bleeding. You have to pull now!"

"I can't. You're too heavy."

"Goddammit, man!" *Useless bastard!* Sweat threatens Josh's vision and he closes his eyes tightly. "I'm going to try something."

"What?"

"The less you know the better. Just hold tightly. I'll tell you when to pull."

Greg panics. "Josh, I can't!"

"You bloody well can. Now shut up and pay attention. I can't stay like this much longer and if you can't fucking well pull, then you're damn well coming with me."

"What do you mean I'm coming with you?"

"For fuck's sake, Greg. You got me into this mess. You've got a backbone like an old woman."

"Look I told you …"

"Greg," Josh yells. "Shut the fuck up and concentrate." He stretches his right leg and slowly maneuvers his foot into a small aperture. "Okay, let's hope it holds."

"You don't believe me!"

Josh's body tenses and Greg cries with pain. "You have to believe me!"

"For God's sake, Greg, please just focus on ... What was that?"

"What?"

"Sounded like someone calling."

"Just the birds ..."

"Listen!"

"Or the wind." Greg lies as his sweat intensifies.

"No, someone's calling. Call back."

"I can't."

"What are you talking about? Just ..." Josh stops. He notices the glazed look in Greg's eyes. "Greg, listen to me. Take a deep breath, we're okay. Everything's okay."

Greg looks past Josh and sees vultures and monstrous waves, smashing and grabbing anything they can to take back to their watery grave. "It's not okay, Josh, it's not!" Tears free-fall, hitting Josh's face.

"Greg, we're fine. Just a bit longer."

"No I can't. You don't believe me." Greg's voice is garbled. Saliva and the perspiration build and hang from his chin like growing stalactites.

Josh stops talking. "There ... There it is again." He hollers.

Greg shudders and a couple of stalactites fell on Josh's face, sliding over his cheek. He yells and yells as Greg's grip slackens and he feels his hand start to slide.

There is no scream. Josh's paralyzed eyes stare up at Greg as he plummets like an unwanted toy tossed from a window. Greg's wail fills the air as Karl reaches the top of the cliff.

What the fuck was that? He moves quickly and sees the fallen bag: the discarded herbs, and his brother face-down at the brink of nothing.

"Greg, what's going on?" Receiving no answer, he inches forward. "Greg ... Greg, listen to me, I'm going to come to you. Don't move; I'll get you, buddy."

"No, stay away. It's not my fault. It's not."

"It's okay, Greg." Karl says calmly. Crawling closer, he grasps hold of Greg's legs. "I'm going to pull you back."

"No! I have to help him."

"Help him? Karl looks helplessly at the endless blue. "Greg, where's Josh?"

Karl carefully pries his brother's fingers off the vines and slowly brings his arm back towards his body. Greg cries with the pain.

"I know, buddy."

"It's not my fault. I didn't mean anything. It was the bee. The damn bee."

Karl slowly pulls his brother towards him. "You're rambling, sit here. Shit, look at your hand."

Greg's rocking intensifies and he spies the chain. Seeing Karl lie down carefully and slide towards the edge, Greg reaches out, picks it up and deposits it in his pocket.

Karl peers over, already knowing what he will find. "Jesus, Greg." A million thoughts run through his mind. *What did he say? 'Not my fault!' 'A bee'? What the fuck does that mean?*

He crawls back, gets up, opens the bag, collects the herbs and stuffs them inside. He takes his rag-doll brother by the arms, pulls him upright and then slaps him. Greg's face drains of color, but his shaking subsides and Karl gently brushes Greg down and eases him towards the track.

"Come on, Greg." He helps Greg all the way back to the

waterfall and stops at the edge of the bush. He sees Terrance nervously striding back and forwards.

"Psst!"

Terrance turns. "Karl?"

"Yeah. You alone?"

"Yep. You got Greg?"

"Yeah …"

Terrance gawks at Greg's frightened, owl-like eyes, darting everywhere in his frozen face "What happened?"

"Josh is dead," replies Karl quietly.

"Dead?"

"Yes, dead. Don't just stand there, give me a hand."

Terrance takes hold of Greg's other arm, places it around his neck and they move towards the pond and gently sit him down.

"Shit, Karl. I've never seen him like this."

Greg's eyes are bloodshot; saliva dribbles from his mouth in little pockets of foam. Terrance grabs a towel and wraps it around Greg's back.

"What the fuck happened?"

Greg offers no response.

"Kept saying it's not his fault."

"Jesus Christ!" Terrance bends down and rubs Greg's arm. "Greggy, come on buddy, what happened?"

Greg's eyes stare, seeing nothing.

Terrance takes hold of Greg's arms. "For fucks sake, Greg, what happened?" His voice is stern, authoritative.

Greg's mouth opens and closes spasmodically, causing his words to gush. "He fell. He fell backwards. I tried to grab him. I did. Got the vines – they cut my hand – see?" He thrusts his hand in front of Terrance's face.

"It's okay, Greg." Terrance's voice is softer, calming. "What were you doing?"

"There was a bee."

"A bee?"

"Yes, I keep telling you ... a bee! It was buzzing around and it landed on his hair. I went to shoo it off and he thought I was ..."

"He thought you were making a pass at him?" Terrance's voice rises. "Why would he think that? Jesus, Greg, you fucking idiot. Is that why you went up there?" Terrance stares at him, feeling nauseated. "Answer me!"

"Yes, no – I don't know. I liked him. I thought he liked me."

"Fucking hell." Karl rubs his forehead. "Shit – we have his stuff." He picks up Josh's bags. "Get your gear, we're leaving."

"What if we meet someone?" Terrance's eyes dart everywhere.

Karl scratches his head. "We won't. We'll go back the way we've come. Greg, get in the water."

"The water?"

"Yes. With any luck it'll knock some sense into you." Karl's voice is thunderous but steady. Greg shuffles towards the pond and keeps walking till he is totally submerged in this watery tomb. He holds his breath and thinks about not re-surfacing but as his chest begins to hurt, he knows he is too much of a coward. He bursts up to see Terrance about to dive in.

"What – thinking of killing yourself now?"

"I wasn't." Greg hates Terrance's face. "I don't blame you for looking like that. I feel terrible – like a criminal."

Terrance swallows back the bile in his throat and nods to Greg to fall in behind Karl.

"What are we going to do?"

Silence.

"We have to let Josh's family know."

"Don't be an idiot. Look at you, for God's sake."

"I mean later, Karl." Greg's breathing intensifies and his whimpering gets louder. "Josh said ... breathing helps and ..."

Karl stops, turns and peers directly into Greg's eyes. Greg shrinks back into Terrance, who stops him retreating further.

"I don't give a fuck what he said. He's not here anymore, is he Greg? So – act normal, keep quiet and maybe, just maybe we'll get back unnoticed and then we can try to sort this mess out."

Back in the cave, Karl tells Greg to change and sit by the fire, while they decide what to do. Greg is physically and mentally exhausted and does what he is told. Terrance gets the first-aid kit and attends to Greg's hand.

"Okay, Greg. Tell us what happened ... all of it." Karl crouches down next to Terrance.

Greg inhales deeply and tells what he remembers. Dumbfounded, Karl and Terrance watch the stream of tears that slide over Greg's blotchy complexion. "I tried to explain. God, it was so horrible. When he stumbled, it was like everything was in slow motion and then he ... it ... felt like forever. Him, hanging on, and me, peering down like that. I couldn't look away. I yelled, honest I did, but you didn't come." Greg pauses. "He was really heavy."

"You couldn't hold him?"

"Yes, he ... he just slipped through my hand. Oh, God, he was reaching out – falling." Greg pinches his nose to stop the waterfall of snot that keeps running into his mouth. "There was nothing (sniff) ... nothing I could do. I knew he was dead. I mean, he is dead, isn't he? Oh, God, (sniff) ... we need to check."

"Of course he's dead. You didn't hear me?"

"No! Oh, God, his poor family. We have to let them know." Greg draws in air, exhaling wearily. "I'm okay, let's go."

"Don't be stupid – you look like shit. You must have heard me?"

"No!" Greg's shoulders slump. "I don't know – maybe – but you were too late. I couldn't hold him."

Karl looks at Terrance.

"I hate myself."

"Yeah, I'm sure you do." Terrance watches his brother. "You should have held on, Greg. Karl was there."

"I couldn't, my arm was hurting … everything was hurting. He was heavy, okay? Really heavy." Greg stands, trying to compose himself. "I'm going to let them know," he says defiantly.

"Oh, for Pete's sake, sit down and don't be ridiculous."

"Why is that ridiculous, Karl?"

"Oh, I don't know Greg. What if he said you liked him, or you'd been coming onto to him? Hell, they might even think you pushed him."

"They wouldn't think that. I'll tell them what happened!"

Karl rubs his face. "Fuck, Greg! Tell them what happened!" His voice is thunderous. "I said, sit down!" Greg recoils in angst, instantly sitting below Karl. Karl crouches in front of him. "You can't tell them what happened. I mean what the hell are you going to say? A bee! Who's going to believe that? Would you believe it?"

Greg's voice is a mere whisper. "But it's the truth."

"Goddammit, Greg! Shut up and let me think." Karl walks to their chest and Greg gets up. "Sit. You're not going anywhere and you are definitely not telling anyone. We'll put his stuff back. I'll open it like it's been dropped. Actually let's open it now, see what's inside."

Terrance opens Josh's bags and finds a first-aid kit, containers, the bird, herbs, some pebbles, a water bottle, binoculars and a slingshot.

"Nice," says Karl. "We'll take this. Might as well get something positive out of today. Don't have to waste time making one now."

"We can't use his. They'll see it!" cries Greg, looking distraught.

"Who? And so what? Anyone could have made it. It's not difficult. I bet some already have."

"We haven't."

"Well, I was going to make one. Terrance, here, didn't 'cause he hates to kill anything and you didn't 'cause you're a girl." Karl's voice is sarcastic, his hand scratches unmercifully at his chin. "If we scatter those pebbles on the ground near where he tripped, it could look like he was using it and it went over with him. Easily washed away with those waves."

Karl gets no response. "So, put the rest of the things back, except the bird. We may as well have that for tea."

"Oh, I don't think I could eat that."

"Well, maybe you will and maybe you won't, but that's what we're doing." Karl puts on gloves and proceeds to wipe down Josh's items.

"Don't look at me like that. I'm getting our fingerprints off. I'll take this back. You two stay put."

"Are you sure there's no other way? We could say we found him."

"Yeah, Greg's right, Karl. What we're doing is wrong."

"I'm sorry, Terrance? If you have a better idea, do tell?"

"I don't. I'm just saying ..."

"He could have fallen."

"Fallen. Oh, yeah, of course, Greg. Why didn't I think of that?" Karl slaps Greg head. "Like he just went to the edge and fell. Perfect. Problem solved."

"Well, he could have been looking at something – not been concentrating."

"Greg, what could possibly be that interesting that he had to go to the edge to see that he couldn't see from a foot or so back, huh? There's nothing out there except ocean."

Greg stares at him blankly.

"That's right, nothing." Karl turns to Terrance. "Well?" He waits. "Okay, then, since neither of you have a better idea, I'm going to get these bags back. Terrance, make sure he doesn't do anything stupid – and that goes for you too."

"This is stupid. It looks like we're guilty."

"You are guilty, Greg. Accident or no accident, a man is dead because of you."

Greg hangs his head.

"Karl, this is some shit we're contemplating. There'll be no going back. If it doesn't work, we'll be in serious trouble."

"I know that, Terrance, but thanks to Greg, we have no alternative." Karl leers at Greg, turns and departs, leaving Terrance and Greg to ponder his words.

"I'm really sorry about this, Terrance." Greg looks small, lost: almost childlike.

"Yeah." Terrance crouches, hands under his chin, elbows digging into his thighs.

"Look, I'll go and tell them. Karl doesn't have to know. I'll take the consequences."

"No, Greg. Karl's right. They'll have to let off a flare and what happens then, huh? They go, we go and where would you go? Maybe to jail, that's where. Maybe we all would. Do you want us to end up in jail for whatever the fuck they would throw at us, cause that's what could happen, Greg – and bye-bye thirty mill."

"Of course not. Sorry, I didn't think."

"You didn't think?" Terrance peers at Greg, his eyes a mixture of pity and disgust.

"I know you're pissed at me. If I could take this back I would, believe me."

"Look ... fuck, Greg, this ... this is ... I don't even know what this is! It was meant to be fun. Jesus, I've got that goddamn Mary on my back – now this."

"I know." Greg gets up. "Here, give me that bird. I'd better cook it."

Terrance looks at Greg, lets out a weary sigh and hands him the bird. Just like that, their lives are changed forever. He hopes they aren't making the situation worse, but has no better solution. Greg is family. He couldn't, wouldn't risk telling Josh's family Greg's version. He wonders what they are doing right now. *Are they waiting for Josh? Are they getting worried? Have they even noticed Josh hasn't returned?*

"Jesus, Terrance, I don't know how I'm going to be able to act normal when we see them."

Terrance rubs his forehead. "Neither do I." He needs a drink. He reaches for a water bottle and downs it in seconds. It does nothing to make him feel better.

An hour later, Karl arrives back with good news. He tells them he's successfully put Josh's bags back and made it look like Josh tripped. He left the binoculars near the edge and smoothed out the soft layer of soil so it looked natural.

"You sure it looks convincing?"

"It's fine. Everything okay here?"

"Yep," answers Greg. "I understand why we can't tell. I won't say a word, but haven't you just done what you said he wouldn't do?"

"What?"

"Well, doesn't it look like he's gone too close to the edge and …"

"Go and change it, then."

"No, no – I meant … I'm sure it's all good."

"Tomorrow, if they haven't already found him, Terrance and I will go to the waterfall as normal. You'll stay here. We'll say you fell on the rocks and hurt yourself while fishing."

"Uh-huh," replies Terrance. "More lies. This just gets better and better."

Karl flashes him a disconcerting look but Terrance is past caring.

"Karl, thanks for this. I don't know how I'll ever replay you guys."

"We don't really have a choice, do we, Greg?"

"I just feel so bad for his family."

"Yes, it's not ideal," replies Karl, sarcastically.

Greg gets on with the meal he is preparing. The smell of cooked meat soon fills the cavern and he gets some rice into a pot. Any other day, they would have been ravenous, but today all three couldn't care less if they were eating meat or bread.

CHAPTER FIFTEEN

Kate begins to feel strange at about the same time as Josh falls to his death. A shiver runs down her body, leaving her heavy, low on energy.

"Hon, you're white as a sheet."

"I just felt as if someone walked over my grave."

Ian puts his arm around her as Logan hands her a mug of coffee.

"What time is it?' asks Kate wearily.

Ian looks at his watch. "Jeepers – nearly five-thirty."

"Where is he, Ian?"

"Don't worry love, he'll be here any moment."

"Yeah, Mum, you know how it is," says Logan, glancing at his dad at a loss.

"He's never late."

"Sure he is, Mum."

"He's not!"

"I'll check the waterfall, if you like."

Ian smiles at his son. "That's a good idea. Don't take too long and be careful."

"I will. See you soon ... with Uncle Josh."

Logan runs off, deciding to head across the beach. He sees no one, so cuts into the bush and follows the stream. He arrives at the waterfall and sees Trudy and Drew.

"Have you guys seen Josh?"

"No. Been here for about an hour, only the girls were here."

"Shit, where the hell is he?"

"Was he meant to be here?" asks Drew.

"Yes, this morning."

"And you haven't seen him since?"

"No. Guess I'd better head back. Told the olds I wouldn't be long."

"If he hasn't shown by morning, go to the main beach – we can start a search. If we see anyone else, we'll let them know." Drew smiles reassuringly while squeezing Logan's shoulder.

"Thanks."

"You know he's probably back with your mum and dad as we speak." Trudy says supportively.

Logan's unconvincing smile hangs between them before he runs off and is swallowed by the greenery. The noise from his heedless footsteps fades and Trudy reaches for Drew's hand.

"Poor thing, he looks so forlorn."

"Yeah, he does. Let's hope Josh has turned up."

"Have a horrible feeling bout this."

"Yeah, me too."

They quickly pack up their things and head for the beach, calling Josh's name as they go. Receiving no response, they turn for their shelter and see Stan and Harvey. Drew tells them the news and Stan says they have been down on the beach for most of the day, fishing off the rocks, and have not seen him.

"Doesn't sound good. He seems a pretty capable guy to me."

"Our thoughts exactly, Stan," says Drew. "Look, spread the word."

"Will do."

Stan and Harvey watch the two figures jog to the other end of the beach. Stan rubs his son's back and gives him a reassuring smile.

"Dad, do you think he's okay?"

"Honestly, Harvey – no."

"What do you think happened?"

"Those cliffs are pretty steep."

"He'd be dead, wouldn't he, if he fell?"

"Yes, I believe he would." Stan walks back with his arm protectively draped across Harvey's shoulders.

"Dad?"

"Yes, son?"

"If Josh is ... you know, they'll have to go."

Stan squeezes his son's shoulder.

Kate hasn't slept and watches as the sun's rays inch their way across the water, making a beeline to where she is sitting, bringing with them the dread of what the day might hold.

"Poor thing. You look exhausted," says Ian, concerned at his wife's state.

"I feel terrible."

"I know. Eat something. It'll help." He offers her an energy bar.

"I don't ..."

"You must, Kate. We could be out all day and you're no good to Josh like a zombie."

"No – guess not." Kate takes the bar and bites into it and quickly takes a sip from her cup. The coffee is only lukewarm, but it helps her get rid of the unappealing stodge. Ian and Logan look on sympathetically.

"All set, love?"

Kate nods, keeping her eyes lowered.

"We'll head to the main beach as arranged."

Ian helps Kate and the three of them make their way to the end of their cove, where Ian spies Rosaline in the water. He waves and she gets out to greet them. They tell her their dilemma and she rushes off to get Jack. Ian and Logan steer Kate on to find Moana and Matt on the rocks.

"You guys early starters, too," chirps Matt, happy as a clam at high tide.

"Josh is missing. Didn't come back last night."

Matt's smile vanishes.

"We've arranged with some of the others to meet at the main beach for a search."

"Oh, you poor things. Matt, wake the boys. Don't worry love, we'll find him."

Kate smiles meekly. Her lips quiver with the onslaught of fresh tears. Ian quickly thanks them and they continue on.

"She's just being kind, love," he says rubbing her shoulder.

"I know but they're just words, aren't they? How many more times am I going to have to hear them?"

"We love him too, darling."

Kate's lip trembles uncontrollably. "I didn't mean ..."

"I know. Come on now, nearly there."

Ian holds her till they get to the main beach. Stan and his family arrive and have started discussing the best way to conduct a search when Rosaline, Jack and the Davidsons appear. The Booths and the Wentworths come moments later. They decide that one third of the group will go to the waterfall, one to the stream that leads to the fruit trees and the remaining third will go across to the other side of the island to see if he has ventured that way. They will meet back on the beach after two hours and rethink, if Josh is not found.

Two hours pass quickly and to everyone's disappointment they find themselves back at the beach.

"God, Kate looks so distraught. It's horrible," says Celia.

"Poor thing and poor Logan – he's trying so hard not to cry," says Trudy, her voice breaking.

"Girls, why don't you go and sit with Kate and Logan. Best we talk to Ian alone."

"What do we say to them?"

"I don't know, just be there for them."

"Come on, Trudy."

"But I'm useless at this sort of thing."

"Everyone is," says Celia, taking Trudy's hand and leading her over to Kate and Logan. Ian thanks them with a dog-tired smile, and walks to the small group huddled together a considerate distance away. He concurs they are now most likely looking for a body.

"He was going to the waterfall. Said he'd found herbs on the cliff."

"Oh, God," utters Rosaline. "If he's fallen ..."

"He'd have no chance," cuts in Jack.

"We should get up there," states Nigel soundly.

"Ian, what about Kate and Logan?"

"I'm afraid they'll want to come, Stan."

"What about the pond?"

"Good thought, Rosaline, but we were up there," says Drew softly. "We'd have seen him. Sun was shining down, water was pretty clear."

"But it's a possibility."

"Rosaline, Drew's right."

"Jesus, Jack, you don't have to sound so dismissive."

Jack raises his eyebrows and gives his wife a condescending smile. "I'm not."

"Actually, it makes sense to me," cuts in Nigel. "Let's search every inch of it."

"We should make a move, then. It's already bloody hot." Stan peers at Ian. "If he's hurt, we need to find him quickly."

Ian goes to inform Kate and Logan. They get up. Ian takes Kate's arm and they make their way to the waiting group.

"I'll stay here," Moana says. "Someone has to, in case the Longs and the others come back."

"Yes, of course. Thanks." Ian appreciates Moana's thoughtfulness. He had completely forgotten about anybody else, his mind preoccupied with thoughts of his best friend. He can do nothing to stop Kate from coming and this distresses him more. He isn't expecting Josh to be found in a state he wants his wife to see.

Stan takes the lead and they trek along the track by the stream. They call Josh's name and look for any odd disturbance, but see nothing to indicate that anybody has trampled their way off the track. They hear water splashing and laughter when they near the waterfall. They come out of the bush to see Terrance and Karl emerging from the pond.

"Howdy," calls out Karl.

"Morning, guys. You haven't seen Josh by any chance, have you? He was coming here yesterday and no one's seen him since."

"No, Stan, we haven't. We were here early but no one arrived before we left," answers Karl quickly.

"We're going to search this entire area." Ian says, sitting Kate down.

"Sure, we'll help." Karl gives Kate a look of pity and sympathy.

Terrance moves over to her. "I'm … I'm really sorry."

"Thank you," mumbles Kate, gazing at him with dazed, unreadable eyes.

Terrance takes hold of Karl's arm. "This is so wrong."

Ignoring him, Karl turns to Ian. "Okay, Ian, what's the plan? Split up – take different sides?"

"Yes, I guess so."

"Rosaline and I and a couple of others can take the east side."

"Okay, that sounds good, Jack."

"We'll go," says Sammy. Zach nods in agreement.

"Good, good. We need to search behind the waterfall. It looks climbable, not too difficult."

"I can do that," says Matt, getting up.

"Harvey, you go with him."

"Sure, Dad."

"I'm staying here with Kate," says Ian. "What about the left side?"

"Well, Yvonne and the girls can search over by the rocks. I'll help Drew and Trudy dive," says Stan.

"Celia and I can go left with Karl and Terrance. We'll go to the top. That okay with you guys?" asks Ritchie.

Karl nods a silent yes and faces his brother. "Don't worry, Terrance. This is good. Act normal."

"That's easier said than done." Terrance sneers at Karl as he puts on his sunglasses. He hopes they will cover the lie trapped in his eyes. Every few meters they stop and call Josh's name. Ritchie and Celia look one side, Karl and Terrance the other. The bush is dense and dim and, hearing nothing, Karl motions for them to head up the cliff.

"I feel like a complete shit."

"I know. Fuck, I'm not insensitive to the situation. We just have to ride it out." Karl stares at his brother. "Jesus, are you purposely trying to look guilty?"

Terrance peers at his brother, knowing exactly what he means. The silence between them hangs heavily in the air.

"Take them off."

Terrance whips off his glasses and tucks them over his t-shirt's neck. "Happy now?"

Karl shakes his head and clambers up the cliff to catch up to Ritchie and Celia. Terrance follows but keeps his distance. They reach the top and find themselves on level ground. Vines twist and wind over the hard soil where the shrubs have ceased to grow, leaving a majestic openness that commands attention.

"What a view," says Karl. "Fantastic." Karl smiles at his brother. Terrance sneers and puts on his sunglasses.

"Yeah, it is something isn't it?" responds Ritchie.

"Sure is!" Karl smiles at Celia. "What d'ya think, Terrance?"

"Yeah, very nice." *Go to the top of the fucking class, Karl!*

Celia looks left, then right. "Look, we'll search over there. Do you two want to check that way?"

"Sure." Karl shoves Terrance right. It takes only a few minutes before they hear Ritchie yelling. Karl grabs Terrance's arm and flashes him an icy warning and pushes him forward. They find Celia and Ritchie standing over Josh's bags.

"Oh, shit – he must have gone over. See those vines, those skid marks …" Ritchie stares at the edge of the cliff. "Do you think he was looking at something with the binoculars and maybe tripped on them?"

"Could have."

"I'm going to lie down – take a look."

"Oh, God, Ritchie." Celia's legs go weak watching Ritchie slide towards the edge.

"Oh, fuck, pull me back."

"Is he dead?" asks Karl, grasping Ritchie's legs.

"Dead?"

"Yeah, how far down is he? Could he be alive?"

"No way. It's a hell of a fall."

"You're sure, hon? People fall off buildings and somehow survive."

"Yes, she's right," says Karl with just enough concern in his voice.

"Fine, you look then," replies Ritchie, irritated.

"Terrance?"

"Why me?"

"Because you're lighter than me and you don't expect Celia to, do you?"

"Jesus Christ!" Terrance crawls to the edge and lies flat, pulling himself forward by his arms. "Hold my legs," he yells closing his eyes and counting. Sweating profusely, he feels light-headed and sucks the air to steady the run of images before him.

"Come on, Terrance, get on with it," shouts Karl.

"Karl," snaps Celia, narrowing her frosty eyes.

Karl gives her a disparaging smile before apologizing and Terrance peers over the edge. He feels the bile rising in his throat and ejects the bilious muck. He watches it fall and his eyes lock on Josh's body. *Christ his legs – those angles and that's got to be blood round his head – it's so dark.* He slides backwards, dislodging his glasses and reaches to grab them just as Karl pulls his legs. Cursing, he kicks himself free, rolls right, feels his stomach churn and throws up his morning's breakfast.

Karl crouches beside him. "Nice. Couldn't have done better myself." He pats Terrance's back and helps him stand as Celia moves closer.

"So, he's dead, then?"

Dead as a doornail! Terrance nods.

"Are you all right?"

Terrance brushes Karl off and ejects what is left in his mouth. "I'm fine." He sways, trying to regain his balance and clear his head. Karl lingers by his side as they watch Ritchie pick up Josh's things.

"We should go." Ritchie takes Celia's hand and heads for the track and Karl falls in line behind them. Terrance keeps well back, spending the entire time contemplating on how they will tell Kate and her family. When they arrive at the waterfall his dread reaches that pivotal point *–fuck it. I'm going to tell them the truth.* He drifts towards Kate, but is blocked by Stan's pacing body. He lowers his eyes to hide the burden of shame he can't escape. He sees Stan's feet step sideways and knows Stan has seen the bags Ritchie is carrying.

"Jessie, blow your whistle."

"Yes, Dad." Jessie blows as hard as she can.

Terrance wants to close his ears to the shrill noise. The tree canopies rustle overhead as birds take flight and then the bush is engulfed with an eerie silence. He raises his head to see Ritchie gently putting down Josh's bags beside Kate.

"I'm afraid he's fallen over the cliff. It's a big fall ... he wouldn't have suffered."

He hears the trepidation in Ritchie's voice and stares as Kate's body deserts her. Ian moves like a man half his age and grabs his wife before she hits the ground.

Terrance bites hard on his upper lip as he watches Logan's helpless misery. He feels someone beside him and catches Stan's glare before a warm hand lands on his shoulder.

"Are you okay?"

"Not really." He removes Mary's hand but his attention remains on her father.

"You don't have to be so brave, Terrance. It must have been horrible up there. Ritchie said you confirmed Josh was dead."

Terrance turns. "I'm not brave, Mary." He falters and closes his eyes to steady himself just as Karl steps beside him.

"It's okay, Karl, I've got this."

"I'm sorry?" Karl's voice is loud, caustic. "Got what exactly?"

"I'm helping Terrance."

"Terrance is fine. Go sit with your sister. She's in more need of you."

"Just go, Mary," sighs Terrance wearily. He sees the hurt in Mary's eyes and opens his mouth to say sorry when Kate appears in front of him. Mary huffs and walks towards her mother and Jessie, leaving him standing uncomfortably naked in front of Kate.

"Terrance," Kate says quietly. "You can't imagine how grateful I am. I know it must have been unpleasant to see Josh that way.

You should go back with Karl and …" She looks around. "Where's Greg?"

"He's back at our place. Hurt himself yesterday," cuts in Karl.

Terrance looks at the ground. *I can't look at her. Lying to her is bad enough.*

"Oh, so he won't know, will he?"

"No, I guess not."

"Well, you two go – tell him. We know Greg liked him. Teased Josh about it, 'cause he's very – well – insular about things. You need to tell Greg that he's … that he's gone." Kate folds her arms across her chest and walks quickly back to Ian and Logan.

"Hey, Terrance, I'm sorry," says Karl loudly. "Thought you had outgrown that vertigo of yours. Let's get you home."

Terrance sees the surprise on everyone's faces. *Jesus, Karl, just stop with all this shit.* He waves and reluctantly follows his brother, disappearing into the safety of the bush. "It's not my vertigo that's making me sick."

"Well, it probably isn't helping mate, but I hear you."

Back at the waterfall, Matt motions Zach and Sammy over to him. "I want you to run ahead. Ask Jessie if you can take her whistle. Get to Mum. We need to let the others know he's been found. Be discreet."

"Sure, Dad." Zach and Sammy go to Jessie and Stan and tell them what their dad has suggested. Stan passes Jessie's whistle over and the two of them depart quickly without Kate and her family noticing.

"Ready to go Kate, Logan?" Ian asks empathetically.

Kate nods and takes Logan's hand.

"Good, no point in hanging around. I want to get that flare up as soon as possible."

"Ian, I don't like the thought of leaving Josh here. We need to get him. I can't leave without knowing he's rescued."

"I know, love. We won't be going anywhere until they've recovered his body. Now, come on, let's go."

The trip back is silent. Kate's eyes are restless and they dart over her surroundings. *How dreary the bush looks when something sinister happens. Everything looks glum.* She thinks of Terrance. *Vertigo must be horrible – poor thing.* She feels tears well up in her eyes and lets them fall freely as she walks.

They reach the beach, consume the condolences on offer and wait for Ian to return with their flare. He ambles back, looking wretched. His hand shakes so badly that Stan offers to light it for him.

They sit and wait, looking out at the emptiness for what seems like an eternity, when finally the dinghy arrives and John and Alison get out.

"Would you like one of us to let them know what's happened?"

"Thanks, Stan, but no." Ian strides quickly towards them. He wants some space for his family. He tells John and Alison all he knows.

"And you're absolutely sure he's dead?" asks Alison.

"One hundred per cent. It's so hard to believe; he was always so cautious. Seems so unlike him. Always the one telling us to be careful."

"Well, we don't know the circumstances yet," replies Alison sympathetically. "How is your wife holding up?"

"Not well. Oh, and she's made it quite clear we're not leaving until his body has been recovered."

"Of course, Ian," says John. "Look, I'm going to need someone to show me where he is. Alison, I would like you to stay here and contact Bill. Let him know what's going on. Once we're back, we can decide on the best action to take."

"I'll go to Kate. I'm terribly sorry, Ian."

"Thank you, Alison. John, Ritchie was one of the ones who found him. I'm sure he won't mind taking you."

"Good, I'll go and ask him. I can imagine you want this over as soon as possible."

"Yes, thank you. I'm feeling my age."

"We'll be as quick as we can."

Ian finds Kate crying as she talks to Alison. He hates it that she has to go through this. He hates it that they all do. He turns to see Ritchie talking to John. John raises his hand and he and Ritchie depart for the cliff.

John and Ritchie arrive back fifty minutes later and John motions Alison over to him.

"He's going to have to be air-lifted out. No way we can get a boat near those rocks. Poor bugger had no chance. Looks to me as if he was looking at something through his binoculars, tripped and lost his footing. There's a bunch of pebbles on the ground. Certainly don't belong up there so he must have brought them."

"I'll stay here John; Bill's expecting you. I'll tell everyone what's happening."

"Okay, and Alison … keep them here."

John departs and Alison explains to the others what he has advised. She asks if anybody has seen the Tillers. Stan says he knows they spend time around the rocks. Alison asks Sammy, Zach and Mark to go and see if they can find them. The boys jump at the chance and run with speed, reach the rocks and spy three figures sitting against the cliff.

"You have to come with us. That guy, John Sedden, said so," shouts Mark, bending over.

"Why's that?" asks Karl.

"Don't know, really. It's to do with Josh. Left Alison what's-her-name on the beach. The posh-looking one."

"We'd better go," Zach says, anxiously.

Karl rises slowly, stretching his arms. "Greg, you okay? We'll walk slowly, if your back's still hurting."

"What's wrong with your back?" inquires Mark, noticing Greg's bandaged hand and scraped arms.

"Greg slipped on the rocks. Got a few cuts and bruises, hurt his back," intervenes Karl.

"It's nothing."

Terrance closes his eyes tightly, trying to steady the thoughts racing around his head. *Why do we all have to be there? Is it just because they want to account for everyone, or is it something worse? Christ, what if we have to describe it all and we say something different? I can't believe this is happening.* He sighs heavily as his mind goes over and over the past day's events. He hopes he can lie convincingly.

They arrive in time to see the dinghy round the cove, carrying four figures. They reach the other families just as John, Bill, Owen and Karen reach them.

John looks over the group before him. "Kate, Ian, Logan and Andrew, our deepest condolences to you. This is a terrible tragedy. All of us are deeply saddened to hear of your loss. I have been in contact with the Papeete police and they will be here as soon as possible. They wish to speak to all of you, so they have asked that you all remain here. It is a death that we are dealing with and they have procedures that have to be carried out. It does not mean that they are looking at this as anything other than a tragic accident. This is all normal practice, so please don't be alarmed.

"Are you all right, Kate? I know this isn't pleasant to hear."

Kate looks at John blankly. "This situation is certainly not all right but I know this has to be done."

"Kate, I don't mean to upset you any more."

Kate looks away and Ian holds her more tightly. "John, please carry on. Kate knows what you mean."

John continues. "While we wait for the police to arrive and when you are ready Ian, Kate and Logan, we would like you to think about any items that you would like to take back. We must leave everything how it is for the time being, but once we have the okay from the police you may go and gather your belongings. Any items that came in your chest must be taken back with us. Any other items that you brought and do not wish to take can be kept and used by the rest of the contestants. Are there any questions?"

There are none. John continues. "Because of the extreme situation, we thought you could all do with some refreshments. We have some coffee, tea and hot chocolate for the younger ones. Also cakes and biscuits. Please help yourselves."

"That's very good of you." Ian looks at his son.

"I'll get you something, Mum." Logan gets up. "Dad?"

"Coffee – maybe a cake."

"Sure thing."

The aroma from the coffee entices Logan. *God I can taste it already. And, man, these cakes look delish. I'm starving and thank you, God, thank you – finally something stodgy.* He fills two plates and takes them to his parents, goes back for drinks and then sits beside them, stuffing his face and gazing out to sea. He quickly spots a speck in the distance and Jessie jumps to her feet beside him, knocking sand over his plate. He feels his father's hand on his back.

"I see it, everyone! I see the helicopter!"

"Sit down, Jessie."

"But Dad, it's exciting."

Stan pulls his daughter down. "Yes, it is, but now's not the time."

Logan hands her his plate and Jessie smiles sheepishly and takes a cake. She takes a bite, screws up her nose and wipes her lips.

John motions everyone to move further up the beach as the roar of the helicopter's engines becomes as invasive as a chainsaw on a Sunday morning. Hands protect ears and eyes as the helicopter lands, depositing three uniformed policemen and one man and one woman, dressed in smart but casual clothes, on the beach.

"Commissioner Andre Belair." says Bill, holding out his hand.

"Bill, good to see you. This is Inspector Claudine Jarnot."

Bill holds out his hand to the Inspector. He sums her up quickly, knowing she will be doing the same to him. *Firm handshake, inquisitive eyes.* He smiles. *Haven't a clue what's she's thinking.* "Inspector Jarnot. Pleasure to meet you."

"Thank you, Bill. Please call me Claudine. I've heard good things about you. Shame you left us. Are you still with the police in Auckland?"

"No. I work for Martin now."

Claudine gives Bill a shallow smile. "So this is everyone I take it, Bill?"

"Yes. John Sedden, Grace Williamson, Owen Mills and Karen Holland over there are part of our crew, not contestants. John's in charge."

"Thanks," replies Andre. "We'll take it from here."

Claudine turns to face the contestants and smiles. "Hello, everyone. My name is Inspector Claudine Jarnot and this is Commissioner Andre Belair. We are from the Papeete Police Force, as are these three gentlemen. Gendarme, or as you say in New Zealand, Constable Marc, Constable Collet and Constable Manon.

"Inspector Jarnot," interrupts Bill. "This is Ian, Kate and Logan Smyth."

"Thank you, Bill. Now while we recover Josh, we will need one of you to go with our constables to your shelter so we can inspect Josh's belongings."

"Yes, of course. I'll come with you," says Ian getting up.

Claudine smiles. "Thank you." She motions for two gendarmes to follow Ian and whispers to them to be respectful.

Inspector Jarnot, Commissioner Belair, John and Bill depart for the waterfall, leaving the group with the other gendarme. They return fifty minutes later and Inspector Jarnot takes Ritchie and Celia off to one side while Commissioner Belair talks to the Tillers.

"Greg, is it?" asks Commissioner Belair. "You have a few nasty bumps and scrapes there. Would you mind telling me how you got them?"

"I was fishing with Karl and Terrance and I slipped on the rocks."

"He wasn't with us at the waterfall as ..."

"Merci beaucoup, Karl," interrupts Commissioner Belair with a wary look. "I am addressing Greg."

Karl smiles. "Sure, sorry."

"So, you didn't know of Josh's death, till when?"

"Till Karl and Terrance came back. Terrance was a bit of a mess."

"Really? Why was that?"

"He had ..."

"As I mentioned before, Karl, I'd like Greg to answer. I'll get to you in a moment."

Karl nods, catching Gendarme Marc's hand moving furiously across his pad.

"If you could continue, Greg."

"Um ... well, Terrance saw him."

"Josh?"

"It upset him." Greg nervously looks at Terrance. "He's not great with heights."

Commissioner Belair looks at Terrance. "But you were the one to confirm he was down there, were you not?" Commissioner

Belair pauses, tapping his fingers on his lips. "Odd, if you hate heights."

"Made sense at the time. Thought I'd outgrown it."

"Please continue, Greg."

"Um, well, we were on the beach. Sammy, Zach and Mark came and said that we had to come to the beach and that's it, really."

Commissioner Belair turns to Karl and Terrance. "And you two are absolutely sure you never saw Josh at all that morning?"

"Yes ... I mean, no we didn't see him."

"Terrance?'

"No."

"And was there anything, anything at all that looked odd up on the cliff?"

"Odd?"

"Out of place?"

"No, I don't think so. Everything looked normal, except maybe the pebbles." Karl looks Commissioner Belair straight in the eye.

"Maybe he collected pebbles."

"Maybe he did, Greg." Commissioner Belair looks them over. "Merci beaucoup, gentlemen. Please stay here with Gendarme Marc." He quickly walks to speak to Inspector Jarnot and Bill. He takes the notes Gendarme Marc gave him, swapping them with the notes Gendarme Manon has taken for Inspector Jarnot.

"Seem to collaborate, Claudine. The only thing puzzling me are the pebbles. We'll have another word with his family."

They walk over and find that Ian and Kate are just as puzzled, but Logan nods his head quickly, his eyes darting from his mother to his father.

"He made a slingshot. No one was meant to know, but I stumbled across him one morning. Was meant to be a surprise – for Mum. I promised not to say unless he didn't catch anything."

"A slingshot! Now, that makes sense. Thank you, Logan." Inspector Jarnot taps her notebook twice then deposits it in her pocket and Inspector Jarnot goes back to Ritchie and Celia while Commissioner Belair talks to the Tillers.

"It has come to our attention that Josh had a slingshot. That would answer the puzzle of the pebbles."

"We didn't see one," says Terrance, glancing at Karl.

"It could have ended up in the sea," offers Greg. "I mean, that's a possibility, right?"

"Yes, it could have – probably something we will never know. Merci beaucoup, gentlemen."

The Papeete Police Force and the members of Martin's team gather together to talk. They compare notes and the gendarmes go back to the helicopter.

"Ian, Kate and Logan, it is time for you to say your goodbyes. You will be taken with Josh to the Papeete Hospital, where he will remain until a post-mortem is complete. Kate, you and your family will stay at Martin's hotel.

"We would like to thank you all for your patience. It has been a long day." Commissioner Belair signals Inspector Jarnot and they accompany Bill to check the contents of the chest and take it down to the dinghy.

"So, Bill, this contest of yours is not turning out that well?"

"No, it isn't. Had one couple leave because the woman was hurt after that storm, but at least she's okay."

"Argh – the lure of money, oui?" says Andre with a wry smile.

"You know, I touched on the subject of suicide with Ian. Couldn't bring myself to ask Kate, but Ian and Logan were adamant on that one."

"I didn't think it looked that way. He was gay and apparently a bit reserved, but was happy enough. I dismissed that theory at the beginning and a guy like that would have absolutely left a letter for the family. No, suicide is out of the question, but you were right to ask."

"It was good seeing you again, Bill." Commissioner Belair shakes Bill's hand and waits for Inspector Jarnot to do the same.

"Yes, good to see you again, Andre, and nice to meet you, Claudine. Let me know if anything unusual turns up." Bill watches his old friend chatting freely to the woman who now has his job. They climb into the helicopter and Commissioner Belair waves. Bill waves back and observes the Smyths saying their goodbyes. He watches the helicopter take off and then wanders over to John and Alison and they depart the island, leaving everyone watching their dinghy till it becomes a tiny speck on the horizon.

"Well, thank goodness that's over. I think we should share these things out quickly."

"I totally agree, Nigel," says Stan, getting up. "This has been unpleasant and Yvonne and I would like to get the kids back and settled."

"Well, for the sake of those who weren't with us when Aron and Helena went ..." Nigel pauses. "I'm sorry." He puckers his lips and sighs. "So, as I was saying, we divided the items up by taking rounds and one member from each team would come up, pick out something, until there was nothing left. I think we should do the same here."

"Sounds good to me," answers Karl.

"Now, as to who goes first? Mark why don't you, Harvey and Peter go and get some twigs. We need eight different lengths."

"Twigs?" questions Jack, sarcastically.

"Sure, Dad," says Mark ignoring Jack's comment. The three boys head down the beach and then to the palms.

"Peter," whispers Harvey, "I think we'd better put off our viewing for a few days. Let's wait till things get back to normal. We'll still run, but the other thing can wait."

"Okay."

"Those police were talking to Ritchie and Celia and the Tillers for ages. Do you think they suspect something?"

"Who knows?"

Mark comes up to them with a handful of twigs. "Hey, what are you two whispering about?"

"Nothing."

"You must have been talking about something."

"What's it to you?"

"Peter, chill. We were just saying it might not have been an accident."

"Police thought it looked like one."

"Yeah, but what if it wasn't?"

"That would mean someone pushed him."

Peter licks his finger and points to the heavens. "Ding dong!"

"Don't be a dick, Peter."

"I'm just saying, that's all." Peter snarls and looks at Mark. "Could have been you for all we know."

Mark pulls back, staggered by Peter's remark.

"Mark, he's just kidding." Harvey intervenes, giving Peter a quick flick of his eyes.

"Yeah, well just for the record – it wasn't." Mark moves in closer, till he stands inches from Peter. "Maybe it was you, dickhead."

"Fuck off."

"You fuck off."

"Jesus, you two."

Peter ignores Harvey, shoving Mark hard and then he sees darkness. His nose throbs and he feels liquid run into his lips. "Shit, you broke my nose."

"I hardly touched you." Mark walks away, leaving Harvey thrown by Peter's sudden aggressiveness.

"Wanker." Peter bellows at the receding figure. Mark gives him the finger.

"Jesus, Peter!"

"What? I don't like him."

"Why?"

"I just don't." Peter gets up, shaking the sand off him. "Is it bad?"

"Not really. Good for you it wasn't hard."

"Yeah, well I wasn't expecting it. Fuck him. Who cares? I'll say I tripped."

Harvey shakes his head and they head back. "You know we probably won't be able to go anywhere now."

"Nah, it'll be cool."

"Maybe, but like I said, the other thing can wait."

"Fine – but not too long. It's boring enough as it is." Peter glances ahead. "Oh, for fuck's sake!"

"Peter," calls Henry, striding towards them. "Peter – are you all right?"

"I'm fine."

"Mark said you hurt yourself."

"Did he? Well then, there you go."

Henry looks at Harvey questioningly then back to his son. "Let's see that nose."

"Don't, Dad. It's nothing."

"What happened?"

"Like he said, I tripped. No big deal."

"On what?"

"I dunno."

"All right, Peter, I was just asking."

"Must have tripped on something Mr. Henderson."

"Something – yes, thank you, Harvey. I guess that must be it."
Henry looks around.

"Well, if I had seen it, Dad, I wouldn't have tripped."

"I guess not, Peter."

"I'm not a child."

"Move."

"I'll walk with Harvey."

"Look, son, you'd better get a handle on these moods. I know
you didn't want to come but you can catch up with your friends
when we're back. It's three months, not forever, and if we win this
thing, you'll be happy we came."

"Win it! Huh, they'd all have to die for that to happen."

Henry grabs Peter's arm, squeezing it tightly. "That's enough."
His voice is sharp. "That sort of comment if completely uncalled
for, young man. If you want to enjoy the rest of the time on this
island then you'd had better damn well change." Henry turns to
Harvey. "Harvey?"

"Yes, Mr. Henderson?"

"I'm sorry you had to witness this. Peter won't be going
anywhere for the next week."

"Look, Dad, I'm sorry, okay. I'm just pissed that I tripped."

"Good to hear, but you're still grounded. Now, get a move on;
everyone's waiting."

Peter scowls, kicks the sand and follows his father. Harvey
walks alongside, looking completely baffled by what he has just
witnessed.

Nancy rushes up to Peter, her hand protectively reaches for his
face.

"Mum, I'm fine."

"Oh, Peter, I think we had better go so I can put something on that. You might have a nasty bruise in the morning."

"Don't fuss."

"Peter, what did I just say to you?"

"All right, all right. Sorry, Mum, but you're making me feel like a baby."

"Well, stop acting like one and your mother won't need to treat you like one. Now pick your things up and get going."

Jack watches Peter with amusement. "Tripped, my arse."

"Jack, you weren't there."

"That's the result of a punch."

"Well, it's nothing to do with you so forget it. I want to leave."

"Yeah, bet it'll be an interesting night in their shelter."

"Oh, I dunno, Jack. These things happen with teenagers. He'll have forgotten it by tomorrow."

"Is that so, Moana?"

"Yes, it is, Jack," Matt intervenes. "I guess you wouldn't know, being as you don't have kids."

"Well, that might be, Matt, but it doesn't change the facts."

"You don't know the facts, Jack."

"Jesus, you can be thick sometimes, woman."

Rosaline stands. "I'm going. Why don't you stay and make friends."

Terrance snickers and feels Karl's elbow in his ribs.

"Time to leave," mutters Greg.

"Yes, that sounds like a sensible move. I think today's events have stressed everyone and we're all tired. Best get their things divided up and get an early night." Nigel rises and helps Linda up, looking at Mark doubtfully. Mark smiles sheepishly back at his father.

The following morning, Jack is out running when he sees Peter sitting on the beach, watching his family and the Downs in the water. Smiling, he sits beside him.

"Pretty girl."

"Uh?"

"Mary – she's a pretty girl."

"Oh, yeah. She's all right, I suppose."

"Come on, son, you must fancy her."

"She's only got eyes for Terrance and that wanker Mark."

"You sure?"

"I'm sure."

"Well, I think you're wrong. It's just what she wants you to think."

"Why would she want that?"

"Girls like her …" Jack watches Mary. "Well, they're a tease. Like to make you jealous."

"She doesn't even know I like her."

Stan smiles and nudges Peter "Oh, she knows, Peter – believe me, she knows."

"You reckon?" Peter's eyes follow Mary.

"Absolutely. I've seen the way she looks at you."

"Really?"

"Really! You should do something about it before Mark gets there first."

"He's such a dork."

"That what the fight was about yesterday?"

Peter looks at Jack for the first time.

Jack grins sympathetically. "Well, then, do something about it. Don't let him get the girl."

"Yeah, I won't – thanks. Think I'll join them. You coming?"

"No, I've got my girl waiting for me."

Peter grins coyly. "Oh, right."

"Bye." Jack watches Peter run down to the water, making a beeline for Mary. Jack laughs and turns to see Terrance, arms crossed, leaning casually on a palm tree.

"Terrance."

"Jack."

"Been there long?"

"Long enough."

"Make a habit of listening to private conversations, do you?"

"Only when they're interesting."

"Well, I'm sure you've been told to mind your own business a couple of times, then."

"As should you, Jack."

"That so! Well we all interpret things differently, Terrance. That's what makes life interesting and on that note, I'll better get back to my wife."

"Yes, you shouldn't leave her alone."

Jack stops. "I'm sorry?"

"Well, you never know who she could be talking too."

"Well Terrance – as long as it's not you, I'm not bothered. Have a nice day."

Terrance raises his eyebrows and the two of them lock eyes before Jack breaks away and disappears into the bush.

"That Jack," says Karl, panting heavily as he pulls up beside Terrance.

"Yep. Tough run?"

"Yeah. Everything okay?"

"Caught him deliberately trying to cause trouble between Peter and Mark."

Karl looks down to the water. "Mary?"

"Yep."

"Well, not our problem, mate. Keep your distance, 'cause I'm pretty sure he's well aware of the way Rosaline looks at you."

Terrance smiles.

"I mean it, Terrance."

"I know. It's just sweet to think he knows. He's a smug bastard and he treats her like shit."

"Well, that may be, but like I said, not our problem."

CHAPTER SIXTEEN

Rosaline is hot and tired. The trek to the fruit trees has taken longer than expected and has done nothing to alter the solemn mood Jack put her in this morning. She crashes out of the vegetation and finds she is not alone.

"Trouble in paradise?"

Rosaline looks at the older woman. She is tempted not to answer, but that would be rude and Moana seems nice. She draws in air, walks over to her and sits down.

"A bit."

"Hmm … Lot of distractions here. Can be hard on a marriage."

"Yes," agrees Rosaline, her voice a mere whisper.

"Even harder if things weren't right beforehand."

"Am I that obvious?"

"No."

"But you've noticed."

"Yes … I've been married a long time."

"Great. If you've noticed, then the others probably have, too."

"Not necessarily. You have to know what to look for. Jack knows though."

Rosaline lowers her head to hide her glassy eyes. "I'm sorry. I don't know what's wrong with me."

"It's okay. Crying's good. You go right ahead. Doesn't bother me."

"I've got no one to talk to."

"Hmm … That's no good."

Rosaline looks at Moana. Her eyes are closed and she looks peaceful. She isn't sure if she wants to burden this woman with her troubles.

"Do you ever get lonely?"

"Lonely? Sometimes. But don't get me wrong, I love my boys and Matt." Moana chuckles. "Well – most of the time."

"You have a good relationship with them, don't you? Matt seems nice. He looks like he's lost weight. Doesn't seem to be limping as much."

"Yes to both. He loves it here. Spending time with the boys … best thing for him." Moana opens her eyes and turns to Rosaline. "I see the man I fell in love with, and I truly thought that man was long gone. So tell me, you been married long?"

"Seven years."

"Seven years … No children?"

"No. Jack wanted them but I didn't."

"Oh, I'm sorry to hear that, luv. Children are wonderful additions to a family."

"Yes, I can imagine. Funny thing is … well, I was changing my mind but then …"

"Then?"

"We had a problem and now I can't see it happening." Rosaline dips her head.

"Oh, dear. Me and my big nose." Moana pats Rosaline's leg. "None of my business. Forgive me."

"Oh, Moana, there's nothing to forgive. I lost my mother a few years ago and I never knew my father – I don't have any sisters or brothers. I can't talk about it to Jack's family or our friends, in case they, well, you know, say something."

"So, you want to talk now?"

"Maybe. It's complicated." Rosaline pauses. "Jack had an affair."

"Argh!"

"It was with his receptionist, Cathy. She was only nineteen."

"Was?"

"Yes, she died. Car accident. It's how I found out. The police came to the door asking for Jack, but he was over at his parents. His dad had come home from hospital – knee replacement. Guess he was meeting her afterwards."

"Cathy?"

"Yes. Told me he had a meeting. Her parents lived overseas. She had Jack's name on her phone, or in her book or whatever, so they came, but he wasn't home."

"Oh, bit awkward?"

"Yes. Jack got back and they told him there had been a fatal accident. The woman driver was killed instantly. Her car collided with a truck. The driver was injured, but survived."

"Oh dear! What did Jack do?"

"He turned white, started to shake. The male officer helped him sit down. I just sat there. It was like watching a film, really. I didn't think it was real, until Jack looked at me. I hated him then. I hated everything about him. He looked pathetic, so hopeless and little, which is kind of funny, 'cause he's not." Rosaline wipes her nose.

"I never even suspected … stupid Rosaline! With her nice house and her career. If I hadn't been so obsessed, Jack mightn't have strayed and Cathy – she might still be alive.

"You know, I never even saw her until the funeral. They had a photo of her. She was very, very pretty, so young. I felt so bad for her parents. It's terrible to see someone's parents bury their child. Just terrible."

"Yes, I can imagine." Moana's hand squeezes Rosaline's leg gently. "You went to the funeral?"

"Yes, Jack was such a mess. I don't know how I did it. You see, I didn't blame her. I blamed him."

"But you and Jack are still together?"

"Yes. I didn't want anything to do with him at first, but he was in a terrible state. Hit the bottle. I let him stay – separate rooms. We hardly spoke. Then his partner broke his leg and Jack was having a hard time coping. He's a tennis coach. I had to step in – help manage things. We had to talk. He's trying really hard. We came here hoping it would be better, but I don't know if I can ever completely forgive him, the way he wants me to."

"Time is a wonderful healer, luv. It might work out."

"Like it has for you?"

Moana smiles compassionately and takes Rosaline's hand in hers. "Well, I think we had better make a start on finding you some herbs."

Rosaline leans over and hugs the older woman.

"Oh, goodness, luv. What's that for?"

"For listening."

"Sharing's good. Any time you need to talk, you come find me. We're at the first cove to the right of the main beach. Just come down and call me. If I'm there, I'll either see or hear you."

"That would be lovely," smiles Rosaline. "Moana, can we keep today a secret."

"Of course. Don't you worry, I know Jack doesn't think much of us."

"Take no notice. He's like that to everyone."

"Yes, I can imagine he is."

Rosaline arrives back to find Jack resting. She looks around and sees he hasn't done much. She puts her bag down and heads outside.

"Going somewhere?"

"No. Thought you were sleeping."

"Enjoy yourself?"

"Yes, got some fruit and herbs."

"See anyone?"

"No, not really."

"So, you did see someone."

"Jesus, Jack, I saw Moana."

"Just asking, 'cause I'd be surprised if you found these by yourself, that's all."

"Okay – yes, she showed me – happy?"

"That's good. Her knowledge could be useful."

"Oh, for God's sake … Please don't be like this, Jack, I really like her."

"You're like chalk and cheese."

"So?"

"Can't see how you'd have much in common."

"No, I don't suppose you can."

"Touchy. Now, how about lying down? Too hot to do much else."

"Promise me you'll be nice to them."

"Sure." Jack reaches out and takes her hand. She closes her eyes knowing that Jack's answer didn't promise anything.

CHAPTER SEVENTEEN

Sunday morning comes, bringing gray skies, colder temperatures and a persistent drizzle of rain. It falls softly, casting a veil over the island, making the bush look like a glossy oil painting. There is no orange scarf flying. The midday lunch is canceled and the rush to prepare something is replaced by a lazy morning's sleep. By the afternoon, the sky is tar black and the rain is heavier, causing the temperature to drop. The wind picks up as thunderclouds threaten to explode with unwanted energy. By evening, the storm intensifies, lashing the island with curtains of water destroying the intense palates of color it created hours ago. Flashes of electrifying forks descend, uprooting the unsuspecting trees in their path, and thunder roars like angry lions, causing the ground to shake as if experiencing a series of tiny earthquakes.

The storm persists its lashing of the island throughout the night and by morning the rain continues to fall, but the winds have abated, taking with them the groans and moans of the bush. The air remains cool and dampness invades everything.

Mary walks to their door and is greeted by an eerie mist. The only sounds she can hear are the relentless drumming of the missiles of rain and the rushing of water. She calls her father.

Yvonne withdraws her body from the warmth her husband offers. "Stan, you had better go or we'll never get any peace. Can you check the fire?"

"Checked it earlier, love." Stan wiggles out of their sleeping bag, shivers and grabs another top.

"What's the matter, Mary?"

"Listen! That's the stream, isn't it? Do you think our stuff's okay?"

"Hope so. Harvey and I will check. Stay here with Mum and Jessie. Keep the fire going and have a nice hot cuppa ready for our return."

Mary grins. "Okay, Dad."

Stan smiles and rubs her hair, laughing at Mary's scowl.

"Get some warmer clothes on, Mary, and make sure our stuff is away in bags. At this rate everything will get wet."

"Will we be okay?"

"'Course. It'll dry out quickly once this rain has stopped."

Stan wakes Harvey and grabs two sets of gumboots. He hands a pair to Harvey, tells him to get dressed, grab a poncho and come with him. They leave, each carrying a spear and bucket and head down to the stream.

"Man, she's overflowing," shouts Stan. "Be careful, Harvey, hang onto the trees."

The rain runs off their hair like a river and slides under their ponchos with ease, soaking their clothes and making them shiver. They reach the rocks where their containers should be to see the stream has grown considerably. Stan kneels down. He feels around in the dirty water, fighting the current wanting to take his hand, till he touches rope and he pulls it towards him, retrieving a couple of containers. Harvey hands him a bucket and Stan places them in it and then his hand is back in the muddied water. "Damn ... rest must have washed away."

"Dad, we should go," Harvey shouts.

Harvey's right. The rain is heavier and the stream is rising. It is now lapping at their knees. He gives Harvey the thumbs up and they start back.

"Dad, look!" Harvey stops. "Over there. Isn't that one of our containers?"

"Could be. Not sure if we can get it. You stay here, I'll make my way over." Stan gives Harvey the bucket but takes the rope and his spear. His feet search blindly for footholds as his free hand grasps trees. Less than two meters from the container, the water reaches over his knees. He curses and ties a rope around the nearest tree and then winds it around his middle, securing it tightly with a reef knot. He looks back at Harvey, moves on half a meter, loses his footing and slithers into the murky water to find he's on the stream's bed. With an effort, he stands and fights against the water swirling around his thighs. Managing to stay upright, he slowly edges towards the dancing container and retrieves it.

He makes his way back to the edge of the stream. Finding it difficult to lift his leg, he turns, pulling the rope taut, and uses his arm to heave himself out, but as he places his foot down, the ground gives way and he falls backwards. The force of the current takes him till the rope yanks him back. He yells out as the container and his spear are ripped from his hand.

Fuck! He pulls himself upright. Grabbing a tree root, he hauls himself up the bank and makes it back to the tree. *Goddammit – stop shaking man, and get this bloody knot undone.*

"Dad, are you all right?"

"I'm fine." *Come on, you fucking rope – come on.* Stan makes his way carefully towards his son and Harvey falls onto his chest, trembling. "It's okay, son. I'm here."

"I thought you were going to be swept away. Thought you might die – like Josh."

"Take more than a little rain to get the better of me." He strokes his son's head. "I lost the container. Think we'll leave that one."

Harvey nods in agreement, still clinging to his father.

"I love you, Harvey. You know that don't you?"

"I know and, Dad ... I don't mean to be, you know, difficult and that. I want to be with you guys but it's ..."

"No need to say any more, son. I was your age once, you know. Now, let's go. Here, tie this rope around your middle."

"Dad, do you think Josh slipped?"

"Must have."

"We need to be more careful."

Stan squeezes his son's shoulder, sweeps back his son's hair, checks the rope holds and nods for Harvey to move. Their progress is slow but they make it back safely. Stan sees their roof is dripping through every gap it can but is relieved that Yvonne and the girls have opened their last tarpaulin and draped it over their belongings and have managed to keep the fire alight.

Stan and Harvey undress and Yvonne brings them dry clothes. They hand the containers to Yvonne and then Mary pours them a hot cup of tea. They sit, letting the warmth of the fire penetrate their skin, drink their tea and listen to the rain attack their home.

CHAPTER EIGHTEEN

Monday brings little change in the weather and Peter is pissed. They have been stuck inside with only a toilet break to relieve the boredom. He is itching to get back with Harvey, now his grounding has been lifted, but the weather has halted his plans, leaving him agitated. He thinks of Mary and decides to try to impress her. He was good at school carpentry and he picks up a small cane and starts cutting off one end. It is tedious work, as the cane is tough. While cutting, his mind conjures up images from the film '*127 hours*' and how the guy cut off his lower arm with his pocketknife. He shivers. *Have I the guts to do that?* He looks at his arm and presses the knife down. Candice screams.

"Oh, my God! What are you doing, Peter?" Nancy shouts.

Peter withdraws the knife. "What's the problem? I was just checking how blunt it is."

"What's the problem?" squeals Henry, sending his neck veins pumping grotesquely. "We see you pushing a knife into your arm and you ask what's the problem?"

"Dad, calm down – you're going to explode. I wasn't going to do anything."

Henry's shoulders slump as he inhales deeply, letting out an inevitable sigh. His fingers trace the lines in his face as he looks back at his son. "Peter, use your brains and test it on something other than your body in future." He gives Nancy's hand a pat and looks at the piece of cane in Peter's lap. "What are you trying to make?"

"A recorder."

"But you said you would help make cards," says Candice towering over him, hands locked on her hips, ready for the oncoming battle.

"No, I didn't."

"You did, too. Mum, he did, didn't he?"

"Well, I think you might have, Peter – and it wouldn't kill you, would it? Pack of cards is a great idea. Give us something to do as a family. God knows how long it's been since we've done that."

"Yeah, well I want to do this first – then I'll help."

"You'll be ages."

Nancy frowns, rubbing her forehead.

"All right, I'll help, but I'm not spending the whole day doing it, okay?"

"Okay."

Exasperated Nancy stares at her children. "Thank you, Peter." She gets up and starts preparing lunch using the leftovers of the fish they had eaten that morning. She reaches for the avocados and fresh fruit and feels Henry's hand on her shoulder.

"I know it's not his fault, Henry. This bloody rain's depressing – everything's so wet. Look at the roof. It's dripping like a tap. Would make anyone irritable."

"I know, love. Can't last much longer. The fog has lifted, so that's a good sign."

"Is it? The wind's stronger."

"Yes, it'll blow itself out, you'll see." He kisses her cheek. "At least our fire's still going. Glad we made that window. Be pretty unpleasant in here without it."

Tuesday morning dawns, with a clear blue sky. The sun is out, already drying the top layer of sand; steam climbs slowly from the ground like snakes in a trance and the earth smells cleansed and oddly sweet. The beaches are soiled with endless coral, seaweed and wood. The rest of the island is awash with debris from the broken bush. The humidity soars, making mosquitoes abundant.

The Booths decide to take everything out of their tree house to air, as moisture has penetrated the roof and walls, making everything damp and smelly. When they have finished, Ritchie, Celia and Trudy go to the beach while Drew heads further into the bush. He wants to do a quick inspection to make sure the stream isn't going to be a problem. He swishes the air as mosquitoes attack his arms and legs. Fallen trees block his way, constantly slowing him down. He comes across the stream to see it has carved a path heading away from them and decides to head back. The mosquitoes are worse, diving at him from all directions, and his arms fly wildly in an attempt to protect his body. He speeds out of the bush and stumbles in the sand.

"Fuck." The sand irritates his reddened bites and he gets up quickly, dashing for the water.

"Hi, babe," says Trudy, running to him.

"Shit – I've been bitten alive."

Trudy laughs.

"It's not funny. They itch like buggery."

"Oh, you poor boy – come to Mama." Trudy holds her arms out and Drew grabs her, taking her under. They surface and he plants a kiss on her lips and then pushes her off. "Fuck, too itchy. You gotta get me something, Trudy."

"Okay. Can't have you avoiding me, now, can we?"

"I'm not joking. It's getting unbearable."

"Men! What would you do without us?" Trudy moves quickly and runs up the beach, kicking sand over Ritchie and Celia.

"Bloody hell, Trudy."

"Sooooorie!"

"Hey, babe, is that Terrance walking towards us?"

"Think so."

"Hope he continues."

"Don't be so rude." Celia sits up straight. "Hi, Terrance."

"Hi." Terrance sees Drew in the water and gives him a wave. "Mind if I join you two?"

"No." Celia nudges Ritchie. "Where's your brothers?"

"Hunting."

"Hunting? Oh, that sounds scary."

Terrance laughs. "Yeah, probably will be with Greg along."

Ritchie and Celia chuckle as Trudy runs past. Her hand clutches a tube of antihistamine cream. The three of them watch as she starts rubbing Drew's neck.

"Hey, guys, stop that – we've got company," bellows Ritchie with a snicker.

"Oh, funny ha ha. Bloody mossies got me good."

"Oh!" laughs Celia. "Poor poppa bear."

"I heard that," says Drew, making his way over. "Look at my bloody ankles. Fucking things."

"You should watch those, mate. Easy to get infected."

"Yeah, I will. Where's your brothers?"

"Oh, they're hunting," giggles Celia.

"Hunting, yeah? What are they hunting?"

"Birds."

"Really?" chirps Trudy. "How are they going to get them?"

"They made a slingshot," mentions Terrance matter-of-factly.

"That's cool. God, why didn't you guys think of that?"

"Why didn't you, Celia?"

"'Cause that's your department, Drew."

"Is that so? Well, I did think of it, but decided against it, 'cause of Josh."

"Oh yeah ... 'course."

"That's ridiculous mate. They caught anything, Terrance?" asks Ritchie.

"I don't know. Guess I'll find out later."

"Oh, so they haven't used it yet?"

"No, Trudy, they haven't."

"We should make one, guys. It's so silly not to."

"Give her a slingshot and she thinks she's Xena," chuckles Drew, causing Ritchie to explode into laughter. Celia looks at them, shaking her head, while Trudy glares at Drew. Terrance watches them, indifferent to their playful banter.

"Sorry, hon. Tell you what, I'll make you one, okay?"

"Don't bother. I'll make one myself."

Drew pushes out his bottom lip, looks at her with puppy-dog eyes, reaches over and tickles Trudy's chin. Trudy erupts in playful laughter.

"So," intervenes Celia locking onto Terrance's eyes. "Are you all right now?"

"I guess. Josh's death ... well, it's just so – pointless." He looks out to sea. "When I was thirteen, my cat died pointlessly."

Ritchie glances at Drew and twirls his finger.

"Mum said I cried for days. I loved that cat. Had a special bond. Then when our parents died, I wasn't as bad, 'cause it happened elsewhere. Didn't have to see them. Saw my cat though. Wasn't nice, just like Josh."

"What was your cat's name?" asks Celia.

"Fergo. He was a pain. Not to me, though. To me he was the best cat ever – to everyone else, he was a pain. Peed in other people's houses; got locked in garages; stuck on roofs. Came home one day, trailing six sausages behind him. Never did find out who they'd belonged to." Terrance laughs. "Yeah, he was one bad cat but I loved him to bits."

"We had a cat when I was young," says Trudy. "Vinegar."

"Vinegar," snorts Ritchie. "What kind of a name is that?"

"It's a cool name. She was run over when I was sixteen. I remember Mum and Dad telling me and my brother – he's younger than me. Boy, did he burst into tears. I held mine in, till I got to my room. I reckon I soaked my pillow through and through, but there was no way I was crying in front of my olds. Never got another one. Mum said we were too old and in a few years we would be gone."

"Yeah, we never got another one, either. I didn't want one. Too hard when they go. Too hard when anything goes," replies Terrance.

Celia reaches out and touches his arm. "Things will get better. We have tomorrow to look forward to. See the flag? The sun is shining?"

"Won't get better for Kate and her family, though, will it? Not for a long time. Look I'd better go."

"See you tomorrow." Celia smiles, hiding the confusion she feels. Watching him walk away, hands in his pockets, reminds her of her first boyfriend and how awkward it all was. She had always felt a pull towards the troubled, but this was different. For one thing, they had been teenage problems. She was now happily married. She had Ritchie and, therefore, no idea how to help Terrance, or why she felt she even should. She decides that however good her intentions, she'd best leave it alone.

"Jesus – that was depressing!"

"Yeah, you'd think he was close to the guy, the way he's acting," agrees Drew.

"Don't be so insensitive. I feel sorry for him."

"Absolutely, Celia."

"Oh, not you, too, Trudy. Bloody hell, give them a pretty face and they go la la."

Trudy whacks Drew on the back. He picks her up, throws her over his shoulders and carries her, kicking and screaming, to the water. Ritchie and Celia follow them down and wade in to their waists.

"So – find Terrance attractive, do you?"

"Ohh, jealous, are we?" Celia splashes him.

Ritchie looks at Celia, a bemused look in his eye.

"Don't be silly."

"Really?"

"Ritchie," says Trudy, overhearing as she playfully swims around them. "Celia's only has eyes for you. Hell – half the female population only have eyes for you and the other half haven't seen you yet."

Ritchie erupts into laughter until he catches Celia's nervous expression.

"Should I be jealous?"

"No." She doesn't look at him. He grabs her arm, forcing her to face him.

"Celia, should I?"

"Of course not. I feel sorry for him. He's nice – in a bad place."

He holds her with his eyes.

"Hon, seriously, I do feel sorry for him. You know what I'm like." She puts her hand up to his face and kisses him.

He wipes a strand of hair off her forehead and smiles tenderly. "Okay. So, I'm hungry. Let's get lunch."

"Sounds good to me." Celia looks back down the beach, but Terrance has vanished. "We have to get going, anyway. Need fruit and you guys have to catch dinner, remember?"

"'Course. You don't think we've got time for …"

"No, I don't. But if you play your cards right, I'm sure we could make time after dinner, in our busy, busy schedule." Celia runs her fingers up Ritchie's chest to his lips causing him to quiver.

It is so unlike him to feel threatened. Still, it won't do him any harm to know how it feels. She has felt the twinge of jealousy numerous times over the years but has learned to cope with it. She trusts her husband completely. *Terrance is attractive, but that doesn't mean anything. It's Ritchie I love.*

The next day presents itself with crystal clear skies and sparkling aquamarine waters, rippling placidly in the gentle, balmy breeze. The beach is an array of colors, with many of the contestants wearing floral shirts, sarongs and wide-brimmed hats. The younger ones wear their swim gear and ignore their parents' badgering about hats and sunscreen.

Lunch consists of fresh fruit salads and Bridget's now famous poisson cru, which today consists of diced tuna, fresh lime juice, coconut milk, shallots, chili and is seasoned with salt and pepper. It smells delicious.

"God, this is just so good. Exactly what we needed," says Nancy.

Drew drops to the sand and takes a tube from his pocket and smoothers his legs.

"Oh, boy, you got hammered there, mate."

"Ya think, Matt? Don't go near the stream; they're everywhere."

"It's this humidity – brings them out in droves," states Moana, practically.

"Is it just me, or is this the hottest day we've had?" asks Bridget, fanning herself with a palm leaf.

"Definitely the hottest," replies Matt, wiping away the sweat persistently rolling down his face. He helps himself to Rosaline's punch. "Hope this cools me down."

"I spent all morning making that, Matt. Oranges, lemons, paw-paw, melons, fresh mint and lime slices but, I'm afraid, no ice-cubes."

"Oh, geez, Rosaline, no ice? Man, that's tough."

"Behave, you," says Moana, winking at Rosaline as Peter helps himself to a drink. He catches Jack grin and smiles before sitting down next to Harvey and Mary. Candice and Jessie are engrossed in conversation with Mark, and Peter nudges Harvey to get his attention.

"Hey, weather's good. Island's drying up, nothing else has happened. How about it? Shall we try for, you know …"

"I was thinking the same thing, old boy," chuckles Harvey. "Your nose looks better. Can't tell if it's red from Mark or just sunburn."

"Never mind that. Can't you just let me know something?"

"Nope. Spoil it. In any case, believe me, it's worth waiting for."

"What are you two on about?" asks Mary, intervening.

"Nothing that concerns you," replies Harvey. "Why don't you go and see lover boy. He looks as if he needs someone to cheer him up."

"You know, I think I will. You two do my head in. I need someone mature to talk to."

"Talk to. Gosh, is that what you call it?"

Peter snickers and Harvey beams a toothy smile.

"Oh, grow up, Harvey. And, by the way, you need to wash your teeth."

"Piss off, Mary."

Mary sneers and stands, shaking the sand off her butt, and then walks provocatively over to Terrance. "Hi. Mind if I sit with you?"

"Depends."

"Oh? On what?"

"On if you're going to behave yourself," says Terrance, not bothering to face her.

It's okay if he doesn't look. He knows I'm showing more flesh than I should. Bet he can feel my heat from here. Mary sits. "Well, yes, I think I could do that. You look nice today with your hair out. Just like a surfer. Do you surf, Terrance?"

"No."

"Shame. Boy, it's hot isn't it?" She stretches her long legs and opens her shirt top. "Care for a swim?"

"I'm good, but don't let me stop you."

"Okay – well I'll just get cool. Won't be long."

"Don't hurry on my account."

Mary gets up and struts slowly down to the water's edge, where she lingers, dipping her toes into the lukewarm, bath-like water while stretching her arms high. She dives under and surfaces a few meters further out. *Oh, I feel like Jessie's beautiful mermaid, bursting out of her underwater world to dazzle in the brilliance of the sun's warmth.* She doesn't look around. She can feel Terrance's eyes on her. She brings her hands to her head and pushes back her hair. *He can't help but think I look good. I've practiced this move often enough in my mirror. If only the others weren't here, I might be able to snare him. He's vulnerable at the moment. Mum and Dad said so last night. I'll have to be careful though; Dad's very aware that I like him.* She runs her hands over her shoulders. *Being here makes me feel so sexy. I have to find out what it's like to kiss him.* She smiles. *Maybe have sex. God, I can't just dream about him. Hmm … I can almost feel his lips.* She trembles and sinks below the surface till her breathing slows and the heat escapes her.

Terrance watches Mary with amusement. *Little vixen. She knows she's a very attractive young lady.* He sighs. *Pity she's young. Could easily pass for eighteen, the way she looks.* He remembers what it was like to have crushes at that age. How intoxicating it could be. He smiles, recalling an old girlfriend, just as Mary comes back to him. He instantly looks away as Mary sits back down, inches from him.

"Good swim?"

"Very. You should have come," she purrs, facing him. Her breath brushes his neck, causing him to turn. His eyes drop momentarily and Mary pushes herself forward.

"Seriously, Mary," he replies, jumping up. "Don't." He looks at her for a moment and heads off towards the others.

Displeased, Mary sulks as she watches Terrance laughing with Ritchie and Celia. *What's she doing being so friendly? She has Ritchie, who is the second most gorgeous guy ever.* A sharp stab of jealousy washes over her.

Rosaline watches them with interest. She sits beside her husband, who is in deep conversation with Stan. *God knows what he's talking about. I may as well not even be here.* She peers at Ritchie and Celia heading for the lagoon and gets up and walks over to Terrance.

"Mary still being a pain?"

"She is."

"Don't be too hard. It's horrible having a crush at that age and not being able to do anything about it," she says, sitting next to him.

"I know." He looks at her. "You liking it here?"

"It has its moments. Finding it hard to forget Aron and Helena – Josh and his family. I never thought things would happen like that."

"No, me either."

An awkward silence lingers. "What would you do with the money, then?"

"Me? Dunno, really. Greg wants a restaurant. You?"

"Not sure. Have things to sort out. Maybe it will make it easier, maybe it won't. Anyway, probably won't win it."

"Yeah." They stare at each other. "Jack's a lucky man."

Rosaline smiles coyly and says nothing.

"You shouldn't let him belittle you."

Terrance's words make Rosaline weak. *I can't deny I desire him.* "I try not to take any notice."

"You should leave him."

"Leave him?" She blinks several times as his words dig deep.

"When this is over. You're too good for him."

She opens her mouth but Jack appears in front of them.

"You two look cozy."

"Jack. I didn't hear you."

"Obviously."

Rosaline hears the sinister tone in her husband's voice. "Terrance and I were just talking about Josh."

"Yeah? How's the ver-ti-go, Terrance?"

"Fine, thanks."

"Nasty ailment, that."

Rosaline smells her husband's jealousy. She gets up, turns her back to him and mouths a silent apology to Terrance. "Jack, let's go for that swim."

"Sure."

Jack gets up, flashing Terrance a contemptuous smile, and takes Rosaline's hand. Terrance sees her flinch and he looks away to find Mary staring at him.

Bridget is chatting away with the ladies, letting them in on her little secrets of how she manages to keep her skin and hair looking fresh. They decide to have a ladies' day in two day's time, so they can spend the morning pampering themselves. Everyone has to bring something useful.

Nigel is busy chatting to Matt about coming down and helping with the raft they are making. Matt explains that Ian had drawn a plan but they haven't made much progress. Nigel volunteers

Mark's services. He feels they have a great deal in common with the Davidsons.

Peter, remembering his recorder, decides to hand it to Mary. She is stunned Peter could make anything and even more stunned that he should make it for her. She thanks him and puts it to her mouth and blows. Its sound is not as sweet as the recorders she has back home, but it somehow seems perfect on this island. Peter is chuffed that she likes it. He tells her Harvey let it slip that she played. She says she is not very good. Peter says it doesn't matter.

CHAPTER NINETEEN

The next morning, Karl, Greg and Terrance arrive at the waterfall and see the Downs already there. It is almost too hot to do anything and as the seawater is lukewarm by mid-morning and does little to keep them cool, the pond beckons. The Hendersons appear moments later, sweat-drenched and feeling lethargic.

Peter and Candice join Harvey, Mary and Jessie at the swing. Jessie leaps out but her hands slip and she falls, landing flat on her stomach. Loud cheers of praise come from her audience. She surfaces, bursting into tears, and Stan dives in, pulls her out, pats her on the back and tells her she has winded herself. Between gulping air and crying, Jessie manages to reach the comfort of her mother's arms.

"I want to go. They're laughing at me."

"No, they're not, darling."

"Yes, they are. I hate them and I hate it here. I want to go home."

"Oh, Jessie, don't be so silly."

Jessie's face crumbles. "My stomach's sore."

"Stan, perhaps we'd better take her back. Maybe she's coming down with something."

"Yvonne she's fine – a little embarrassed maybe, but she'll survive."

"All the same, she's had a fright. You stay – I'll take her back."

"No, I'll come. Jessie, get your things." Stan watches his daughter amble over to her belongings and turns to his wife. "This is silly. Why do you always give in?"

"I don't. She's miserable, Stan."

"Okay – I'll get Harvey and Mary." Stan tells Harvey and Mary to get out of the pond and pack up their belongings. Between the whining and pleading, Stan relents and let them stay, but they are to leave with the Hendersons. He storms back and snatches up his bag.

Yvonne smiles, "Wow, you really told them, didn't you?"

Stan opens his mouth to answer when a noise behind him grabs his attention.

"Geronimo!" bellows Karl, as he somersaults head first into the water.

"Karl's a complete idiot," says Terrance empathetically.

"He's very natural with kids – has he any of his own?"

"Not that I know of."

"Oh God – sorry. I didn't mean to pry"

Terrance laughs, "It's fine, Nancy."

"You sure that thing is safe?"

"Perfectly," pipes in Greg, bending to pick up his towel. "Hey, Henry, Peter's nose looks better."

"Tunnel vision, that boy."

"He's not that bad, Henry," replies Nancy defensively.

"Unbelievable – it was probably the only bloody rock on the beach and he had to go and trip over it."

Terrance and Greg exchange bemused looks.

"He's a teenager, darling. It's what they do."

"Yeah, I remember, Nancy," says Terrance, sympathetically.

"Sure am glad that Mary isn't our daughter."

"Oh, yeah, she's got it bad for Terrance," offers Greg, sheepishly grinning.

"Oh, that's good." Nancy purses her lips. "Um, I mean – that's not good for you, but it's good she … she likes you …"

"Instead of Peter."

"Oh, hell, sorry Terrance. I'm not usually so, um ... forthright."

"You should watch her. She knows I'm not interested."

"Does she?" Nancy's gaze shifts to Mary. "I'm not so sure about that, Terrance."

Karl emerges from the water, wanting to go back for their nets. Greg says he'll go with him while Terrance decides to stay. He remains idly chatting to Henry and Nancy. The conversation is no more than the occasional pleasantries one might say when surrounded by friends on a lazy afternoon.

Nancy nudges Henry. "Time to go, darling. It's been over an hour since Stan and Yvonne left."

The kids grudgingly oblige, pack up and say goodbye to Terrance, who gives them a lazy wave as he spreads himself out on the grass.

"Oh, damn it," cries Mary. "I can't find my sunglasses. I'll have to go back."

"We'll wait, Mary," says Nancy.

"Oh, no, I'm fine, you go on. Harvey, I'll catch you up."

"Think I'd better wait."

"Honestly Harvey. I'm just going to get my glasses and come back. It'll take five minutes. Don't treat me like a baby."

Harvey shrugs. "Fine, what do I care?"

"Well, if you're sure, we'll be on our way."

"Perfectly and thanks, Mr. and Mrs. Henderson," answers Mary with an angelic smile. She turns to her brother with a victorious smirk. She takes off without another thought and arrives to see Terrance, bare chested, dozing peacefully on the grass. *Oh, if only I had my phone, everyone would be so jealous.* She carefully takes her sunglasses out of her pocket, places them on her head and quietly lies down beside him.

Terrance springs to his feet.

"I came back to see if you're all right."

"Mary, I'm not in the mood."

"Don't be like that, Terrance. You see, I have this problem."

"Well, I suggest you speak to your mother, then."

"Oh, that's good," says Mary giggling. "You know, you can be very funny."

"Yeah, so I'm told."

"Well, the thing is. I'm stuck here while my friends are, like, having fun. You see, don't you? I can't, 'cause I'm here. But I could if you'd, like, help me."

"What are you talking about?"

'Well, my friends and I know these boys and they like us and we were, like, going to go out with them and, like … you know, let them do things. Only, now they will have done – well, those things, and I haven't and I will be the one left out, and that's going to be, like, so horrible."

"Look, Mary, I can't help you. I mean, you're what – sixteen? Go ask Mark or Logan … or Peter."

"He's a child. I want a man."

Terrance guffaws. "Oh, you're priceless … you really are."

"Look, Terrance. Just kiss me, okay? That's it. Then I'll leave. I just have to know what it's like. Just one little kiss. What's so bad about that?"

Terrance emits a long breath.

"Well?"

"Oh, for God's sake, Mary. One kiss – that's it."

Mary's eyes flutter and her lips glisten as her tongue slowly traces over them. "I promise."

Terrance puts his hand on the back of her head, pulls her towards him and her eyes close. *Oh, my God!* She moans as her heart quickens, making her body burn with desire. She quickly pushes her body into him and his hand finds her hair and pulls her away.

"Get off, Mary."

"You wanted me."

"I wasn't thinking of you." Terrance's voice is low, filled with resentment and shame.

She takes no notice. *Touch me!* She is so close to him. *Please, Terrance, touch me now!* She reaches for his face and he grabs her wrist tightly. *Ouch!* "That hurts! Let go."

"Let go! Let go!" he hisses at her. "But isn't this what you want? Me holding you like this, touching you." He pulls her tight and plants a hard kiss on her lips.

God! Mary is caught between desire and panic.

Meanwhile, Harvey is getting blasted for leaving Mary behind. Yvonne calms Stan down by saying that Nancy and Henry are there. Stan tells Harvey to go back and get her. Harvey takes off as fast as he can. He doesn't want to stay near his father.

Karl reaches the pond, stopping as though he has hit an invisible wall. It takes a moment for the scene in front of him to register and then he is running, screaming at his brother to let go. He reaches Terrance and yanks him off. "What the fuck are you doing?"

"Giving her what she wants."

"Are you mad?" Karl shoves Terrance and turns to Mary.

"He was trying to rape me," she yells. "He's insane."

"You came on to me, Mary," hisses Terrance. "Don't turn this around."

"Oh, you knew what you were doing," spits Mary.

At the edge of the bush a solitary figure stands, mouth gaping, eyes wide.

"Oh, shit," says Karl. "Harvey, it's not what you think."

"Yes, it is," cries Mary. "Harvey, he was trying to rape me."

"That's a fucking lie. You wanted me. You've wanted me since you got here. Always pestering me with your seductive ways. You're nothing but a stupid little girl. I told you to get lost but you wouldn't. Just a kiss you said and then you'd leave. Ha! Well, I gave you what you wanted, but you wanted more." Terrance's face is distorted with rage; spit flies from his mouth.

Harvey stares, unsure whether to stay or run.

"Harvey, come here." Karl's voice is stern, commanding. "We need to talk."

Harvey finds himself moving. *I don't want to. I just want to get Mary so I'm not in trouble.*

"Harvey, you have to believe me," cries Mary as tears flow from her bulging eyes. "He tried to rape me, honestly. I came back here for my sunglasses and he just went nuts."

"That's a fucking lie."

"All right, Terrance. Calm down," says Karl commandingly, causing an awkward silence to hang in the air, ready to suffocate those beneath it.

Are those crocodile tears? Harvey stares at his sister. "Why were you doing that to my sister?" he asks gingerly.

"Oh, great. Ask him, why don't you?" hisses Mary.

"Oh, shut up, Mary," snaps Harvey. He catches Mary's dumbstruck expression. *You're not so mature now, are you?*

"I was just lying here." Terrance's eyes are cold, distant. "Minding my own business. Said she came back to see how I was."

"She told us she left her sunglasses," interrupts Harvey.

"She didn't even mention them. Actually – they were on her head. I noticed them because the sun caught the lens, made her hair coppery." He peers at Mary.

"Christ," says Karl, shaking his head.

"Said she had this problem about being stuck here and not with her friends and shit like that. She wanted a kiss, then she'd stop all this crap and go."

Karl continues shaking his head. "And you kissed her?"

Harvey's eyes never leave Mary.

"Yeah, I did. Then she wanted more. It pissed me off. I jumped up and she pulled my head closer. I got mad, really mad, and thought, fuck it, I'll give her what she wants, then see how she likes it."

"See," whines Mary. "He was going to rape me."

"I wasn't going to rape you. I don't even like you."

"Typical," sighs Harvey.

"What?" gasps Mary, stunned by her brother's remark.

"Mary, if you think no one's noticed how you've been acting round Terrance then you're dumber than I thought. Christ, even Mum and Dad have. Oh, wait a minute, that thing about the sunglasses ... oh man – that's another lie, isn't it?"

"No. I found them when I got here and put them on my head."

"Mary," says Karl softly. "I think it's time to admit you may have exaggerated, don't you? Let's put this down to some misunderstanding – on both your parts. Best not mention it again. I can't see any good coming from this."

"I guess not," says Mary timidly. "You won't say anything?"

"Nothing, but you are to leave my brother alone, is that clear?"

Mary nods her head, glancing at Terrance. Karl pats her back and asks if she is okay to go with Harvey. She nods again and gets up.

Karl looks at Harvey and tells him to take care of her. She has stepped over the mark, but has also got a shock. Harvey thanks him, and puts his arm around his sister and they walk back slowly towards the track.

"I want to die, Harvey. I like him so much it hurts." She leans into her brother and his hand rubs her arm.

Terrance watches them go. "I know, I know. I can't take back what's happened."

"No, you can't. Let's just hope this door has finally closed. Jesus, Terrance, what the hell were you thinking? Please tell me, you weren't going to do anything? 'Cause that would have been really dumb."

"To be honest, Karl, I don't know what I was going to do."

Karl puts his hand on his shoulder. "Well, it's over, bud. Now, Greg wants shrimp – you want to help?"

They slip into the water, swim over to the rocks and Karl dives down. Terrance starts to feel better, letting the water cleanse him. He feels more at peace with himself than he has done for the past few days. Taking his emotions out on Mary has helped clear his head. He still doesn't feel good about Josh but he doesn't feel guilty, either. It was an accident. He can see that now. He watches the glassy water, waiting for Karl to emerge.

Mary has listened to Harvey telling her how stupid she's been the whole way home. How she will put on a brave face and act as though she is fine. If their parents suspect anything, anything at all, they will be grounded or worse. She'll say she fell.

They arrive at their shelter and Mary does the talking, telling them how she tripped. Yvonne rushes over to make sure she is okay.

"I'm so silly. Look at my top. It's ruined."

"Perfect," whispers Harvey.

Yvonne tells her to get cleaned up and have a lie down. Mary follows her mother, turns back to Harvey and grins sheepishly. Harvey nods and sees his father watching them.

Stan pats him on the back. "Want to come for a swim? Keep your old man company. Give your mum and sisters some space."

"Sure, Dad." Harvey gives his mum a quick kiss and follows

his dad down to the beach. Stan whistles away, making Harvey nervous.

"Giving your mum a kiss was nice. So, what really happened, son?"

Harvey immediately tenses, making his hairs stand to attention. "Nothing."

"Well, here's the thing. I don't quite believe Mary's story. Something else happened up there and I'd like to think you could tell your old man. I know you probably didn't want to say anything around your mother. So come on, spill."

"Chill, Dad. Honestly, nothing happened. I got there and found Mary on her bum. She was dirty but fine. Fussing over her sunglasses."

"I see," says Stan putting his arm around Harvey's neck. "I'm not angry Harvey, I just want to know what really happened."

"I understand Dad, but it's like she said."

"Okay, then let me put it this way. If you don't tell me and I find out then you're going to be in a bundle of trouble." Stan continues to steer Harvey towards the water.

Harvey isn't all that sure he wants to go swimming but is too wary to say otherwise. They walk in and his father pushes him. He falls face down and comes up spluttering to see his dad smiling amusedly before disappearing. Harvey's eyes nervously dart over the water. He urinates and quickly moves, leaving the warm water behind, hoping his father won't notice. He hears his father surface behind him and finds himself under water again. He thinks about Mary and his promise to her and the Tillers, but isn't entirely sure he can keep it. He doesn't want to end up on the wrong side of his father's temper. *If I tell Dad, what will he do to Terrance? Can I convince him it was Mary's fault? Should I? No, it's too late and — worse — what would that Karl do to me if what happened came out?* He surfaces, gasping for air as his legs are yanked back and he finds himself trapped. His lungs burn as his father pins him down. His head is screaming, his ears roar and his eyes sting from keeping them open but he is too afraid to shut them. As he stops struggling, his father's hands pull him up. He surfaces, coughing and spluttering. Tears spill down his face and he gives way, telling his father everything.

Karl and Greg watch from the edge of the cave.

"I'm really amazed Terrance acted like that."

"Yeah, bit of a shock."

"It's not like him at all."

"No, it's not. Maybe Mary reminds him of Sharon."

"You think? She doesn't look like her."

"Greg, I don't mean physically."

"Oh, right."

"She came on to him. Was young and carefree and, like Mary, overbearing."

"You think he still feels guilty, then."

"Maybe."

"Poor Terrance."

"Yeah."

"Well, we gotta help him."

"Thought this contest would do that."

"Oh, Christ, Karl. You don't think she's suicidal do you?"

"Jesus, Greg, don't be ridiculous. Jack's more of a worry."

"Jack? Oh … 'cause of Rosaline?"

"Uh-huh."

"Well, they haven't done anything."

"They don't have to."

"Oh, boy – Mary and Jack."

"Mary won't be a problem. Stan, on the other hand, will, if that little encounter we just witnessed ended with Harvey telling his dad."

"But you were there."

"He's her father, Greg. Who's he more likely to believe?"

"So we add Stan to the list, too?"

"Greg, this isn't a game." Karl sees the hurt expression on Greg's face. "Sorry buddy – I didn't mean that."

"I know. I'll keep my eyes and ears open."

"Yeah, that'd be good. Hey what-a you say we go and cheer Terrance up?"

CHAPTER TWENTY

The next day, Peter is allowed to go with Harvey. He gets up early, has breakfast, puts on a smidgen of sunscreen and grabs his bag. He has a good feeling about today and hopes that Harvey is there, waiting for him in their usual spot.

It takes him less than fifteen minutes to get to the beach. He sees Harvey perched on their rock so he races over and they decide on a quick dip. Flinging off their shirts they run at speed, behaving like two young children hitting the water for the first time. They flop down, sprawl out like starfish and Harvey's eyebrows dance in time with his devilish grin, and Peter knows that his curiosity might finally be put to rest.

They get out, stuff their shirts in their bags and put on their sneakers and sunglasses. Harvey gets out his hat.

"Better wear yours, Peter. It's heating up."

"Nah, I'm good."

"Rub this on, then."

"Already done."

Harvey shrugs, telling him about Mary and Terrance.

"Savage."

"Yeah – as if he'd be into her?"

"Guess she's kinda hot." Peter sees Harvey's look. "I mean – you know with her tits and all that."

"Oh, yeah, she's stacked – double D or whatever," Harvey smirks. "You fancy her?"

"God, no! Just saying she's … well, not ugly or anything."

"She's all right I suppose, but she's dumb. You know, like really dumb, dude."

"Yeah."

"I mean, shit, she'd have to be to think Terrance's interested with all the other babes here. Like Rosaline – you know, Jack's wife. She's hot."

"Yeah, I'll say and those Booth women are ass-kicking."

"Whoop whoop." Harvey elbows Peter. "Couple of bottom-bitches." Harvey and Peter crack up and swagger up the beach. It doesn't take them long to climb the path Harvey remembers and they take their position, hidden by shrubs. Harvey checks his watch and tells Peter to get out his binoculars.

After an hour, Peter is restless and sore. He stands to stretch his muscles when suddenly he is pulled down. He raises his binoculars and sees Ritchie and Celia on the beach.

Harvey nudges him. "This is nothing, Peter. Keep watching."

Peter blushes and glances around nervously. He peers through his binoculars just as Ritchie lifts a naked Celia out of the water, lays her on the sand and enters her.

"Jesus," croaks Peter, exploding.

"You, too?" snorts Harvey as they fall onto their backs.

"Oh, boy – that was insane."

Harvey glares at Peter. "Ace, huh? Come on, let's bail. You got those extra pair of shorts?"

"Yeah."

"Okay, put them on. Shove those motherfuckers in ya bag. We'll wash them up there."

Peter snickers. "How many times have you done that?"

"Only once. Been here a few times but no show. Think she saw me. Couldn't have, though, could she?"

"No way. Have you hooked up?"

"Yeah, heaps of times."

"Really?"

"Nah!" Harvey giggles. "A few but it didn't mean anything. There was this girl that was smokin' and got her in the back of my dad's car, but I forgot a rubber. Wouldn't let me do it, stupid cow. Another time I was just about to when her dad came outside – we freaked. We were in my car – well, Dad's again – and … got her naked."

"What happened?"

"Oh, his wife came to the door with the phone. I nearly had a heart attack. She was too scared and got dressed as quickly as she could and said next time – LOL."

"I've never really done anything with a girl."

"Dude?" Harvey smiles mischievously. "You fancy Mary though, don't you? It's okay; most of my mates do."

"Really?"

"Totally."

"What about Terrance?"

"Yeah, like I said, she's stupid. She's got no chance. Specially after what happened."

"Oh, yeah."

"You should go for her."

"You don't mind?"

"Nah, just don't tell her I said so."

"'Course." *She is pretty. Maybe I should get to know her more. Find out what it's like to kiss. She might let me go further. She certainly seems the type and if Harvey doesn't mind, what do I have to lose?* He squashes a bug beneath his foot, pumps his fist, (*yeah, come on*) and whistles happily behind his friend.

They make it to the waterfall and see Karl, Greg and Harvey's family. Peter knows his are not far away.

"Hi, guys," says Harvey as they walk to where his parents are sitting. "Been here long?"

"About fifteen minutes. Good run, boys?"

"Yeah, pretty good, Dad. We're just going for a shower." Harvey slaps Peter's back and they dump their bags and run to the pond.

Karl yells, 'look out below' as he launches himself and Jessie off the bank. They fall together, turning Jessie into a screaming machine as they hit the water. Yvonne moves quickly towards the pond but they surface with Jessie in fits of laughter.

"Mum, Mum, can I do it by myself?" she asks running towards her mother.

"By yourself, darling?"

"I know, Jess. I'll come up with you and if I think it's okay then you can go by yourself. How's that?"

"Okay, Dad. Let's go." Jessie takes her father's hand and pulls him along.

"She's a great kid, Yvonne," says Karl shedding water from his hair.

"I know," says Yvonne, smiling as she watches her husband holding her daughter's hand. "Thanks for doing this, Karl. It's a terrific idea."

"Yeah, it's pretty good, isn't it? Not just for the kids, either. You game?"

"Oh, I don't think so. I couldn't."

"Sure, you could. Bet Jessie would just love to see her mum do it."

"Well, I guess she would. Okay, then, I'll just put my glasses down and ... no, wait, we had better watch her. She would be terribly disappointed if I wasn't watching."

"Of course." Karl sits down to wait with Yvonne, and Terrance arrives. Stan and Jessie plummet down, giggling and shrieking and they pop up and swim to the bank. Jessie goes to make sure her mother was watching while Stan walks over to Terrance.

"Like a quiet word, mate."

"Sure, what's up?"

"Don't ever touch my daughter again."

"Look …"

"I know what happened."

"I seriously doubt it."

Terrance takes in Stan's breath as he inches closer and pulls back to give himself space.

Stan's lip curls as his eyes close to slits. "Touch her again and I'll kill you." He slaps Terrance on the back, walks back to his family and peers at Mary. He watches the penny drop as his daughter registers the fact that her father knows. He flashes her a smile and she heads after Harvey and Peter.

Mary gets out from behind the veil of cascading water just as Harvey dives back in and she finds herself alone with Peter.

"Thank you for the recorder, Peter."

"No worries."

"You like me, don't you?" Mary leans back against the wall, noting his awkwardness. "Kiss me!"

"Huh?"

Licking her lips, she smiles seductively. "I said, kiss me." His eyes tell her all she needs to know. "Don't be nervous."

Mary inches forward and puts his shaking hand on her waist. She can feel him trembling as she guides his right hand up to her cheek. She plants a kiss on his quivering lips and feels his body instantly tighten. She pulls back and looks into his eyes. She presses her body against him and feels his hardness and brings her mouth to his ear.

"Oh, that feels good, Peter," she purrs. "Does it feel good for you?"

"Uh-huh." He kisses her again. "You done this before?"

"Of course. You?"

"'Course."

She feels his clumsy hand creep around her breast and her nipple hardens. Her breast feels like a warm sponge as he rubs and squeezes her and then his fingers move downwards and she moans and pushes her fingers into his buttocks.

"Got them," yells Harvey, climbing up onto the ledge. Peter's face burns as he feverishly untangles himself and steps away.

Mary giggles and hovers over her brother "What are you doing?"

"Washing."

"Why?"

"Because Mum will get mad. She just washed these yesterday."

She looks at her nails. "Oh, did the naughty boy dirty his pants again?"

"Piss off, Mary. We got muddy on our run."

"Really – how boring. Oh, well, think I might swim back, have something to eat. Peter –looks like your olds and Candice have arrived." She walks past Peter, brushing his lips with her fingers and gives him her sexiest smile, then dives into the pond, leisurely swims back, rolls out her towel and plops herself down next to Candice.

"Hi. Where's the Tillers?"

"They left. You're lucky you got Jessie."

"Yeah, like she's such good company." Mary looks back over to the waterfall. "Hey, guess what?"

"What?"

"You know what we were talking about the other day?"

Candice nods.

"Well, I just let Peter kiss me."

"I thought you liked Terrance?"

"He's too old really, isn't he? And Peter's keen. It's kind of funny. I know he's your brother and that, but he's quite good-looking."

"You like him?"

"He's okay, and it's not like there's a lot of choice, is there?"

"Suppose."

"Said he'd done it before."

Candice looks shocked.

"He was lying. And then bloody Harvey came back before anything happened, but he did touch my breast."

"Oh, gross."

Mary winds a strand of Candice's hair around her finger and whispers, "You should try it."

"Me?"

Mary can feel Candice's apprehension and pulls her finger back.

"Yeah, why not? You said you like Mark. Oh, better still, do it with Harvey."

"Harvey?"

"Does it really matter? I mean it's not like it's serious or anything. Just a bit of fun – you'll get some experience. Harvey's quite good-looking."

"Yeah, but I like Mark."

"Harvey, Mark, who cares? Go for Mark, then. Yeah, at least he's not my brother." Mary's eyes grow wickedly brighter. "Let's see who goes the furthest."

The girls watch Peter and Harvey coming back. Mary smiles at Peter and he smiles back. They sit down and Peter shuffles towards Mary so that their legs are almost touching.

"Thought we might bring my boat along on Sunday. We could go out over the coral."

"Cool. You like, Candice?"

"Do you think we'll be allowed?"

"Sure. Dad and I went out there. Might see if Mark wants to come too."

Mary smiles at Candice.

"Can we fit that many in the boat?" asks Peter dropping his eyebrows.

"Says four adults, so I reckon it's okay."

"But there's five of us."

"Duh, Mary, we don't weigh as much."

"Well, we might have to bring Jessie."

"Fab." Mary flashes Peter a teasing grin and casually lies back. Peter props himself on one elbow and brushes her silky skin with his finger. She strokes his arm softly while Candice talks to Harvey about going to the swing. Harvey asks if they want to come, but they shake their heads. Harvey shrugs, gets up and takes Candice's hand.

"LOL. Isn't that sweet, Peter?"

Peter nods, his eyes focused on their parents. "They're all watching Jessie." Mary smiles. He rolls onto his stomach and brings his left hand up along her waist and over her breasts. She quivers and closes her eyes as he slips his thumb under her bikini top.

"That's nice."

He circles her nipple and grasps her plentiful breast, squeezing her tightly, and a moan escapes her. She rolls over onto her side. Her breast slips out of her top and she feels him grow hard.

"Peter," she moans as she feels his tongue circle her nipple. He sucks hard and she groans and reaches between his legs. Her fingers run the length of his throbbing organ and she hears a throaty gasp. She pushes his hand down between her legs and his fingers slide under her bikini pants to the moist treasure awaiting him. She feels him quiver, hears his moan and then he is off her. She opens her eyes to see him staring beyond her and she turns her head to see her father getting up. Panicking, she grabs his hand and they dash for the pool.

They dive in and she laughs as Peter frantically tries to loosen his shorts. She grins devilishly, and sinks beneath the surface and takes hold of him. He pushes her off and she resurfaces, smiling. Her eyes scan the grass and, seeing no one is taking any notice, she sinks down and tugs his shorts down. Her hand encases him, working quickly. She looks into his glazed eyes. *Yes! I knew I would be good at this.* Pulling her bikini bottoms down with her free hand, she grabs his unresisting hand and pushes it between her legs, where his fingers find her warmth. She widens her legs just as Peter shudders, sending warm goo over the hand that holds his manhood. *Oh, that's not so bad!* She suddenly stiffens as pain breaks her passion.

"Are you okay?"

"Perfect."

The afternoon goes by quickly. Nancy checks her watch and smiles at the kids "It's so nice to see them all getting on."

"Maybe I should go and join them. Make sure they're not up to no good."

"Don't you dare, Henry. We'd never hear the end of it."

Jessie trudges up from the water looking miserable, plants herself between her parents and snuggles into her mother.

"What's wrong, darling?"

She starts crying and Stan looks down to the pond and sees Harvey and Mary raise their hands.

"Great. Dad thinks we've done something."

"Oh, for God's sake, Harvey, she's crying."

"Maybe you two should go up."

"No way, Peter."

"Perhaps she's sick," says Candice, looking worried.

"Oh, my gosh, yes. That would be perfect."

"Mary?"

"What, Candice?"

"Crap. Your dad's coming this way," says Peter, moving away.

Stan stops at the edge of the pond. "Out, you two. Jessie wants to go back, she's not feeling well."

"What's wrong with her, Mr. Downs?"

"Funny tummy, Candice. Probably something she ate."

"Dad, can we stay up here a bit longer? We're having so much fun."

"Only if it's okay with Peter's parents."

"Sweet. You're the best, Dad." Mary winks at Peter.

Stan comes back down and tells them they have one hour. Candice and Peter's parents are leaving but will leave them their towels. They watch their parents depart and wave goodbye.

"Oh, my God, I can't believe it." Mary's eyes sparkle, full of expectation. "One hour to ourselves."

They get out and flop down on the grass. Peter heedlessly pulls Mary towards him.

"We're going for a little privacy." Mary smiles mischievously at Candice as she wraps her arm around Peter's waist. They walk off and Mary swings her hips brazenly as she looks back at them.

"So!" says Harvey. "What do you want to do, Candice?"

"I don't know," she replies nervously.

He smiles and her eyes follow his hand as he gently brings it up to her cheek and traces his finger along her lips. She freezes.

"Look, Candice, we don't have to do anything you don't want to. I'm not going to force you. We can just hang out. I know you're not like Mary."

Candice smiles tentatively. "I like her, I really do but she's so

… forward. I … I've never done anything with a boy." Her voice lowers. "I don't have her body."

"All tits and arse."

"Isn't that what guys like?"

Harvey laughs. "Well, yeah. Maybe when you're with your mates."

"Oh, you're just saying that," smiles Candice, pushing him gently.

"No, I'm not." Harvey grins and takes her hand. "Personally I like legs and you've a great pair of legs."

Candice looks at Harvey and hits him.

"I'm serious."

"Seriously funny," she giggles and starts to relax, "… but thanks."

They lie down, looking skywards. She feels happy and content as Harvey gently plays with her hair and tells her of how they caught a big fish out over the coral and how his dad gutted it and put the waste back and all these fish appeared out of nowhere. All kinds of fish that he promises to show her on Sunday.

Half an hour later, Mary and Peter stumble out of the bush. Candice takes in their flushed faces and, coupled with the delight radiating from their eyes, she is unsure whether she is jealous or offended.

"Oh, my God!" cries Mary. "That was amazing. I feel so … oh … I don't know what I feel," she bursts out laughing. "It's the best high."

"Like you'd know," says Harvey shaking his head.

"Oh shut up, Harvey." Mary yanks Peter towards the pool.

Candice feels small, out of her depth. "Harvey, do you think they, you know, did it?"

"Probably."

"Really?" Candice watches them. Her body shivers as Peter circles Mary, as though he's done nothing wrong.

"Yep."

"It'll be all right, won't it? Being her first time?"

"I don't know … do you really know it's her first time? Go tell her to pee."

"What?"

"Candice, don't get all shy. It might lessen the chance. And tell Peter to come here," says Harvey stroking her arm.

Candice smiles and goes to speak to Mary. She tells Peter to go and have a word with Harvey. She says it's important and Peter grudgingly leaves. She tells Mary what Harvey said then leaves Mary alone.

Mary's face drains of color. She swims to the waterfall, climbs out and squats. She curses. She's too tense. She puts her head under the cascading water, gulping as much as she can. Feeling bloated she strains and feels a trickle. *This is silly. I'm fine, my period's due any day.* She gets up. *Chances of getting pregnant are tiny – absolutely tiny.* She pushes the idea out of her mind and showers while humming a tune.

"I'm going for a swim," says Candice, not wishing to be part of the conversation Harvey is trying to have with her brother. "And then we better head back."

"Okay – make it quick and tell Mary to hurry up."

Candice dives into the pond swimming strongly towards the waterfall. She sees Mary, waves and points to her wrist. Mary nods and, happy Mary has understood, Candice turns back but stays in the water as Harvey is still talking to Peter.

"Look, Peter, I can give you a couple of rubbers."

"Thanks."

"Better to be safe than sorry."

"Yeah, absolutely."

"Don't worry, mate. You'll be fine. Just wear one next time … if there is a next time."

"Don't you need them?"

"Keep your voice down. No, I like your sister, but she's not like Mary."

"No, she's not."

Harvey pats his back. "So I don't think I'll be using them. Besides the olds would go spare if Mary got pregnant."

Peter shudders. "You won't do it with Candice?"

Harvey sees the worry in Peter's eyes. "Nope. Might kiss her, if that's okay with you?"

Peter shrugs. "'Course. Just don't …'"

"Have sex with her."

"Yeah."

CHAPTER TWENTY-ONE

The morning is hot, with little breeze, and Bridget and Sara sit fanning themselves while they wait for the women to arrive. Sara has laid out a circle of coconut shell bowls and placed a deep red hibiscus flower in the center of them. Each bowl sits on a fan of fresh, green leaves with one lemon, lime and mango.

"This is such a good idea, Mum."

"Yes, I suppose, but I really shouldn't have suggested it. We're in this to win and when you think about it, we shouldn't be helping everyone feel better."

"You sound like Dad and Warren. What's the harm of having a little beauty session?"

"Well ... let's not give away too many secrets."

"Secrets? Seriously, Mum, it's just a nice relaxing day, so enjoy."

"Oh ... I plan to, darling, but I also plan to be cautious."

Sara wraps her arm through her mother's. "Whatever. Now – do you like?" she says, gliding her hand over her presentation.

"Yes, darling, it's beautiful."

"Good." Sara hugs her mother and Bridget smiles tenderly. "Now be nice, Mum – here's our first customer."

"Hi, Nancy."

"Hi, there. Sorry, Candice didn't want to come. Rather be with the young ones."

"Ahhh, of course. Exploring the island will be good for them."

"Honestly, Mum, I think they're a bit old for Peter Pan. Probably more like show and tell."

"Oh, I don't think so. Peter's keen on some girl back home, apparently, and in any case Mary's infatuated with Terrance and Candice hasn't shown any interest in boys yet."

Sara smiles warmly at Nancy. "Hmm – Terrance."

"He is one attractive man."

"Mum?"

"Oh, look," grins Bridget avoiding her daughter's eyes. "Here's Rosaline and Moana".

"Hi. Sorry we're late."

"Actually, it's perfect timing, Rosaline," replies Bridget. "And, Moana, I swear you're looking younger by the day. Island life suits you!"

"Thank you, Bridget, I do feel good. Love it here. What more could you want?"

"Well, a night with Ritchie or Terrance wouldn't go amiss," laughs Bridget, as Linda arrives looking fresh and neat under her floppy gray sun hat.

"God, Mum … in your dreams."

"That may be so, darling, but they're very good dreams. Oh, and on that note, Nancy, I'd keep an eye on the young ones if I were you. Not a lot to do here and they are entering some very inquisitive years."

"Yes, of course, Bridget. We never really know what Peter's been up to. He never tells us anything and it's pointless asking."

"Yes, it's a tricky time," states Bridget glancing at her daughter.

"Yes, indeed," concurs Linda, taking a place next to Sara as Celia and Trudy arrive looking hot and uncomfortable. They sit and immediately start fanning themselves.

"So, then, who would you fancy if you had the chance of any of the guys here, Rosaline?"

"Oh – gosh, Sara. I think … maybe Ritchie." Rosaline's

cheeks burn and she rubs her neck. "I mean, Celia, he's gorgeous. Those dark smoldering looks and ..."

Sara raises her eyebrows.

"Oh, I don't mean I fancy him."

"It's okay, Rosaline." Sara exchanges coy smiles with the women. "Everyone fancies him."

"So, Sara, who would you choose?" Bridget intervenes; the tease in her voice accompanied by her finger curling her hair.

"Stop it, Mum – you look stupid."

Bridget chuckles and laughter erupts from the older women.

"Just for the record, though," cuts in Sara, "Terrance or Ritchie would be my pick."

Moana gives a loud chortle. "Yeah, they can light my fire anytime."

"I think Stan is nice." Linda remarks, blushing. "I mean in that mature, still handsome sort of way."

"Well, well. Hey, it's a shame Greg is gay, 'cause he's not bad, either. I mean, have you seen his skin? It's like a baby's bottom," says Nancy, as the women chuckle.

"Oh, this is going to be fun. We ladies can have a good old chin wag," says Moana, stretching her legs.

"Oh, look, there's Yvonne. She's got nothing with her – that's a bit cheeky," voices Sara.

"Hi, ladies, I'm afraid I can't stay. Jessie got her period. It's her first and she's a little mortified. I sent Harvey and Mary to the waterfall to be with Candice and Peter and Stan is waiting for me to get back."

"Oh, poor love," says Bridget. "You can always bring her down later. We can fuss over her – might cheer her up."

"Yes, maybe. I'm just glad they thought to put those bins here. She is so worried someone might find something."

"Indeed," answers Moana. "Tell her we miss her."

"Thanks." Yvonne tiredly walks up the beach and melts into the palms.

"Oh, poor little mite. What rotten luck, getting it here."

"Yes it is, Linda, but she'll be fine. Now, ladies, let's get on with our day," says Bridget "This heat's going to make everything too runny if we wait any longer."

"Is this coconut milk, Bridget?"

"Yes, Linda, with a bit of oil. Makes amazing moisturizer. Just rub it in and leave. We'll wash it off later. You all brought some water?"

The women nod and are soon busy massaging one another, while their hair soaks in the goodness of the coconut liquid and Bridget's coconut goo-like cream penetrates their skin, making it feel softer than it has for days. Bridget then hands out her avocado mix for the face. Instead of cucumber for the eyes she uses cut up watermelon and the ladies lie back, letting nature take over.

While the ladies pamper themselves, Nigel and Mark go to help finish the Davidsons' raft. Being near completion, they are tying the last vines in place. Stepping back, they look at their achievement with approval. Matt goes inside their shelter and brings out three cans of beer.

"Only three left. Saving them for a special occasion but I reckon this is as good as any. Don't mind sharing do you, guys?"

"Not at all, Matt. Perfect way to finish." Nigel sits down, opens a can and takes a generous swallow. "Cold, too."

"Put them in a rock pool."

"Smart," says Mark taking a much-wanted gulp before handing the can to his father. "Nearly forgotten how this tastes."

"So, guess the only thing left to do is test that she floats?"

"I reckon, Nigel," answers Zach, taking his last sip. The five of them sit in silence looking at their masterpiece. "Shame the Smyths couldn't be here. Wonder how they're doing?"

"Yes, unfortunate business," reflects Nigel.

"True." Matt takes the cans and places them in their rubbish sack. "Come on, guys, enough of the gloom. We've got a raft to sail."

"You first," says Nigel patting Matt on the back.

"I'll get our oars." Sammy picks up a couple of thin bamboo canes, which have several weaved palm leaves tied together on the ends for paddles.

"That's interesting!" says Nigel. "Moana's work?"

Matt nods proudly and Nigel smiles as he helps push the raft off. It floats well and they row out over the coral bank to the clear, deep water of the outer lagoon.

Zach leans over and watches the fish swimming back and forth. "Wow, this water's so clear. It's like being in an aquarium."

"Dad, we should come back with our goggles and flippers."

"You two can," answers Matt, "but let's give our helpers a go first."

"'Course. Here, Sammy, give me the oars, I'll take her back."

While Zach rows, Sammy watches several clownfish dart in and out of the polyps that sway back and forth in the gentle current. He remembers from school that the anemones the clownfish hide in have deadly stinging tentacles. Clownfish skin has special protection that allows them to nestle into the dangerous anemones, while other fish avoid them. He also remembers that while beautiful, due to their bright orange, white and black bars, clownfish are inedible.

"I am definitely going snorkeling here."

"With you there, bro." Zachs the raft back to the beach and brings it up beside Nigel and Mark.

"Oh, man – out there – amazing," says Sammy handing Mark

the oars. Matt, Sammy and Zach stand with folded arms and faces beaming with satisfaction.

"Shame your mum isn't here to see her launched, boys."

"Yeah it is, Dad," answers Sammy. "I reckon she'd be pretty proud."

"I reckon she would."

Ritchie and Drew wander down onto the beach and come alongside Matt, Sammy and Zach.

"Hey, you guys make that?"

"We all did, Ritchie," responds Sammy.

"Bamboo?"

"Yep. Light, waterproof – good buoyancy."

"Yeah, we can see that, Matt."

"Interesting." Ritchie looks at Drew.

Matt's hand goes to his chest as he belches. "Had a beer to celebrate."

"A beer?"

"Yeah, Dad bought some."

"Nice. Any left?"

"All gone. Have to make do with something else."

"Now, there's a thought. Wonder if we could make anything alcoholic here? Do you think Moana might know, Matt?"

"Might."

"Sweet!" answers Ritchie watching Nigel and Mark pull the raft up. "Hey, maybe we should do a dinner. All bring our sleeping bags and sleep under the stars. Have a big fire. It'd be choice."

"Maybe," says Drew heading down to inspect the raft.

"Hi, Nigel, Mark," calls Ritchie following his brother. "Hey, what do you think about a night feast, with a big fire on the beach and sleeping bags? Sound cool?"

"Lunch, now dinner?"

"Nothing else to do, Drew. It could be fun."

"Exactly, Nigel. Maybe some music, a wee dance – something to drink," winks Ritchie to Mark. "Might even get the girl."

Mark smiles sheepishly and takes a couple of steps away from the raft and his father. Ritchie sits beside him and peers out to sea. He weighs up Ritchie's words and wonders if he might be right. *Hell, Ritchie's probably had more girls than I'll ever have. He should be an actor. It wouldn't matter what shit he was in, the film would still be a hit.* "Dad will be going over everything. He takes forever explaining things."

"So does Drew," grins Ritchie.

Mark smiles back and they sit together, arms resting on their knees, like two surfers waiting for the perfect wave.

"Ritchie, they're taking it out again if you want to join them," calls out Matt as he and Nigel walk towards them.

"Son, it's too damn hot for me. I'm off home. You coming?"

"Sure, Dad."

"Okay, see you later." Ritchie picks up a spear and heads down to the raft, jumps on and they head out, leaving Matt, Nigel and Mark surveying them. Matt takes off his hat, wiping away the perspiration that drips down his forehead.

"I'm stuffed. Think I'll have a rest."

"Sure, Matt, thanks for letting us have a ride."

"Anytime, Nigel – anytime."

Nigel and Mark trudge up the beach and walk along the bush's edge for shade.

"Dad, think I'll go to the waterfall. See if Harvey and the others are there."

"Okay, son. Take care."

"I will." Mark squeezes his father's arm and runs off in the opposite direction. Nigel watches him go and continues on, eager to get back for a lie down.

After the morning's beauty therapy, the ladies say their goodbyes and look forward to catching up again on Sunday. Rosaline strolls back with Moana.

"I could live here with Matt. In fact, I don't really want to go back. Matt's leg seems better and he's changed. I have, too."

"Yes, I know what you mean."

"Oh, I know I'm not a looker like you, but I am what I guess some would describe as 'handsome'. I'm feeling good and I'm happy – that's enough for me. Now you, you are truly beautiful. You were bloody lovely when you arrived, but now you're just sensational."

"Oh, go on."

"You got it, girl, you enjoy it. And I'll tell you something else; I've seen the men here look at you and I know what they've been thinking."

"Stop it. I won't be able to look them in the eye."

"Oh, it's all harmless, love. You be good and think of repairing this marriage of yours."

Rosaline squeezes Moana's hand and they stroll on, happy in each other's company. When they get to Moana's shelter, she gives Moana a kiss on the cheek and leaves.

Watching her go, Moana catches sight of the boys in the lagoon, realizing she's missed the launching. Seeing no sign of Matt, she heads indoors to find him snoring peacefully on his back, water trickling out of the upturned bottle on his stomach. She gently removes it, picks up her book and sits down to read.

CHAPTER TWENTY-TWO

Rosaline sits mesmerized by the fire. Even as a child, the bewitching flames took her somewhere else. Somewhere peaceful, where everything is as it should be; where everything is perfect. Her thoughts turn to Terrance and, without thinking, her gaze shifts to him. He looks at home, laughing away with his brothers, and she glances at Jack. His hand loosely holds his cup and her eyes shift to his face. His blurry gaze and ruddy cheeks confirm he has had too much of Bridget's concoction. She touches his cup, but his hand tightens around it and she withdraws, hugs her knees and hopes he will not spoil the evening. She turns her attention back to the conversation.

"Bloody good idea, this."

"Yes, Karl," says Bridget, matter-of-factly.

Eric holds his cup out in a celebratory salute, spilling some of its contents onto Jack's legs.

Jack huffs. "You do know that this is a competition, right?"

"Yes, Jack, I think everyone's aware of that."

"Really?" answers Jack, nonplussed. "Being nice and friendly isn't exactly competition material."

Rosaline instantly lays a hand on his arm. "Jack, please – not now."

Jack brushes her off and she catches the contempt lurking in Terrance's eyes.

"No one's keeping you here."

"True, Terrance." Jack's disdain back at Terrance is obvious and the mood within the group shifts. "But I wouldn't want to miss out on all this fun."

"For God's sake, Jack, I think you've drunk enough."

"Don't patronize me, woman."

"I didn't mean to be ..."

"I don't care what you meant."

"Actually, your wife's right. This stuff's strong," cuts in Karl. "Kava?"

"Try Moana's instead, if you don't like it," Bridget says in a voice that entirely betrays her feelings.

"Bridget, I'm not complaining," Karl says apologetically.

"No, of course you're not, I apologize, Karl."

"What's the big deal? It's not as if we have to drive."

"Hey," hollers Greg chuckling. "That's quite funny, Jack."

Rosaline leers at her husband, delivering a silent warning. She feels a hand touch her arm and turns to see Nigel's sympathetic face.

"You know," he announces with an air of authority that catches the others attention. "I'm impressed with you, Peter. I would never have thought to make those." He winks discretely at Rosaline and she nods her head in appreciation, seeing that everyone's eyes are now focused on what Peter has in front of him.

"Oh, thanks, Mr. Wentworth. Did this sort of thing at school a couple of years ago. It was kinda boring."

"Ah – well there you go. Not so boring now, is it?"

Peter's upper lip rises. "I guess."

"Things that seem boring are almost always handy later in life," remarks Linda supportively.

"Maracas?" scoffs Jack.

"I beg your pardon?"

"Oh, come on, Linda. Knowing how to make maracas isn't going to help him in life."

Rosaline hears Celia and Trudy titter and bites her lip, seeing the others' amusement. "Jack …"

"What?" Jack glares, stone-faced. "If Peter wasn't here he'd never make them in a million years."

"True, but he is here", voices Nigel triumphantly, releasing approving smiles amongst the group.

"Thank you, darling, but I was merely meaning that school work in general, boring as it may well be at the time, comes in very useful once you're out in the big, wide world."

"Whatever, Linda," replies Jack rolling his eyes. "Guess they'll go with those drums that lot made. Wonder if they learned that in school?"

Rosaline notices Jack's wink at Peter and grabs her husband's arm. "That's enough. Come and get some food."

Jack shrugs, reluctantly stands and walks unsteadily behind his wife. "What's your problem?"

"You've made everyone uncomfortable."

"Well, that woman's a pain."

"What?"

"Linda … Mrs. Bloody Mother of the Nation! Jesus, they're so righteous, it's pathetic."

"I don't understand you sometimes, Jack. They're perfectly fine."

"They're boring. Look at her in her gray cotton shirt and walk shorts and those whiter than white socks – that, by the way, never look dirty … and he looks like some dorky twat on safari."

"Cut it out, Jack."

"Why, what you gonna do?" Jack's face contorts into a patronizing grin and Rosaline, resisting the urge to slap him, turns her back. She notices Terrance watching her and hesitantly makes her way towards Moana, where she and her boys are entrancing others with their unpretentious music. Jessie runs past and picks up Mary's recorder. The high–pitched noise she makes sounds dreadful. Rosaline bursts out laughing and walks on to see that Nigel and Linda have moved, leaving a space beside Terrance. Hesitating, she looks to Jack, who is now sitting beside Karl. He raises his cup lazily and flashes her a sickening smile. She ignores his careless disposition and sits watching the dancing flames.

Greg gets up to refill his cup, and seeing that Jack is preoccupied talking to Stan, Rosaline turns to Terrance. The warmth of the fire penetrates pleasantly into her skin, making her feel uninhibited, slightly reckless. The gravity between them intensifies. Terrance locks his blue eyes on hers and she is helpless to control the heat radiating from her.

"Do you still think about Josh?"

Momentarily caught off guard, she shakes her head. "Jack tells me to stop being naive." Her voice wavers as her trembling hands rub her legs. "Says these things are going to happen. I guess I just try not to think about it."

"I suppose we all do."

"This place gives you a sense of false security."

"Sure does."

"This is good, though, isn't it?"

"Yeah, it is." Terrance's eyes hold her gaze and immense pleasure consumes her before cloaked feelings of betrayal make her look away. There is something unsaid between them, but for now it is enough to just be here with him and she gazes back into the fire, letting the warmth invade her.

Jack has been watching his wife while amusing himself in conversation with Yvonne, Stan and Karl. He hates the way she seems comfortable and somehow flirtatious sitting next to Terrance. Irritated, he knows it partly to be his fault. She just didn't do it for him anymore. No one did. But she was still his. He didn't exactly want her but he didn't want anybody else to have her either. It wasn't that he didn't still find her attractive, but he blamed her for what had happened. Every time he felt the slightest hint of desire, Cathy popped into his head and his sexual drive was back in neutral. *I can see that prick's appeal. Bastard's attractive — if you like the long blond hair, blue-eyed beach look.* He glances at Stan and Yvonne, whose attention is on the kids. *Mary seems intoxicated by him.* He laughs, causing Stan and Yvonne to peer at him. He smiles back. "Young ones — good to see them enjoying themselves."

"Yes," answers Stan dubiously.

Jack's eyes follow Harvey, Peter and Mark as they run past him. He watches them huddling together. *They're up to no good!* He looks back at the girls dancing. *How can they move to that dreadful music?* He smirks, wondering how long their supposed friendship will last.

Peter watches the group of adults joking and relaxing around the fire. "All good, they're engrossed in conver-fucking-sation."

"Hurry up then, Peter. Pour it."

"Hey, that's enough."

"Piss off, Mark. Don't be such a dork."

"Piss off yourself. It's too much for Candice."

"Whoa — you her baby-sitter?"

"No."

"You're blushing."

"Am not. She's just — not like your sister."

"Oh, you got that right, didn't he, Peter?"

"Shit, yeah." Peter and Harvey burst out laughing.

"What's so funny?"

"Nothing," snickers Peter, impolitely.

"I'll give Candice hers."

"Bugger off. I'm her brother, I'll give it to her."

"Chill, Mark. Better Peter does … less suspicious."

Rosaline spies her husband watching the boys handing the cups to the girls. She smiles, thinking it nice to see some manners still prevail, until she notices Jack's smug grin. Her eyes dart back and shadow Mary as she drains her cup and throws it away carelessly. She has an uncomfortable feeling that something is going to happen and that Jack may well have something to do with it. Her eyes trace Peter and Mark as they hustle around Mary. Jessie flutters through them, causing Rosaline to giggle. *Oh, Jessie, you look like a beautiful, yet awkward young butterfly.*

Terrance gives a loud amused laugh. "She's completely oblivious to the nuisance she's making of herself."

"Oh, to be young again."

"It's very amusing." Terrance's eyes find hers.

Fireworks explode in her head, causing her cheeks to burn. Her mind goes blank, wiping her vocabulary clean. She feels naked. The silence between them is deafening until she hears Karl roar with laughter and she turns her focus to the circle of adults, following their gaze down to the teenagers.

"Heavens." Rosaline utters loudly, raising her hand to her chest.

Stan sits upright. "What the hell is Mary doing? She looks like some whore."

"Keep your voice down, Stan." Yvonne's eyes are on her daughter. "They're just having fun. You remember what that was like?"

Rosaline bites her nail, catching the look Stan gives his wife before his eyes divert back to his daughter.

"Shit, Yvonne, look at her. Give her a pole – she'd be right at home. Where the hell did she even learn to move like that?"

Rosaline glances around. All eyes are on Mary, except for Terrance's. He is staring at Stan. She feels uneasy catching the gloating smile spreading across his face.

"Fuck this, Yvonne. I'm having a word."

"She'll be mortified. We'll keep an eye on her, make sure she doesn't do anything silly."

"I'd call what she's doing now pretty silly, if she was my daughter."

"I wasn't talking to you, Jack."

"He's right, though."

"And I didn't ask for your opinion, Terrance."

"Just saying what everyone's thinking."

"Is that right?"

Rosaline is startled at the venom in Stan's voice and she catches her breath as Stan rises. Terrance and Karl stand instantly as the mood around the fire darkens.

"Stan – stop it," Yvonne shouts, reaching for her husband.

Ignoring her, Stan faces Terrance. "Stop watching my daughter."

"Mate, everyone's watching your daughter," says Terrance unfazed by Stan's threatening disposition.

Stan's cheeks glow red as the fire inside him burns. The blood races through his veins, making him explode. "You conceited bastard."

"Stan, stop it. He's done nothing."

"Oh, yes he has, Yvonne."

Rosaline gasps as Stan's fist comes quickly but Terrance is faster, leaving Stan punching air. She watches Yvonne pulling at her husband's arm, hears Jack's brash laugh and her stomach turns.

"Back off." Karl looks fixedly at Stan, his arm out as a warning. "It's your daughter you should be watching."

"Mary!" Yvonne's head swivels right and her hand instinctively covers her mouth. "Good God, what's she doing now?"

Irritated, Stan looks from Terrance to his daughter. She unbuttons her shirt and slowly takes it off, hoisting it high over her head. Spinning around, she laughs wildly, tossing her head back, making her hair dance about her seductively.

"This stops here," Stan roars as Mary whips off her bikini top.

"Oh, boy, this is better than a sex bar," hollers Jack.

"Oh, God! Do something Stan," screams Yvonne, mortified.

"Mary!" shouts Stan racing around the fire. Mary looks at him, laughs and dances away, weaving in and out between the people in her way.

"Fucking hell! This is just priceless," chortles Karl.

Rosaline stares wide-eyed as Stan runs after his daughter. *This is terrible.* Her mouth gapes as Mary heads to the water, discarding her bikini bottoms. *Oh, God, Stan looks like a huge warrior. Steam will start to blow from him any moment now.* His thunderous voice sends chills down her body and she wraps her arms around her legs, wishing she wasn't witnessing this.

Mary's voice is slurry, carefree. "Dad, get in – water's amazing."

"Get your arse out of there, young lady. If I have to get in and drag you out, you'll be sorry."

"Oh, poo. You're such a spoil sport."

Rosaline's hand goes to her mouth. *I don't want to join the others laughing, but this is getting pretty funny. I've never seen anyone dog paddle quite like that.*

Stan storms into the water, lunges for his daughter and clutches her arm. Yvonne waits at the water's edge with a towel.

"Whoops!" Mary giggles. "This sand's a bit wobbly."

"What the hell do you think you're playing at, making an exhibition of yourself like that?" Stan drags Mary up the beach, passing the other teenagers.

"Bet she doesn't feel so mature now," whispers Harvey to Peter as Mary gives them a big cheery smile.

"Oh, Dad, chill. It's all good, isn't it? The moon, the food, the fire, the music – the boys."

Yvonne gasps. "I don't believe it. She's had that drink. Oh, you silly, silly girl."

"Harvey, Jessie, get your things," shouts Stan without looking at them. "We're leaving. Mary's done enough partying for one night."

"That's not fair," whines Harvey. "Why can't I stay?"

"Because you can't," Stan barks.

Incensed, Harvey goes with Jessie to collect their gear.

"Is Mary drunk, Harvey?"

"She's a bloody pain. She ruins everything."

"What do you mean?"

"It doesn't matter. You wouldn't understand."

Rosaline watches as they follow their parents back up the beach. She sees Harvey look back at Mark sitting closely beside Candice. *Poor Harvey. His jealousy is seeping out of him like sweat.* She catches sight of Stan looking at Terrance and is perturbed when Terrance tilts his cup; a grin plastered on his face like a Cheshire cat. Matt's voice interrupts her thoughts.

"Holy mother of God. That was truly unexpected."

"Wonder what he'll do?" says Jack. "If I had a daughter like that, I'd lock her up and throw away the key. Good set of tits though, if you like them big."

"What's not to like?" bursts out Matt. "Hey, bet she won't be showing those again for a while."

"Let's not forget that *that* was not all that was on show," chuckles Karl blinking furiously.

The three of them erupt into laughter, causing chuckling and stifled murmurs around the fire.

"Okay, you lot, you've had your fun," intervenes Moana. "She wouldn't do that sort of thing normally."

"Oh, I think she would, Moana," says Karl. "I really think she would."

"You know something we don't?"

"Yeah, Jack I do, as it so happens. The other day she swung off the rope. Only had her bikini on and, well, when she emerged, it wasn't – on, that is!" The men launch into hysterical laughter. "We had a good eyeful, I can tell you," Karl's head shakes. "She didn't even flinch. Just walked out, straight up to Terrance."

"I don't believe it," says Moana, shocked. "She didn't?"

"She bloody well did!' states Karl.

"Well I never."

Rosaline scans the party around her. Terrance is silent, looking like he could thump someone. She looks at Moana, who is looking over at Mark sitting protectively next to Candice. Peter is beside him with his hands on his head, staring blindly into the sand. Zach and Sammy are lying down next to them with the Booths. Linda and Nigel sit tightly together, listening but saying nothing. She is glad to see not everyone found Karl's story entertaining.

"Well, I just hope Stan isn't too hard on her."

"Look, Rosaline, that girl's trouble. She needs a good spanking."

"You offering, Karl?" laughs Jack, feeling his wife's fist.

"Nope. Don't want a bar of it. Makes you wonder why she's the way she is, though? Hey, Terrance, bet you're glad you weren't to blame this time, huh?"

Rosaline gasps. "This time?"

"Stan had words to Terrance about touching Mary. He's so wrong about that one."

"What do you mean, touching?"

Terrance sighs heavily. "Jesus, Greg. It's nothing, Rosaline."

"It wasn't nothing, Terrance," bursts out Greg. "Mary was

coming onto him and then Harvey showed up and the little vixen said Terrance was attacking her, which was complete bullshit. Anyway, Mary must have told her dad differently. Said he'd kill him if he touched her again."

"Greg – drop it?"

"Well, I was just telling them what ..."

"Ah, so that explains his aggression towards you," cuts in Jack. Terrance's silence tells everything.

"Well, well." Jack sighs. "It's all becoming clearer now."

"Oh, my God ..."

"Rosaline," cuts in Jack. "It's not your problem."

Rosaline edges away from her husband and closer to Moana. She feels Moana's hand rub her back as silence descends on the group. Looking around, she is mortified to find everyone looking at her. She knows she might have appeared too familiar. Nerves run through her body as Jack comes and sits next to her. She wills herself to sit calmly as his condescending smile cocoons her. His arm finds her waist and she feels like his prisoner.

The fire is still going early the next morning. It has kept everyone warm during the night. Linda and Nigel are up, making coffee, and its aroma soon wakes the others. Most help themselves to a drink before leaving. No one suggests they do another dinner.

Up at the Downs' shelter the air is filled with an uneasy presence. Mary is told to go with Harvey and get some milk from the stream for breakfast. Feeling lost and alone, she trails behind her brother, hating the silence she has caused between them.

"Harvey, please talk to me. I know you're angry but I need your help. I don't know how to make this better. Jessie is clearly avoiding me and Mum and Dad are watching me like hawks." She frowns sadly. *How am I going to find my way back?* "Mum's my best bet, don't you think?"

"Figure it out yourself."

"God, you're such a pain. Fine, don't help then. I'll get Mum on side myself." *You'll come round. You'll want my help with Candice. It's just a matter of time before you speak to me.*

They walk on together in solitude and when they return, Mary sees her mother putting dishes into a bucket outside their door.

"Mum, would you like me to do those?"

"Look, Mary, if you are sincere about helping then that's great, but if this is just another ploy to make me buckle and feel sorry for you, then don't bother."

She looks at her mother with a timid smile. "It's not, Mum, I'm truly sorry."

"Good to hear it. Now, Harvey and Jessie are coming with me to the fruit trees. You are to stay here with your father."

Mary shivers as she watches her mother shuffle Jessie and Harvey out the door. *Please, Mum – I don't want to be alone with him.*

"Right then, young lady, you can tidy up out here, and put a decent top on. One that covers you up."

Mary sidesteps past her father, retreats into their shelter and reappears in a red t-shirt. "That better?"

"Much. From now on you're to wear a top over your bikini, do you understand? I'm not having anyone else gawking at you."

"Does that go for you as well?"

"I beg you pardon?" Stan clutches Mary's arm.

"You're hurting."

"Mary, how many times? It was a misunderstanding."

"Oh, so it's like all right for you to go and get drunk and do something inappropriate but it's a different story for me, then, is it?"

"Yes, it bloody well is, young lady. I am an adult; you are a child. I have already explained what happened."

"It was sick."

"I thought you were Yvonne. You know that. We've been over this again and again and let's not forget you were the one in my bed, Mary."

"Mum said I could 'cause mine wasn't dry. You knew that, and you knew she was staying the night at her friend's," Mary hisses at him.

"I forgot. Jesus, I was drunk – it was dark. I was more mortified than you, believe me."

"Oh, like I seriously doubt that, Dad." Mary stares, her hard eyes ablaze with disgust.

Stan exhales deeply. "Mary, it was an unfortunate mistake. Nothing happened. I've apologized. It was as much your fault as mine and you know it."

"You're the adult."

Stan's hand whips up so fast Mary has no time to move. She reels as the harsh sting penetrates her cheek. Tears pool in her eyes.

"That is enough! You are not to mention this again and as for last night, well, you'll have to deal with that yourself. You acted like a little slut. You want us to treat you like an adult. You bloody well better start behaving like one. Now get inside and do the floor."

Mary slips inside the protection of their shelter.

"And have some respect, for God's sake."

She wants to run. *I know he's right, but even so, he should have known. We're so different in builds. How could he not have known?* She wipes the tears away from her eyes. She thinks about Peter. *He likes me. I know he does. I wish I was with him.* She thinks about telling her mother about what happened that night, three months ago, when her mother had stayed over at her friend's for the first time ever, but she knows she won't. *Would Mum believe me? Especially now! She will think I'm making it up to help her my situation*

and, more importantly, it will hurt her so much and I don't want that.
She loves her mother more than anything in the world. *I will just
have to grin and bear whatever comes my way and if I'm extra good and
help more, then Mum will come around and let me go with Harvey again.
I can be with Peter and if Peter doesn't want me – there's always Mark.
He wants me. He was practically dribbling as he watched, and Peter's
aware of it, too. Hated me dancing with Mark first, getting close.* She
smiles.

Stan pokes his head inside. "Grab what you need. We're going
to the waterfall. Be ready in five."

"All right, Dad," she says sweetly.

"And wear something sensible on your bottom."

Later in the afternoon when they return to their shelter, Yvonne
says it looks like rain and Stan and Harvey go down to the beach
to check the horizon. There are no ominous-looking clouds, but
the sky is gray. The breeze has picked up and Stan thinks Yvonne
might be right. He looks back at the caves and asks Harvey if he
has been in them.

"Nope. Peter and I peered in one day but it stunk and Karl said
they're full of bats."

"Bats, huh?"

"Yeah. Hey, Dad, can I go out with Peter tomorrow for a run?"

"Maybe. We'll wait and see what the weather's doing."

"You know it wasn't all Mary's fault."

"Look, Harvey, I know what you're saying but what she did
was really stupid."

"Yeah, I know, but don't be too hard on her, Dad. We're stuck
here for two more months."

"Yes, but she has to know that what she did is unacceptable
and if that means she has to stay with us – then so be it. We have
to be able to trust her and until we do, she doesn't go anywhere."

Walking back up, Stan thinks he had better cut Mary some slack. He couldn't afford for her to say anything to Yvonne. It had taken long enough after her sister had stuck the knife in for Yvonne to be herself with him again.

He remembers the dinner party they had for Yvonne's sister, Carly's, thirty-second birthday. She brought along a chap that she had been seeing for all of two minutes. Stan had instantly disliked him and found they had little in common. The evening had been a complete disaster from the word go. Jessie had caught a cold the day before and was not well. Mary had started to come down with it and Harvey had been upset that he couldn't go to his friend's house for the night. They had been worn out before the guests had even arrived.

Yvonne had over-cooked the lamb roast and the potatoes were slightly charred. The beans were soggy and unpleasant and the gravy looked like someone had thrown it back up. She had been near tears but he had said that no one would notice. A lie. Gavin, Carly's friend, had asked if they had liked their meat well done, saying that they should try it medium rare. He said the meal took him back to his childhood dinners with his parents and how his mother used to cook. Still did in fact. Always ended the night in bed, farting all hours.

Stan could have thumped him – and Carly, for that matter.

"So, what do you do Gavin?" he had asked, trying to steer the conversation in another direction.

"Oh, this and that." Gavin had replied, while downing yet another glass of wine.

'This and that.' – What sort of reply is that? "And what exactly is 'this and that'?" he had asked, watching the bemused look on Carly's face.

"Bit of this, bit of that. You know."

"No, I don't, Gavin. *That's* why I'm asking. I mean, have you got a job or do you mean you haven't got a job and you just do anything?"

"Well, Stan, it's like this," said Gavin, pouring the last bit of wine into his glass. "I do whatever I feel like, when I feel like it, and therefore it's a bit of this and that."

"So, are we talking legal or illegal?"

"Oh, Stan, I don't know if you really should be asking Gavin that sort of thing."

Stan had looked at Carly. He remembered the look on her face. She had loved how it had ruined the night even more, if that had been possible.

"No worries, babe. Like I said Stan, I do what I want, when I want."

Stan remembered how he slouched back in his chair, with his wine glass raised and gave him a look that said 'don't go any further with this, asshole'. Stan pushed his chair back and said he would take the plates out and bring in the dessert. Yvonne had started to get up but he had told her to relax. In truth he wanted to get out of the room so he could take some deep breaths and calm down. That guy was a bum and Carly knew it. He knew she only brought him here to make them uncomfortable. She was a bitch. He had put the plates in the sink when he heard the door open. Carly had come into the kitchen asking for wine. He grabbed a bottle and opened it for her to take back and she said that he was mighty tense. She started massaging his shoulders and then moved to his front and planted a kiss on his lips. He had dropped the wine bottle when he heard the swing door open and saw Yvonne standing there, white faced.

"It's not what it looks like, Yvonne," he had said as he shoved Carly off. She just smiled at him: a long, slow, devious smile. He felt like hitting her, hard. Hard enough to break some bones, but she just walked towards Yvonne and said in that sarcastic voice of hers, "It's not what it seems, Yvonne." She went through the swing door and left them looking at one another. He immediately went over and told her what had happened and Yvonne replied that she knew what her sister was like, but it didn't make it any easier seeing her lips on his. She wanted them gone and she wanted to go to bed, alone. He gave her the space she needed and went back into the dining room and told them to fuck off. Those were his words. He could remember that clearly. He told her sister to fuck off and not to bother coming back – ever!' Gavin had whistled and got up, saying something like 'bummer, man,' but he couldn't really remember and he didn't really care. He had just wanted them out of their house and out of their lives. He had shut the door and locked it and had heard Yvonne going upstairs. He was sure she was crying and he stayed downstairs and cleaned up, got out a pillow and a blanket and slept on the couch.

It had taken nearly three weeks for Yvonne to let him back in and even though she said she believed him, he knew that what had happened had damaged his marriage. He didn't blame Yvonne, but he did blame her sister. He knew that Harvey and Mary had heard what had gone on and with this and the other incident he had with Mary, he now wonders if they are partly to blame for her behavior.

CHAPTER TWENTY-THREE

The next morning brings persistent but gentle rain, which encloses the island in a misty veil and continues to fall for the next two days. By Wednesday the sun begins to peek through the clouds while the breeze picks up, blowing briskly from the east. Mary's little exhibition has changed the easy-going nature of things and there is now an unsaid awkwardness between some of the families. The rain has helped the Downs' plight, as many have stayed indoors. Harvey and Jessie can't wait till Sunday, when they will meet up with everyone for lunch. Stan has backed down towards Mary, hoping she has learned her lesson.

Sunday arrives and instead of eating first, a game of volleyball is underway, bringing with it much needed laughter and shouting. After an hour, the game comes to a halt and they gather together for lunch. The sun is relentless under the sky's clear blue canopy and appetites are not what they were. The younger ones pick at their food, wanting to take out Harvey's boat. Given permission, Harvey and Peter drag it down to the water's edge with Mark and the girls in tow.

"Here, Mark, you first."

"Why me?"

"'Cause it's Harvey's and I asked."

"That's hardly fair, Peter."

"No, it's not," concludes Harvey, "but that's the deal. Take it or leave it."

Beaten, Mark grabs the pump and reluctantly makes a start. Peter hi-fives Harvey, while Mary, Candice and Jessie exchange wary looks.

"You kids be careful and stay where we can see you," Stan yells, seeing the boat inflated and the kids eager to go.

Harvey waves and takes the oars. The others guide him around the coral-laden rocks and out to the coral bank and they soon reach the deeper indigo water. Mark dives in, followed by Peter. Jessie jumps off, holding her nose. She spies clownfish darting around and surfaces, her eyes alive with delight. They take turns, leaving someone on the boat so it doesn't float away, and spend their time diving as the fish circle around them, curious about the strange creatures entering their world.

Peter is amazed at the different plants growing on the coral bank. Careful not to touch any of them he stares, fascinated by the clownfish darting in and out of the anemones' tentacles. He spies two vibrant, royal blue starfish on some sponges and then two yellow-belly damsels swimming by as he watches a pufferfish inflate itself to several times its normal size. Knowing pufferfish are deadly poisonous, he stays still while it casually floats by.

Coming up for air, he is greeted by Jessie's excited chatting. She is talking so quickly that she is hard to understand, but he joins in her enthusiasm and they go below the surface for another look. He shows her the clownfish and they see a butterfly fish pecking the coral for food and then he spots one of the many varieties of parrotfish, remembering that, on the sheet they were given, parrotfish are considered 'royal food' in the islands.

Surfacing, they get back on the boat with Mark and Harvey. Mary swims over and climbs in as Mark, Harvey and Candice dive off.

"Jessie, go with them."

"No, I'm tired. I want to go back."

"Please, Jessie," says Mary, growing increasingly annoyed.

"No, I don't want to."

"I'll push you in if you don't go."

"Mary, I'm not feeling well."

"Oh, for Pete's sake. What's the matter with you now?" She sees Harvey swimming back. "Oh, Harvey, thank God. Take Jessie with you?"

"But I'm not …"

"Be quiet," says Mary with a hiss in her voice, making Jessie whimper.

"I was about to climb aboard."

"Oh, for fuck's sake. Mary – let's get back in." Peter grabs her hand and together they jump into the water, leaving Harvey with Jessie. Jessie looks at him, whimpering, and Harvey feels her forehead.

"Hey, guys, think we should take her in."

Mary and Peter ignore him, swimming further away. Mark reaches the boat, gets in, grabs the oars and focuses his attention to the left of them. Harvey pulls Candice into the boat and she sits next to Jessie, wrapping her in a towel.

"We should get her back, Mark. She's shivering like crazy."

"Oh, fuck!"

"What?" says Harvey, irritated.

"I think I saw a shark."

"Oh yeah, good one." Harvey scoffs. "That'll get them out."

"You're joking, right?" Candice's voice is a mere whisper. Jessie's face drains of color as she draws in air. Her shivering gets worse.

Mark doesn't answer; his eyes focus on the rippling water. Harvey peeks at Candice. He sees his own fear in her eyes. "I don't see anything, Mark."

"I see it, I see it," shrieks Jessie. "Over there Harvey, over there." Jessie points and Harvey and Candice freeze.

"Oh … m-my … God," stutters Candice.

Harvey yells. Peter looks over and raises his arms. Mark screams, "shark!"

Jessie stands, transfixed. "I don't want to die, Harvey … I don't want to die."

Back on land Terrance has been watching the youngsters. He becomes alarmed when the raft rocks dangerously and Jessie is yanked down. Sensing that something is wrong, he reaches for his binoculars. Scanning the water, he sees nothing. He glides the binoculars back to the boat and concentrates on Jessie's face. He follows her gaze back around to Mary and Peter in the water and then he sees a fin.

"Shark!" he shouts, throwing down the binoculars.

Everyone stops what they are doing and looks out at the boat. Harvey and Mark are frantically waving their arms. Stan holds Yvonne while Henry struggles with Nancy. She repeatedly calls Peter's name as she tries to get free. Karl grabs Terrance's arm, telling him it might be wise for him to stay and keep the others on the beach and let Ritchie, Drew and himself swim out.

"Christ, Jessie's an idiot, jumping up and down like that. She'll tip the boat."

"What's she yelling, Peter, and why's Mark waving like that?"

"Maybe Jessie might really be sick." Peter freezes. "Are they yelling shark?"

"Shark?" Mary turns frantically. "I can't see anything."

"Stay still." Peter looks back to the boat. "They're coming."

"Peter," Mary wails, rotating around him, her eyes transfixed on the glassy water.

"Quit splashing."

Mary panics, pushing Peter under. He resurfaces, gulping for air as Mary shoves him and starts swimming for the boat. He doesn't move – he can't. He watches Mary leave him. The water around her disturbingly white. His eyes dart left and right but he sees nothing.

Mary reaches the boat and Mark takes her hand to pull her up. Harvey puts down the oars and is grabbing her bottom when she is suddenly dragged backwards. Mary screams and Harvey and Mark pull harder as the water changes color. Jessie blubbers uncontrollably and Candice freezes.

"We're going to die!" Jessie's voice is shrill, almost unrecognizable.

"Be quiet," shouts Harvey as he and Mark strain to lift Mary. They get her body over the side and she falls onto the floor, causing the boat to rock, spilling water inside.

"The water's red ... it's so red!" screams Jessie, howling. Harvey quickly takes off his t-shirt and places it over Mary's leg.

"Oh, God," whimpers Candice, her eyes frozen with fear.

The shark has taken a huge chunk out of Mary's thigh and has bitten her badly around her calf. Blood seeps from her and pools around their feet.

"Mark, take your shirt off and tie it round the top of her leg – tightly."

Mark instantly whips his t-shirt off and has it around Mary's leg in seconds. "She's in shock.

"Peter," whimpers Candice.

"Fuck, Harvey. Peter's still in there."

Peter watches the boat getting closer. His eyes dart nervously around him as his feet tread water. The boat glides alongside him and Mark grabs Peter's arms and tries to lift his unresponsive body. Peter is like lead and Mark dives in and pushes Peter from below and Harvey manages to haul him in. Peter falls face down next to the crimson t-shirt covering Mary's leg. Harvey helps Mark aboard and then Jessie starts to heave. She spills her lunch into the boat. Harvey yells at Candice to do something. She pushes Jessie to the side of the boat and Jessie, trembling uncontrollably, vomits again.

"Oh, for fuck's sake!" yells Harvey, exasperated. "Pull her back. Vomit attracts sharks, you stupid girl."

"I didn't know that," shrieks Candice. Fresh tears stream down her face like fast flowing rivers.

The boat shudders and groans.

"What was that?" shrieks Jessie.

"Keep still," hollers Mark.

"It's the shark," screams Jessie. "I want Mum." Her screeching turns to sobbing as water rises in the boat. Harvey rows insanely. They take another knock and Jessie shrieks hysterically.

"Shit, Harvey, you've gone over the coral," says Mark, desperately pressing on a rip in the boat's bottom. Water flows through in an alarming rate, mixing with Mary's blood, turning the boat's floor into an artist's canvas.

Harvey doesn't care. He focuses on the figures swimming towards him and closes his mind to the chaos around him. He thinks the whole thing has taken ages but realizes it can have been only a matter of minutes as he hears Karl tell Ritchie and Drew to grab the ropes. Karl swims behind them and somehow manages to push the boat forward and Harvey stops rowing, exhaustion overwhelming him, as the boat is pulled towards the shore.

Mary's eyelids feel heavy. She has no idea of the time. It seems to flow forward and backward and then blur together. She is cold, but there is warmth around her legs. *Something has happened and it must have happened to me. I'm the only one lying down.* She forces her eyes open and looks at Candice cradling Jessie. *God, they look awful!* She tries to say something but her mouth is dry and tastes like sick. A shadow descends over her and she blinks and sees Mark. *What's that you're saying?* Her ears roar and she looks at Harvey, but he turns away. *Why did you do that?* She feels sleepy but the hot, dull ache in her leg keeps her awake. She tries to sit, but Mark pushes her back down and then she hears splashing. Faces peer down at her, but they are not her parents. Someone is stroking her hair and she watches as Candice and Jessie are lifted out. Her hand brushes her leg and she pulls at the cloth. It is damp and warm and red. She screams as hands reach out and she sees a familiar watch.

"No, Stan, don't move her," shouts Linda, rushing next to him. "Please," she says touching his arm. "Let me see, before she's moved."

Mary watches her dad move back. His face is miserable. She sees her mother grab his arm. Her eyes are red and wracked with pain and in this moment Mary thinks of her grandmother, who was taken from them five years ago, suffering from cancer. It was the only other time Mary had seen her mother look utterly terrible, utterly broken and she looks back to find Linda clutching another dripping brilliant-red cloth. *Oh, Mum, please don't cry. Ouch, that hurts, Linda. Don't press so hard.*

Linda whispers something to her father and he nods and draws her mother into him.

"Lift her up the beach. Use the boat as a stretcher." Linda's instructions are clear and authoritative.

"Yvonne, Linda knows what she's doing. She was an excellent nurse. Mary couldn't be in better hands," says Nigel supportively.

Mary stares at her mother's head bobbing, and the tears trickling into her quivering mouth, before Linda's no-nonsense voice takes her attention.

"Need that fire built up. Stan, keep holding her hand. Harvey, I want you to go with your mother and sister and sit by the fire, keep warm. Get someone to make something hot to drink."

"We'll help," says Nancy, holding onto Candice while Henry cradles his son.

"Good … get Peter and Candice up there, too. They're in shock."

Peter! Peter's okay! Mary closes her eyes. A hand touches her forehead and she opens her eyes to see Linda's caring face. *Oh, God, I was such a bitch to think you were old and boring.* She smiles meekly and Linda's hand kindly brushes her forehead again, wiping away her dampened hair.

"It's time, Stan. You should do it now."

Do what now? Mary sees her father nod and he unclasps his hand, giving her a kiss on her cheek.

"Be back soon, Princess. Be brave. Linda will look after you."

Where are you going? "Dad," she croaks, but he doesn't hear as he briskly walks away.

"Sweetheart, don't fret. Your dad's gone to get a flare."

Mary's body tenses and Linda rubs her shoulder compassionately. "It's all right. You need to go to hospital. I don't have the equipment here to fix you up, but you're going to be fine – you hear me? Just fine."

Mary's eyes blink back the tears. *"Everyone says that – oh, God, what's happened to me?"*

"Good girl. Now I'm going to clean you up and make you more comfortable."

Rosaline arrives with some water and pain-relief and Linda gives them to Mary. Nigel and Moana bring down a couple of first-aid kits and Mary hears Linda telling them to find the sterile water, pads and bandages.

"Take some deep breaths, sweetie. I'm going to need you to be strong. Do you think you can do that for me?"

No! Mary nods. Fear strangles her body, making her stiff. Only her lips quiver as she feels Linda's hands on her leg. She bites down, causing blood to drip into her mouth. Biting harder, she concentrates on the pain. It doesn't stop the sizzling fire that intensifies in her leg and then everything fades.

Linda gets to work. When finished, Yvonne, sits holding her daughter's hand. Linda knowingly rubs her shoulder and leaves them alone to speak to the others.

"How bad is it?"

"It's not pretty, Sara, but she'll survive. Need skin grafts and plastic surgery but she shouldn't lose her leg."

"Shit, we shouldn't have let them go out there."

"No one knew this would happen, Terrance."

"What were we thinking?" whimpers Rosaline, looking at the huddled figures of Peter and Candice clinging to their parents.

"Well, at least Mary's out of your hair now," announces Jack.

Terrance's hand is so quick that Jack is on the ground before he knows what hit him. Stunned, Jack struggles to sit.

"You deserved that, Jack," roars Matt.

"What the hell is wrong with you?" Rosaline spits, towering over her husband.

Jack gawks at her, saying nothing. He tastes blood. He looks past his wife to where Karl is talking to Terrance and sees the threat in his eyes. He shifts his gaze to the Booths and the Davidsons, who show their disgust and look away.

Stan and Harvey arrive back and let off their flare. Ironically, the red flare lights up the afternoon sky beautifully and they all sit, scattered like tombstones in a graveyard, waiting for Martin's team.

CHAPTER TWENTY-FOUR

John, Bill and Alison leave Martin's launch after seeing the red glow hovering over the island. The rest of the team watch the dinghy merge into the distance and Grace goes below to inform Martin. She hesitantly steps into his room, inhales deeply and advances towards his bed. She glances at Ella holding Martin's hand. Her tongue runs over her parched mouth and she swallows noisily. She tells Martin the news and watches his shaking hand lift off his oxygen mask.

"My folder."

Ella picks up the manila folder on the bedside table and hands it to Martin. Grace's pity builds and she focuses her attention on the crisp white walls, the minimal yet expensive furniture, mostly covered with medical items, and then on the open window. The breeze blows in and out of the stuffy room, helping to take the smell of death with it. She wonders how Martin feels, trapped in his bed. A lump forms in her throat and she swallows hard as she watches Martin's frustrated finger wobble down the page.

"The Downs." Martin's croaky voice is a mere whisper.

"Oh. That is a shame, Martin," says Ella. "I really liked that family. The kids were so excited; so full of adventure."

"Yes. I liked …" Martin coughs and Ella quickly hands him his glass of cold water. "Jessie … the little one." He struggles for breath and Ella places her hand on his head, soothing what little hair he has left. "I liked her." He looks at the window. "Young and … healthy."

Grace wants to leave but instead takes his free hand. He is weak and it is like holding a damp sponge. She looks at Ella in despair.

"Ahem … Martin, John, Bill and Alison have left. They will be in touch shortly."

Martin coughs and Ella holds a glass with a straw to his lips.

"Damn … cough."

"I'll go, Ella. I don't want to tire him." *Christ, that's a lame excuse.*

Ella gives the smallest of nods and Grace leaves. Breathing a sigh of relief, she closes the door behind her and quickly makes her way to the upper deck and fresh air.

"How is he?" asks Owen, looking up from his book.

"Much the same. He looks so old and small. I know he didn't want to end up in hospital but honestly, Owen, it's really awful in there."

"Is Ella okay?"

"Yes, Ben. I don't know how she does it."

"No, it can't be easy. I guess she's used to this sort of thing, though," says Karen, placing her hand on Owen's leg. "He knows we care, Owen. He's better off without us all looking in on him."

"Poor Ella, she loves him so much."

"Yes, she'll miss him terribly. We all will." Ben helps himself to a juice just as the radio buzzes. "Hello, John. What's up?" Ben listens carefully. He clicks off the radio receiver. "Owen, we need to get the helicopter. Mary's been attacked by a shark. I spoke to Linda. Mary's stable, but losing a lot of blood."

"Oh, the poor girl. Did they say what her injuries are?" asks Penny.

"No. Alison is staying there and John and Bill are on their way here. They need a dry blanket, pillow and a stretcher. Owen, can you go below with Karen and find them?"

Phil shakes his head. "Did we really hammer that one home?"

"I know what you're thinking, Phil, but it's not our fault. They knew the risks. They have to take responsibility, especially Mary's parents."

Phil gets up takes a pair of binoculars and looks towards the island. "True, Ben, but I feel bad."

Penny rubs Phil's back. "Phil, come on. It's unfortunate but it is what it is. They can leave anytime."

Grace knows what Penny has said is true but as she looks over at her teammates, she can see the doubt setting in. She closes her eyes and thinks that maybe Martin's rapid decline is not such a bad thing. *He won't be here to be accountable for their broken lives. God, I wish I was somewhere else, rather than here, bobbing away in the middle of nowhere, waiting for more bad news.*

Back on the island Stan, Harvey, Rosaline and Jessie make their way to the Down's shelter to gather their things. Stan is thankful for Rosaline's offer to help. He isn't thinking clearly; Harvey is still way too quiet and Jessie continues to breakdown at any given moment. They step into the shelter that has been their home for the past month.

"This is nice," comments Rosaline.

"Thanks," says Stan trying to sound appreciative. "Could you help Jessie get her things?"

"Of course."

Stan sees Harvey venting his frustration on the fire. He reaches out to him but Harvey pulls away.

"I'm all right!" Harvey turns his back and goes about picking up anything he can see.

"Son, we don't need those. Just get your own things. Don't worry about anything else." Stan's heart is heavy and he leaves Harvey and steps into his tent to sort through Yvonne's and his belongings. He bundles what he can into their bags and watches Rosaline and Jessie come out of her tent and steps inside. He sees

Mary's bed and slumps down, crying. He hears Rosaline telling Harvey and Jessie to give him a moment.

He wipes his eyes and emerges looking wretched and Jessie rushes into his arms. He holds her tight as they start back.

"Wait!" yells Jessie, stopping.

Stan kneels down in front of her. "What's wrong, Pumpkin?"

"I forgot something."

"Well, go and get it, then."

"It's not in there."

"What do you mean?"

"I mean it's a secret." Jessie looks at her dad, her mouth quivering.

"A secret huh? Where is it, Jessie?"

"Over there," she says pointing through the bush. "Will you come with me, Dad?"

"Of course I will."

They walk a few meters and Jessie goes behind a large tree and bends down. Her hand descends into the darkness of the small shrubs

"I made a diary."

Stan hugs her. "Clever you."

"Am I, Dad?"

"Yes," he says kissing her cheek. "You are."

"You can't read it, Dad."

"Why not?"

"'Cause it's private stuff."

Stan ruffles his daughter's hair. "I know that, just teasing you. Come on, we'd better get ourselves back." He takes his daughter's hand and they walk back to Harvey and Rosaline. Jessie closes the door of their shelter for the last time.

"Dad?"

"Yes, Harvey?"

"What about the stuff in the stream?"

Stan sighs. "Rosaline, there are some containers attached to a rope in the stream." He points left. "Most are by those trees. You and the others are welcome to them."

"Thank you, Stan. I'll let everyone know," says Rosaline respectfully.

Stan appreciates her thoughtfulness in not inquiring as to what they hold. They arrive at the beach to find Yvonne comforting Mary as she slips in and out of consciousness. Stan and Rosaline take Harvey and Jessie to join the others and leave Peter with Yvonne.

"You and Mary like each other?"

"Yes."

"Will you keep in touch, Peter?"

"I ... guess."

"She's going to need friends now. Real friends, Peter, not just friends that come and go, but friends she can depend on. Know what she's gone through. Are you one of those friends, Peter?" Yvonne senses his indecision as he looks at Mary.

"Sure, Mrs. Downs."

"I hope so, Peter. Here, I wrote our phone number down for you. Keep it safe."

Peter blushes just as Mary opens her eyes.

"Mary, it's Peter! I'm here! I'm so sorry." Tears fall onto Mary's face and he wipes them away tenderly. He kisses her hand and holds it close to his cheek.

"Peter"

"I'm here, Mary."

"Peter?"

"Yes, Mary?"

Yvonne watches them, her heart breaking. She feels old, completely drained. *What a nightmare!* She glances towards Stan and her other children. Rosaline is holding Jessie's hand. *That's nice, Jessie needs that.* She stares at her son, Harvey. *When did he get to be so grown up?* She lets out a small whimper and wipes her nose. A flashback of the moment when Terrance yelled 'shark' pops into her head. She had been frozen with terror. A deep, unspeakable terror. A terror one feels when they are totally incapable of protecting their children. She had felt completely useless. But Harvey had been there. Harvey had saved Mary. "My hero!"

"Pardon?"

"Oh, Peter, sorry ... thinking out loud."

"It's okay, Mrs. Downs."

Yvonne squeezes his leg and starts to weep. She can see Peter's awkwardness. Mary has slipped back into unconsciousness. Yvonne puts a hand on Peter's shoulder and stares at her daughter, wishing she could take her place.

John, Bill and Alison arrive carrying a stretcher. Alison and Linda manage to get Yvonne and Peter to move away and John, Bill, Matt and Drew gently lift Mary onto the stretcher and tie her in securely. Alison then places a thermal blanket over her and Linda puts a soft pillow under her head. She shows Alison the bandages. They are tinged pink and Alison gets out a bigger bandage and they wrap her leg from thigh to ankle.

Everything happens so fast and when the helicopter has been and taken the Downs away and John and his crew have left, the remaining families sit trapped on the beach.

"It's a terrible thing to watch one's child and not being able to do anything."

"Oh, Moana, it's the worst," says Nancy, bringing Candice closer to her. "You two were so brave!" She reaches over to Peter and rubs his arm. "We're very proud of you."

Peter glances at his mother and gives her a small smile. *Mary's gone and Harvey. I want to go, too.* Mark comes over and sits with him. Peter gets up and goes to sit with his father.

"Give him time, Mark," says Moana. "He's had a nasty shock."

Rosaline hesitantly tells Jack about the containers in the stream.

"For Pete's sake, woman, this is meant to be a contest. If it means we get a bit of help then so be it. Do you think they would let on?"

A small chill runs down her body. She agrees to remain silent and leaves Jack to see what Henry, Ritchie, Karl and Nigel are laying out on the sand. She looks back at Jack, feeling more distant than she ever thought possible.

Once again, the ritual of dividing up someone else's belongings is completed and just as the sun is setting, they all make their way back to their own shelters. The mood on the island is at an all time low. Mary's attack has affected them all.

CHAPTER TWENTY-FIVE

Rosaline and Jack decide moving to the Downs' shelter makes perfect sense. They pack up quickly. Jack wants to get there before anybody else claims it. He tells Rosaline to take as much as she can and they set off and arrive to find it empty. The fire is still glowing and Jack piles on more dry grass and twigs. He puts shoes outside the door and they trudge back for their chest. It is heavy and carrying it takes time. They reach the shelter and Rosaline slumps with exhaustion. Jack tells her to stay put while he goes back for their final items. It is close to midnight when he returns, bringing the final bits and pieces and they lie down on the bed Rosaline has made.

"Thank God they're gone."

"I'm tired, Jack."

"Oh, come on, Roz. After Mary's dancing show everyone's uncomfortable."

"That would have changed."

"Maybe, maybe not. We can't stay pally-wally forever."

"You think we might be in for another storm?"

"Christ, I don't know! It's not a problem now, in any case." Jack smiles as Rosaline turns her back to him. "That tired, huh? Pleasant dreams, then." He can't see her face but he doesn't have to. He knows she doesn't want to be here with him but she can't do anything about it. He closes his eyes and is snoring within minutes.

The Tillers spotted Jack and Rosaline earlier and guessed they were taking over the Downs' place.

"Typical." Karl looks west. The breeze catches his hair and fills his nostrils with the salty air. "Smell rain."

"Yeah – why don't I get the fruit while you two hunt?"

"Sounds good to me, Terrance," says Greg. "If we get more than one bird I can cook one up for Sunday."

"Greg, let's not get too enthusiastic. We've been here for a month and there's still seven of us left. Anything we get, we keep."

"Karl's right, Greg."

"You think so, Terrance?"

"Yeah, I do. Look, we have to start thinking that this is a contest and not some bloody holiday."

"Exactly. Be friendly, just not too friendly and remember – watch and listen."

Greg looks at his brothers. "Well then, Terrance, you should be careful with Rosaline."

"Yeah, Greg's got a point there, mate."

"Jack's a prick. He treats her like shit."

"I agree but no need to antagonize him."

"Point taken, Karl, but I'm not going to ignore her."

"Well, you may just have to, buddy. That guy's got some serious anger and we don't want it coming our way."

"I can handle him." Terrance sees the quick exchange between his brothers. "Look, I'm well aware of the situation. I'm not going to do anything stupid, okay?"

Karl raises his eyebrows. "Well, Greg – guess we'd better make a move. Be 'bout a couple of hours. We'll meet you back at the cave."

"Fine."

Terrance sits watching the water. Tiny ripples flow rhythmically, making their way towards him. They keep the images of Mary's attack alive, causing a dull persistent throbbing in his forehead and, between that and the heat, he is beginning to feel a little nauseous.

He hears footsteps and turns to see Karl and Greg. He rubs his forehead and looks back out to sea. He knows what is coming.

"Forget something?"

"Look mate, we're a little concerned."

"'Bout what?" Terrance glances at Karl before his eyes travel to Greg, who stands behind Karl, a mixture of pity and concern spread across his face. He hates that face and looks away.

"We think you should come with us."

"No, thanks."

"Come on, bud, it'll be good for you."

"I said no."

"Okay, Karl, he wants to be alone."

"No, he doesn't, Greg – he just thinks he does."

Terrance glances sideways. *It's always the same isn't it? You thinking you know what's best and Greg follows along like a lost puppy. Come on – hit me with the next question.*

"Um … Karl, we should go."

"We need to talk."

"I don't, Karl."

"Is it Mary?"

Jesus Christ! Terrance exhales slowly.

"Is it?"

"Yeah. I was thinking about her. I just can't wipe it away like you."

"I haven't 'wiped it away' as you put it, but what's the use of going over and over it? It happened. Wasn't anyone's fault."

"Wasn't it?"

"What's that supposed to mean?"

"Karl, let's go."

"Shut up, Greg. Jesus, Terrance, you don't seriously think it's your fault do you?"

"We should have been more careful."

"You're not her father. If you want to blame someone, blame her parents."

"So you do think it's someone's fault then?"

"Oh, for Pete's sake – their responsibility."

"And what about Josh?"

"Josh?"

"If we're talking responsibility." Terrance sees the confusion on Karl's face, the hurt in Greg's eyes. *Too bad – they just can't keep sweeping it under the carpet and forget about it.* He watches Karl from the corner of his eye. Karl's lips twitch as he attempts to find the right words. Greg stands statue-like. *Muted again, Greg? What a surprise!*

Karl closes his eyes. "What can we do?"

"Nothing."

"You have to get this sorted, Terrance."

"I will, Karl."

Karl's hand finds Terrance's knee and squeezes it compassionately. "Okay then – see you later."

Terrance gives them the faintest of nods and watches them trudge up the sand. He knows they are worried but he won't say anything. It's not his secret to tell.

He gets up, puts his bag over his shoulder and strides into the bush, carelessly stomping on the attacking plants in his path. He can't stop thinking about Mary and Josh. People die around him. It didn't matter that he hadn't killed them. He just felt, rightly or wrongly, that he was in some way to blame. Peter comes into his view and stops in front of him, looking vexed and steamy. "Peter … You look hot."

"So?"

"Alone?"

"I'm running."

"Good for you."

"Takes my mind off things."

Terrance nods. "Look, Peter, I'm really sorry about Mary."

"Really?" Peter's voice is mocking. "I would have thought you'd be happy she's gone."

Terrance sighs. "No, Peter I ..."

"She told me what you did." Peter's voice is frosty. "Yeah, that's right – you fucking creep." Peter's eyes narrow as he inches forward. "You're lucky I don't say anything. I could, though." His head nods quickly. "Yeah, and then you wouldn't be so popular, would you?"

Terrance eyeballs Peter. "Say what you like, Peter, just make sure of the facts." Again he thinks of death as he steps around Peter. He doesn't look back. He knows Peter is still watching him. *Little shit better not say anything.* He thinks of Rosaline. *Would she believe it? Jack certainly would. Would make his day.*

He exits the bush and the bright light hits him hard. Closing his eyes he draws in air, exhales slowly, dumps his bag on the ground and rips off his sweat-laden t-shirt.

"Oh, my God, Celia, look at that."

Celia looks up lazily from the orange she is peeling. "Is he real?"

Trudy laughs quietly. "Oh, yes." They watch, bewitched, taking in the way the sun catches Terrance's sweat, making his skin glisten. His eyes open and he waves, seemingly oblivious of the effect he has created. Celia offers him her orange.

"Thanks." He wipes his forehead and crouches before them. "Can I ask you something?"

"Sure."

"Do you think about Josh and Mary?"

"Oh, wow, sometimes. She had a thing for you, didn't she?" Celia looks straight at Terrance.

"Yeah, bit of a crush."

"That can't have been easy."

"No, it wasn't." Terrance rises. "Sorry – I'm busting. Be back in a mo." Terrance walks a generous distance away from the girls and relieves himself behind the cover of the trees.

"Oh, man – he's got the sexiest eyes."

"Eyes that draw you in, if you let them." Trudy raises her eyebrows. "Could drown in those if you wanted." They giggle together and Trudy licks at the trickle of juice that escapes her mouth.

"Behave!" snickers Celia as Terrance wanders back.

Trudy yawns. "Wonder what's taking the boys so long?"

"Hmm, thought they'd be back by now."

Trudy looks at her watch. "Been gone nearly two hours." She watches Terrance. "We'd better go find them."

"I'll come with you, if you like. See those clouds rolling in? Storm's on its way."

"Okay – thanks."

Terrance notices Celia's nervous smile and he follows them down the southwest track, which brings them out further around the cove, onto a rocky beach to find Drew and Ritchie downing oysters.

"Oh, you rotters," yells Trudy. "We thought you might be in trouble and here you are having a bloody feast."

"Here, have one," replies Drew, cutting around the shell and then opening the oyster for her. The oyster quickly slides down her throat, making her gag.

"Yuck, you could have washed it."

"Oh, you're too fussy, Trudy," says Ritchie. "Celia, you want one?"

"No, thanks, hon. I'm with Trudy. Don't like them unwashed and no lemon."

"I'll try one, thanks," says Terrance taking the shell Ritchie holds out for his wife. He brings the shell to his lips and tips it so the oyster glides into his mouth effortlessly. "Beautiful!"

Celia blushes. "Terrance was getting fruit. He came with us in case something happened to you two."

"That was thoughtful of you, mate."

"No problem."

"Well, thanks anyway," says Drew packing his bag. "We better get going."

"So, Terrance," says Ritchie as he puts the last few items into his bag. "What's your line of work?"

"Electrician."

"You any good?"

"Well, I guess you'd have to ask the people I've worked for that question."

"Guess we would. Might need an electrician when we win."

Terrance sees the look Celia gives her husband. Ritchie ignores her, pulling out a slingshot.

"Made this after Josh. It's quite fun from what I remember. Pull it back, let the stone go and wham, you've got your prey ... or not, if you're a bad shot."

Terrance's heart skips a beat. "I'm not really into it."

"Put it away, Ritchie," says Celia's looking agitated.

Ritchie shoves it into his shorts pocket. "Might see something on the way back."

"Duh, too much noise, dude," says Drew taking the lead. They walk to the fruit trees in silence.

"Well see you Sunday, weather permitting." Ritchie extends his hand and Terrance warily accepts it. Ritchie's grip is strong and they hold each other for a moment before releasing. Celia looks on nervously and Terrance smiles, waves and heads back into the bush.

"What was that?" spits Ritchie.

"What?"

"That little exchange."

"It was nothing. And what's with the questions?"

"I don't like him sniffing around."

"Oh, don't be so crass. He's not sniffing around. Jealous are we?"

"Like I said before. Should I be?"

Celia sighs. "Don't be stupid. Why would I fancy him when I have you?"

"I don't know, you tell me." Ritchie walks on, catching up to Drew, leaving Celia behind with Trudy.

"Everything okay?"

"'Course. He's just being stupid."

"God, it was just a bit of fun."

Celia shrugs her shoulders. "I know."

"How dare he make you feel guilty?"

"I don't. Well, not really."

Trudy takes Celia's hand. By the time they reach their tree house, rain is falling. The drops are heavy and they land on the tree house with a thud. Before long, small puddles appear on the floor. Trudy rushes and grabs two buckets.

It rains all afternoon and into the night but by the next morning the sun makes its appearance, ready to dry the sodden bush. Trunks, which lay where they fell from the previous storm, have rotted and insects appear and scurry about, finding new homes or rebuilding sodden ones.

Ritchie wakes feeling nauseous and a little achy. He goes outside to relieve himself, where he sees Drew. Drew tells him he has been up during the night, thinking he is going to vomit. They stoke up the fire and Trudy emerges, looking pale, and sits with them.

Celia pokes her head out the door, takes one look at the three of them and shakes her head. "Wonder if those oysters were okay?"

"They were fine. You didn't eat the rest of that fish stew, did you?"

"No, I didn't fancy it."

"Yeah," says Ritchie, bending his head towards his bucket. "'Member I said it sort of smelt."

"Can I get you anything?"

"Buckets."

"Okay, Trudy." Celia grabs two buckets and fills some coconut bowls with water.

"Look, I'm going to get more lemons. Nothing I can do for you now and you know I can't stand being around sick."

"Yeah, you go."

She squeezes Ritchie's shoulder and leaves them sitting shivering and moaning around the fire, faces bent down and buckets held tight.

Celia moves quickly by herself, gets what she needs at the fruit trees and decides to go down to the beach in the hope of seeing either Bridget or Moana. They might be able to suggest something to help. The beach is deserted. She sits, letting the sun warm her body. Before she knows it, tears are flowing from her eyes and she hugs her knees into her torso and rocks back and forth. She feels something on her shoulder and turns to find Terrance crouching beside her. Flustered she wipes her eyes and tries to still her shaking body.

"What's wrong?"

"I'm ... I don't ..."

"It's okay – I'll go."

Her hand grabs his shirt. "No, I don't want to be alone."

"Has something happened?"

His voice is tender and she relaxes. "Not really." She looks at him. His eyes are full of concern. "They're sick."

"Do you need help?"

"I'm just feeling sorry for myself." She wipes her eyes and gazes at his sympathetic face. "Sorry you had to see me like this."

"Doesn't matter."

"Of course it does. Oh, shit." Her eyes mist over and she shuts them tightly. She clenches her fists and feels Terrance's arm on her shoulder.

"I'll go."

She nods and stands.

"Steady there."

"I'm fine."

"You sure?"

She tilts her head and looks at him. Her hand brushes the strand of hair that has found its way across his face and she tucks it behind his ear. His hair is soft, his skin is warm and smooth and her hand moves down to his neck.

"Celia?"

She looks at his mouth.

"You should go, you're upset. You don't want this."

"I know. I love Ritchie."

"So go."

"I can't." Fresh tears flow as she pulls his head towards her.

Terrance tenses. A vision of Mary and her provocative ways confronts him and then Rosaline is before him. Common sense is replaced by desire and he picks Celia up and takes her into the cover of the palm trees.

Peter crouches. He is only meters away but they haven't seen him. He watches through the protective leaves of the shrubbery.

Feeling aroused, he moves with them and when they come together he explodes and drops to the ground, panting.

He stares as they dress hastily. Terrance is talking to her. His hand takes hers and she hugs him and leaves. He watches Terrance turn and head back along the path towards him. Peter lies still until Terrance passes and he can no longer see him. He gets up and runs. Every little sound in the bush seems amplified. *Good – she won't hear me.* He sees her figure ahead and stops running.

"Hello."

"Oh, hello, Peter."

"Been over at the main beach?"

"Yes, I'm going home."

"Saw Terrance on the beach."

He sees Celia tense and grins. Her face tells him she knows.

"Were you watching us?"

"Yes, and it's not the first time. Only, this is the first time I've watched you with someone else. Does Ritchie know?"

"What?"

"I said …"

"I heard what you said, Peter, and it's not funny."

"No, it's not, is it?"

"What do you want?"

"What I want is what Terrance wanted."

Celia gasps and takes a step back.

"You see, Mary and I did it and now she's gone. Ritchie doesn't need to know a thing about this morning. You give me what I want and I'll keep quiet. Deal?"

"I'm not going to have sex with you, you stupid little boy."

"Oh, Celia." Peter laughs. "You see, I have Jessie's camera. She left it for me. It's very good – takes videos."

Tears fall down her face. "You little prick."

"So, we got a deal then?"

"I'll tell your parents, Peter."

"I'll show Ritchie and he'll know his wife's a whore."

"Fuck you."

Peter reaches out and Celia's hand comes up fast but he is faster. He thrusts her back against the tree, jamming his leg between hers and holds her arms above her head. He is tall and he kisses her hard.

"I like it when you fight." He feels her strength but it is not enough.

"Please, Peter, don't do this. Not like this. It's wrong."

Peter jams his arm under her neck and thrusts his other hand under her top. His fingers find her breasts. She struggles fruitlessly and he feels her nipples harden. He yanks her away from the tree, slaps her cheek and she trips and falls. Her head hits the ground with a sickening thud. His desire surges and he kneels over her and bends to lick her throat while his hands pull her shirt apart. *This is easy – struggle, damn you.*

A small moan escapes her as he shoves his hand under her skirt. He fumbles with his shorts and yanks them down, entering her quickly. He brutally thrusts again and again, thinking of Mary and then he explodes and falls onto her. Panting, he gets up, brushes himself down and takes a photo.

He pulls on his shorts and steps away. He hears her retch and something in his mind snaps.

"Celia." He bends over her. "Please, Celia, I didn't mean it."

She sits extending her hand out. He bends down, but doesn't touch her. "I don't know what to say. I couldn't help it," he splutters. Tears spill from his eyes. "Please, tell me I didn't hurt you. Please," he pleads.

She looks repulsed and says nothing.

"Oh, shit, what have I done?"

Celia remains silent.

"I know you must hate me so much and I don't … I don't blame you, Celia. I truly don't, but I …"

"Be quiet, Peter." Her voice is icy. "I don't hate you as much as I hate myself."

"I can't forget Mary. It should have been me."

He sees her puzzled eyes.

"It should have. It should have. It should have got me, not Mary."

"Oh, Peter."

"I didn't help her. I couldn't … I wanted to but I couldn't."

"Oh, my God, Peter."

He hears her hate dissolving, sees the pity in her eyes.

"We're not going to talk about this again. Never! Do you understand me, Peter? Grief does horrible things to people."

He nods his head repeatedly as his hand fumbles around in his bag. "Here," he says holding the camera. "You can wipe off the video and the pictures. I haven't watched them, honest."

He thrusts the camera into her hands and she turns it on and presses trash. She hands the camera back.

"Mary will still be there when you leave. She's going to need you. The boy she liked when she was here. Go back to that boy, Peter, and forget … this."

"I will, I promise. I really do." Peter bites his nails as he watches Celia walk away. *This bloody place has changed my life forever.* Instead of making him feel wiser and independent, he feels even more like a child and wants nothing more than to be back in the safe company of his parents.

Celia arrives back at their tree house, expecting to see heads over buckets, but it is quiet and there is no one in sight. She goes inside to see all three of them lying on their beds, sleeping soundly. The air is hot, trapping the sickening smell and she pulls up the blind on the sea side to let in the breeze before going outside to suck in the clean, fresh air. She desperately wants a shower but she doesn't want company so she picks up a towel and heads for the beach. A swim in the sea will have to do.

CHAPTER TWENTY-SIX

Greg watches his follow contestants arrive for their Sunday lunch as he cooks his birds. The atmosphere between some of the teams remains uneasy. The Hendersons arrive last, with Peter dragging his heels. Greg thinks Peter looks agitated and watches him closely as Peter's eyes dart around the group nervously and then go to his feet, where he carelessly kicks the sand. *He looks like trouble and trouble is something I can do without after Karl went ape-shit at me yesterday, and Terrance didn't help.*

The words are still fresh in his mind as though he was right back in the cave with Terrance acting as though he was sick of everything.

"Sorry."

"You're sorry?" Terrance said flatly.

Oh, man, that was stupid. "Yes."

"What about?"

Greg remembered Terrance's stone-face. It made him feel small; made his lips twitch. It was a 'tick' of his, one of many.

"Well?"

Greg sucked in so much air that his lungs hurt. He began to cough, his throat felt tight and swallowing was hard. When he spoke, his voice was nothing more than a squeal.

"About Josh." Greg wished he hadn't lowered his eyes but it was as though Terrance could see through them; see his shame.

"Look at me."

No way.

"Look at me."

He sheepishly did.

"I don't get it. You and Karl wander around as if nothing has happened."

"I do not. I think about him."

He got the raised eyebrows.

"I do. I feel terrible but if I don't talk about it … it's like … like it wasn't real."

"Wasn't real? Jesus, Greg."

Terrance had looked disgusted and had stormed out. Karl returned, said he wasn't hungry and got into his sleeping bag and when Terrance finally appeared, he did the same. *Boy, did I get the silent treatment.*

He turns the birds and steals a look at Celia as she walks past. *Nice. Say hello, why don't you?* She stops next to Peter and Candice. *Interesting!* He casually moves closer and helps himself to a drink.

"How are you, Peter?"

"Fine thanks, Celia."

"Good."

Greg nods to Celia and senses her discomfort. She briskly turns and heads back to Ritchie. He sees Peter and Candice ogling him and Peter swiftly grabs the ball and runs off. Candice looks at Greg, screws up her nose and takes off after her brother.

"That Celia's very rude. Why didn't she ask me how I was?"

"Because I was with Mary, numbskull."

"Oh, I hadn't thought of that." Candice frowns. "Then that was nice of her."

Peter's gaze goes to where Terrance is talking to the Booths. A slow contemptuous smile spreads across his face as he remembers what he did earlier.

He had been out running, made it to the rocks and saw the Booths gathering oysters. He was becoming increasingly nervous over his actions with Celia and fear of her telling tormented his thoughts. He wished she wasn't around. He remained hidden, observing them putting oysters into buckets. He watched as they took a break, hearing them laughing as if without a care in the world, and as they casually lay basking in the sun, Peter's mind grew dark. He quietly made his way to their buckets, unnoticed.

"Lunch," shouts Linda, interrupting his thoughts. He whips Candice aside.

"Don't have the oysters."

"Why not? Just 'cause you don't like them, why shouldn't I have them?"

"'Cause …" Peter interrupts her, whispering in her ear, "… I might have peed in them."

"Why'd you do that?"

"People drink their urine – like on those survivor shows. I didn't think they would bring them here."

Candice gapes as Peter holds her arm tight and they stand watching the oysters being loaded onto plates.

"Peter, you have to tell Mum and Dad. Someone might get sick."

"That's the point, stupid."

"I'm going to tell Mum." Candice puckers her lips. "And don't call me stupid."

"You tell and I'll tell about you and Harvey."

"We haven't done anything."

"Yeah, well, they don't know that, do they?"

"Peter – you have to say something."

"No, it's too late now. Anyway, Mum and Dad don't like them and nothing's gonna happen. No one's even noticed."

"I don't understand why you're being so horrible," she says quietly, looking up at him.

He does not look at her. His eyes stare ahead. He lets her arm go and shoves her forward.

"I'm not. Go get some food and act normal."

"Oh, boy, you got chili in these?" asks Nigel, blinking repeatedly.

"A bit. Sorry – they're a bit spicy, aren't they?"

"Are you sure they are okay?" inquires Linda, her tongue darting over her lips.

Peter snickers. Candice's face is a mixture of worry and guilt.

"Drew is very fussy and knows his shellfish. He's not a fool."

"I didn't mean it like that, Trudy," says Linda.

"They're fine," says Drew smiling warmly.

"Taste good to me. A beer would go down well about now," says Eric licking his fingers. Jack chuckles in agreement.

Henry puts his plate down, leaving his oysters. "Five weeks gone."

"Yep, seven to go," responds Karl casually surveying the group.

"Maybe we'll end up doing that competition thing," says Mark.

"Yeah, like that survivor stuff on TV!" Peter's eyes glow under his jiggering eyebrows.

"Well, I for one, don't like that program and I certainly don't fancy some of the things they have to do."

Nigel squeezes Linda's arm.

"Yeah, could be interesting, though, couldn't it?" Karl's eyes travel again over the people around him. "Probably how this is going to pan out."

"Well, it's still a way away. Want to do another dinner?" asks Nancy.

"Suppose," says Drew lackadaisically.

"What's for entertainment this time?" snorts Jack. Rosaline elbows him. The conversation grinds to a halt. Moana suggests they do dinner that night and they decide to pack up and leave to make their preparations.

Later that afternoon, Celia is out gathering seaweed and reaches the second cove to see Moana and her sons working hard. She ambles down to say hello.

"Hi. That looks interesting, guys."

"Yeah, Mum's idea," chuckles Zach.

"Really?"

"Yes, love, we're making an umbrella."

"Matt not helping?"

"No, I sent him for a rest. He's a bit tired and I want him to enjoy himself tonight."

"Yes, he did look a little weary at lunch."

"Too much sun and too much fishing."

"Yes, probably."

"So Celia, what do you think?" asks Sammy, stepping back.

"I think your mum's awfully clever."

Moana beams. "I'm bringing it along tonight for Matt and me." She ties the last vine around the bamboo cane and gestures for the boys to raise it up.

"Well, would you look at that! It works?"

"Never any doubt, Mum," says Zach, rubbing his mother's arm.

No, I don't suppose there was, Zach. Your mum knows much more than we give her credit for.

"Did you want something, luv?"

"Oh, no, Moana," says Celia smiling. "I'm good. I'll get off. See you tonight."

Celia walks further along the beach for privacy. She goes over the dates of the month in her head as she has been doing for the last three days. She is sure her period had been due two days ago. She is never late. The day it is expected is the day she gets it. Has been that way from the day she got the damn thing twelve years ago. She tells herself that with everything that has gone on, it's probably okay. *I can't be pregnant and, if I am, it must be Ritchie's. The chances that Terrance, or – God forbid, Peter – could have impregnated me is ridiculous. I'm being an idiot to even consider it.* But consider it she does. She is beginning to make herself sick with worry. She has a quick dip and makes her way back to their shelter.

"Hey," says Ritchie, drawing her into his arms and kissing her.

She notices Trudy and Drew staring. *Come on, girl, you have to act normal.* She knows Trudy senses something amiss and stiffens when she sees her lean into Drew.

"Boy, Celia looks tense."

"Yeah, does a bit. Nothing she's talked to you about?" asks Drew, preparing the nets and containers for their trip to the waterfall.

"Nope. Poor thing must have her period."

"So?"

"So … they're trying for a baby, duh."

"Oh, yeah."

"God, Drew."

"Sorry."

"Honestly, don't you notice anything?" Trudy sighs. "I'll ask if she's okay later."

"Aye, aye, cap-it-tan."

"Idiot," laughs Trudy, swiping his bum. "I do love you, you know." Trudy reaches up on tiptoes and plonks his sun hat on as he bends down and kisses her.

"Shame we have to go. Couldn't we just …"

"Nope." Trudy hands him the containers and picks up her bag, shoving him in the direction of the waterfall.

"You're no fun."

She smiles, shoving him again. "I'll remind you of that later, shall I?"

Drew lets out a throaty laugh as they wander off, happy in each other's company.

The Tillers have been out crayfish catching and have been lucky. They have five large crayfish. Greg is boiling them up so he can make cold salads. He figures Moana or Bridget will be making one of their curries.

"Smells good, Greggy boy," says Karl, returning from a dip at the waterfall.

"Where's Terrance?"

"Oh, he's still up there with the Hendersons. Henry's not too keen on the swing and neither is Nancy, so Terrance is going on it with Candice. She's a bit shy after the other day. Peter's been nice to her. Poor kid, he's been through enough. Become very protective of Candice. Maybe something good has come out of Mary's accident, after all."

Terrance arrives back an hour later and says they should get to the beach early. He can smell Greg's cooking outside.

"Good point. Candice okay now?"

"Yep. Funny thing, though, caught Peter giving me the evil eye."

"Maybe he's still a bit jealous of you."

"Maybe."

"Hey, Greg, you want to go and see if the beach is clear?"

"Sure, Karl."

Karl and Terrance pack up and Greg comes back, saying it's good, so they take their bags and sleeping gear and Karl and Greg go back for the food, leaving Terrance to get the fire going.

The Hendersons arrive and Candice runs past, dumping her things onto the sand on her way to the water.

"Idiot," calls Peter as Candice's run turns more awkward with each step.

"It's so hot," she bellows as she reaches the water and falls face down, rolls over and rubs her feet furiously.

"What a bum," laughs Peter, walking towards her. He kicks off his flip-flops as he reaches the water and casually walks in towards Her. She shrieks and madly sweeps at the water to fend him off.

"Oh, to be young again," laughs Karl, as he and Greg arrive back.

"Yes, it's good to see them enjoying themselves." Nancy says, smiling.

"Yeah, it is. How are you?"

"We're coping."

Karl's attention focuses behind Nancy. "What the hell are they carrying?"

Nancy turns her head to see Matt, Moana, Zach and Sammy. The boys have their hands full while Matt and Moana carry something big. "It's an umbrella."

Terrance jumps up, runs over and offers to help.

"Thank you, Terrance. Can you help Matt put it in up there by those palms? Boys, get some rocks to put around it?"

"Sure, Mum. We'll just dump this lot first."

Karl wanders over. "That's smart. Who thought of it?"

"Mum did. She's amazing."

"She is."

The others arrive and set-up their belongings and, before long, cups are filled with Bridget's and Moana's drinks. Greg's cold crayfish salad is a snapped up quickly, together with the green salad

Rosaline spent the afternoon preparing. Linda's fresh fruit platter and Nancy and Candice's lemon fish compliment the curried rice dish Moana has made. Bridget and Sara's breadfruit chips are a hit. Even the oysters the Booths brought disappear quickly and as the sun begins to set they sit contentedly around the fire.

Matt is having a hard job keeping awake and decides to retire. He says goodnight and gives Moana a kiss, telling her to stay and enjoy herself, and wanders slowly up to their umbrella and his awaiting sleeping bag.

Bridget had Eric and Warren bring down several coconuts earlier from which she removed the outer Layers. She has placed them down on the harder sand with a pebble the size of a golf ball.

"Now, who's up for a game of bowls?"

"Oh, you're brilliant, Mum," says Sara. "But I don't think I will. It's so nice by the fire."

Warren and Eric decline and carry on talking to Karl, Henry and Nancy. Peter and Candice are in an argument with Mark and Nigel and Linda say they are happy just relaxing. Zach and Sammy say they're too comfortable and Moana waves them on, shaking her head in decline.

"I'll play," replies Rosaline. "Always liked marbles when I was a kid. How much harder can it be?"

Jack tips his cup, belches and gets to his feet. "Well, Roz, if you're as good as you are at tennis, then I'd say pretty hard."

Terrance shakes his head at Karl and Greg but before he can say anything Rosaline is in front of her husband. "Well, I guess that just shows what a shitty coach I had, doesn't it, darling?"

Bridget stands with her hands on her hips. "Jack, maybe you should sit down. You might have had one too many."

"Nope, I'm good." He looks at the others. "Fuck it, it's something to do," he says picking up Bridget's drink container. "Even if it's naff."

Ritchie and Drew drag Celia and Trudy down and Terrance pulls Greg up and ambles behind.

"How are we going to tell which is whose?" snorts Jack derisively.

"I've colored the tops of them," replies Bridget matter-of-factly.

"Really? Someone bring a torch, 'cause I'm having a hard time seeing your handiwork, love."

"Pay attention, Jack," replies Bridget frostily. "I'm sure you all know the rules. Bowl and the closest wins. Who wants to go first?"

"I will," says Trudy, taking the coconut closest to her. "Mine's red." She brings her arm back and slowly releases her coconut. It wobbles slowly towards the pebble and stops within half a meter of it. "Yes!" she squeals, jumping up and down.

"Trudy's a bit competitive."

"Really, Drew? Can't tell," says Terrance, smiling. He launches his coconut. It hits its mark and Trudy's coconut is bumped away.

"Oh, you bugger," says Trudy despondently, rubbing her stomach.

"Bloody hell, it's going to take all night if that's how they roll," voices Jack re-filling his cup.

"So," says Celia, handing a coconut to Drew.

Jack curtsies, spilling drink over Greg. "Whoops."

"You don't have to play."

"Oh, you'd like that, wouldn't you, Terrance? But then I'd miss out on the pleasure of beating you."

"Yeah, well you just keep drinking, Jack, 'cause you got no chance."

"My turn," cuts in Drew, launching his coconut.

"Oh, for heaven's sake, Drew."

The men burst out laughing as Trudy storms towards the water to retrieve her coconut. Annoyed with the atmosphere, Celia aims carelessly and her coconut rolls quickly past its target. Rosaline goes next. She lets her coconut go and it travels on a diagonal line down to the water. "Oh, blast."

"Ha! Told you, she's bloody useless," howls Jack, snatching a coconut. "Where's the color?" He turns it over. "Oh, here it is … pink." Jack snickers. "Hey, Greg, you want this one?"

"Knock if off."

"Ohhh, that's nice." Jack drapes his arm over Greg's shoulder. "Brotherly love and all that."

"Get off him."

"Whooh there, Goldilocks," Jack slurps back more drink. "Greggy boy's not my type."

Terrance steps forward. "I said get off him."

"Geez, calm down. Hey, Bridget, you got any chill pills in that bag of yours?"

Trudy yanks the coconut out of Jack's hand and shoves another one at him. "Look, can we just get on with the game and be civil to one another, please?"

"Green, huh," smiles Jack.

Greg, seeing his opportunity, ducks out from under Jack's hold and steps beside his brother.

Jack raises his hands. "My go." He bends and lazily takes aim. "No pressure, then." His aim is surprisingly good. He stands tall, pleased with himself and leans into Rosaline.

"You really are a jerk, Jack," she hisses before moving away.

"I do believe it's my turn," says Bridget taking careful aim. She lets her coconut slide out of her hand and along the sand. It hits the pebble and rolls it down the sand, away from Jack's coconut and towards Terrance's. Bridget gives Jack a triumphant smile as Greg takes his coconut.

"No worries here, people," murmurs Terrance.

"Oh, ha-de-ha." Greg carefully lets his go. It looks good, until it hits a shell and veers left. "That's just bloody typical."

Laughter escapes those playing and Ritchie takes aim. Dead on target, his coconut slows down and comes to a stop alongside the pebble.

"Yes." Ritchie raises a fist and turns around. "Round one to me."

"Fucking show-off," laughs Drew, shoving his brother away. "Only round you're gonna get, bro."

"You wish. I'm pretty good with my aim, aren't I, Celia?"

Celia smiles meekly and goes with Trudy and Bridget to pick up their coconuts. Rosaline follows and picks up her own.

"Hey, babe, get mine would you?" yells Jack. "I need a piss."

"Tell him to get his own, Rosaline," says Bridget seething. "He's ruining this."

"He's drunk too much."

"It's no excuse, Rosaline. If he were my husband I'll tell him where to go."

Rosaline smiles thinly. Bridget puts an arm on her back. "You know what? Let's have some fun." She gets out her pocketknife.

Celia goes first this time, with Trudy after her. Both of their coconuts stop near the pebble. Terrance is next with another good bowl.

"Awesome, bro," says Greg, as he lets his go. It bangs into Trudy's and sends it down to the water.

"Oh, for Pete's sake, not again." She goes to retrieve it before it gets waterlogged. Drew and Ritchie shake their heads while Jack eyeballs Terrance. He pushes Drew out of the way and sends his coconut rolling. It wobbles in an ungainly manner and then splits in half.

"Fucking thing."

"Must have been a second," bellows Drew, as everyone bursts into irrepressible laughter.

Jack grabs Rosaline's arm. "What did you do?"

"Nothing."

Trudy takes Rosaline's free arm. "Leave her alone."

"Piss off, woman," says Jack, his voice pitching higher as his neck muscles thicken.

"Let her go."

"I told you to piss off." Jack's hand shoves Trudy and she trips and falls flat on her stomach. Ritchie and Drew rush to help Trudy to her feet. She grabs her stomach and moans.

Jack wobbles, tries to still himself and then his smile widens. "Oh, here they are, Prince fucking Charming and Pansy to the rescue."

"Terrance, don't, I can handle him."

"Terrance, don't ... " says Jack, caustically, swaying on his feet.

"Take your hand off her and pull yourself together," says Terrance with loathing. Rosaline breaks free of Jack's grasp and Jack's face turns clown-like before he leans forward and throws up at Terrance's feet. The splattering of his vomit stops everyone.

"Oh, God, Jack," says Rosaline, near tears.

Jack rolls onto his side, moaning. Ritchie takes his cup and hands it to Rosaline. "Best leave him be – let him sleep it off."

Terrance takes Rosaline's arm and gently pulls her away. Ritchie and Drew help Trudy up and she instantly doubles over.

"Oh, Drew, my stomach hurts."

"Okay, love, we'll take you up."

"No, Drew, I mean I think I'm going to have to ..."

"Move," says Bridget coming to her side. "She's cramping."

"Ohhhh," moans Trudy. "I'm not going to make it."

Drew picks Trudy up and heads towards the fire. Ritchie and Celia follow, leaving the others standing bewildered.

Trudy's moans echo down the beach and Terrance quickly grabs Rosaline's hand.

Reaching the safety of the fire, Bridget swallows deeply. "Well, that was not the outcome I expected."

"What happened down there?"

Bridget sighs deeply. "I really have no idea to be honest, Karl."

"Oh, Mum, come and sit down. You look exhausted."

"Yes, I am, Sara. I don't think my idea was such a good one after all."

"Don't blame yourself for Jack's actions. He's been in a foul mood for days. I'm just so sorry you had to witness that."

"He's a prick, Rosaline."

"It's like he's drunk, Terrance," she sighs but doesn't look at him. "It's me he's angry with. Everything else is just in the way."

Terrance raises his eyebrows. *You mean me. Man, I don't get it. Don't do this, Rosaline; don't defend him. I know you feel this.*

Moana's voice interrupts his uncertainties. "Never mind, Bridget. It was all rather entertaining from up here, but now I think I'll go and join Matt." She yawns. "I'm feeling a little tired so I'll say goodnight." She gets up, wearily walks back to their umbrella and slowly gets into her sleeping bag. She gives Matt a quick kiss and covers him with another blanket, closes her eyes and drifts off.

Linda helps Nigel to his sleeping bag. He has a headache and as she gets him settled she notices Mark still sitting near the fire. She goes to him and feels his head. It is cool and damp. She checks her watch. 1:50 a.m. She puts her arm around him and they sit dozily, transfixed by the flames, until Mark turns and vomits. Linda helps him stand and takes him to one side, gets some water and her bag, pulls out a facecloth, dampens it and hands it to him.

Nigel stumbles over to her, holding his stomach, collapses and spills his dinner. Karl and Terrance go to help while Greg gets cups of water.

By morning, several are sick. Karl and Terrance keep the fire going while Linda and Rosaline nurse the unwell. They look up to see Moana running towards them.

"Moana, whatever's the matter?"

"It's Matt. I can't wake him up … and he's so cold."

Linda stands, sways, blinks several times to clear her head and moves as quickly as she can. Matt is on his back. Linda carefully touches his forehead, and feeling that it is indeed very cold, tries to find a pulse. Rosaline arrives and cradles Moana.

Linda places her hand under Matt's nose. She looks up at Moana and back at Matt, and although she knows he has been dead for some time, she opens Matt's mouth and checks his airway. *Good, his tongue has not flopped back.* She starts CPR. *I'll need a miracle here, Lord.* She starts pumping but after several attempts she looks at Rosaline and at Moana's desperate face and regretfully shakes her head.

Linda places Matt's hands across his chest and arranges the blankets neatly around him as tears of despair fall from her eyes. She leaves Moana with Rosaline and goes to find Sammy and Zach. She can see them in the water with Peter and Candice. She feels slightly dizzy but walks on, with a heavy heart, to deliver the sad news. She tells Peter and Candice to go and help their parents and finds she barely has the energy to talk.

"I'm so sorry, boys, but your father has … has passed away."

"Oh, no!" wails Sammy. He runs up the beach, leaving Zach open-mouthed.

"I don't understand."

"Heart attack is most likely."

"Heart attack? But he was okay. He was better than he's ever been."

Linda feels useless. She rubs his shoulder but Zach shrugs her off. His face contorts with the effort of holding back tears. "I'm going to Mum."

"Of course." She watches him trudge up the sand. Her stomach churns and she feels queasy. She makes her way to Mark and Nigel.

"Mum?"

"I'm afraid Matt died during the night. Heart attack, I think."

"Shit!"

"I have to sit down. I'm very tired."

"Yeah, you look beat. You rest, Mum. I'll feeling better so I'll look after Dad."

Peter and Candice tell their parents what they heard. Nancy informs Karl, Terrance and Greg. Rosaline walks down to them and confirms what they have been told.

"Shit, you don't think this is some tropical virus thing, do you?" asks Greg, anxiously.

"Moana thinks Matt died of a heart attack."

"Heart attack? Shit, the poor bugger," ponders Greg.

"She thinks the others are sick from something they ate."

"Yeah, that would make sense."

"Well, it's not my crayfish salad."

Karl sighs. "Did any of you have the oysters?"

"No, I didn't, Jack did though."

Terrance smirks.

"Okay, so it looks like a case of food poisoning. Better ask Linda what's best."

"She doesn't look too good, either," says Rosaline peering at Linda, huddled by the fire.

"We just need her advice on what to do."

"Okay. I'll go ask," volunteers Greg.

"I'm going to go to Moana. Zach is sick and I'm not sure how Sammy feels. She needs someone with her."

"I'll go with you, Rosaline."

"I don't think that's a good idea, Terrance."

"I don't care. Jack won't even notice, state he's in."

Before Karl can say anything Terrance takes Rosaline's hand and walks away.

"Christ, he can be reckless sometimes. Okay then, Greg, lets clear this up. Smells like shit around here."

Greg screws his nose up and picks up an empty container and starts spooning the vomit up.

"Jesus, Greg, you'll be here all day at that rate. Just scoop the container through it and dump it in the bucket and I'll go and chuck it over the rocks."

Nancy and Henry come over and offer to help while Peter and Candice sleep.

"So none of you had the oysters, then?"

"No, Greg, we didn't."

"I'll boil some water. Boiled water is better on the stomach."

"Thanks, Nancy. Henry, can you help clear this up?"

"Anything, mate."

"How are Moana and the boys?" Nancy asks.

"Not good. Terrance and Rosaline are with them."

"Poor buggers!" Henry shakes his head. "We should let off their flare soon."

"Yeah, I know, mate, but a bit longer won't hurt."

"No, of course not. Karl, it's a bit strange that so many are sick. I mean you usually get one or two bad oysters but there must have been lots to cause this."

"The Booths brought them, didn't they?"

"I'm not accusing them, Nancy. Hardly likely they'd eat something they fiddled with and end up throwing their guts out."

"Yes, of course."

"Trudy's had it the worst. Non-stop both ends. Ritchie wasn't affected and he says Drew and Celia vomited a couple of times but seem better," says Greg biting his nail.

"Poor Trudy. Do you think I should go and help Henry?"

"No. I spoke to Ritchie earlier and he thinks the worst is over. They're sleeping." Henry looks at Karl and Greg. "I'll be more watchful from now on. Thank God, Peter and Candice are okay."

"Yeah, you're lucky there. That could have been nasty."

Greg is perplexed. "So you really think someone did this then?"

Henry shrugs. "Yes. I hate to say it but it's a possibility."

"Well, it wasn't us."

"It's okay, Greg, I didn't think it was."

"Shit, perhaps these dinners are not such a good idea."

"Probably not, Greg. Then again, don't think anyone will be in a hurry to have another."

Terrance and Rosaline return to the fire. Rosaline makes no attempt to hide the steady stream of tears that are beginning to soak her top. Terrance sits her down and crouches beside her protectively. Nancy and Henry have gone to Peter and Candice to take them back to their shelter. Karl asks Greg to make a brew of tea and goes to join Terrance.

"I'm sorry, Rosaline. I know you and Moana got on well."

Rosaline nods. "She is so nice. It's just not fair. He was doing so well, was so happy," she sniffs, wiping her hand across her nose. "Sammy's really upset – Zach's trying to hold it together."

"We really do have to let off their flare."

"Yeah, they know. I'm going with Zach in a mo', Karl."

"I'll go, Terrance. You stay with Rosaline. I've checked on Jack, in case you're worried."

Rosaline looks mortified. "Oh, God, thank you, Karl. I just don't feel …"

"He'll survive. Linda checked him. She's more worried about Nigel. Thinks he may be having an allergic reaction. He's pretty bad and she's not too good either."

"Shit," Terrance looks across the fire to the huddled figures and sees Greg advancing, carrying a tray of steaming cups.

"Here you are, guys."

"Thanks, Greg."

"Not for me, buddy," says Karl standing. "Zach's coming down so I'm off. Sooner this is done the better."

Terrance and Rosaline watch the two figures diminish down the beach as the sky changes to an impressionist painting. The rising sun's yellow rays lengthen out like broken brush strokes reaching for the shimmering aqua sea.

The silence between them is awkward. Terrance wants to say something but the leap is too great. He is certain about how she feels but the certainty overwhelms him. None of it makes sense anymore.

"God, how can there be so much beauty and so much ugliness?" She stares in the direction of where Jack lies. "I should be with him."

His emotions soar. "Why?"

She rubs her forehead. "Oh, Terrance, if only things were … that easy."

Terrance stares at her. *Shit, do I say anything? Do I really want to change my life – her life?* "Do you still love him?"

Greg sits himself down and the moment is gone.

"How is Linda?" asks Rosaline quickly.

"She thinks she's over the worst."

"That's a relief."

"Yeah, I guess."

"What's on your mind, Greg?" asks Terrance in a voice that doesn't hide his annoyance.

Greg hesitates. He looks to Rosaline and back to Terrance. "I'll tell you later."

"Is it something to do with me?" asks Rosaline.

Greg's eyes plead with Terrance.

"Look, Greg, just say it." Terrance's voice deepens further.

"Well ... it's just Karl was saying ..."

"Yes?"

"Well, that he thinks it could be ..."

Greg looks squarely at Rosaline.

"Jack?" says Rosaline for him.

"And you."

"What?"

"All right, Terrance, don't get pissed. He just said that it could be a little charade of theirs. You know, get you off-side – make it look like they've got problems."

"That's ridiculous. Why would I do that?"

"Thirty million dollars."

"Piss off, Greg. Jack's a prick but she wouldn't do this."

"Okay, calm down. I didn't think she would, either. I'm just saying what was said, that's all." Greg blinks several times, looking uncomfortably guilty.

"Fuck Karl. He's so wrong."

"It's okay, Terrance. Like Greg said, it could be anyone and I guess Karl's right to wonder."

"He might be right about Jack though, mightn't he?"

"Greg, he's thrown his guts out over there," says Rosaline defensively.

"So?"

"Terrance," her voice softens. "He would have told me not to eat them."

"Fucking hell!" Terrance sneers. "You don't need to keep defending him."

"I don't!"

"Yeah, you do, actually."

Greg lifts his eyebrows. "Karl says it might appear logical to be someone that isn't sick."

"Jesus Christ, Greg! Are you saying that's what we're meant to think?"

"Yes."

"Then just say so, then."

"I did, Terrance." Greg scowls and faces Rosaline. "Anyway, you need to be careful."

"He's not going to hurt me, Greg. Like you said, he wants the money and, besides, you don't know it was him."

Terrance's eyes penetrate deep into Rosaline's. "And you don't know it's not."

She flinches. "Like I said, he won't hurt me – he wants the money."

Terrance looks away from her. "Everyone wants the money, Rosaline."

Karl and Zach return. Karl leaves Zach to let off the flare and goes to his brothers and Rosaline.

"All right?" asks Greg.

"Yeah. He's pretty cut-up but says at least his dad was happy again and that's got to be a good time to die."

"Shit!"

"Yeah, I didn't know what to say to him. Told me they don't care about leaving. Said that even if they won, what would they do with the money?"

"Shit."

"Christ, Greg – is that all you can say?"

"Sorry, it's just … you know, really sad."

"Yes, it is," says Karl, his eyes wandering from Greg to Terrance's somber face and Rosaline's strained expression.

"Should we go to him?"

"No, Greg, it's his final act on the island and he wants to be alone."

"Shit."

"He's not the only one." Terrance gets up and walks away.

"What the hell's wrong with him?"

"I think he's tired."

"Yeah, well, we're all tired, Greg. Think I'll get that cuppa now."

Greg is up like a shot. "No, I'll get it for you. Want another one myself."

"Fine." Karl sits down, smiles warily at Rosaline and rubs his eyes.

"Yeah, you rest. You look beat." Greg looks timidly at Rosaline and quickly walks away.

CHAPTER TWENTY-SEVEN

The flare lights up the mid-morning sky, tingeing it with a pinkish-fawn glow that hangs over the island like a Portobello mushroom. Several kilometers offshore the launch is completing its morning sweep and a solitary figure stands on deck.

"Shit!" Karen lowers the binoculars and goes below. John's head is immersed in a magazine. 'Madame Butterfly' plays from his phone. She sees he has not noticed her, so she lingers at the bottom step and takes a huge breath, before disturbing him.

"John?"

"Hmm?"

"There's a pink flare."

"You sure?"

She nods.

He slams the magazine shut, hits the stop button on his phone and wipes his eyes. "We were only there the other day."

"I know."

He clears his throat and takes a sip of his coffee. "Hell, must have been sitting here longer than I thought."

"Would you like a fresh cup?"

"No – but thanks. Can you go and tell Bill and Alison to be ready in five?"

"Sure." Karen squeezes John's shoulder. "It's the Davidsons isn't it?"

"Yes."

"Are you going to tell Martin?"

"I am but I don't know if he'll understand."

John feels his shoulder squeezed again and watches Karen walk down the hall. He runs his hands through his hair, stands and takes a quick look in the mirror that hangs by the entrance of the hallway. He needs sleep. His eyes are bloodshot, half-closed. He moves to the sink and splashes his face with water, inhales deeply and heads down the hall. Reaching Martin's door he knocks lightly. The door opens and Ella gestures him in. The open window does little against the heavy, death-like air. The Grim Reaper is already at work, using the trapped light to cast ghostly shadows over the motionless bed. John can hear the air being sucked into Martin's laboring lungs. His eyes go to Martin's bony chest and he is staggered by how translucent his friend's skin has become. Yellow patches stain the folds of skin under his eyes and around his shriveled lips. In this moment, John feels completely useless.

"Can he hear me?"

"I talk to him, hold his hand. Sometimes he opens his eyes."

John sniffs, clenching his teeth. "He looks so much worse than last night."

"It won't be long now."

"He should be in hospital."

"John, you know his wishes. He's dying and that isn't going to change whether he's here or there."

"I know. It's just …"

"Hard?"

John nods, bites his lip and takes his friend's hand. "Martin, it's John. The Davidsons' flare is up." Martin's eyes flicker and John feels the faintest pressure in his palm.

"I'm taking Alison and Bill. I'll be back as soon as I can." John places Martin's hand down carefully and follows Ella into the hallway. His throat feels constricted and swallowing is hard. "I'm scared to go in case …"

"I know, but you have a job to do and that's what he would want." She bites her trembling lip. "Oh, John, he won't even know us soon."

"He's a lucky man, Ella." He kisses the top of her head. She touches his cheek and he leaves her and bumps into Phil.

"John, you sure you don't want me to go?"

"No, I'm fine." John pats Phil's shoulder and they get back to find Grace sitting at the table waiting for them.

"Grace, could you see if Ella wants anything? She's worn out and won't leave him."

"Of course. How he is?"

"Bad."

"You go, John. We'll look after them."

"Thanks – talk soon, Phil."

John finds Bill and Alison waiting in the dinghy. He sits next to Alison. She places her hand on his leg. No one speaks; there is nothing to say.

Arriving at the beach they see Henry and Karl at the water's edge. Karl gives them a quick account of what has happened. The others are over the worst but Nigel doesn't seem any better. Alison goes to assess Nigel, leaving John and Bill to take care of Matt and his family.

"Moana, Sammy, Zach … we're so sorry."

"Thank you, John. It's so hard to believe."

Sammy hugs his mother.

"He was so much better, you know. His limb, his weight." Moana shakes her head. "Now he's gone."

"He loved it here," Zach bursts out.

John feels for the young man standing bravely by his mother's side, struggling to regain his composure. *Poor lad – he looks a little manic.*

"He didn't want to … leave."

Moana rubs Zach's back. Her face contorts with grief and her eyes find John's. "I … I want to thank you."

"Thank us?"

"Yes, I got my husband back. The boys got their father." She pauses, swiping the line of mucus that runs onto her lips. "It was the best time we've had for years."

John feels Bill's hand on his back, swallows hard at the lump forming in his throat and tenses his body to stop the flood of emotion wanting to escape. Then Bill is gone with Sammy and Zach to pack up their chest and get their belongings.

John gathers the remaining contestants together, tells them the now-familiar procedure and Peter raises his hand. "Excuse me Mr. Sedden, but do you know if Mary's all right?"

"Mary is doing well."

"Really?"

"Yes, she's got plenty of support."

"John, can you give her our love?" asks Nancy. "Tell her Peter is thinking of her. We all are."

Peter takes his mother's hand. John catches the smile she gives her son and he wishes he wasn't here, with these people, on Martin's island. He feels someone beside him and turns to see Alison.

"I'm certain Nigel's having an allergic reaction. Linda said he had oyster poisoning about seven months ago. He's terribly dehydrated and weak. Needs to be in hospital."

"Have you told them?"

"Yes, Mark's devastated of course."

"Bet he is. We'll get Matt, Moana and the boys back first. Bill can take Mark to get their things. I'll get Phil to come back with me. Can you stay with Nigel?"

"Of course. I'll tell them what's happening. Linda's pleased to be going. She thinks there's more to this than meets the eye."

"She said something?"

"No." Alison raises her eyes. "Isn't that always the problem?" She leaves him before he can respond and then Rosaline's voice takes his attention.

"Oh, Moana, I'm so sorry."

"Hush now, we'll be fine." Moana tucks Rosaline's hair behind her ear. "There, that's better. Don't want to hide that beautiful face of yours. Now I want you to listen to me."

Rosaline bites her lip. Her eyes lock on Moana's face.

"Money's not everything. Don't be miserable. If there's someone else, then let him know." Moana winks. "Be happy!" Moana kisses her hand and walks down to join her boys. John's and Rosaline's eyes lock.

"I feel like I've lost a mother all over again."

Embarrassed, feeling as though he has intruded their private moment, he smiles sympathetically and quickly walks away. *I don't need this. I just want to get back for Martin.* He gets into the dinghy and carefully makes his way out of the lagoon, then puts the dinghy into full throttle, heading for the launch.

He climbs aboard and is met by Phil and Ben. He can tell by their faces that he is too late. He covers his face with his hands. "Fuck, fuck, fuck."

Phil steps beside him. "Penny's with Ella. Grace is really upset … wants to be alone." He sighs. "John, hate to ask, but what's the story over there?"

John sniffs and exhales through his mouth. "It's not good, Ben, Matt's dead."

"Shit."

"Heart attack."

Ben takes a moment. "Poor bugger!"

"The Wentworths are leaving, too. Nigel's got oyster poisoning or some allergic reaction."

"Well, I'm not surprised," says Ben.

"No, guess it was bound to happen. Odd that most of them were sick."

"Really?" says Phil looking at Ben.

"Really." answers John wearily.

"Do we do anything?"

"Nothing we can do," John leans over the table. "For now, we need two stretchers, one body-bag and thermal blankets, quick as you can."

"Do you want to see Ella first? Duncan's emailed the hospital."

"No, best sort this out, leave her to grieve."

"Okay, meet you on deck in five."

It is dark by the time everyone is on the launch, fed and settled down for the night. John walks wearily to Martin's cabin. He opens the door and the warm air stops him like a wall. The room is dark. A small lamp on the bedside table casts faint light and shadows still hover over his friend's body. John notices an envelope on the table. It is marked 'Davidsons'. His hand shakes as he picks it up. Ella can't see him tonight and he respects her wishes. He puts the envelope into his jeans pocket.

He lingers by the bed. He wants to touch his friend but it doesn't seem right, so he stands weeping, looking at the face that once smiled and laughed with him. He knows there is nothing he can do so he leaves, closing the door gently behind him. His watch says ten thirty-two and he makes his way down the hall to his room. He notices light under the room Moana is in and remembers the envelope. He knocks softly, Moana opens the door and he hands it to her and carries on. Reaching his room he kicks off his shoes and collapses on his bed. He stares at the ceiling, hoping that Martin's compensation to the families that leave the contest isn't an insult to Moana and her boys. *Was Matt's life only worth ten thousand dollars? Was any of theirs?*

The next morning, John and Ben are up early making arrangements for their visitors to be transferred to the mainland. Nigel will recover in the Papeete hospital and Martin and Matt will be transferred to the hospital's small morgue, where a postmortem will be carried out. Both family members will stay in Martin's hotel and, when possible, they will all be flown back to New Zealand.

John hands Ben an envelope. "Ben, take Ella, Grace and Duncan and meet Edward at Martin's hotel. Here is a list of Martin's instructions he wishes you and Grace to carry out. Ella and Duncan will look after the medical side.

"The rest of us will stay here and make sure everything is still running according to plan. We can keep in contact by the launch radio, email or Skype. I guess you'll be gone for a week, maybe two, now that we have Matt to deal with. Keep me up-to-date, and I'll do the same. Oh, and Ben, make sure they know that we'll be paying for any funeral costs – whatever they need. Numbers to call are in their envelopes."

"Of course. Is anyone else up?"

"No, although I did hear some shuffling earlier so I'm guessing we'll have company soon."

"ETA for the boat?"

"Around eleven. Gives everyone time to get packed and have something to eat." John sits back. "Interesting – radars picked up another boat west and it looks like we have a storm brewing."

"Terrific."

"We'll go around to the east, get some shelter if it comes to anything."

"You want another coffee? You look beat."

"Thanks," replies John, putting an A4 envelope on the table for Ben. "End of an era, Ben. End of an era!"

CHAPTER TWENTY-EIGHT

Saturday morning is a scorcher. The easterly breeze blows warm and provides little relief. The sky's palette is a mix of pale blue and gray. The flag hangs limply at half-mast.

"Bloody annoying," says Bridget, fumbling with a lock on her bag. "Pass me that oil, Sara." She sprays a little into the hole and then inserts her key. Again it starts to turn but stops. "Goddamn thing!"

"Still no luck then?"

"No, Warren. Bloody thing's stubborn."

"Well, I did say it was silly with all this salty air."

"Yes, thank you, Eric." Bridget rams the key back and forth. Click. "There – done it."

"Well, that's a relief," says Eric, wiping his brow. "Now, Warren, we still going west?"

"Yep."

"Good. You two still getting fruit?"

"Yes, we said we would, didn't we?"

Eric steps back from his wife. "Think we should go," he whispers to Warren.

"Sure you still want oysters after the other day?"

"Yes, Sara."

"Geez, Dad. Just asking."

Eric looks at Bridget. "Sorry, guess we're all a bit irritable." Bridget takes no notice and he turns to Warren. "Ready?"

"Ready. See you, hon." Warren gives Sara a kiss. Eric waves to his wife, but she has her back turned and is emptying the contents of her bag. He shrugs to Sara and follows Warren.

Eric and Warren reach their destination to find the waves pounding the rocks, causing froth and spray to fly meters into the air. When it is full tide, the pools are invisible, but as the tide is still coming in, they make their way easily to the lower, bigger pools. They only have an hour before high tide so they quickly get to work.

Three-quarters of an hour pass. Warren checks his watch, looks at the advancing water and then at the sky. "Stratus clouds, looking darker by the sec."

"Yes, we may be in for a thunderstorm. Look at those ones … Cumulonimbus, wouldn't you say?"

"Appear to be building that way. Wind's westerly now, getting colder. We should make a move."

"Saw a cray down here. Might try to get that. If we get a storm, we need something to tide us over."

"Better make it quick, then."

Eric puts on his goggles, jumps in, dives down and spreads away the dancing seaweed. He unfurls a clump with his foot and then feels pressure around his lower leg. Stretching, he gets half of his head above water and quickly waves his snorkel.

"What's wrong?"

Eric points below and Warren descends, brushing apart the seaweed. What he sees is virtually unheard of, almost inconceivable. *Fuck!* He resurfaces. "Clam."

Eric closes his eyes. *Clams are notoriously hard to open.*

"What do I do?" asks Warren. His voice quavers with the absurdity of their situation. "Can I open it with our knives?"

Eric shakes his head.

"Fuck!"

Eric points to the bush.

"Find something." Warren looks left and right.

Eric points to his watch and out to sea.

"Tide."

"Eric nods.

"Goddammit! Okay, I'm going. Don't worry, I'll get something."

Warren clambers over the rocks. Glancing back, images of a hippopotamus flash before him while his heart thumps like a drum, trying to escape his tightening chest. He sniffs the air. The rain is close. "Fuck," he yells, frantically searching between rocks. "Think, you fucking idiot." He thumps his skull. "Christ there's gotta be something!" He scratches his scalp, rubs his eyes, looks around but sees nothing. "For fuck's sake, use your head." The rain starts falling. Beaten, he retraces his steps. He reaches Eric as waves begin to crash over the lower rocks.

"I'm going to get help."

Eric clutches his shoulder and squeezes. His hand is cold, shaky and Warren knows he has little time. Leaving Eric is one of the hardest things he has ever done. He moves hastily, trips and falls, smashing his knee. Wincing in pain, he curses as blood pours from the ugly cut. He takes out his knife and cuts his shorts, ripping a length of fabric big enough to tie around his knee. He limps on. Each step he takes sends pockets of pain down his leg. He refocuses and reaches the fork in the track and decides to go left, hoping he can cut across the bush where it flattens out and be on the beach in twenty minutes. He checks his watch. *Thirty-five minutes to get here – no!*

"God, help me." The bush moans and he reaches for his backpack. "Oh, fuck, you idiot," he screams at the darkening sky. He closes his eyes. *It's on the rocks!* He punches his forehead and veers off the path, heading for the beach. Fear distorts his vision as trees attack with their claw-like branches. Razor sharp leaves slice his skin, but he barely notices as the pain from his burning knee throbs with every step. He pushes himself on and makes it out of the bush. He stumbles, dazed and confused, as the wind circles him, howling like a pack of wolves. The beach is deserted and he sways as missiles of rain pelt against him. He checks his watch again. He has been gone nearly an hour. His mind goes blank and he collapses.

Terrance emerges from the bush. "Warren?

"Eric?"

"It's Terrance, mate."

Warren's mind whirls. "Oh, thank God." His body shudders with fatigue as he struggles to stand.

"Shit, your leg's a mess."

"It's not important." Warren strains with the effort to be heard above the growing storm. "Eric needs help."

Karl and Greg arrive.

"Eric's caught ... a clam. He's got ... half his head out ... of water ... At least, he did have." Warren's head hangs. "Can't open it."

"Oh, Jesus."

"Where is he, Warren?" cuts in Karl.

"Southwest ... last cove ... We can reach ..."

"Let's go."

Warren winces, sucking in breath as Karl and Terrance lift him and support him between them. Greg follows behind. When they reach the rocks they see the end of Eric's snorkel poking out of the water.

"Oh, God," whimpers Warren, sitting. He watches Karl grab his goggles and make his way down.

"It's okay," Karl shouts. "He's breathing through his snorkel." Karl dives, resurfaces and gestures to Eric that he will be right back.

Warren sees the wind whip around Karl's body, pushing against him like an unseen wall. Karl gets back to them and Warren sees the despair evident in Karl's eyes.

"No way we're going to be able to open it. He's cold – stiff," shouts Karl.

"What the hell do we do?"

"We cut his foot off," answers Terrance looking down at Warren's face. "We gotta mate. It's the only way."

Warren's head gives a small nod and Karl, Terrance and Greg leave him. They know time is against them.

A huge wave smashes over the rocks and rushes towards them, obliterating any sign of Eric. Slowly, the top of Eric's snorkel becomes visible and they rush into the pool. The sea spray stings their eyes as the wind threatens to take their hair. The sound of rain hitting the rocks deafens them, as thunder rumbles overhead. Karl takes out his knife.

"Why don't we break his leg?" shouts Greg.

"What?" yells Terrance.

"Break his leg. Then we wouldn't have to cut the bone."

Karl looks from his knife to Terrance. "Okay, Greg, you hold him."

Greg awkwardly takes hold under Eric's armpits. Karl nods to Terrance and they disappear into the swirling dark water. Another wave batters them and Eric's snorkel is taken.

Karl and Terrance's attempts to break Eric's bone are futile and in desperation they frantically slice his flesh. Blood and skin dance around them, making their plight more arduous. Karl's lungs burn and he surfaces for breath. Greg's hand touches his shoulder.

Warren watches Karl's fist slam the water just as Terrance resurfaces. He sees Greg shaking his head and Karl throw his bloodied knife onto the rocks. A wave takes it on its retreat to the sea. Warren stands and glares at Eric's lifeless body swaying eerily, trapped in its tomb. The wind battles with him and, beaten and broken, he slumps back onto the rocks and waits for the Tillers to reach him.

"Sorry, Warren," bellows Karl grabbing the two bags he sees. "Storm's getting worse; we have to go."

Warren watches Terrance tend to his leg as if it were happening to someone else. Karl takes off his t-shirt and hands it over. Terrance works quickly, removing the stained cloth. He ties Karl's t-shirt as tightly as he can, and then they are helping him up and supporting him again. Greg takes the bags and they slowly make their way back.

"What am I going to say to Bridget? To Sara?"

Warren receives no answer. They walk on as the storm intensifies around them. Flashes of lightning illuminate the bush. Trees scream as the wind whips their limbs and sends them crashing to the ground. Shivering badly and near exhaustion, they finally make it to the tree house. Bridget and Sara are inside, huddled by the fire. Bridget looks, blinks twice and rises.

"Good God, Warren, you look terrible. What on earth have you done?"

"I ..." Warren's voice fails him. "We ..."

"I'm so sorry, Bridget, Sara," cuts in Karl. "Eric's had a terrible accident. He's gone."

"Gone? I don't understand!" Bridget's eyes bulge. "Gone; gone where?"

"He's dead, Bridget," says Greg, gently.

"Oh, Mum!" cries Sara. Warren slumps and Karl and Terrance carefully sit him by the fire. Sara cradles her husband and Karl takes Bridget's hand.

"We tried everything. His foot was in a clam and with the tide – the rain – we couldn't save him."

"I don't believe it," questions Sara. "A clam? Does that even happen?"

"I think I read of one diver – his arm was caught." Warren's voice is barely audible. He puts his head in his hands. "It rarely happens. They don't just slam ..."

"God, I thought that was just a myth," says Sara aghast, furiously rubbing Warren's back.

Bridget gazes at Warren's leg. Her face pales, she wipes her eyes and clears her throat. "Let me see."

Terrance unwraps the cloth.

"Did he suffer much?" asks Bridget, her voice devoid of emotion.

Warren winces as the air finds its way into his wound.

"I don't think so," answers Greg. "He was so cold – barely conscious."

"Drowned, then?"

"Yes, Bridget," says Karl compassionately, sending a silent message to Terrance and Greg.

"Poor Dad." Sara no longer holds back her grief and Warren pulls her into him.

"It's getting very wet in here," says Bridget to no one in particular.

"Come with us," says Terrance. "If this rain keeps up, this place is going to be drenched. Pack up the stuff you need. You can stay with us till we can let off your flare."

"But what about Dad? He's out there alone ... We can't just leave him?"

"Sara, he's dead." Bridget's eyes pool and she rises and walks over to their chest. "Thank you, Terrance, appreciate it." She starts to gather their possessions, moving unemotionally around their shelter. Greg pinches his nose and clenches his teeth. Karl pats him on the back and nods for help with the chest.

"Your mum's right, darling. Gather up our stuff. Take the sleeping bags, rugs."

Nodding, Sara gives her husband a heartbroken smile.

Warren squeezes her hand. "Put what you can in the chest, Sara."

"Won't be needing any of these," says Bridget picking up Eric's clothes.

"Oh, Mum." Sara unfolds herself from Warren and moves to her mother.

"Don't, Sara. I'm fine. If you do that, you really will start me off. Warren, is there anything here you might like?"

"Oh, I don't think I could Bridget."

"No, of course not. Sorry ... I wasn't thinking."

"Bridget? Is there anything of Eric's – something personal?"

"Yes ... his watch. Oh, God, he's probably wearing it."

No one speaks.

"Then no, there's nothing."

"Okay. We should make a move. Greg, can you and Sara help Warren? Terrance and I will take the chest and these bags. Bridget, can you manage your bag?"

"I was so offish with him this morning."

Sara squeezes her mother's hand. Bridget flinches, brushing her off, and picks up her bag. They leave the tree house for the last time. Their silence makes the rain heavier, the light darker. They decide to head towards the beach to make walking easier but find they are too exposed. They trek back into the bush. The trees talk to one another, screaming as the wind re-shapes them.

"Blimey, how much further are you?"

"Actually, Sara, we're nearly there."

"Really? You must be well covered."

Greg winks. "You could say that, Warren."

They carry on, battling the storm to reach the end of the

beach. Taking them around the back of the cliff, Karl stops and pulls back a clump of overhanging foliage. Bridget and Sara gasp.

Warren shakes his head. "Shit – a goddamn tunnel!"

"Yep!" says Terrance, as Karl leads them down to their cavern. Their fire is still glowing and Karl piles dry grass on it, until it is radiating enough warmth to ease their shivering. They sit, drawing in the much-needed heat. The silence between them is heavy, full of misery. Greg picks himself up and attends to the pot over the fire. The pheasant they caught yesterday simmers away with vegetables in a watery gravy. It has been cooking while they were out and is almost ready. He washes some rice and puts it on to boil and then busies himself cutting up coriander. A task that takes longer than it should.

Terrance rests his hand on his brother's shoulder. "I'll get bowls, Greg."

"I can get them, Terrance."

"No problem, you carry on there."

Greg continues to chop the coriander, his knife slicing with a life of its own.

"Greg, that's enough mate. It's kind of irritating."

"Sorry." Greg puts down the knife.

"I'll get our bowls, shall I?" Bridget says, uncomfortably loudly. She marches briskly to her bag, fumbles around and takes out four bowls. She strides over to Greg and lays them out. She picks one up and throws it as far as she can across the cavern.

No one moves. She lets out a big sigh and then clasps Greg's arm.

"You've cut your arm, Greg."

"Oh, that. Yeah, must have scraped it on the rocks."

"Let me see."

"I'm fine, Bridget."

"Let me see."

Greg turns his arm and Bridget's fingers lightly touch his skin. He winces.

"Terrance, get me a lemon, please."

"Really, Bridget, it's fine."

"Terrance, a lemon."

Terrance hands her a lemon and she takes the knife and cuts it in two. She squeezes one half over Greg's upturned arm, letting the juice drip onto his cut. Greg instantly pulls his arm back."

"Don't be such a baby," says Bridget, harshly.

"Mum!"

Bridget stops. She takes Greg's hand and closes her eyes. "I'm sorry, Greg. I didn't mean that."

"It's okay."

"I'll go and sit down. Did I give you those bowls?"

"Yes."

She turns and wearily walks to the fire.

Greg glances at Terrance standing apprehensively next to him, as he tentatively fills up a bowl and hands it to his brother. Terrance silently takes the bowl to Bridget and returns for the others. Greg removes the pot from the fire and goes to join them.

"Tuck in," says Greg, handing Karl his bowl.

"This is good," says Sara, softly.

"Love my meat," chirps Greg. "No way could I be a vege."

"Oh, God, me, neither, Greg," Sara swallows quickly. "Ironic, isn't it, that we're supposed to think it's healthy but honestly, some of them are the most anemic looking people I've ever seen."

"Hey, Karl," says Terrance, chuckling. "Remember those two you worked with years ago, who were into the lifestyle thing. They only ate vegetables, took all those pills. Shit, they looked like death warmed up. Really, really pale – and so skinny."

Karl twirls his fork. "Made you wonder what planet they were on."

"Yeah, they were strange, all right."

Greg snorts, laughing. "Yeah, and Karl, remember when Catherine – was that her name? Anyway she gave you that herbal tea when you said you had a funny tummy."

"Upset stomach."

"Yeah, whatever … But 'member she said it would cure you?"

"Cure me! It fucking well nearly killed me," chortles Karl.

"Yeah, yeah, I remember having to go and pick you up 'cause you couldn't leave. Oh, man, that was so bad."

"I don't know how the others stayed in the building," snickers Terrance.

Warren laughs.

"Yeah, yeah, and then …" Greg roars. "Then you just left it for someone else to deal with."

"Okay Greg, calm down. I was on a toilet and …" Karl smiles, "… I have learned to flush."

Terrance erupts. "Fat lot of good that would have done!"

Sara and Warren exchange amused looks. Bridget smiles appreciatively.

"Surprised you went back there," roars Greg, holding his stomach.

Karl snickers. "Small minds and all that, Greggy boy. Now, make yourself useful and get us some more stew."

With their bowls refilled, they sit eating while listening to the storm hammer the cave walls. The water starts to pour in from the cavern's opening, bringing with it torn leaves and broken twigs.

"Don't worry, this happened before," smiles Karl. "We'll be fine."

The next morning is no different. The rain and wind constantly batter the island, lowering the temperature. The waterfall is cascading heavily, causing the pool to overflow and the stream to rise quickly. It has burst its banks in several places, turning the ground to mush. The birds have retreated into the safety of the tree canopies further inland and the insects and rodents have found cover in tree trunks and rocks.

Karl returns from the tunnel. "Sorry, Bridget, no point in letting off your flare. I doubt they could make it here."

"Of course, Karl. It's just awful knowing he's still out there."

"Promise the first signs of this letting up, we'll let it off." Karl rubs his hands and helps himself to another coffee. "Anyone want another?"

"Yes, please, Karl," says Warren, while Bridget and Sara attend to his knee.

"Looking a bit better this morning," says Bridget. "Probably should have it stitched when we get back. Will leave a nasty scar."

Karl hands Warren his coffee. "So, what do you guys do on days like this?"

"Well, Greg usually cooks up something that takes half a day. We sleep – make things. Have a couple of magazines, if you want a read."

"Thanks."

Bridget gets up and opens her bag. "I've just the thing."

"Oh, Mum," says Sara, sympathetically.

Terrance's eyebrows rise. "You brought Monopoly?"

Bridget sits down and runs her hand over the board. "This is the first present I ever gave Eric." She inhales deeply. "We played it all the time. Said he imaged he was rich." She looks at Sara. "Didn't he, Sara?"

"Yes, but we don't have to play it now, Mum."

"Why not? He would want us to and there's nothing else to do, is there?" Bridget's tone is sharp, emotional.

"Great idea," says Karl opening up the box.

"You know this could take all day?" chips in Greg.

"I think that's the point, Greg," says Terrance, lying on his side, elbow propped in the sand. "Haven't played since I was a kid. 'Member Dad hated it because it took so long. Had some pretty good arguments."

"Yeah, that was because Greg cheats."

"I do not, Karl. You can talk: You're so competitive."

"Ha! You're so full of shit, Greg. Now, listen up, guys, keep your eyes peeled. He's a slimy bugger."

"He's joking," says Greg uncomfortably.

Terrance places his money in a stack. "Boy, this is going to be fun."

"You shouldn't do that, Terrance," states Greg, placing his money into different piles. "How can you tell what you have?"

"Duh – that's the whole point, Greg."

Sara and Warren glance at Bridget.

"I'll go first?" says Greg looking round.

"Yeah, whatever, Greg, just get a move on," replies Terrance.

Greg takes the dice and puts them in his cup.

"Greg, just roll the dice."

"I am."

"Fucking hell, if you're going to take this long, we'll never even get round the block."

"Oh, very funny, Karl." The dice roll out. "Yes!" Greg squeals, causing Sara and Bridget to smile.

"Typical," laughs Karl.

Greg moves forward. He picks up the dice and rolls again. Two fives. He moves and rolls again. Two threes.

"Ha!" says Karl. "You're in jail."

"No, I'm not. You can't go to jail on the first go, everyone knows that!"

"Fuck off, you can so. You rolled three doubles, you're in jail." Karl snickers, picks up Greg's iron and places it down.

"Put that back."

"Yep, it's all coming back to me now," says Terrance scratching his ear.

"But … I'm right, aren't I, guys?" asks Greg, looking at Bridget, Sara and Bill.

"To be honest, Greg, I think you do have to go. We've always played that if you throw three doubles, you go to jail." Bridget says, empathetically.

"See, in you go." Karl chuckles as Greg's face glows with indignation.

"Nothing like a game of Monopoly to bring out the best in people," says Terrance, sarcastically.

CHAPTER TWENTY-NINE

The following morning dawns with no rain and very little wind. The sun peeps through the lingering clouds. The air is muggy and pockets of steam rise from the black rocks, giving the island a ghostly appearance. Terrance watches the sky darken over the lagoon. Earlier he released the Booths' flare and his thoughts turn to Rosaline.

"Oh, I'm sorry. I didn't know you were here."

He smiles quietly at the woman before him. "That's okay."

"You lit it, then?"

She looks utterly miserable and he lowers his eyes. "I did."

"It's quite pretty, really."

He says nothing.

"Do you think they'll be long?"

"Hard to say. Depends where they are."

"Of course." Sara clears her throat. "Was it bad, Terrance?"

His eyes shut. *No, not this!*

"Please, I need to know." Her voice pleads and he looks into her sorrowful, puffy, blood-shot eyes.

"Yes."

She bites her quivering lip.

"Not for your Dad. He wouldn't have felt much."

"Honestly?"

"Honestly."

She nods quickly. Her body shudders and he takes her in his arms. She sobs into his chest and his hand strokes her hair. They stay like this till she regains her composure. She washes her face in the closest pool.

"It's just so hard to believe."

"I know." He stands behind her, eyes locked on the reflection staring back at him.

"I don't want Mum to see him." Her voice is small, lost.

"I'll make sure she doesn't."

She stands, raises her heels and kisses him gently on his cheek. He feels her misery sink into his skin but before he can speak, she is walking back to the tunnel.

His thoughts return to Rosaline as he makes his way over the slippery rocks to wait for John. The urge to find Rosaline is great, but he wills himself to sit. He can feel the heat from the sun starting to burn his bare skin, but today it feels right.

He doesn't know how long he has been sitting before he sees Karl wandering down carrying his shirt and sunglasses. "Any lotion?"

"Sorry."

"Hat?"

"Nope."

They share a private laugh and wait together for what seems like hours before the dinghy enters the lagoon. They don't move as John, Bill and Alison get out and stride towards them.

"Did the Longs let off their flare?"

"Yes," answers Karl. "They're with us. Eric's dead."

"The storm?" inquires Bill.

"Sort of." Karl's voice matches his solemn face. "He got his leg jammed in a clam. Couldn't budge it. Tried to cut his foot off but it was too late."

"Oh shit. Where is he now?"

"Still there; weather closed in fast."

"Christ!" John bites his gum. "How's the family?"

"Okay, I guess. Warren's hurt his knee."

"John," intervenes Terrance. "I don't think it would be good for them to see Eric. He's been in there for a day and a half and we kind of made a mess of his leg."

"Right, we'll take them back first – come back for Eric. We have a hacksaw on board so we'll bring it back. Have you managed to get their things?"

"Pretty much."

"Good. Better take us to them."

The five of them make their way into the cave. John tells Bridget, Sara and Warren how sorry they are, while Alison attends to Warren's leg.

"Nasty cut. Can't see any infection, though."

"Good." John turns to Bill. "So, we need to get the rest of the items that came in your chest."

"Karl or I can go. We know where their hut is," intervenes Terrance.

"John, why don't you and Alison take the Longs back to the launch and get what we need. I'll stay and get the chest ready."

"Makes sense, Bill. I'll radio Ben, tell him what's happened and ask when they're coming back."

"Okay. Terrance, you ready?"

"Sure." Terrance goes to Warren and shakes his hand and gives Sara and Bridget a small hug, then disappears down the tunnel with Bill. Karl and Greg help John and Alison get the Longs' belongings packed.

"Thank you," says Bridget. She picks up the Monopoly game and looks at Greg. "I don't want this anymore."

"Are you sure?"

"Positive – it would only remind me of our time here and I don't want that."

"But Dad loved that, Mum. You may regret leaving it."

Bridget's hand shakes. "No, Sara. I don't want it. It was his. I shan't want to play it again."

"I'll look after it, Bridget."

"I know you will. Now, I think I might go outside. I want some time alone before we go."

"Of course, Bridget. Have you got everything?"

"Yes, thank you, John." Bridget takes Karl's hand. "Thank you for everything." She smiles, stoops to pick up her hat and marches down the tunnel.

After packing what they need, Karl and John support Warren, and Sara and Alison bring their bags down to the beach. They get Warren and Sara and their gear into the dinghy as Bridget walks over. She gives Karl's and Greg's hands a squeeze and climbs on board. John takes them through the lagoon for the last time. Karl, Greg and Alison sit and wait for Terrance and Bill, who arrive minutes later, carrying the chest between them. Half an hour later, the dinghy speeds across the lagoon and John beaches it beside them.

"How far can we take the dinghy?"

"Should be able to make it to the west of the second cove, John. It's pretty close."

"Will need one of you to show us where he is."

"I'll go."

"Thanks, Karl. Alison, you better stay."

"Of course, John."

"See you soon." John, Bill and Karl depart and soon vanish behind the small cliff dividing the beach from the next cove. Terrance, Greg and Alison sit patiently, letting the water lap at their feet. Alison hands Terrance some sunscreen. "You're beginning to look like a lobster."

"Thanks. We should move under the palms." He rubs his face and arms. They sting and he curses. They move up the beach and Terrance hands the lotion to Greg, who is constantly checking his watch.

"Three-quarters of an hour. Maybe we should head over."

"We'll wait another fifteen minutes, Greg," replies Alison, stretching her legs. She stands and they hear the dinghy's motor. Terrance and Greg lift the chest and follow Alison down. John keeps the motor running and Karl jumps out, takes the chest from Greg and they get it on board. Alison gets in and John reverses the dinghy and within minutes they are gone.

"Well, glad that's over."

"I don't want to know, Karl."

"What a mess his leg was. Was bloated up like ..."

"Karl, I said I don't want to know," shouts Greg.

"Oh, man-up, Greg."

"Knock it off, you two," huffs Terrance. "I'm going for a dip."

"Good idea, Terrance," says Karl, dismissing his brother's attitude. "Hey, it's only us, the Hendersons, Jack and Rosaline and the Booths left now. How many more weeks, Greg?"

"'Bout four. You should keep track." Greg storms down to the water.

"You shouldn't go on at him, Karl."

"He knows I don't really mean it."

"Even so, he deserves some respect."

Karl's arm finds Terrance's shoulder. "Yeah, he does." They walk into the water and join Greg. The three of them float together in silence and then decide to head up under the palms to dry off. Within minutes, the roar of an engine has Greg standing.

"Hey, guys, the dinghy's back!"

"No way." Terrance stands.

"Oh, Christ, what now?" shouts Karl jumping up. The brothers walk down the beach. John stops the motor and he, Bill and Alison jump out.

"Quick," yells John. "Help us get this out of sight."

"Why have you still got Eric?"

"Pirates."

"Pirates?" questions Greg. "What do you mean, pirates?"

"I mean we've been visited by pirates. Could be on their way here. Shit, you had a fire over there?"

"Yeah, so?"

"Cover it with sand. Want it looking as if no one's here."

Covering the fire as best they can, Terrance and Alison join Karl, John, Greg and Bill just as they are attempting to put the dinghy into the tunnel. They manage to squeeze it in sideways, leaving Eric's body jammed against the wall.

"Where are the others?"

"Jack and Rosaline are not far."

"Can you get to them under cover?"

"Yes."

"One of you go with Bill and bring them here."

"I'll go," says Terrance quickly. He and Bill leave the tunnel and run along the track to the waterfall.

"Is this bad?" asks Terrance.

"Could be," replies Bill. "We noticed their boat alongside ours, and Johns been trying to radio. Don't know the state of the launch or if they're okay?"

"Shit."

"If they're on board when we radioed, they'll have heard … Could be looking for us."

"Jesus." Terrance stops Bill. "That's their shelter."

Bill runs and bangs on the door. It opens slowly.

"Jack is Rosaline with you?"

Jack's eyes settle on Terrance. "She's in our bed."

"Good. Pack your bags, you're coming with us. Move fast, we have to get out of here."

"What's he doing with you?"

"He knew where you where. I'll explain later."

"Explain now."

"We came to take the Longs back and ..."

"What's happened to the Longs?"

"Eric's dead. He got caught in a clam."

"A clam?"

"Jesus, Jack, he said he'll tell you later."

"I'm talking to Bill. What fucking idiot gets caught in a clam?"

"Jack," says Bill harshly. "We've spotted pirates, so get your wife and grab some things."

Jack eyeballs Bill. He scrunches his nose. "You serious?"

"Deadly!"

"Need any help?"

Jack looks at Terrance. "No, thanks." He retreats into the shelter, leaving Bill and Terrance waiting anxiously. Rosaline comes out with a small bag.

"What's this about?"

"All I can tell you is that there are pirates in the area. We need to get you safe. Terrance has the perfect place."

"Of course he does." Jack looks at Terrance with a grin that stretches his top lip flush across his teeth. Bill starts making his way back.

"Ever thought of going for the role of The Joker?" scoffs Terrance.

"Only if you play Batman," sneers Jack right back at him.

Rosaline steps past them and catches up to Bill. Jack steps in front of Terrance. *Fucking bastard!* His eyes go to his wife. He saw the relief on her face when she saw Terrance and caught whatever that was on Terrance's face. *They definitely have something going on.* He glares at the back of his wife as she hesitantly walks in front. *Think I didn't notice you helping him and that pain of a woman Moana, instead of me. Hanging around her and that prick like a bad smell while I was puking my guts out. What sort of a wife does that? Well, fuck you, Rosaline. You agreed to come here. You're my wife and there's no fucking way I'm letting you and that bastard get together.*

His eyes travel down her body. *Still sexy as hell!* He wanted to knock her down and take her, kicking and screaming, until she was begging for it. *Wouldn't be me she'd be wanting. It would be that son-of-a-bitch.*

Spitting, he tries to rid himself of the bilious taste forming in his mouth. He smirks. *Why the hell is Bill ferreting around like a lost boy?*

"Something amusing you, Jack?"

"Just you, Terrance." He hears Rosaline's sigh and leans in close. "Don't do that, darling. It doesn't become you." He smiles at the hurt in her eyes and puts his arm around her shoulders. She flinches but doesn't move away. He knows it is not because she doesn't want to. *Don't want things getting nasty. Oh no, can't have that!* His anger deepens.

Bill signals to Terrance and he moves right and pushes back the foliage and disappears.

"Well I'll be … This really is Peter Pan stuff."

"Quiet, Jack." Bill ushers them in past the dinghy and they walk down the tunnel. Bill calls John's name and they emerge into the cavern to see John, Alison, Karl and Greg.

"This is very cozy."

"Jack!"

John pays no attention. "The Longs have left because Eric has unfortunately died."

Rosaline gasps.

"Oh, yeah, the clam story."

"It is no story, Jack. When we went back to the launch with Eric we saw another boat. Probably pirates."

"Oh, my God!"

"It's okay, Rosaline – for now anyway. We don't think they saw us."

"But you can't be sure."

"No, we can't."

"You said you had Eric?"

"Yes. He's still in the dinghy."

Rosaline gasps again.

"What ... He's up there in the tunnel?"

"Yes, Jack, we know it's not ideal but ..."

"Jesus! And what – we're supposed to believe all this – first a clam, now pirates?"

"We were there," intervenes Terrance. "We tried to save Eric but we couldn't."

"Is that right."

"Jack, stop it!"

"Why? I'm sick of you taking his side."

"Don't be ridiculous."

"I'm not a fool, woman."

"That's enough," cuts in John. "I don't know what's going on here but you believing us or not isn't our concern. You're free to leave anytime."

"I'm so sorry, John." Rosaline turns to her husband.

"She wouldn't dream of leaving now, would you?"

"Look," John's voice is harsh. "If we want to get out of this in one piece I suggest you put your differences aside for the time being. I personally couldn't give a fuck who's fucking whom, but I want to survive today and so do my friends, so if you're going to make this any harder then you can piss off right now."

Jack looks at John. His eyes blink repeatedly as his fingers rub his chin. "Well, if you're going to be like that John, then I guess I have to believe you. Won't get any trouble out of me, mate."

"Terrance?"

Terrance nods his head. His eyes never leave Jack's face.

"Good."

"John?"

"Yes, Rosaline?"

"What about Sara, Warren and Bridget?"

John swirls his tongue over his teeth. "I – we don't know. I won't lie to you. Pirates are mercenaries. They pillage, rape or worse."

"Worse?" interrupts Rosaline, "What could be worse?"

Jack looks at his wife. A small hiss escapes his lips. "Never was the brightest spark, were you, Roz?" He watches her face drain of color. She looks small, frightened; somehow needy. He moves closer but Alison steps between them.

"That's not going to happen."

"Pardon me, love, if I'm not convinced. So, John, I take it you have a plan?"

"John, we have to get the other families," intervenes Bill.

"Yes, of course."

"The Booths are just back off the main beach, in a banyan tree. I'll go."

"Karl, wait. No one's going alone. Jack?"

"Fine."

"Good – take your spears. Where are the Hendersons?"

"Further round, we think. I'll go."

"Thanks, Terrance. Alison and Bill, stay here with Greg and Rosaline. Bill, keep watch on the tunnel. They can't get to that sea-side one and you can easily see if someone tries to enter through the small one."

"You have to crawl through there."

"Perfect. Thanks, Greg."

"Right, everyone be careful and be quick. Keep hidden – don't take risks."

They depart down the tunnel, make their way into the bush and reach the track. Jack and Karl go left and Terrance and John continue right to the smaller coves.

Jack and Karl reach the Booths' tree house and crouch in the shrubbery.

"Everything looks okay."

"Best wait a bit."

"If you think so, Karl." *Can't remember who made you boss, but I've no bone to pick with you and waiting isn't such a dumb idea.*

"Grass is trodden flat in the front of their shelter, but it's thick to the right. Obviously no one's been there," whispers Karl.

Twigs and small logs are stacked up against the base of the tree and they can see rope hanging to the left, inside the barrier of roots that hang down like arms, reaching for the ground. They smell smoke.

Karl taps Jack's arm and they creep forward and reach the entrance. Karl knocks quietly and Ritchie appears before him.

"Mate," Karl whispers. "John sent us to get you. They think pirates might be here. You need to grab your stuff and come with us. Everyone here?"

"Celia is, but Drew and Trudy went to the waterfall."

"Shit, how long ago?"

"'Bout an hour."

"I'll go," says Jack.

"No! We do what John said. We might run into them on the track. If not, then we'll head up."

"What if they come back via the beach?"

"Bill's keeping a look out, Ritchie. Come on, we'll help you pack. John said bring everything."

The four of them hurriedly stuff whatever they can into any bag they can carry. Karl and Jack find most of the items that came in the chest. Karl then tears down the screens and kicks the walls, leaving gaping holes. Jack uses his spear and rips parts of the roof so that it hangs suspended.

"Right, that'll do. We need to move."

Ritchie nods, throwing water over the fire. Karl kicks dirt and leaves over the pit to kill the smoke.

"We'd better go," says Karl, taking the lead with Jack as they carry the chest between them. Celia follows behind, struggling to hold the two bags she has and Ritchie follows at the back, knife tied to his leg in case they hit trouble. They arrive at the cave and enter, having seen no sign of Drew and Trudy.

"I'll go," volunteers Karl.

"Look, I should be going to get my brother, man," says Ritchie, agitated.

"No, Ritchie, I want you to stay here."

"Celia, I have to go."

"Celia's right, Ritchie," says John, stepping in. "You need to stay with her. Greg, can you go?"

"I guess."

"Okay, bro, come on."

Karl looks at John. John nods and hands Karl a revolver. Karl tucks it into his belt, hidden by his t-shirt.

Bill and Terrance make it to the Hendersons' but the shelter is empty.

"Fuck. Where the hell are they?"

"I dunno. Oh, hell, they might be at the fruit trees. I'll go."

"No, Terrance, we stick together."

"Bill, we don't have time. It's not far. I'll be careful."

"All right. I'll rough this up a bit. If I see anything I'm not hanging around."

"Fair enough."

Bill watches Terrance disappear into the bush. He madly stuffs anything he can into bags. He rolls up the sleeping bags and puts them into the chest with a couple of rugs. He tears down some of the blinds Nancy has carefully made and leaves some hanging, ripped and broken. He throws plant debris inside. He scans the area and checks his watch. Terrance has been gone for over half an hour. He hears something snap and his hand goes to his gun.

Terrance breaks through the foliage. "No sign."

They load the bags on their backs and carry the chest between them. Every few meters they stop and listen. Making it to the second cove, Bill goes ahead to check the beach. He carefully steps his way towards the exposed palms and brings the binoculars up to his eyes. He scans the sea. It appears clear. He rubs his eyes and takes another quick sweep. He freezes. He sees a boat appear from behind the cliff that separates the two coves. He lowers the binoculars and withdraws back into the bush.

"We have to move. There's a boat outside the lagoon."

"Jesus. How big?"

"What?"

"How big's the boat?"

"I don't know! I didn't wait around to measure it."

Terrance's mind races like a go-cart. *Shit. Are they like they are in the movies, with machine guns and God knows what else? Drug traffickers, gun smugglers, it doesn't matter … They don't seem to have any morals whatsoever. Fuck, if we're caught our best hope is death.* He pictures Rosaline and begins to feel sick. He must make it back.

"Stop!" says Bill. "Quiet."

They step off the track and crouch in the cover of the trees. A solitary figure appears before them.

"Fuck – it's Karl," mumbles Terrance.

"You alone?" asks Bill, his eyes scanning the area.

"Yeah, came to get you. We've got company."

"We know. Here, help us with this lot. Couldn't find the Hendersons."

"They're safe. Were up at the waterfall but Drew and Trudy weren't."

"Damn. We'll see what John wants to do when we get this lot back."

The three of them navigate the track less cautiously. They know it won't take much time for the boat to get to the lagoon. They re-enter the cave and Celia runs to them.

"Sorry, Celia, no sign of them."

Karl turns to John. "We have to go back to their shelter."

Nancy and Henry hold Peter and Candice close. Celia throws her arms around Ritchie, sobbing.

"Babe, I have to go. I'll find them, bring them back."

"No, you can't. It's too dangerous."

"I have to, Celia, he's my brother."

The mood in the cavern darkens as Celia untangles herself, wraps her arms around her torso and stares at her husband coldly. Her silence hangs heavily between the two of them like an invisible barrier, trapping their feelings.

"I'll be fine, promise. You'll be safe with John and Bill."

Celia looks away as Rosaline puts a caring hand on her arm.

"I'm coming," says John, taking out his revolver.

Ritchie's fingers lift Celia's head. "Love you," He kisses her tenderly and she wraps herself into him. He disentangles himself and Rosaline takes hold of her as he grabs a spear and follows Karl and John into the tunnel. They leave the chilling sound of Celia's moans and make their way along the track, stopping when they reach the beach. John edges down to see if the boat is in sight. It is anchored in the lagoon and a dinghy is up on the sand. He crawls back and tells them what he's seen. They move on in silence.

Drew and Trudy arrive back at their shelter, exhausted and hot.

"What the fuck?"

Trudy can't believe her eyes. "Where's our stuff? And where's Ritchie and Celia?"

Drew shakes his head.

"Drew, this is strange. I mean, really strange."

Drew moves to the window and Trudy screams. Three men stand in the doorway loaded with machine guns and knives. Their skin is as black as night and Drew's mouth opens in disbelief and he inches closer to Trudy.

"Stay where ya are!" says the one in front. "Any more of ya?"

Drew shakes his head.

"Ya messing with us?"

"No, it's just us."

"Whot ya been doing here, den?" says the same man.

"We look after the island," says Drew.

"Don't have much stuff."

Drew stares straight at him. "Day trip."

The men stare with their cold, metallic eyes.

"Dat your launch out there?"

Drew's eyes dart to Trudy.

"Yes," she says quickly.

"Whot ya name?"

"Trudy," she says, screwing up her face.

"Trudy, huh, dat true?" Trudy nods frantically. One man slowly moves towards her. "Ya?" He points his gun under her chin, lifting her head so she is forced to look him in the eyes. She gives the faintest nod.

"Lost ya voice, bootaful?" He smiles a sickening grin. She recoils as his breath hits her nostrils, making her retch.

"Don't!" calls out Drew.

"Don't! Don't! Oh, man, I'll do whot I like. Don't say another word, asshole."

Trudy looks at Drew with begging eyes.

"So, Trudy, whot ya do for fun round here den?"

"Noth ... nothing." She darts her eyes over the two silent men behind him and tears pool, as her lip begins to quiver uncontrollably.

"Nothing! Well we can fix dat. Bit of fun, sound good, Trudy," he says bringing his hand up. He yanks her band from her hair. "Nice," he says, licking his lips. "Trudy – take dat top off. Ya sweating."

Trudy's hands shake wildly as her fingers try to grasp a button. Her assailant grins and licks his knife.

"Leave her alone!" shouts Drew. A deafening buzzing sound fills the air and Drew's knee explodes like an over-ripe tomato. He screams and falls to the floor, rolling to his side. His hands clutch at his leg and instantly turn crimson. His eyes bulge grotesquely as he gapes at the saliva dripping from Trudy's open mouth.

"Now ... dat ... was ... stupid ... asshole."

Terrified, Trudy starts to wail. Her arm is grabbed and she looks to Drew. He tries to come to her but his leg holds him back. He reaches out and the man holding her laughs.

"Please," Drew's voice is strained. "Leave ..."

The man grins, revealing his tobacco-stained teeth. "I taught I told ya to shut up, asshole. Hey, didn't I tell him ta shut up?"

"Ya did!" says one of his mates.

"Then ya were warned." He steps forward, raises a pistol, fires and hits Drew between the eyes. Trudy screams.

"Fuck!' says John. "Get down, get down."

They crouch behind trees, as the screaming intensifies.

"That's Trudy." Ritchie jumps up, but Karl grabs him, holding him still.

"Don't be an idiot. We don't know how many there are."

"Drew's in there?"

"Quiet. I'm going to take a look, see what the situation is." John moves like a ghost to the side window and peers in. He sees Drew and his eyes travel quickly to Trudy. She lies on the floor. A knife picks off the buttons of her shirt. He notes the other two men near the door, guns ready at their chests. He silently drops to the ground and heads back.

"Drew's been shot."

Karl holds Ritchie firm.

John continues. "There's three of them. Saw machine guns – knives. Two at the door and one of them is …" He looks at Ritchie. "Undressing Trudy."

Ritchie struggles against Karl. John clasps his hand on Ritchie's chin.

"Listen, Ritchie," his voice is stern, steady. "They don't know we're here. When we go," he waits for Ritchie's full attention, "… it will be our only chance."

Ritchie nods. "What can we do against machine guns?"

"Use our brains." John releases his hand. "Karl, you don't have to do this."

"He's right, Karl. Get back to your brothers."

"I'm staying." Karl squeezes Ritchie's shoulder. "If I don't make it, then so be it."

"Positive?"

"Yes, John. Couldn't save Josh but might be able to save them."

Ritchie frowns. "Of course, you couldn't save Josh."

"I'm staying." Karl glimpses John's questioning eyes. "What's the plan, John?"

"Karl, you get to the window. I've got a gun, so Ritchie and I will make our way to the door. Signal us when to go in."

"Okay."

Ritchie, how good are you with that spear?"

"Guess we'll find out."

Karl reaches into his pocket and pulls out a slingshot. "I'm pretty handy with this." *Oh, shit. Why did I bring up Josh?"*

John frowns and then breaks his gaze. "Ritchie, ready?"

"Ready."

"All right – quiet."

The bush is silent apart from the wind rustling the trees and they move vigilantly forward. Karl reaches the window and waits for John and Ritchie to get to the door. Trudy's screams are now terrified whimpers and Karl slowly inches his head up.

Trudy lies facing him. Her face contorts as she tries to open her swollen, red eyes. Her lips are caked with blood. Her shirt lies open. She wears no bra. The skin of her breasts is blotchy and red welts rise like judder bars. There is a bloodied graze under her left rib.

Karl sees one man holding her arms, another at her legs and the third man dropping his shorts. He lifts his slingshot and aims. "Now!" He yells, sending a pebble speeding. The man holding Trudy's legs falls back into his companion as John enters the room. John shoots them both and aims at the man still holding Trudy. Eyes dark as night stare up at John and Ritchie. They hear the explosion of bullets and Trudy's body jerks uncontrollably as her chest bursts. Skin and blood coat her twitching assailant. His tongue slides along his victorious grin as John takes aim and shoots him through the heart, killing him instantly.

"Noooooo!" screams Ritchie, darting forward.

John and Karl watch Ritchie's desperate hands but blood flows over his fingers, creating rivers in seconds. Ritchie cradles Trudy's head in his bloodied hands, kisses her forehead and gently lays her down. Scrambling over to his brother, he puts his ear to Drew's face. He breathes into Drew's mouth and starts pumping his chest. Karl moves but John stops him.

"Leave him, get their weapons. The noise will bring others."

Karl looks at Richie.

"He'll come. He's got Celia to think about."

Karl moves quickly. He takes the machine guns and knives from the two men nearest Drew. John moves to the man who shot Trudy and removes his machine gun. He rolls him over, searching for weapons. He finds the pistol and two knives. He wipes them on the dead man's clothes and slides the knife into his boot, slings the machine gun over his shoulder and hands the pistol to Karl.

"Ritchie, time to go."

"Why did they do this?"

John squeezes his shoulder. "Think about Celia."

Ritchie closes his brother's eyes, kisses his forehead and rises. "Wait!" He pulls Drew over to Trudy, grabs their picnic rug and covers them. He joins John and Karl at the door, doesn't look back and follows them in silence until John stops them as they reach the stream.

"Cover your face and arms with mud."

"How many do you think are here?"

"At least three, maybe more. Stay close and drop if you see or hear anything."

They keep off the track and use the trees as camouflage, stopping every few minutes. The air is suffocating and sweat drips like water, draining their bodies of energy. They continue on and finally reach the cave's entrance. John quietly calls out. The foliage draws back and they go inside.

"What's happened?"

"Three of them. Drew and Trudy are dead."

"Oh, Jesus."

"They'll be more."

"What the hell do we do?"

"We'll, we don't panic, Jack. We've got their weapons. We're safe enough for now."

"Safe? There's God knows how many fuckers out there and you're telling me we're safe?"

"For now."

Jack slides his hand through his hair. "Some fucking contest this is turning out to be."

"Yeah, we hear you, Jack, but this isn't part of the plan."

"Is that so, Bill? So then, guys, what exactly is your plan?"

"Our plan, Jack," cuts in John frostily, "is to let everyone know the situation. I'm not going to lie, but I don't want to scare the kids and women unnecessarily."

"Huh, good luck with that."

"Shut up, Jack, and let him speak." Karl turns to Ritchie. "I'll come with you to tell Celia."

"No, thanks, Karl. Rather do it alone."

"I'm so sorry, Ritchie," says Bill compassionately.

"Yeah." Ritchie looks at his wife and makes his way towards her.

The contestants huddle together around the fire, hardly comprehending what John is telling them. He finishes talking, looks at their bewildered faces, nudges Bill and stands. "Okay, everyone, Bill and I will go and see if the dinghy's still beached and set up watch."

"Do you want me to come, John?"

"No, Karl. If we spot anything, one of us will come back."

"We have your dinghy. We could go out – reach their boat?"

"Already thought of that, Jack."

"What about tonight, then?"

"Maybe. You ready, Bill?"

"Ready."

John and Bill leave and take up watch at the side of the cliff, camouflaged by the rocks and the shrubbery. Back inside the cave, Ritchie and Celia sit alone while Karl talks to the others.

"Oh, Christ. Poor Drew and Trudy," says Rosaline.

"Drew was shot in the leg and head."

"And Trudy?"

"Trudy was ..." Karl scratches his chin. He looks at Peter and Candice huddled close to their parents, "... shot in the chest."

"Oh, God!" cries Nancy, pulling Candice tighter and placing her hands over her ears.

"She wouldn't have known a thing."

"That's it, Henry. We're not staying here any longer. I don't care about the money. They're kids, Henry, just kids. When did we forget that?"

"I ... I don't know. Of course we'll leave." Henry glares at the people before him. "We should all leave. He pulls Peter closer.

"Oh, Dad," says Candice sobbing. "I want to go home."

"I know, honey."

"Me, too." Henry pulls Peter close. Peter doesn't resist.

At 7:00 p.m. Jack says he is going to the beach to check on John and Bill. No one argues. Henry, Nancy, Peter and Candice are busy packing up what they want to take back. Karl and Greg have gone down the tunnel to keep guard. Ritchie cradles Celia by the fire. Terrance sits himself next to Rosaline.

"You okay?"

"I can't believe ..."

Terrance touches her hand gently. "I won't let anything happen to you." His heart drums so loudly he is sure she can hear it. She clasps his hand and his heart nearly leaves his chest.

"I'm still with Jack, Terrance."

Just like that, back to Earth. "Yeah, of course, but you can't want to stay with him."

"No, but …"

"The money?"

Rosaline sighs, leans on her elbow and looks at him. "It hardly seems important at the moment."

He holds her hand tight and Rosaline places her other hand over his, unaware that Jack has returned and is heading towards them. The impact of Jack's foot knocks Terrance sideways.

"Jack!" screams Rosaline." What the hell are you doing?"

"Keep your fucking hands off my wife."

"Stop it." She grips his arm. "Please!"

Henry and Alison rush over as Terrance stands, holding his side.

"Jack, you need to calm down." Henry's voice is stern. "We don't need any more trouble."

"For Christ's sake, she's scared. I was trying to reassure her."

"I just bet you were."

"Jack, please don't do this."

"Goddammit, Jack, listen to your wife. I don't want my kids any more frightened than they already are," Henry says, getting agitated.

Jack's eyes narrow to slits. "He wants my wife."

"From what I saw he was just talking to her." Henry raises his hand; his fingers sweep through the air. "We're all on edge."

Jack cocks his eyebrow as if Henry's words are somewhat incredulous. Henry's head moves up and down as he pushes out his lower lip. "We must help each other when we can."

"I know what I saw, Henry."

"Jack," cuts in Alison, her voice low, commanding. "Drop it."

Jack takes in the determined look in her eyes, her hand moving to her holster. His eyes move to Rosaline and he lingers as though, if he waits long enough, he might see some sympathy in those emerald eyes of hers. She looks away.

"Fine." He raises his hands.

"Oh, God, Terrance, you're bleeding," says Nancy.

"It's a scratch, he'll live."

"What's the matter with you, Jack?" Rosaline's voice cracks. "I don't know you anymore. I'm not even sure I want to."

"Well, too fucking bad."

Rosaline's slap cuts through the heavy silence like a knife. "You make me sick."

Jack teeters backwards, the stinging slap turning his cheek red.

"Apologize," Rosaline says in a voice like steel but nothing more than a whisper.

Footsteps break the tension and Karl and Greg enter the cavern. Henry moves his family over to the fire and Alison and Rosaline follow. Karl and Greg look questioningly at Terrance.

"What's going on?"

"He's crazy. She's better off without him."

"Oh, Terrance."

"Can it, Greg." Karl's tone is harsh.

"Don't talk to him like that."

"Now you listen to me, Terrance. This is some shit we're in and now's not the time to fuck with Jack."

Terrance huffs!

"I mean it, Terrance. Do not …"

His words are cut off by the sound of running footsteps. Bill enters the cavern. He looks at the scene before him. "Everything all right?"

"No!" Terrance watches Henry pinch his lips; raise his eyebrows and side-glance at Jack. Terrance looks back to Bill. "A misunderstanding."

Bill glances at Jack, Alison and Rosaline. Alison gives a small shake of her head. "Okay, then, I'll assume whatever this was is sorted, because we have a bigger problem." Bill's eyes sweep over the tense group as Jack shuffles close to Rosaline.

"Those left on the boat must be getting suspicious that their mates haven't returned. So ... I need someone to come with me. The rest of you wait here. Two of you guard each tunnel. I need the machine guns but you can have my gun. Alison, – you have yours."

Alison nods.

"I'll come," says Karl stepping forward.

"Good man. Rest of you stay quiet and wait for our return."

"Like we have a choice?"

"There's always a choice, Jack."

"I'll guard the tunnel then, Bill. Care to join me, Terrance?"

"I'll come with you," cuts in Henry before Terrance can answer.

"Thank you, Henry," whispers Alison.

"Let's go, Karl." Bill makes his way to the tunnel and Karl follows, stops, looks back and then is gone. Terrance looks at Greg but Greg is still watching the empty space where Karl had been seconds ago. He moves forward and is draping an arm around Greg's shoulders when they hear noise from the tunnel and then Karl bursts into the cavern, panting like a dog out of breath.

"Two men – on the beach." He pauses, drawing in air. "'Nother dinghy." Karl grabs the revolver out of Greg's hand. "John says to stay put. Terrance – come with me." Karl hands him the revolver.

Running behind Karl, Terrance is filled with dread. The revolver is cold and heavy in his hand. He shoves it in his pocket. He takes it out. He wipes his forehead. He is hot and sweat sprays from him like a sprinkler. Nerves make him alert to every sound. He constantly looks left then right and then Karl is telling him to duck. They crawl to the edge of the bush, where he sees John and Bill squatting, eyes focused on two figures beyond, machine guns ready, standing by the dinghy.

John's voice is low. "We can't fire. The sound will carry to the launch."

"So we wait?" asks Karl.

John nods.

Terrance feels Karl's hand squeeze his shoulder, but it brings him little comfort. The day has been long, the night still needy. The minutes tick by slowly and Terrance feels his limbs start to lock. He stretches one leg out behind him as Karl thumps his shoulder. He freezes as he watches their targets striding towards the bush, heading east. John beckons and they follow, tracking the men easily, and Terrance wonders if this boldness is a self-assured trait of theirs. A smugness that comes from years of experience.

The air is uncomfortably sticky and Terrance's sweat falls like a river, turning his clothes to cling-wrap. He becomes fixated on the intimidating, slippery revolver and walks straight into Karl. Karl grasps his wrist and pushes him to the ground just as his shaking intensifies.

He edges his head around Karl's shoulder and sees they are at a shelter. John turns and sends Bill a signal and Bill creeps sideways and positions himself to the left of John. Bill kneels on one leg, rests his elbow on his other and takes aim. Terrance's eyes go back to John. He understands that he and Karl are there for backup. He sees Karl ready himself and he forces himself into position and points his revolver. He can't swallow; his throat constricts and he clamps his left hand on his right one to try to stop his shaking.

For a moment, Terrance thinks he is at a fireworks display. His ears buzz as he watches the men collapse. He rigorously wriggles his earlobes back and forth, but it does no good. He sees John and Bill already at the bodies. Karl's pistol is raised and Terrance suddenly thinks of Greg. *Christ, I'm no different from him.* He hangs his head in shame, puts the revolver down and stretches his fingers till they hurt. His eyes watch John and Bill rip what they can from the dead men's hands before heading back over.

"That's five of them. That means five of us need to be in those dinghies. Bill, when we get back, go and get Jack."

"Jack?"

"I know it's not ideal with whatever you two have going on but we can't take Henry. Ritchie needs to be with his wife and, from what I've seen, I don't think Greg is up to it."

"John's right, Terrance."

"I agree." Bill looks at John. "Give him the revolver; Terrance can have a machine gun."

Terrance opens his mouth, but Karl's look stops him short. He hands the revolver to Bill and reluctantly makes the exchange.

They move quickly and quietly and arrive at the beach to find nothing has changed. Bill leaves them huddled together in the concealment of the palms. He returns with Jack in tow.

"Okay, I'll keep this simple." John looks at the faces staring at him. "Jack, you're with me – you three take the other dinghy. Looks like the noise didn't carry this far and it's quite cloudy, so that's good. No one talks and if you see any raised guns, fire."

Jack aims at Terrance. "Bang."

Bill's hand is fast. Jack's wrist is lowered. "This is not a game, Jack."

They start the motors and proceed slowly toward the boat. Terrance pulls the machine gun up to his chest and notices Karl's look. He gives his brother his best reassuring grin. The machine gun feels cold and foreign in his sweaty hand.

Karl leans over. "Don't over-think it."

Terrance looks at him blankly.

"Look … just stay behind me."

"Okay, you two, no more talking," intervenes Bill. "Karl, what are you doing?"

"I'm holding the gun up. Thought it might look more natural."

Karl catches Bill frown before a cloud takes their light.

"Just be ready to use it." Bill slows the dinghy to keep behind John and they come up alongside the boat. A man leans over the side and casually drops a ladder. John steadies the dinghy, reaches for it and throws a rope up. The man catches it and starts winding it around the cleat as John starts to climb. Reaching the top, he draws his knife, grabs the man around the neck and slits his throat. He pushes him overboard and the man hits the water face-down.

Jack climbs next and Bill jumps onto the front dinghy and ties their dinghy to it. He motions for Karl and Terrance to follow as Terrance moves he glimpses movement at the back of the boat. The moon reappears and his eyes widen.

His stomach tightens and his chest hurts as his adrenalin fires. His eyes narrow as he raises the machine gun. Aiming is difficult. His finger tightens and his arm jiggles as shells pop around him and bullets slice the air. He feels Karl clasp his arm and his finger relaxes. His ears ring, muffling his world. He follows his brother's lead and crawls to the ladder and sees John and Bill racing towards his target. He climbs on board after Karl and Bill motions them to stay put. The clouds part and in the moonlight he sees Jack cowering against the cabin's wall, before his eyes fix on John and Bill as they reach the door of the bridge. Without warning, John opens fire and disappears into the cabin with Bill close behind.

Karl's hand holds him still. They stay crouched together, their eyes flicking left to right, trying to find movement, until Bill appears at the door.

"All clear," Bill mouths slowly, raising his hand and signaling forward.

Terrance hears the relief in Karl's sigh and they follow Bill inside and see John sitting at the table.

"You three okay?" asks John.

Terrance wiggles his ear and takes a seat next to Karl. Jack wanders in, hitting his ears and leans against the wall.

"Terrance, you sure?"

He finds his voice. "Yeah, but ..."

"You didn't kill him, Terrance."

John looks at the man beside him.

"You got him good, but you didn't kill him." Bill sits back. "I did."

Karl pats his brother's back, nodding to Bill. Jack shakes his head and remains silent as John's and Bill's eyes lock on his. The boat shudders and they stand quickly.

"Bill, come with me, you three stay here." John and Bill go to the door and cautiously make their way out onto the deck. Peering over, they see several sharks attacking the man Terrance shot with a savageness that turns their blood cold. As they head back they almost collide with Karl, Terrance and Jack.

"Poor Mary," says Terrance to no one.

John takes the machine gun from Terrance's hand. "I thought I asked you guys to stay put." He ushers them inside and they sit, exhausted, while John and Bill go through what few cupboards there are. John pulls out a bottle, undoes the lid and takes a long drink. He passes it to Bill.

"There's no sense going to the launch tonight. Any more of them and we'd know about it by now. We'll go tomorrow."

"These guys need to go back to the island."

"I agree, Bill. You take them back, I'll stay."

"I'll stay with you," says Karl.

"No, you won't."

"What if another boat shows up?"

"Highly unlikely, Karl. They mostly travel by themselves. Easier to get in and out with only one boat." John takes the bottle and takes another drink. "May as well take anything you want in the way of food – you guys have earned it."

"You know the Hendersons want to leave," says Bill, looking at Karl, Terrance and Jack.

"They have kids," says Karl. "Makes a difference"

"I suppose the likelihood of this happening again must be pretty slim?"

"Yes, I would think so, Terrance. Once we get back to the launch, I'll contact Ben and the police. Anyone else in the area would be stupid to stay."

"How about you, Jack? You have Rosaline to think of."

"She'll stay."

"She must be tougher than she looks."

"Not really." Jack finishes his glass and gets up. He opens cupboards and pulls out bags of rice, three cartons of coconut milk, two cans of coke, four packets of dried noodles and another bottle of rum.

"You'd better go." John leans over. "I'm really sorry about all this."

Jack walks out the door ignoring John's words. Karl and Terrance shake John's hand and Karl looks at the machine gun lying on the table.

"Keep it. We'll collect it tomorrow. Bill and I will go out to the launch early. If you don't see us before noon, then you can assume there are others."

Bill starts the motor and Terrance watches the boat fade into the night. "What a fucking nightmare." He hears the motor quieten, waits for Bill to stop and jumps out behind a solemn Jack and a subdued Karl. Bill departs without a word and the three of them drag themselves up the beach.

"Were there others and where's John and Bill?"

"Three, they're dead. John and Bill are staying on the boat. They're going to the launch early tomorrow," says Karl, his voice heavy with fatigue.

"By themselves?" asks Henry.

"Yes." Karl puts down the machine gun.

"Why do you still have that?" asks Rosaline.

"John said we should keep them over night."

"So there's more of them?"

"Hon, I don't think so. They would have made themselves visible by now."

"Jack's right, so how about we open that bottle of rum and have a well deserved drink?" says Karl. "Got some coke for you two as well. Here, Peter … give one to your sister."

Terrance watches as Peter takes the cans and opens them. He hands one to Candice and they gulp down the liquid noisily. He smiles as a trickle of coke runs down Candice's chin and how she cleverly flicks out her tongue to clean it up. *So innocent!* He looks at Rosaline and she smiles back. Karl hands him the rum and he takes a swig and passes it to Greg.

"You guys still leaving?" asks Greg.

"Yes, we're not putting the kids through any more. We could have been killed today."

"True, Nancy, but we weren't."

"Yes, Jack but nevertheless …"

Jack cuts in. "Bill says the police will keep an eye on things. Pirates would be stupid enough to hang around."

"What about the launch?" asks Peter, burping. Candice giggles and the tension in the room dissipates briefly.

"Don't know. What do you think, Alison?"

"We'll just have to wait and see."

"John said if they're not back by noon, we should assume something's gone wrong."

"Then what did he say to do, Karl?"

"He didn't, Alison. I guess he figures that will be our choice."

"Then we need to make a plan. If they don't show, we take the dinghy and go and see for ourselves."

"Is that wise?" interrupts Rosaline. "We don't know how many of them are out there."

"Can't see any other way."

"Karl's right. We can't just stay here and wait. Jack, you up to it?"

"Of course, Alison."

"I'll come," says Ritchie.

"Ritchie, mate, you need to stay with Celia."

"Karl's right. You can't go now …" she lowers her voice. "We might have a baby to think about."

"What?" Ritchie asks with a quizzical look.

"I wasn't going to say anything. It's still so early."

"You're pregnant?"

Celia's eyes dart over the people staring back at her. "I … I could be." Celia touches Ritchie's cheek. "Maybe!" Fresh tears fall as Ritchie takes her in his arms. Terrance locks eyes with Celia and she quickly buries her head into her husband's neck.

"You all right there, Terrance?" asks Karl, leaning into his brother.

"Fine." Terrance's voice is low. He catches Peter's alarmed face.

"I'll take first watch," says Greg. "I'm not tired."

"I'll come with you," offers Henry. "Rest of you should try to sleep. We may have a big day tomorrow."

CHAPTER THIRTY

John and Bill arrive at the launch at 5:30 a.m. They search the upper deck thoroughly but find no one and go below. Bill notices a foot protruding from behind the counter and proceeds forward cautiously. Owen is lying flat on his stomach. A dark stain has formed on his shirt between his shoulder blades. Bill kneels and checks his wrist. Nothing. They proceed down the corridor and find Karen, with a crimson hole in the middle of her forehead. Bill bends down and gently closes her lifeless eyes. John signals for them to continue and Bill opens the next door. Finding them empty, they check the adjacent cabins.

"Let's go below before we check Martin's rooms," whispers John. They discover Phil propped against the toilet wall, two bullet holes in his stomach, his throat slit.

"Shit! Fucking bastards," curses John, closing Phil's eyes. He reaches for a towel and covers his friend's head and torso.

"There's still Penny and the Longs," says Bill. "Martin's quarters are the only places left."

John nods and they make their way back to the second level where Martin's rooms are. John opens the door slowly. The dimmed light in Martin's bedroom has a surreal feel and as he opens the door wider he sees complete chaos.

Clothes hang from open drawers, the floor is scattered with items. John tries the bathroom door but it only budges a few inches. He pushes his weight against it and the door moves to reveal Warren Long's half-draped body. His un-bandaged knee is a bloody pulp of ripped tissue. Several bullet holes have stained his torso. His eyes stare sightlessly at the ceiling and one hand clutches a soiled towel. The shower curtain lies against the door.

"Oh, fuck!" says Bill as he peers in. His stomach turns and he leans against the wall to steady himself.

John's voice is weary. "Where the hell are Penny, Sara and Bridget?" He closes the bathroom door and stands beside Bill. They stay like this for a few minutes and then John straightens and heads for the bed. "Bill ... we haven't tried Martin's safe-room."

"Of course." Bill strides over and helps push the mattress back. John presses his ear down on the wooden base.

"Penny, it's John. Knock if you can hear me."

There is no sound and Bill raises his gun as John lifts the small latch. The light streams down and Sara screams. Penny recognizes John and bursts into tears.

"Give me your hand."

Penny pushes Sara up and John grabs her arms. Bill leans over and helps lift her out and John reaches for Penny. She sinks into his arms, sobbing violently.

Sara looks at them with bulging eyes. "Where's Warren and Mum?"

Bill and John exchange looks.

"Where are they?"

"I'm so sorry, Sara. Warren's dead. We haven't found your mum."

"Oh, God, they shot her. She told us to hide." Sara wails. "Oh, Mum."

Bill looks at her compassionately. "You go with John and I'll find her." He puts a tender hand on her shoulder. "I promise."

"Okay, Bill, we'll go upstairs, radio the police."

"I want to see Warren."

"Sara, you don't need to see him."

"I have to. Where is he?"

John places his hands on Sara's rigid upper arms. " It won't do you any good to see him."

"I can't just leave him … I love him."

John can't deny her request. He takes her to the bathroom and gently pushes the door ajar.

"Don't come in."

Her voice is cold and John remains at the door. He hears her gasp and his hand tightens on the doorknob.

Sara emerges, her face a torment of sorrow and rage. "This is your fault. You and this bloody contest."

The venom in her voice hits him hard. *It was their fault – Martin's fault!*

Sara pushes her finger into his chest. "Well?"

"I'm sorry, Sara." His voice trembles as he forces himself to look at her. She looks utterly broken and his mind frantically searches for something to say that will make this better.

"No. I'm sorry, John." She backs away. "I didn't mean it."

His mouth is dry. Words escape him.

"Mum's dead, isn't she?"

"I … I don't know." He wishes he could give her some hope, but his mind won't work. Bill enters the room and pulls him aside.

"Found more blood."

John looks at Sara.

"Tell me. She's dead, isn't she?"

"I didn't find her, Sara."

Sara runs past them and up the stairs. John and Bill follow and join her next to Penny, where a pool of blood has stained the deck. She collapses onto her knees and places her hand over it.

"There's blood on the seat," whispers Penny to John and Bill. "If you look closely it's down the sides in a couple of places as well."

"Penny, hold Sara back."

"You think she's in there?"

"I do."

Bill gently helps Sara up and Penny takes hold of her. John and Bill lift the wooden lid. Bridget lies huddled, her chest straining to rise with each labored breath. The left side of her shirt is crimson and John and Bill gently lift her out. Her pulse is weak, barely noticeable. Sara breaks free of Penny's hold and collapses beside her mother, brushing her limb, bloodstained hair from her face.

John takes Penny aside. "Can you get blankets and the first-aid kit?"

Penny leaves in a flash and is back within seconds, draping a thermo blanket over Bridget. She gives Bill the first-aid kit and puts another blanket around Sara.

"Try to stop the bleeding, Bill. I'm going to radio this in. Penny, can you make some tea and coffee?"

"On to it." Penny and John go below and John makes a call to the police. He tells them what has taken place, signs off and clicks on mail. He sees several emails from Ben and opens the first one. It tells him they are coming back on Saturday. Saturday is tomorrow. John hits reply and gives a brief outline of what has happened. He tells them to wait for his email saying it is safe before they leave. He pushes send and joins the others on deck.

"Bill, I'm going to take her into the lagoon. We don't want them coming here."

"Good idea," says Bill. He leaves Bridget with Sara and walks to John. "I've done my best to stem the bleeding. She's stable for now, but I'm not sure she'll make it."

John squeezes his shoulder, takes the coffee Penny hands him and goes to start the launch. He drops anchor beside the pirates' boat and asks Bill if he wants to go ashore. Bill sets off in the dinghy and arrives to see Terrance, Alison and Greg running down the beach.

"Bill, thank God. I take it John is okay?"

"He's fine, Alison. Penny and Sara are safe. Bridget's been shot but she's alive. No one else made it."

"Jesus."

"John's got the police and a medical team on the way. How's everyone here?"

"Okay, I guess. Poor Sara must be a mess."

"Yeah, she's not good. Look, we've got a bit to do. Are the Hendersons still wanting to leave?"

"As far as I know."

"You sure you guys want to stay?"

"There's no way you're going to get Karl to leave if Jack stays."

Bill looks at Greg.

"We'll be okay."

Terrance fists his brother. "Yeah, we'll be fine."

Greg smiles back meekly as they see Henry walking towards them.

"Thank heavens you're back."

"Terrance can fill you in, Henry. I need to go and talk to the others."

Bill pats Terrance on the back and heads to the cave. Terrance tells Henry what Bill has told them. He sees Henry's frown as the disbelief forms in his eyes. The five of them stand in anguished silence as they try to come to terms with the fact that more of the people they have come to know are no longer with them.

CHAPTER THIRTY-ONE

The helicopters arrive and Commissionaire Andre Belair and Inspector Claudine Jarnot disembark, followed by five gendarmes.

"Bill – wish I could say nice to see you again."

"I know, Andre, dreadful situation. John's on the launch, waiting for Inspector Tate and the medical crew."

"Yes, we have that information. How is everyone coping?"

"Hard to say, really. The Hendersons are leaving."

"No one else?"

"No, the other two teams want to stay."

"Fools!" says Claudine.

"Agreed," says Andre, motioning for the gendarmes to follow him. "Give me a quick summary of what happened here, Bill?"

Bill goes over his account of events as quickly and precisely as he can, still trying to make sense of it all.

"You say Terrance Tiller killed one?" inquires Claudine.

"Yes, self-defense. I told him he didn't kill the bastard. He doesn't need the guilt."

"Did he believe you?"

"Not sure."

"Right then, we'll get the bodies first."

"You need to take Karl. He knows where their shelter is."

Bill and Karl leave with the three gendarmes. Karl informs them what happened and when they arrive at the Booths' tree house the three gendarmes enter first. They take photos and measure distances between the bodies, walls and door.

"We moved Drew," announces Karl sheepishly. "Seemed right they should be together."

Karl watches one of the gendarme's pen running back and forth as another gendarme lifts the closest dead man's shirt. "No markings to say they're with any organized group."

"Is that how you tell?"

"Usually, Karl. Their clothes, their boat – especially the tats. I'd say considering their ages ... just opportunists trying to make a quick buck."

"Fucking bastards!"

"We are all not so fortunate to be born into a comfortable life, Mr. Tiller. Poverty breeds contempt and corruption."

"Yeah, but not everyone goes around killing people!" snaps Karl watching the gendarmes examine Drew and Trudy.

"Karl, why don't we wait outside?"

Karl nods, already on his way.

"Look, I know I've asked, but are you sure you won't reconsider?"

"Jack's not going to hand us the money so there's no way we're letting him get it."

"Catch twenty-two, then."

"Catch twenty-two, Bill. And thanks for what you tried to do for Terrance."

Their conversation stops as two of the gendarmes appear, carrying a body enclosed in a shiny black body bag.

"I don't give a fuck how you treat those bastards, but be careful with Drew and Trudy."

"Of course, Mr. Reese. We'll take Mr. and Mrs. Booth now and come back for them."

When they arrive at the beach, Drew and Trudy's bodies are immediately put into the helicopter and the gendarmes go back for the three men. Ritchie and Celia get ready to leave. Karl helps Ritchie get their things on board and Celia wanders over to where Terrance is sitting.

"Um, about me being pregnant."

"Yes?"

"The chances that …"

"I know what the chances are, Celia."

"Please," she swallows loudly. "Ritchie needs this."

He sees her quivering lip. Knows how hard this is. "I'm not going to say anything." His hand touches her arm softly. "I'm sorry … this is such a fucking disaster."

She peers into his eyes. "I need this so badly, Terrance."

He smiles at her and looks back to sea. "Go and have a good life – be happy."

"Please leave."

"Can't."

She takes his hand and squeezes it tightly. Her kiss is warm on his cheek. "You're a good person, Terrance – stay safe." She leaves him and he watches her walk back to her husband. His eyes mist over and he looks away.

Greg walks over to Karl as Celia and Ritchie board the helicopter. They both glance over at their brother.

"Should I go to him?"

"No, he'll be fine. It's a lot to digest and I didn't help by telling him I mentioned the slingshot."

"The slingshot?"

"Don't worry, Greg. When we went to find Drew and Trudy, John told me I needn't stay – and I stupidly said I couldn't save Josh but maybe I could save them."

"Oh, Karl."

"Then I took out the slingshot …" he pauses, rubbing his scalp, "… John just stared at me and I could feel his mind working overtime. He made me nervous and he knew it. I threw the damn thing away."

Greg's face drains of color.

"It's no big deal. He won't say anything."

"How do you know?"

"Because John's a very clever man. He may think we know something about Josh but he's got no proof and after the debacle this contest has turned into, he's not going to want to rock the boat. He'll want this thing wrapped up and over as soon as possible."

Bill walks over and sits with Terrance.

"The police are nearly through, won't be long till they go."

"That's good."

Bill studies the man below him. "Look, Terrance, Karl inferred that you know I was lying. I wish I could say something to help. Killing someone, justified – and believe me you were – or not does something to you. Eats you up if you let it."

"You're speaking from experience, I take it?"

Bill ignores the slight hint of disparagement in Terrance's voice. "Yes, I am."

"People die around me, Bill."

"People die every day."

"Not like this."

"No death is ever easy."

"I came here to get away from it."

"Who died?"

"My girlfriend." Terrance smirks. "Actually she was a bit more than that, she was my fiancé."

"I'm sorry."

"Yeah, me too. We were going to get married the next day. Been together for three years."

"Must have been hard."

"It was my fault. I didn't want to marry her but I never told her. I just went along with everything. She was so happy, her parents were so happy – my parents were happy. Everyone was so fucking happy. And then we went to this swanky restaurant for lunch – kind of like our last one as single people and I just blurted out that I didn't want to marry her." He picks at his chin. "Fuck, can you imagine what that did to her?"

"Must have rocked her world."

"Oh, yeah. I took her dreams away from her in a few seconds – just like that. I couldn't have been more brutal if I tried."

"What did she do?"

Terrance huffs. "She covered me with wine and stormed out. I heard her crying in the foyer but I just sat there with the whole fucking restaurant looking at me as though I was a piece of shit." He clamps his eyes. "Am a piece of shit, and what did I do? I left and walked around. I phoned her, but she wasn't answering. I called her parents … no answer. I sat till it got dark and then I walked home. All I wanted was a shower. I opened the door and there she was. This beautiful, white porcelain doll floating in a crimson bath."

"Jesus!"

"Yeah, so that bit about death changing you, believe me, I know. Didn't talk to anyone then but I did date a lot of girls. Didn't care who I hurt, but then Greg's partner dumped him. It was like something changed in me and my misery became his. I stopped the girls and spent my time helping him and then Karl entered us into this fucking contest."

"Wow. That's some story you're carrying around."

"Yep."

"I'll talk to Karl."

"No, we're not leaving."

"If you think money's going to …"

"It's not the money."

"Rosaline?"

"Yep."

"Look, Terrance. I don't know Jack, but I've watched him and he's carrying a lot of anger."

"He treats her like shit."

"Yeah – well, that doesn't surprise me."

They hear Alison calling.

"Police are leaving, I better get over there."

"Yeah." Terrance gets up and shakes Bill's hand. "Thanks. I didn't mean to dump that on you."

"Look, in case we don't get a chance to talk again. Take care – I hope it works out for you."

Terrance takes his hand back. "Bill?"

"Yes?"

"Killing that bastard …"

"Look, mate, it's never easy, but if I don't have a choice and they're scum then it sits right. I feel good because I've stopped them and the world's a safer place." Bill cocks an eyebrow and Terrance smiles as Bill turns and walks off.

Night passes and the sun rises in an innocent, clear blue sky, bringing with it an uplifting atmosphere desperately needed by the small group. Bill and Alison rise early and get the Hendersons' gear down to the beach.

"Do you think we should leave them the pistol, Bill?"

Bill laughs. "You want to give it to Jack or Terrance?"

Alison gives a nonchalant shrug.

"Seriously, you know we can't. Andre was quite clear about taking the guns."

"Yes, I know, but what if there is someone out there?"

"We've done a search and I personally think it's highly unlikely that anyone else is still here."

"This doesn't feel right anymore. Are you sure we can't we let them share the money?"

"Unfortunately, Martin gave us no room to move on this. One team has to win or the money goes off to charities."

"But there must be some sort of loophole?"

"Believe me, there's not. John and I have been over and over it and it's tight."

"We stuffed up, Bill."

"Perhaps. Look, Alison, I feel bad, I really do, but this was something no one saw coming."

"Shouldn't we take this as a lesson then?"

"We can't force them to leave. They're adults, Alison, not children."

"I know that. I'm not getting at you, but I hate feeling responsible."

"Did seem like a good idea at the time."

"Yes, it did."

Bill looks at Alison. "You going to be all right?"

"Have to be, don't I?" Alison takes hold of Bill's arm. "Bill, don't tell John about this. He has enough on his plate without worrying about us."

"It's nothing he doesn't feel himself, Alison, but I'll not say a word."

Alison let's go of Bill's arm. "I'll stay and wait for John. You go and get them up. The sooner we leave the sooner this thing ends."

Within an hour, John has returned and picked up the Hendersons, Bill and Alison and disappeared out to the sea.

Karl, Greg, Terrance, Jack and Rosaline sit watching the tranquility surrounding them until the sun's relentless heat burns their skin and they retreat into the cavern. Rosaline looks right to the three men sitting beside her. They look weary, beaten, Karl especially. His eyes are shut and his finger traces little circles on his temple. She is glad he is here. He makes her feel safe. She can clearly see the resemblance to Terrance as they sit together. Karl is just an older, rougher and darker version of the man she now loves.

She can't settle the fear of what might happen. It consumes her and she begins to shake and clamps her arms around her legs, hugging them tight to her pounding chest. She feels a warm hand on her back and she glances at Greg. She likes Greg: this funny, awkward, gay version of his brothers. He has kept his brown hair short, his skin is still clean and clear but his once happy face now carries a look of uncertainty.

"Are you all right?"

She wishes Greg hadn't asked. She will now have to speak and she isn't sure if her voice will hold the emotion tormenting her. She swallows deeply and draws in air.

"I don't want to … leave the cave."

Karl rubs his tired eyes. "There's no hurry."

She smiles meekly as her lip dances up and down. "I mean, I don't want to leave at all."

"Well, too fucking bad. We can't stay."

"She can." Terrance cuts in.

"No, she can't. You know the rules."

"Fuck the rules, Jack."

"Calm down, Terrance. Look, Jack, I don't think you guys staying here for a day or so is a problem."

"Exactly, Karl. It's not like we'd say anything and if it makes Rosaline feel better, then what's the problem?"

"The problem, Greg, is that your brother wants my wife and I'm not too keen on that."

"Please, Jack. Terrance has done nothing."

"You need to stay until it's safe."

"And when would that be, Karl?"

"When we feel it is."

"And what if we don't."

"Well, you can piss off back to your place if you want," snarls Terrance. "And Rosaline can stay here."

Rosaline can hold her tears in no longer and they explode into streams, running down her face and onto her chest. Her voice quavers as her fear takes over. "I can't go."

"Fine, we'll stay then." Jack glares at Terrance. "Till it's safe."

"Thank you."

"Don't thank him, Rosaline," says Terrance, his irritation evident. "This shouldn't have even been a debate, for Christ's sake."

Jack smiles smugly.

"Look," yells Karl. "This is only going to work if we all get on."

"Please, Jack?" Rosaline glares at her husband.

"No problem from my end."

"Good."

"Unless he makes a move ..."

"Oh, my God," Rosaline brings her hands to her face, shaking her head.

Greg puts his arm around her. "It will work, Rosaline. We'll make it work."

"Absolutely," grins Jack.

"Terrance?"

"Yes, Greg."

"Stay away from my wife and everything will be hunky-dory."

"I'll stay away from Rosaline if that's what she wants."

Karl steps in. "I think what Terrance means is that …"

"What I mean, Karl, is that if he treats her right then I'll not interfere but if he treats her like shit again, then I'm not going to sit back."

"Fair enough, mate." Jack extends his arm.

"I'm not shaking your hand. I don't like you and I'm sure as hell not going to pretend I do, but for the sake of Rosaline I'll do what's needed so she's not terrified every fucking day we have left here."

"That's the spirit, Terrance," says Greg, almost singing. "Now, how about I cook us up something to eat?"

"I'd like to help, Greg."

"Thanks, Rosaline."

"I'm going for some air."

"Don't go far, Terrance."

"End of the tunnel okay with you, Karl?"

"Fine. Fresh air might do you good." Karl watches his brother storm off and takes the opportunity to speak to Jack, while Greg and Rosaline are occupied.

"Let's just get one thing straight, mate. If there's any trouble, Rosaline can stay but you are out."

"Reading you loud and clear there, Karl." Jack's caustic smile widens. "You won't even know I'm here."

They sit together eating the remains of the fish Greg and Rosaline have made into a stew. They have enough food to last a few days and decide to stay within the caves perimeter. Everyone will take a turn doing a three-hourly watch, positioning themselves at the start of the tunnel that leads to the bush.

It is early morning when Rosaline wakes. She listens to the heavy snoring to her right. She raises her head and looks left to Karl and Greg. *Dead to the world!* She carefully gets out of her sleeping bag and crawls towards Terrance. She knows he is watching and she places herself beside him and leans back on the cavern's cool wall.

"Sure this is wise?"

"Jack's out to it. He could sleep through an earthquake when he's snoring like that."

She hears Terrance snicker and trembles. His body is millimeters from hers and the heat she feels between them escalates quickly. She desperately wants to touch his skin but she is scared to move.

"I want to say thank you."

"Pleasure."

His voice is husky and low and goose bumps cover her skin, making her shiver. Terrance's hand whips in front of her, his palm gently turns her face and his lips find hers and she knows she is lost.

"I can't be with him, Terrance."

"I know." He pulls her close. "I'll think of something."

His words penetrate deeply, clamping her chest around her heart. She feels slightly sick, light-headed and she swallows repeatedly as saliva vanishes from her mouth. She buries her head into his chest. He smells of the sea and she runs her hand over his warm chest and then his lips are in her hair.

Terrance turns her face up to his. She can't answer so she nods and he kisses her again, holding her tight, as if they were one.

"Okay, I want you to go and lie down. I'm going to fix this. If I'm not back in half an hour, wake Karl."

"What are you going to do?"

"I've got something in mind."

"Please be careful."

"I will." He bends down, kisses her and is gone. Rosaline does what he has requested and she lies with her eyes on her watch. She pushes the button every few seconds to illuminate the numbers. She knows this will be the longest half hour of her life.

Rosaline sees Terrance burst into the cavern and quickly wake Karl and Greg. He whispers to her to wake Jack. Jack rolls over, cursing, and Rosaline thumps him.

"Jesus Christ, woman ..."

"I heard something out there," cuts in Terrance. "Rustling – something snapping."

Jack yawns. "Probably just a bloody rodent."

"Too loud."

"Okay, it's getting light," says Karl looking up to the ceiling. "Greg, you stay in here with Rosaline. Jack, you guard the tunnel and Terrance and I'll go and look around."

"Do you think you should? I mean, shouldn't we all stick together?"

"We won't go far."

Rosaline looks at Terrance and catches the look he gives her. She glances to Jack and is well aware that Jack caught their little exchange. She lowers her eyes. Greg hands her a pocketknife and she watches Karl and Terrance run down the tunnel.

Rosaline and Greg lean on the edge of the tunnel wall. She peers at her watch. Forty minutes. She feels a dread unlike any she has ever felt before when a noise from within the tunnel startles them.

Greg jumps to his feet and raises his hand. The knife shimmers in the early morning light and despite their situation Rosaline feels like laughing. *Dear Greg! Does he really expect to do any damage with that?*

Karl and Terrance appear with Jack following behind. Karl motions them all towards the fire.

"Okay, we couldn't see anyone. Didn't hear a thing, but ..." he looks at Greg and then Rosaline. "We found blood."

Rosaline gasps.

"No way!" Jack's face beams with bewilderment.

"Fresh blood?" asks Greg.

"Fresh enough."

"Human?"

"Jesus, Greg! We don't know!"

Rosaline looks at Terrance. His face tells her all she needs to know, her heart calms down and her breathing returns to normal.

"Right, from now on, we stick together, stay in here as long as we can. We know the tunnel to the rocks is safe, so we can go out there. We'll have two on watch at night – three-hourly shifts – and we don't leave here till we absolutely have to."

"So, Karl, what do we do about the contest?"

"We haven't long to go, Jack. We'll worry about that later."

"Presuming we're all alive." Greg stops. "Oh, shit, sorry, Rosaline. I didn't mean to say that."

"It's okay, Greg. It's the truth isn't it? We have no guns – just these stupid pocketknives."

"We have spears and we have the advantage of being here." Karl glances around. "Terrance and I will go and get shells."

"Shells?"

"Yes, Jack. We'll scatter them at the entrance of the tunnel. If someone should find it then we'll hear them."

"Great idea, Karl."

"Thank you, Greg."

"Regular little Boy Scouts aren't you?"

"I don't hear you making any suggestions."

"Looks like you got it covered."

"Oh, grow-up, Jack."

Jack bursts into laughter. "What, Rosaline? And spoil all the fun? I don't think so."

CHAPTER THIRTY-TWO

The next few days are spent in the cavern but their food supplies are running out and they need fresh water. The weather has been hot and, with little to no breeze, the air is humid and stale, making them fatigued and irritable.

"We should split the thirty mill and be done with it."

"Rules are rules, Terrance."

"Yeah, well, Jack, the rules are fucked."

"You agreed to stay."

"None of us want to be here."

"I'm not handing you the money just like that," Jack answers nonchalantly. "Besides, people have died – if we left, makes their deaths seem rather pointless, doesn't it?"

"Well, you'd have to ask their families that, wouldn't you?" spits Terrance.

"Terrance is right," says Rosaline quietly. "We're crazy to stay."

"This is getting us nowhere."

"Okay, Greg, keep your shirt on," says Karl. "Things will get back to normal."

"Normal?" shouts Terrance. "And just what the fuck is normal, Karl?"

"Jesus, Terrance, back to how we were before."

"What? Before Eric drowned or before Mary got attacked or Josh was sent to his death ..."

"Shut up, Terrance." Karl's eyes divert to Jack but it is too late. "I meant back to how we were before the pirates."

"They weren't pirates," states Greg. "And I don't see how we can do that. We're trapped in this cave like animals."

Karl peers at each of them. 'Okay, then, tomorrow we'll search every inch of this fucking place."

"Finally," says Greg sighing.

"What about Rosaline?"

"What about me, Jack?"

"This isn't high school, hon."

"We stick together." Karl's voice is soft yet thunderous.

Rain falls during the night but the next morning brings a cloudless sky and the sun heats the island quickly. They collect their weapons and depart. Rosaline suggests they wear dark clothes. They slather on insect repellent and sunscreen and smear mud over their bare skin. Before long they arrive safely at Jack's and Rosaline's shelter. Terrance, Greg and Rosaline keep watch while Jack and Karl enter. Jack tells Karl nothing has changed.

They carry on following the trail to the waterfall. Once there, they split into two groups. Karl and Terrance swim over to the waterfall. It is deserted. Jack, Rosaline and Greg survey around the area to the left, find nothing and join Karl and Terrance up the bank to the left of the waterfall. They decide to head up to the spot where Josh met his fate. The thought sets them on edge, slowing them down, and the climb becomes hard, but once they reach the top they find nothing out of the ordinary.

"Wow, only been up here to find Josh. Didn't notice how beautiful it is."

Greg leans over and whispers to Terrance. "Clever Karl."

Terrance stares at his brother, unmoved by his words.

Rosaline kneels. "Wonder what made Josh go so near the edge."

"Maybe he was pushed?"

"Who would have pushed him?"

Karl gives a half-suppressed laugh. "Rosaline, I don't think Jack's serious."

"Might have been one of those bastards here all the time."

"Jack, you're scaring your wife."

Jack scoffs. "Sorry, love – me and my big mouth."

Terrance looks at Karl and shakes his head. "We should move and check what we can before it gets too hot."

"I agree. We don't have time to waste admiring the view," says Jack, sarcastically.

Karl gives his brothers a silent warning and heads for the safety of the bush. They descend quickly, trek along the stream's path and reach the Booths' decaying shelter.

"Jesus," says Greg, stunned to find it looking so dilapidated.

"Don't panic, this is our doing. Tried to make it look like it hadn't been used for ages."

"Well, you did a pretty good job, Karl."

"Rosaline, you and Greg wait here. We'll check it out."

Karl, Terrance and Jack cautiously move forward and enter. The smell of rotting debris mixed with blood fills their nostrils and, seeing nothing to suggest anybody has disturbed what remains, they exist quickly. The group advances on to the second cove and along to the Davidsons' shelter.

"It's as cozy as when they left," says Rosaline sadly, running her hands over Moana's flax walls. "I hope she and the boys are all right."

"To be honest, I thought they'd be here till the end."

"Did you really, Terrance?"

"Yes, Jack, I did. She was one smart lady."

"She was wonderful." Rosaline sighs. "I'm going to look her up when we're out of here."

"What for?"

"Because I like her, Jack."

"We need to move," interrupts Karl, his agitation evident. "It's already two and we've still got to get the damn fruit and search the other side."

They drag themselves back up the beach and head deep into the bush. Pockets of steam rise from the damp carpet of moss and rotting debris. Endless perspiration falls from them, sapping their energy, and mosquitoes dive from every direction.

They approach the fruit trees and quickly search the area, find nothing and collapse under the shade of the closest tree. Rosaline looks at her legs, sees red lumps growing in size, and feels the first signs of unbearable itching.

"They got you too?"

"Uh-huh."

Greg shows her the backs of his legs. "They love my blood. It's not fair. Karl and Terrance never get bothered, but I swell up like I've got mumps."

"Me too, Greg." Rosaline looks to where her husband stands. "It's completely unfair."

They leave the comfort of the fruit trees and check out the Jenners', the Smyths' and the Hendersons' shelters. All are empty, showing no signs of human activity. They leave for the next cove but again it is deserted. From there they make their way through the rocky terrain around the back of the island and then divert inland. There is no sign of anybody so they turn back, making their way through the center of the bush where the air is thicker and more humid. The plant life becomes lethal and nasty cuts grow on their legs and arms. They make it back to the second cove and drop down onto the beach, exhausted.

"Get in the water; it will cleanse these cuts," says Greg, wading in. The water is warm and he closes his eyes and lets his body relax. He hears a splash and looks to see Terrance diving under him, with Karl in pursuit, and then he is under water.

"Hi, Greg. Thought we'd join you," says Karl, surfacing, a devilish grin on his face.

"Great!"

Whooping like kids, Terrance and Karl raise Greg skywards and dump him like a slobbery fish. He surfaces, coughing and gasping. "Growing old is inevitable, Karl, but growing up is optional."

"Whooh!" laughs Karl loudly. "When did you think of that one?"

Greg shakes his head at his brother's laughter and joins Rosaline and Jack, sitting uncomfortably apart at the water's edge.

"It's nice, you know," smiles Rosaline.

"What is?"

"Seeing you guys having a bit of fun."

"Yeah, I guess. Hey – you want to help me cook tonight?"

"Love to."

"Sure that's wise, hon?"

Rosaline doesn't look at Jack. "Why don't you go for a swim?"

"You know, I think I might just do that."

Rosaline and Greg watch him keep his distance from Karl and Terrance. "How's this going to work, Greg?"

CHAPTER THIRTY-THREE

"Well, it's another brilliant morning," says Greg, rubbing his hair.

"Where the hell have you been?" asks Karl.

"Wanted a swim."

"Greg, no one goes anywhere by themselves."

"I just wanted a quick dip, no harm done."

"Greg, Karl's right."

"It's okay, Rosaline. Didn't we come to the conclusion that it's pretty safe?"

"Just take someone next time."

"Geez Karl, sorrrrie. Anyone for breakfast? I'm famished."

"You've probably got worms," says Terrance, poking Greg's stomach.

"Very funny."

"What do we have?" asks Rosaline, smiling at Greg.

"Well ... plenty of fruit. I found a jar of honey in the Booths bag."

"Oh, my God – we had honey in there?" says Rosaline.

"Yeah, Greg, what's the story there?" Karl walks past him, emitting a thunderous fart.

"Karl."

"What?"

"He's such a pig, Rosaline."

"It's okay, Greg." Rosaline looks over at Jack. "I'm used to it."

Greg chuckles. "So, are we going to the waterfall?"

"Yes, Greg, we're going." Karl stretches and heads down the tunnel. Jack gets up and follows him, leaving Terrance free to talk.

"Feeling tired?"

"A bit. A swim will do us good."

"Yes, it will."

She nods. "You okay?"

"I am now." Terrance touches her hand but hears footsteps and retreats. He can't wait to wash. He has been wearing the same t-shirt for two days and it stinks of sweat and salt. His skin feels like leather coated with sand and sends shivers down his body every time he touches it. He puts his hand to his hair, but it feels like straw and he decides to leave it tied until he gets under the waterfall. His stubble feels like it has a week's growth and he is glad there is no mirror on the wall. He walks back over and helps himself to a few slices of mango, which he washes down with the small amount of coconut milk Greg has poured into his cup. His mouth is dry and everything tastes the same.

"You look incredibly sexy in that sort of beach bum kinda way." She winks at him and strolls off towards her bags. He can't help the smile that grows on his face. She knows what he was thinking. Knows he is feeling dirty, unattractive, and her words fill him with an elation he can't describe.

"Okay, everyone," yells Karl, interrupting his thoughts. "Grab what you need. We're off."

They fill their backpacks with empty water bottles, soap and towels and head out.

"Oh, shit. I forgot the sunscreen."

"Don't worry, 'bout it, Greg."

"No, I better get it." Greg dashes back down the tunnel.

"Seriously, no one's going to use it."

"No argument there, Jack."

"Quite picky about his appearance, isn't he?" laughs Rosaline.

"Aren't they all?"

Terrance turns to Jack. "What's that supposed to mean?"

"Queers – they like to look good, don't they?"

Rosaline peers at her husband. "You're not queer."

Jack smirks. "You're not funny, Ros."

"What the hell's taking him so long?" says Karl checking his watch.

"Tell you what Terrance, I'll go see."

Jack runs into the cavern to see Greg on his knees, hands searching the sand around his bags. He creeps up behind him.

"What are you doing?"

Greg's body shudders. "Jesus, Jack, you nearly gave me a heart attack."

"What are you looking for?"

"Um, I dropped a shell …"

"A shell?"

"Yes, I found it ages ago and have been carrying it around." Greg registers the disapproval on Jack's face. "I know, I know, but it makes me feel better."

"Wouldn't have picked you for the superstitious type."

"Well, I'm not usually but with everything's that happened here, it just makes me feel better." Greg looks around and his eyes spot what he is looking for. "Okay, I'll look for it later. Can you get the sunscreen from Karl's bag and I'll get mine as well."

"Jesus, Greg, I don't think anyone wants it but if it gets you out of here then fine."

Greg waits for Jack to turn his back and deposits his find into his shorts pocket. He pats his thigh and gets up.

"Aren't you forgetting something?"

"What?"

"Your sunscreen."

"Oh … one will be enough. Like you said, no one will use it."

Jack scratches his head. "Let's just go, shall we?"

They reach the waterfall, are greeted by a whirlwind of flies, disturbed from their work at a rotting carcass, and proceed to set their gear down at the opposite end of the bank. They grab their soap and head for the fresh water. Conservation goes out the window and white foam soon floats in little mounds on the surface.

Terrance slips into the water and removes his clothes. He leaves them on the ledge and dives down. The colder water clears his head and he emerges in the middle of the pool. He sees Rosaline's eyes on him and swims towards her. She nods her head as Jack steps out from the falling water.

"God, that feels good," says Jack almost cheerily.

Terrance leers at Jack. *Idiot looks like he's just stepped out of a shower commercial – all squeaky-clean, totally misleading.* He pulls his shorts under the water and puts them back on and grabs the soap and lathers his hair. He manages to yank his band out and surfaces with his hair swept off his face for the first time in days. He grabs his shirt and swims over to the bank, gets out, spreads out his shirt to dry, opens his bag and pulls out shaving foam and his pocketknife.

He finishes just as Jack emerges from the pool.

"Can I use that?"

Terrance is watching Rosaline get out and casually hands Jack his kit. "Don't cut yourself." He waits till Jack is occupied, walks to Rosaline and sits with her.

"So – feeling better?"

"Uh-huh."

"You look amazingly beautiful with the sun in your hair." He leans closer. "You smell so good."

"Terrance, please stop." Rosaline moans as she peers behind him.

"We're just talking." His eyes dance before her and she looks away.

"Please," she moans quietly.

"I'm not doing anything." His smile teases as she feels the heat rise between them. "You're making me crazy." His voice is husky, a mere whisper. "I want you."

"I want you, too."

He feels her finger circle his hand and shuts his eyes. "I have to move." He runs and dives into the pool. The water calms the passion mounting inside him. He swims and reaches the waterfall, rests his arms on the rocky ledge and presses his body hard against the rocks.

He thinks about how much longer they have. *Is it a week or slightly longer?* He has lost track of time. Each minute around her is like torture. He wants to ask if she loves him but is too scared that what she feels is just the effects of what they have gone through; that it will all change once they leave this place. He jumps out and goes behind the blanket of water, drops his shorts and pulls at the bandage he put on the other day. The cut looks clean. His blood kept them together till now. *Please, God, let it be enough for the remaining days we have left in this god-forsaken place.*

CHAPTER THIRTY-FOUR

Three days pass without any further tension within the group. Terrance has done his best to keep contact with Rosaline short by busying himself making spears and, early this morning, he and Karl risked diving for crayfish, catching two. They decide to eat them for lunch on the beach and Greg boils them. When they are ready, Rosaline gets the fruit she has cut up and Terrance and Jack bring plates, utensils and towels. Karl surprises them with a half-empty bottle of rum and they set up under the shade of the coconut palms at the bush's edge.

The crayfish is eaten quickly and Rosaline passes the fruit around. They sit sucking on mango slices and swigging the rum as the bottle is passed between them. The combination of rum and the relentless sun makes them lethargic and careless.

"Shit, I'm beat." Karl lies back and within minutes is asleep. Jack and Greg lie down and drift off instantly. Terrance can feel his eyelids getting heavy as he looks at his brothers. He wipes away the little stream of saliva running out the side of Greg's mouth, making Rosaline chuckle.

"He's a lovely man."

"Yes, he is." Terrance lifts his gaze and Rosaline wraps her hands around her legs.

He stares at her with a longing that stretches far beyond anything he has ever felt. "I wish I could hold you and make love to you on this beautiful fucking beach." His eyes search her face. "But I can't. I can't even stand being close to you because it's killing me that I can't touch you." He watches her face.

She gazes back with her drowning emerald eyes and his heart feels like lead. "Jack wants to leave the cave."

She unclasps her legs and moves closer.

"You can't."

Rosaline crawls until she is inches from him. She places her finger on his lips and traces his lip-line then runs her finger slowly down his chin and onto his neck. She brings her face down and licks his cheek and slides her tongue to his ear. He shivers and grabs her hair.

"I love you, Terrance Tiller."

Between the heat and the softness of her voice, he nearly misses her words. He pulls her face to his and kisses her so tenderly that her body collapses into his and they sink to the ground together. His face is wet and he can't tell if it is from her tears or his own. She is all he can think of; all he wants. He hears nothing but his pounding heart and he hurriedly checks the sleeping bodies beside them before kissing her again. His hand moves with a mind of its own as it caresses her warm, silky flesh that rises to his touch as if it has been waiting for him. He is bending his head into her chest when he hears coughing.

Terrance scrambles off Rosaline so fast that his head swims. He looks at the ground, drawing in deep breaths. When his light-headedness settles he slowly looks left. Rosaline has moved back to where she was sitting and his brothers and Jack haven't moved. He looks at her. She mouths the words 'I love you' and blows him a kiss. He lies back with his arms folded over his forehead and closes his eyes. She makes him feel like he is fifteen again. All at once, a deep dread of losing her begins to manifest itself and tighten around his heart.

Terrance wakes first and checks his watch – 3:45 p.m. His

mouth feels dry and he reaches for his bottle. The warm water does nothing to quench his thirst. Beside him he hears Karl's snoring and notices his pink legs. He picks up a towel and covers them. Karl stirs but doesn't wake. Greg is zonked. Has never been able to drink during the day.

They stay for another hour before Terrance wakes Karl and Greg and says they should make a move. Rosaline wakes Jack and they amble back.

"I'm just going to get some food underway. You want to help, Rosaline?"

"Yes, thanks, Greg. I'll just go for a wee and be right back."

"Terrance," Karl says stepping in front of him. "A word."

Terrance follows his brother over to where Greg is standing, looking sheepish.

"What's going on here, Terrance?"

"Nothing."

"Terrance, you and her couldn't be more obvious if you tried."

"I love her."

Terrance watches Karl and Greg exchange a look.

"You love her?" Karl's voice is full of ridicule, tinged with laughing sarcasm. "For fuck's sake, what the hell is wrong with you?"

"Karl, he can't help who he falls in love with."

Terrance can almost feel the punch that Karl wants to dish out to Greg. "Greg, it's okay." He turns to his brother. "Sorry, Karl, but it's how I feel."

Karl's eyes bore into him as he feels Karl's finger press hard into his chest.

"Look, I don't give a fuck if you like ..."

Terrance glares at his brother, unmoved.

"... pardon me ... love her, but this is neither the time nor the place. If you want sexual relations with her, then wait till we're out of here."

"I'm not stupid, Karl."

"Really?"

"Cut it out, both of you," Greg wipes his mouth. "Come on, Karl, it's obvious she doesn't want to be with Jack, and I think they make a great couple."

"Are you fucking serious?" Karl looks from Greg to Terrance. "Oh, to hell with it – I give up. Quite frankly, I'm amazed he hasn't decked you already."

"Yeah, I am too." Terrance's grin matches the jeering in his eyes.

Greg puts his arms around his brothers. "We good, then, guys?"

"We're good." Terrance half-smiles at Karl as Rosaline walks out of the tunnel.

Dinner is eaten quickly and quietly. They sit around their fire. The tension between them fuels their weariness and the necessity to be civil gives way to careless honestly.

"I'm leaving you, Jack."

"Oh, boy," says Greg, shifting away from Jack and towards Karl.

Jack leans forward. "I beg your pardon?"

"You heard me." Rosaline's voice is softly distressed. "I'm sorry, but this isn't working."

"It would be if he wasn't here sniffing around."

Karl clasps his hand on Terrance's knee.

"It was over between us before Terrance, Jack. We just couldn't see it."

"That's a lie. He's wormed his way between us and ..."

"I love him."

Jack's erupts. "You love him?" He shakes his head. "You don't know what love is!"

"Please don't!"

"Oh, you're priceless." Jack turns to Terrance. "She doesn't love you. She's just getting me back and you're the poor bastard she's using."

"Jack, stop it." Rosaline's voice trembles as she looks at Terrance.

"'Jack, stop it'! Why Roz? Afraid lover boy here might doubt you?"

Terrance frees himself from Karl and moves closer to Rosaline. "What the hell's he talking about?"

"I love you, Terrance. He's just being a prick."

"She's getting me back because I had an affair."

Terrance's mind goes blank. He can feel Karl readying himself; can hear Greg's silent plea for logic. He turns to Jack.

"She's using you, for Christ's sake."

Terrance looks into Rosaline's eyes, finds what he is looking for and takes her hand. "I don't think so."

Jack leers at Terrance "Your funeral, mate." His face is split by a conceited grin. "Bit of a pickle we're in then, isn't it?"

Karl exhales loudly. "Not really, Jack. You can stay, but if you do anything – and I mean anything – we don't like, then you're out." Karl's finger circles his mouth. "On the other hand, I guess Rosaline and you aren't a team anymore, so that kind of disqualifies you."

"No fucking way I'm handing the money to that prick."

"Please," says Rosaline, stepping forward. "Nothing will change till this is over." She glances at the brothers. "Whoever wins this thing wins it fair and square."

"That your idea of a joke?" Jack sneers. " But since the alternative's not very attractive, then I guess that'll have to do."

"And I give you my word that Terrance and I won't do anything while we're here."

Jack turns and walks towards the tunnel to the rocks.

Terrance watches Greg busying himself getting together the pieces of fruit they have left. Rosaline goes to Greg and gives him a quick hug. Terrance smiles as Greg puts his arm around her and kisses her head. Karl slaps his back and he gives him a half-hearted smile.

"I don't trust that prick for a second, Terrance. Are you going to be able to stay away from her?"

"'Course."

Karl cocks an eyebrow. "So, you fucked her yet?"

"No, we'll wait."

"That's decent of you."

"Karl, I love her." Terrance searches his brother's eyes. "I mean, I *really*, love her."

"Okay, then, we stay sharp and watch him like a hawk. He doesn't go anywhere by himself and we don't leave him alone."

"Agreed."

"Yeah, well I just hope she's worth it, buddy."

The next morning, Terrance is up and dressed first. He pulls out his backpack and fills it with the empty water bottle he still has, his mangled toothbrush and a bar of soap that now resembles someone's unfortunate attempt at clay modeling. He hears Greg stir and nods. Greg screws up his nose and untangles himself from his sleeping bag.

"Shit, Greg – your legs been bleeding."

"Yeah?" Greg looks down. His leg is red and caked with spots of blood. "Bloody mossies."

"You must have scratched yourself in the night. Where's the antiseptic cream?"

"Gave the last of it to Rosaline yesterday."

Terrance wanders to their chest and takes out a jar. "This will have to do then."

"I don't think …" Greg yawns, "that normal honey works the same as manuka."

"Well, maybe it will stop the itch." Terrance runs his fingers inside the jar, and pulls out a small lug and slaps it on Greg's bite."

"Shit, stings a bit."

"Must be working, then." He sees Rosaline stir and goes back to his backpack.

"Morning."

"Morning, Rosaline." Greg rolls up his sleeping bag as Karl and Jack wake. Karl clears his throat and Jack sits, emptying his lungs with a hacking cough.

"Christ. We got anything to drink."

"Nope," answers Greg.

"Throat feels like sandpaper."

"There is a God," whispers Greg. Rosaline looks at him and they share a private chuckle.

"Fuck, we must have something."

"Nothing, unless you want a bit of coconut, but it's pretty dry."

Terrance puts his backpack on and stands, ready to leave. Jack kicks his sleeping bag to the side, stoops, picking up his t-shirt, and throws it over his head. The sleeve catches and he curses as he pulls it down, ripping it open under the arm. "Fucking thing."

"I suggest we go. Sooner we get there, sooner we get food."

"Yeah, think we can work that out for ourselves, Terrance." Jack plucks his hat off his bag, puts his sneakers on and throws his bag over his shoulder.

Terrance looks at Karl, who has been unusually quiet. Karl heads down the tunnel and Terrance follows quickly. He can hear Greg chatting to Rosaline behind him about how it's all going to be all right, because Karl will make sure nothing happens to them. He glances back and notes Jack's somber face.

Jack's head feels heavy with the amount of rum he put away and the revelations that transpired last night. He is surprised he isn't filled with more anger towards Rosaline. Deep down, he knows that what happened would happen eventually. They can't go back. He realizes that now. He can't love her properly after Cathy and she can't forgive him for the affair; game over.

His mind turns to Greg. *What was he really looking for? I don't buy that cock-and-bull story about a shell. For one thing he'd have a bulge in his pocket.*

"Something amusing, Jack?"

"No, Rosaline, nothing." He sees her skeptical gaze before she dismisses him. *So easy for her now! I'm not her concern anymore.* He feels the start of the green eyed-monster lurking and concentrates on planting his feet where his wife has stepped.

They make it to the waterfall and he watches Karl and Terrance step into the pond with their nets. He's sick of hearing how Karl reckons early morning and late afternoon is the best time to catch the buggers, but he doesn't argue; he simply doesn't care. *If they want to waste their energy providing me with food then that's fine with me!* He sits close to Greg and Rosaline, listening to Greg's boring details about some herbs that grow around here somewhere.

"So, Greg, what did you plan to do with the money?"

Greg huffs. "I want my own restaurant. Be my own boss – head chef, with all the little wanna-be chefs under me."

Rosaline wipes her brow. "What would you call it, Greg?"

"I don't know."

"Would you include your name?"

Greg ponders. "I want it to sound classy."

"That would be a no, then," says Jack, snorting.

"Just ignore him, Greg."

"Oh, come on, Rosaline. He wants something classy. Greg's ... whatever, doesn't exactly ring up 'Michelin Star', does it?"

"I probably won't use my name. I'll get Terrance to help me come up with something."

"Jesus, it's your restaurant."

"It's no big deal." Hurt, Greg turns to Rosaline. "What about you, Rosaline?"

"Hmm?"

"Come on, what would you do with it?"

Jack snarls. "Half of it."

Rosaline dismisses her husband's remark. "I'd buy some land and design an amazing house."

"Wow, really!" Greg eyes widen. "That's exactly what Terrance wants to do."

"Are you sure?"

"Oh, for fuck's sake."

"No, it's true, Jack. He talked about it before we left. He'd design it and he and Karl would build it."

"Pretty basic, then."

"Ignore him, Greg."

"Actually, Jack," says Greg puffing out his chest. "Terrance did an architecture degree."

"I thought he was an electrician?"

"Well, yes he is, but he does have a degree in architecture."

"Seriously?"

"A mate of his wanted to start his own electrical business and asked Terrance to help. His friend was offering good money and so he said he'd help get it off the ground. They were really popular."

"Yes, I can imagine," cuts in Rosaline, without thought.

Greg laughs. "Yeah, Marcy was pretty easy on the eyes as well. Sure ladies deliberately found faults just to get them back."

"Absolutely," giggles Rosaline.

Jack folds his arms under his head. "Did he actually do any work?"

"He's a bloody good electrician," answers Greg, defensively.

Jack's smile widens, pleased at Greg's irritation. His eyes travel to Greg's shorts, where Greg's hand is lost in his moving pocket.

"Found your shell, then?" He sees Greg stiffen.

"No."

"What shell's this?"

"He has a shell." Jack raises his eyebrows. "*Had* a shell. A lucky shell."

"Oh, I see," Rosaline smiles demurely.

"It wasn't a lucky shell, I just liked it."

Jack and Rosaline exchange looks. He can tell his wife is suppressing her amusement. He smiles at her, but the laughter in her face disappears in a flash.

"What would you do with the money, then?" asks Greg, his voice curt.

"Me – oh, I don't know. Invest some; travel heaps. Do all the things I've wanted to, but never could."

"I'm going for a swim," says Rosaline coldly. "Coming, Greg?"

"No, I think I might collect those herbs I was telling you about."

"Oh, then I better come with you."

"No, you go for your swim and I'll go with Greg." Jack is standing before Greg can protest. He revels in Greg's uneasiness and slaps Greg's back. "Come on, buddy. I'm guessing you want to use them for lunch."

"Yes."

Jack smiles, watching the brief exchange between Greg and Rosaline. He hears Rosaline whisper that if they're not back soon, she'll get Karl and Terrance to come with her and look for them.

"Okey dokey, Greg. Let's move."

"Blimey, I haven't heard those words for years."

"Really? Don't you bum-chums use words like that all the time?"

"Not really."

"Oh, come on. Stuff like dandy and peachy and ..."

"No, can't say we do, Jack."

"Well, I'll be," Jack places an arm around Greg's shoulder and guides him on. "So it's just on TV, then, is it?"

"Look," says Greg, trying to wriggle out of Jack's hold. "I say and do the same things you do, okay?"

Jack snickers. "Well, not really, Greg." He winks. "I'm pretty sure you do one thing differently."

Greg shrugs off Jack's arm. "You should stay."

"Hey, come on – lighten up, I'm just teasing you."

"Is it just that you don't like gay men or is it me in particular?"

"Um, well, let me see ..." Jack watches the way Greg's face turns blotchy. "Hey, I don't dislike you." Jack looks out to where Terrance has perched himself on a rock. "But your brother – now that's a different story."

"Look, Jack, I might take a swim instead."

"Don't be silly." Jack places his hand on Greg's shoulder. "Come on, I'll help get what you need ... and I'll behave." He draws a silent cross in front of his chest.

"Let's just hurry this up, then."

"Good man. You go first."

"No, thanks. I'll follow you."

Rosaline checks her watch. They have been gone for over thirty minutes. Her eyes dart over to see Karl and Terrance swimming back. She shivers and wraps her arms across her chest. *I shouldn't have let them go.* Karl and Terrance emerge from the pond with huge smiles, each carrying a full net.

"Hey, Rosaline – where's Greg and Jack?"

She hesitates. "They went to the top. Greg wanted to get herbs." Her words are rushed. "I knew I shouldn't have let them go but I didn't know what to do!"

"How long have they been gone?" asks Karl dumping his net.

"Over half an hour."

"Okay, let's get up there."

"I'm so sorry."

"It's not your fault," Terrance takes her hand. "Greg could have stayed."

"Jack was, ..." she ponders. "I don't know, nasty then apologetic. It was hard for Greg to say no. I was just going to call you."

"Come on," yells Karl, sprinting, and Terrance grabs Rosaline's hand as they run after him. They know the route to the top but Rosaline's legs feel like lead and her feet betray her, causing Terrance to slow down. Terrance guides her in front of him, gently pushing her up the bank towards Karl's outstretched hand, and clambers up after her. She feels sick, emotionally drained. He tells her to breathe deeply, that he is right behind her.

At the cliff top the air is unbearably hot and still. Jack is crouched where Josh fell, surveying the ground. Greg has collected his herbs and is sitting back from Jack, breathing hard, fanning himself with his hat.

"Wonder what the hell he must have seen to go over?"

"Maybe he saw whales." Greg squints out to sea. The cobalt ocean sparkles under the cloudless sky. He wipes his forehead and sucks the sweat from his hand.

"Maybe, but why would he go to the edge?"

"Maybe he wanted to see how far up he was."

"Hey, lets take a look."

"Oh ... no, thanks."

"No?" interrupts Jack. "Oh, come on, Greg. You must have wondered?"

"Yeah, of course, but I don't want to go near the edge."

"Scared you'll go over?"

"No – 'course not."

"You don't need to look do you?"

"No."

"No – 'cause you know what's down there don't you?"

"No." Greg stands and his hand automatically goes to his pocket. "Why would you say that?"

Jack walks over to him and puts his hand on his shoulder and squeezes lightly. "No reason."

"Then why say it?"

"Just a theory." Jack sees Greg's trembling pocket. "What you got in there, Greg?"

"Nothing."

"Do you always fiddle with nothing?"

"When I'm nervous."

"Why are you nervous?"

"You're making me nervous."

"Show me what's in your pocket."

"No. Why should I?"

"Thought you said you didn't have anything in there?"

"I did. I don't. I'm heading back."

"Not so fast, buddy." Jack whips Greg's arm up, bends it behind Greg's back, slides his hand into Greg's pocket and feels something cold. He pulls it out and opens his hand.

"A chain?"

Greg doesn't answer.

"Can't recall ever seeing you wear this."

"I told you, it's been in my pocket. Give it back, Jack."

"What's on it?

"Nothing that concerns you." Greg tries to snatch it but Jack holds him firm. He dangles the chain up to their faces and takes a long look.

"Is that the letter 'J'?

Greg stiffens.

"Fuck me! It's Josh's, isn't it?"

Greg offers no answer.

"Is this Josh's, you little faggot?" Jack shouts into Greg's face, his spit landing on Greg's cheek. "Answer me!"

"What the hell is going on here?"

Jack whips Greg around, surprised to see Karl, Terrance and Rosaline standing behind them.

"Let him go, Jack."

Jack looks at the panic in his wife's eyes. "Fuck off. This little bastard has Josh's chain. I knew it. I knew you three had something to do with his death."

"Look, Jack, calm down. Let Greg go and we'll sort this out."

"Fuck, you're unbelievable. I've found the fucking chain."

"What chain?" Karl advances but Jack takes a step backwards, taking Greg with him. He sees Terrance reach out to Karl and clasp his arm.

He dangles the chain in front of Greg. It glistens in the sun's light and momentarily mesmerizes Karl, Terrance and Rosaline.

Terrance shakes his head and his eyes search Greg's face for answers. "Greg?"

"I forgot about it," answers Greg, timidly.

"Forgot about it. How could you forget about it? It was in your pocket, you fucking liar."

Terrance stands resolute as Rosaline touches his hand. Karl's eyes travel quickly from Jack to Terrance and Rosaline.

"Oh, I get it. You're going to tell me you didn't know?"

"Shut up, Jack," shouts Karl, moving forward. Jack clasps Greg more securely.

"Jack, let him go," shouts Rosaline.

Greg squirms like a pig in Jack's grip.

"Stay still, you little shit." Jack further tightens his hold around Greg's neck. "You said you broke it?"

Greg's tears crash down his face. His mouth quivers. "It ... it broke when I tried to grab him. I was going to give it to ... to Kate, but I forgot."

"What are you talking about?" snaps Jack.

"You're hurting me. I can't breathe."

"When did you try to grab him?"

Terrance cuts in. "Jesus Christ. Look, Jack, Greg was there but it's not what you think."

"What?" gasps Rosaline.

"Jack, step away from the edge and we'll tell you what happened. Let's just all calm down and get some perspective on this."

"Some perspective?"

"Come on, man, Greg didn't kill him. He tried to save him." Terrance inches forward.

"Save him? Boy, this had better be good, as from where I'm standing, Greg looks guilty as hell."

"I did try to save him. I ..."

"Look," intervenes Karl. "Josh fell and Greg grabbed him but couldn't hold on. He tried but just couldn't!"

"Really?"

"Be quiet, Jack."

Jack looks at Rosaline and slightly relaxes his hold on Greg.

"Well, Greg?"

"I tried to save him but he was too heavy." Greg words are barely audible.

"I got to the top and found Greg lying at the edge."

"Hang on Karl – you were there, too?"

"No, not at first, but I went up and heard yelling."

"So you don't know what happened."

"Greg told us what happened."

"But you weren't there?"

"No, I wasn't but ..."

"But what? You weren't there!" hollers Jack.

"Look, I told you," screams Greg. "He slipped and I grabbed him and then I couldn't hang on and he slid out of my hand."

"Why was he near the edge and why have you got his chain?"

"I caught it when I tried to grab him and it broke."

"What was he doing at the edge?"

"He spotted something."

"What?"

"I don't know. I moved a bit closer to him but I couldn't see anything – and then he sort of tripped and he reached out and grabbed me and I don't know, next thing I knew he was pulling me over." Greg wipes his eyes and rubs his nose. "He was heavy ... I couldn't hold him. It happened so fast. He didn't believe me. It was horrible."

Terrance gawks at his brother.

"What do you mean he didn't believe you?" snaps Jack.

"What?"

"You just said he didn't believe you."

"Jesus Christ," cuts in Karl. "Okay, there was this thing with a bee."

"A bee?" Jack's malevolent laugh bellows around them. "Are you fucking serious?"

"They were doing some form of yoga and Josh had his eyes closed and Greg tried to get a bee off him and he got startled, stood up and tripped backwards."

"Hot damn, this just gets better and better." Jack shakes his head, snickering. "Come on, you really expect me to believe that? You make a pass at him, Greg?"

"No, 'course not."

"Jack, we know how it sounds. It's why we didn't say anything, but Greg's no liar."

"Terrance is right, Jack. We didn't say anything because of this exact reaction. It's a terrible accident and nothing was going to change that. Greg had a hell of a shock and we didn't want to put him through more."

"Put him through more. How do you know he didn't let go deliberately?"

"Why the hell would he do that?"

"Maybe 'cause he made a pass at Josh and Josh told him to fuck off. Maybe he thought it better to let go."

Greg's body stiffens.

"What – have I got it right, Greg?"

"No. Stop it. My head hurts."

"You let go on purpose." Jack squeezes him tighter. "Didn't you?"

Greg frantically looks to his brothers, his eyes pleading for help.

"Greg?" Terrance's voice is questioning and he moves forward. Jack yanks Greg back, causing them to stumble. Greg's hands wildly lash the ground, trying to get hold of anything, as his body slides over the edge, taking Jack's head and torso with him. He clings onto Jack's shirt for dear life. Jack grabs a clump of vines as Karl dives and seizes his legs.

"Terrance!" shouts Karl, as the weight of Greg hanging onto Jack begins to slide them closer to the edge. Terrance clutches at

Karl's legs and tries to find a foothold. Rosaline pulls at a clump of vines and stretches them over to him. He wraps what he can around his free arm and tries to anchor himself. Rosaline scrambles over and holds Terrance around the middle. She knows her action will have little effect but can't think of anything else to do.

Jack watches the terror change Greg's face, as Greg's free hand desperately tries to find his shoulder.

"Keep still, you stupid bastard; you'll pull us over." Jack feels the blood filling his head, making it heavy. Greg's frantic fingers clutch at his t-shirt. "Fuck, stop it. You're going to strangle me." His neck burns as he tries to dislodge Greg's fingers with his head.

"Stop moving," howls Karl.

"Tell that to your asshole of a brother; he's squirming like a pig." Jack feels the edge of the cliff crumbling. "Stop it, you little prick." *Fucking faggot.* His skin burns where the neck of his t-shirt digs in, as his body is slowly dragged backwards. He feels something sharp scratch his chest and hears the noise of ripping material. The tension around his neck releases. He knows what it means and smiles.

"Bye-bye, Greggy boy," he mouths.

Greg stops moving. He feels himself drop, sees the tear and screams. "Karl! Karl!"

"Fuck, Terrance, pull."

Jack can feel the pressure mount as his body inches backwards. The hole in his t-shirt widens and he watches Greg's fingers slither from the material and then Greg is falling, getting smaller and smaller, till his body smacks the rocks below and lies broken, but still in one piece. Then he is thrust back and he can no longer see over the cliff.

Jack wiggles himself up and away from the edge. Karl, Terrance and Rosaline stare wide-eyed. Karl moves so fast that Jack has no time to register Karl's hand before it smacks into his nose, breaking it instantly.

"You fucking bastard."

Blood pours from Jack's nostrils. "My t-shirt ripped – I couldn't hold him." He pinches his nose and shuts his eyes tightly. The pain is intense. "Shit, I think my nose is broken."

"I don't give a shit about your fucking nose," spits Terrance. Rosaline places her hand on his arm.

"I'm so sorry." Tears fall down her face. "So, so sorry."

Jack watches them carefully. He slides himself further away from the cliff. His nose aches and his eyes blur with pain and moisture. "He …"

"I don't want to hear it." Karl's voice is thunderous. Jack closes his mouth.

"Is this what you wanted?" Rosaline asks. "Does it make you feel good?" She starts to cry. "How could you?"

He looks at Rosaline. "I didn't do anything – he let go."

"If it wasn't for you, none of this would have happened." Rosaline snarls. "You caused his death. He was a nice person and you … you had to go and … oh, Jack – what have you done?"

"He as good as admitted he let Josh fall." Jack stares at them. "They shouldn't be here. Should have gone ages ago. The money's ours – always was."

"The money – I don't care about the money. Greg is dead, for God's sake."

"Yeah, I'm sorry 'bout that."

"You fucking conceited bastard," hisses Terrance. His red eyes spill as he walks over to Jack and spits in his face. Karl pulls him back and Rosaline takes him into her arms. He slumps to the ground, pulling her with him.

"You fucking move and I'll send you over to join our brother." Karl's voice is choked but unforgiving. He turns his back on Jack and walks to Terrance and Rosaline. He crouches beside them. "Come on, let's go."

Terrance rises and walks a couple of steps towards Jack. "You may get the money but you've got nothing Jack – nothing!"

Jack fixes his gaze on Terrance, licks the blood from his lips and spits as he watches Terrance turn and take hold of his wife's waist as the three of them walk slowly towards the trees. He stays watching them till they disappear. He spots the chain lying half-covered by vines and Terrance's words echo in his brain.

EPILOGUE

Rosaline gets up after sleeping to relieve the headache she often gets when she thinks about the past five years and the guilt that consumes her. The guilt that just won't go away. She looks out the bedroom window at Karl playing with her son, Greg, and her gaze shifts to her husband, Terrance, sitting, eyes forever watching, protecting.

Jack agreed to a divorce in exchange for her lie. All she had to do was pretend to be with him, so they won the money. When the divorce came through, Terrance married her without hesitation. It was too quick, but necessary, both trying to eliminate the despair they felt. They loved each other but the wounds were great, their grief deep. They had their half-share of the money. There was no way Jack was getting it all. She didn't want it, but it wasn't for her. She took it for Karl, for Terrance. To make things better. It didn't.

Karl and Terrance each dealt silently with their own guilt. They said they did not in any way blame her and they all wanted to believe it could be so, but there was an unspoken awkwardness between them. They smiled, hugged and acted like any normal family, but it was like they were constantly acting out role after role after role. It never really felt completely real, completely honest.

When Greg was born, it had felt like a new beginning, but as she watches them now, she knows time will never heal them. They will never be able to forget or totally forgive. She wipes the tear away from her cheek and inhales several deep breaths, much as actors do before going on stage, goes out of the bedroom, down the hallway and out the French doors to join her family.

ACKNOWLEDGMENTS

I would like to thank my family for putting up with me while I was working on this project and the wonderful people who became my 'guinea pigs' by reading the second draft, so that I could convince myself that this story was good enough to print.

These people are: My daughter, Hayley Maxwell; my mother, Irene Kingwill; my tennis coach, Dennis Bolotovski; my good friend, Julia Mead; my sister-in-law, Heather Falkenstein, and my physiotherapist, Jonathan Ward, whose enthusiasm and excitement blew me away.

Thank you to Lel Scott of Hawkeyeproofreading.co.nz, for being such a great proofreader/editor; Giles Scott, and the wonderful team at Publishme.co.nz and my good friend, Kevin Wildman, for his help with the technical side of setting up my website.

Lastly, I would like to thank, you, the reader. I hope you have enjoyed reading this book as much as I enjoyed writing it.